FALKIRK COMMUNITY TRUS

30124 02696774 7

D1756750

JAN 202

MAKING WISHES AT BAY VIEW

WELCOME TO WHITSBOROUGH BAY BOOK 1

JESSICA REDLAND

Boldwood

FALKIRK COMMUNITY
TRUST LIBRARIES

First published in Great Britain in 2020 by Boldwood Books Ltd.

Copyright © Jessica Redland, 2020

Cover Design by Charlotte Abrams-Simpson

Cover Photography: iStock

The moral right of Jessica Redland to be identified as the author of this work has been asserted in accordance with the Copyright, Designs and Patents Act 1988.

All rights reserved. No part of this book may be reproduced in any form or by any electronic or mechanical means, including information storage and retrieval systems, without written permission from the author, except for the use of brief quotations in a book review.

This book is a work of fiction and, except in the case of historical fact, any resemblance to actual persons, living or dead, is purely coincidental.

Every effort has been made to obtain the necessary permissions with reference to copyright material, both illustrative and quoted. We apologise for any omissions in this respect and will be pleased to make the appropriate acknowledgements in any future edition.

A CIP catalogue record for this book is available from the British Library.

Paperback ISBN 978-1-83889-195-4

FALKIRK COUNCIL LIBRARIES

Large Print ISBN 978-1-83889-662-1

Hardback ISBN 978-1-80162-571-5

Ebook ISBN 978-1-83889-196-1

Kindle ISBN 978-1-83889-197-8

Audio CD ISBN 978-1-83889-249-4

MP3 CD ISBN 978-1-83889-683-6

Digital audio download ISBN 978-1-83889-194-7

Boldwood Books Ltd
23 Bowerdean Street
London SW6 3TN
www.boldwoodbooks.com

To Beatrice – nurse, midwife, councillor, mayor, mother, grandmother and inspiration. May you rest in peace xx

1

I blame it on my dad. If he hadn't died when I was only six, I don't think I'd have been so obsessed with older men. Don't get me wrong, Nick did a brilliant job at being the man in my life. I don't know what Mum and I would have done without him. But ceasing to be the brother and becoming the dad instead is a big ask for anyone, especially when they're only ten themselves when it happens.

Let me be really clear for a moment. I wasn't looking for an older man to be a replacement father or anything weird like that. It's just that I was drawn to them more than to anyone close to my age. There was a confidence about them. Maturity. Experience.

They were attentive. They knew what they wanted. In some cases they knew what was best for me too and I kind of liked not having to make decisions for myself. Sometimes. So, on reflection, perhaps they were filling some sort of dad-shaped void in my life.

The thing is, my relationships always seemed to go wrong. Very wrong. I swore every time that I wasn't going to get involved with an older man again. Then the next one would come along and I'd be right back to square one, thinking that this time would be different.

What's that phrase? You have to kiss a few frogs before you find your prince? Believe me, I've kissed more than my fair share of frogs. And toads. And snakes. But I'd finally got there. I'd found my prince and he answered to the name of Tony Sinclair. Forty-five. Divorced. No kids. Still had his own hair. Still had the body and sex drive of a man in his twenties. Perfect. Or it would have been if he wasn't constantly on the road with his job and I didn't work shifts. Time together was rare and precious.

'Are you still courting that sugar daddy of yours?' Ruby asked as she watched me lay out the tables for afternoon bingo.

I smiled at my favourite resident. I knew I shouldn't have favourites, but Ruby had led such a fascinating life and I loved hearing all about it. She'd run away to join the circus at age fourteen, then toured the world as an exotic dancer in her late teens and early twenties. Seriously. I'd seen the photographic evidence. She'd been a looker back then and still was. She'd gathered a few wrinkles in her eighty-four years, but her grey eyes still sparkled with mischief, her thick white hair was always elegantly pinned up, and she dressed immaculately in calf-length satin and lace dresses, crocheted floaty cardigans, and pearls. She reminded me of a flapper from the twenties.

'Tony? Yes, Ruby, we're still courting.'

'No more accusations of being clingy?'

I shook my head. 'All dealt with and forgotten a couple of months ago.' We'd split up in April after I'd gone overboard on texting and phoning him around my twenty-fifth birthday. He was working away on my actual birthday, which I completely accepted, and this had been my way of feeling close to him. He wasn't impressed, his boss wasn't impressed, and I wasn't impressed at being called 'childish and clingy'.

So I childishly dumped him. I regretted it immediately and pleaded for another chance. He made me stew a bit before forgiving me but everything was back on track a fortnight later. Lesson learned.

Ruby took a seat at her regular table overlooking the gardens and straightened her lilac frock. 'How long is it now, Callie?'

I started distributing the bingo cards. 'Coming up eleven months. Bit of a record for me. It usually goes tits-up within three.' I gasped and put my hand over my mouth. 'Please don't tell anyone I said rude words. Especially Denise.'

Denise Kimble, aka the She-Devil, was the Day Manager of Bay View Care Home and not my biggest fan. I'd been hauled into her office only the week before and lectured on the 'inappropriateness' of shouting out, 'Who's farted?' during film night. It didn't matter to her that the residents had found it hilarious or that it had prompted Jack Laine to do the decent thing and leave the room to evacuate his bowels instead of steadily overcoming the residents' lounge with noxious gases. Apparently, 'The elderly frequently suffer from flatulence issues and staff should know better than to draw attention to it using vulgar language'. That was me told.

Ruby picked up the bingo card I'd given her, frowned and swapped it with one from across the table. 'No lucky seven on it,' she announced when she saw me watching. 'Nearly eleven months, you say? Congratulations. Let's hope he's a keeper.'

I grinned. 'Oh, he is, Ruby. He definitely is.'

'I like sugar daddies. Did I tell you about my first one? I was sixteen and he was the fifty-eight-year-old lion tamer at the circus. There was nothing that man couldn't do with a whip...'

* * *

'Tony!' I ran across the car park at the end of my shift, grinning. He drew me into a tender kiss.

'Get a room, you two!' yelled Maria, my best friend and colleague, as she walked past.

I waved to her and giggled. 'She's only jealous. Where are you taking me tonight?'

'I thought we could have a night in. I've got some wine and I can order a takeaway.' He stepped back and frowned. 'What's up, angel?'

'Nothing,' I said in a tone that clearly meant 'something'.

'Callie...?'

'Well, it's just that you promised we'd go out somewhere nice for once.'

Tony took my hands. 'It's Monday. Who goes out on a Monday night?'

'But you said...'

'I'm tired too. I've driven miles today.'

Tony's job took him all over the country looking at care homes to add to his company's portfolio and finding suitable sites for new ones. It was how we met. He'd visited Bay View last summer but one of the residents keeled over with a heart attack shortly after he arrived and I was the only staff member available to give Tony the tour while the She-Devil dealt with the emergency. 'No flirting, Carolyn,' she'd hissed. 'He's a professional and I expect you to try and behave like one in front of him.' And I did. It's not my fault that I have a naturally friendly, bubbly personality that older men seem drawn towards. Thank God it had been Maria who discovered us in the laundry room together and not the She-Devil or I'd have been sacked on the spot.

I looked into Tony's hazel eyes and had to concede that he did look shattered. 'Okay. A night in it is. I bought some new underwear, but if you're really that exhausted...'

His eyes lit up and he kissed me again. 'Not *that* exhausted,' he murmured. 'Come on. Let's get you home.'

* * *

Tony wrapped his strong arms around me an hour or so later. I backed up against his chest as he kissed the top of my head. 'I didn't get to show you my new underwear,' I whispered.

'Next time. Besides, I prefer this look.' He lifted the duvet up and whistled appreciatively. 'Yep, I definitely prefer the natural look.'

'Stop it! You're embarrassing me.'

'There's nobody here except the two of us. Unless Sir Teddington has suddenly come to life and turned into a voyeur.' He indicated my childhood teddy sat on the bedside cabinet. 'Because, if he has, we can put on a better show for him than we've just done. Really give him his money's worth.' He began circling his hands over my breasts. My body arched at his teasing touch.

'Tony! It's half nine. I've only had a sandwich all day. Shouldn't we get something to eat?'

'The only thing I'm hungry for is you.' He lightly ran his right hand down the curve of my stomach.

'I mean it. I'm starving.'

'Food can wait. It's not like you're wasting away, is it?'

I stiffened. 'What's that supposed to mean?' I was a size sixteen and proud of my curves. A physical job and a love of swimming kept me toned but this wasn't the first time Tony had made a comment suggesting I was fat rather than curvaceous. Feeling irritated, I flicked his arms off me and wriggled out of the bed.

'What's up?' The surprised look on his face suggested he really hadn't a clue.

'I need the loo.' I grabbed my robe off the wardrobe door and scuttled through the living area towards the tiny bathroom.

Chewing on my thumbnail as I sat on the toilet, I replayed the conversation. He hadn't actually called me fat and it was the sort of comment I'd normally have brushed aside as a joke, so why had it got to me just now? Was my irritation less to do with the comment and more to do with another broken promise around going out? Not that I was complaining about how we'd spent the evening – he certainly knew what he was doing – but surely after eleven months we should be developing more as a couple? I was no expert, having never made it past three months before – but wouldn't a normal couple have developed common interests during that time that weren't just confined to the bedroom? Or the sofa. Or the shower.

I looked at myself in the mirror as I washed my hands. My thick shoulder-length dark hair was sticking up in all directions. I grabbed a brush and tried to tame it, but to no avail. I sighed. I was going to have to say something to Tony, but I'd never had to have 'the talk' before and the thought of being all serious wasn't appealing.

When I returned to the living area, Tony was fully-dressed and fastening his shoelaces. *He's finally going out for food. Yippee!* My stomach growled on cue.

He straightened up but didn't smile. 'I've got a meeting in Manchester first thing so I'm going to head over there now.'

My stomach churned. 'You're not staying?'

'Not tonight. No.'

'But I thought...'

He picked up his laptop and overnight bag. 'You thought what?'

'I thought you were staying. You brought your bag in.'

He shrugged. 'I was, but I've changed my mind about the early start. I'd rather drive to Manchester now.'

'But you said you're tired. And you haven't eaten.' I wrapped my arms around him and gently kissed his neck, eager to get him back onside. 'Why don't we get food delivered and have an early night?'

He stepped back and hitched his bag onto his shoulder. 'For God's sake, what's wrong with you tonight? Talk about high-maintenance. You want to go out. You don't want sex. You want food. You want to stay in. You want to go back to bed. You're doing my head in.'

'I'm sorry. It's just that—'

Tony put his hand up to silence me. 'I haven't got time for this. I've got a long drive. Good night.'

As the front door slammed a moment later, I

wrapped my robe more tightly around my body and shivered. What the hell had just happened? Had I just been dumped? He hadn't lost his temper like that since the incident in April and he'd certainly never walked out on me.

2

'How was your evening with your sugar daddy?' Ruby asked the next morning as I called at her room with her medication.

'Not good. I think I've been dumped.'

'How can you *think* you've been dumped. You either have or you haven't.'

I shrugged. 'I don't really understand what happened. He accused me of being high-maintenance and stormed out.'

She shook her head. 'You don't need him, darling. When I was your age, I had six suitors on the go. One for each day of the week and Sunday off—'

'To repent your sins?'

Ruby laughed, her eyes twinkling with mischief. 'Goodness, no! Sunday was for whomever had pleased me best during the week. I wanted to spend my day off pleasurably.'

'Are you not finished your rounds yet, Carolyn?' The She-Devil's pitchy voice bore into me, wiping the smile from my face.

'Nearly.'

'Nearly isn't good enough. You should have finished ten minutes ago.'

'It was my fault,' Ruby said. 'I had a funny turn. Callie had to help me out.'

The She-Devil's eyes bore into me. 'Is this true?'

I nodded and crossed my fingers behind my back. 'Ruby went a bit dizzy.'

She turned to Ruby. 'You're fine now?'

'Yes. Much better. Callie was amazing as always. She's such a gem.'

I had to look away. The She-Devil would *not* have appreciated the compliment.

'Yes, well, finish your rounds, Carolyn, then report to my office. One of the residents has only just advised us that they had an accident in the night. I'll need you to strip their bed.'

I could imagine the grin on her face as she sashayed down the corridor towards her office, delighted that I had a soggy mattress to deal with. Or worse. I bet she'd been saving that task especially for me, as usual. Cow.

'Thanks for defending me, Ruby,' I said.

'Any time. Couldn't have you dumped and sacked in the space of twenty-four hours, could we?'

I smiled. 'Will you be down for dominoes this afternoon?'

'Of course. I need to beat that Iris Davies this week. I'm sure she's cheating.'

'She was the North Yorkshire Pub Dominoes Champion for a decade, Ruby.'

'Yes. No doubt by cheating. I'm onto her.' She pointed two fingers at her eyes, then flicked them away, then back again.

'I'll see you later.' I laughed as I kicked the brake off the trolley and started to push it away.

'Callie!' she called. 'If you really have parted company with your sugar daddy, you could always court my grandson, Rhys.'

I turned to face her. The cheeky grin on her face

matched her playful tone. 'Would this be the illusive grandson who never visits?

'It might be.'

'Are you sure he exists?'

She laughed as she tapped the side of her nose. 'That's for me to know and you to find out.'

'See you for dominoes,' I called as I set off down the corridor again. I wasn't convinced Ruby had a grandson, mainly because she never spoke of children. The only photos in her rooms were black and white images from her own youth. She occasionally mentioned a grandson yet he never seemed to show up. Either he was fiction or he was completely unreliable. I wasn't sure which idea I preferred.

* * *

'The She-Devil's on the warpath,' whispered Maria, stopping me in the corridor three days later.

My heart sank. 'With me? What have I done now?'

'A delivery arrived that she thought was for her but was actually for you.'

'What sort of delivery?'

'A floral sort of delivery.'

I grinned. 'Tony?'

'Presumably. I told you he'd get over his childish little man-strop and come grovelling.'

I hoped that was the case. I'd texted him and left a couple of messages – careful not to bombard him – but he hadn't responded.

'Why's she on the warpath?' I asked. 'Aren't we allowed deliveries?'

'It's not that. Pete was in reception when they arrived. Apparently it's her wedding anniversary today so she assumed they were from Mr She-Devil.'

'Awk-ward!'

Maria continued on her way and I headed towards the front of the building where Denise's office was positioned behind the reception desk. Had Tony really sent me flowers? He'd never done that before which meant he must be feeling really guilty about his behaviour. Good.

The She-Devil must have seen me approach. Either that or her satanic sixth sense had been in operation. 'These came for you.' She thrust a large bouquet of yellow and white roses in my direction.

'Put them in the staffroom then get back to your work.'

'Yes, Mrs Kimble. Thank you.' I sped down the corridor with the flowers, fighting the urge to grab the card and read it. For a brief moment, I felt sorry for the She-Devil. It must be awful having flowers arrive for someone else on your wedding anniversary. But then I felt sorrier for Mr She-Devil. The poor bloke probably didn't have much to celebrate while being married to a bully like her, unless she was very different at home, which I seriously doubted.

As soon as I entered the staffroom, I dumped the flowers on the table and ripped open the card. 'Sorry about Monday,' I read. 'Can I make it up to you tonight?' Not exactly romantic but it would have to do. I'd text him after lunch. Didn't want to appear too desperate.

* * *

'I hear your sugar daddy sent you flowers. Not dumped after all, then?' Ruby asked that afternoon, looking up from playing Scrabble with Iris.

I added a splash of milk into cups of tea for them both. 'No. Not dumped.'

'Shame,' she said. 'My grandson's visiting this evening.'

'Is that right? What time can we expect the mysterious Rhys?'

'About six o'clock. He'd be a perfect suitor for you, darling, although he's the same age as you so not a sugar daddy.'

I smiled. 'That's no good then. You know I like my older men. Besides, as we've just established, I haven't been dumped.'

'You should make him work harder for forgiveness, you know. I used to make my men work very hard.'

'I bet you did,' I said, laughing at her cheeky wink.

'Triple word score,' Iris declared, helping herself to some more Scrabble tiles.

'You can't have!' Ruby cried. 'Iris Davies, you little cheat. That is *not* a word.'

'I assure you it is.'

'Callie! She's making that up, isn't she?'

I had to laugh at Ruby's incredulous expression. 'I haven't a clue. Look it up in the dictionary.'

'I will. Where is it?'

I rolled my eyes at Iris then retrieved the dictionary for Ruby from the nearby games cabinet. 'I'm on shift until eight tonight,' I said. 'So I look forward to *finally* meeting Rhys. If he turns up this time.'

'Oh, he will. I'll be sure to introduce you. He's such a lovely young man.'

'I've never met Rhys either,' Iris said.

'That's because I only introduce him to people who don't cheat at Scrabble.'

I giggled as I left them to it.

'I didn't know Ruby had children,' Maria said once the residents' lounge had emptied, leaving us free to clear away the cups and plates.

'She doesn't. I checked her file.' Curiosity had overcome me when I'd filed the report for her fake dizzy spell on Tuesday and her file clearly stated no children.

'Then why was she telling you she's got a grandson?'

I shrugged as I tipped a dish of used teabags into the small bin on the trolley. 'When I was younger, we used to call our next-door neighbours Auntie Pat and Uncle Keith even though they weren't relations.'

Maria nodded. 'We did that. We called the old lady opposite us Granny Jayne. You think this grandson is a non-relation like that?'

'Either that or she's making him up.'

'Why would she do that?'

'I don't know,' I said, emptying a couple of cold cups of tea into the slop bucket. 'She's always going on about what a great grandson this Rhys is, but he can't be that great because I've never known him to visit. She could be lonely.'

'Or she could be losing her marbles.'

I frowned. 'I hope not. She's always seemed so lucid.'

'She's eighty-four. That's a lot of years' worth of data and experiences to keep in your mind. Things are bound to get mixed up sooner or later.' She gently touched my arm. 'I wish you wouldn't get so close to them. You know it makes it harder when...'

'When what?' I snapped, knowing exactly what she meant.

'You know. When they die or whatever. Come on. Let's get these to the kitchen.'

I stomped after Maria down the corridor. Much as I adored her, I hated how detached she could be from the residents. She detested listening to stories of their childhood, their families, their lost loves, or their time in the military, whereas I found it fascinating. She didn't see the point in building relationships with visiting friends or family and she never stayed after a shift to join in a game or a sing-song. However, when a resident took ill or died and I was sobbing my heart out, I envied Maria's ability to move on. Did that mean she was in the wrong job because she didn't seem to care enough or was I in the wrong job for caring too much?

As we cleared the tea trolley, I wondered if she was right about Ruby. Could she be showing early signs of dementia? Nothing else suggested it, though. She wasn't forgetful. She wasn't confused. She just had a potentially fictional grandson.

* * *

'Angel!'

I couldn't bring myself to run up to Tony at the end of my shift that evening. Instead, I walked slowly towards him and, on my tiptoes, gave him a gentle kiss on the cheek.

'I said I was sorry,' he snapped. 'Are you still pissed off with me?'

I bristled. Yes, I was pissed off with a grown man for walking out on me like he had, but sometimes it wasn't about him. 'I'm upset about one of the residents, Ruby.'

He put his arm round me and steered me towards his car. 'I'm sorry, angel, but death's an inevitable part of your job.'

'She's not dead.'

'Illness, then.'

'She's not ill either. Or at least, I hope she isn't.'

Tony released a loud, exaggerated sigh. 'Then do we *really* need to let it affect our evening?' He stared at me, eyes narrowed. I didn't recognise him for a moment as my gentle, loving partner. Then he smiled and his whole face changed. 'I've missed you. Where's my bubbly girl gone?'

As he opened the car door for me, I bit on my lip

to stop me from telling him that sometimes even the bubbliest person had the sparkle knocked out of them and needed a little sympathy. Where would it get me, though? Another strop?

I pasted a smile on my face and tried to keep the sarcasm out of my voice as I sat in the passenger seat. 'She's right here and she loves her flowers. Thank you. How was your week?'

Tony closed my door then dashed round to his side and got in. 'Amazing week. I had a good meeting in Manchester on Tuesday and I've found a great site in Liverpool where...'

I zoned out as we pulled past the front of Bay View. All I could think about was Ruby in her best dress – a stunning satin coral number with cream lace – all alone in the residents' lounge, waiting again for the grandson who'd never appeared. It broke my heart to see the look of disappointment on her face.

'Are you listening to me?' Tony said.

'Of course I am.' I hoped he wasn't going to test me by asking me what he'd just said. 'It's really interesting. Please continue.'

So he did. I nodded my head and made noises of

approval in all the right places, but I felt in a daze, like my body was there but my heart and mind weren't.

'You said you were going to make it up to me tonight?' I prompted when Tony finally stopped jabbering about his week. 'Are we going out?'

'Out? Of course not.'

I tensed. What was it with him always wanting to stay in? 'Why do you say "of course not" as if it was a really stupid suggestion? It's Friday night. People go out on Friday nights.'

'Yes, and I bet those people don't finish a twelve-hour shift at eight o'clock.'

'That's sweet of you, but I promise I'm not too tired. I could jump in the shower and be ready in fifteen minutes.'

Tony laughed. 'Maybe another time, angel. I've just driven up from Nottingham. I want to lie on the sofa with my gorgeous girl and make it up to her with her favourite wine and some Belgian chocolates.'

So he wasn't really thinking of me at all. He was the tired one. As usual. He was also the wine drinker. I'm more of a lager kind of girl. And he was the Belgian chocolates fan too. Personally, a bar of Galaxy was more my thing – a box of fancy nut-topped truffle-y crap did nothing for me. Not wanting to cause another rift, though, I smiled and said, 'Sounds great.'

'And, of course, a spot of make-up sex,' he added.

Also thinking of him.

Just like I'd done in the car, I made the right noises in the right places. Lots off oohs, aahs and soft moans to make him believe I was in the moment. But I was really back in the residents' lounge with Ruby. It was possible her grandson had shown after I left, but that would have made him over two hours late, so a no-show was far more likely. Or no grandson. Should I speak to the She-Devil about it? If this was the start of dementia, I owed it to Ruby to flag it up.

'I'm nearly done, angel,' gasped Tony.

Oops. Back in the room. 'Ooh, yeah, oh, that's it. Yes! Yes!' *No! No!*

He grunted then rolled off and disappeared to the bathroom. I thumped my head against the pillow a few times before getting up, pulling on my robe, and going into the kitchenette to gulp down some water.

'Are you staying the night?' I asked when Tony re-appeared. I hoped he'd say no. My worries about Ruby were making me feel irritated by his presence and I longed to be alone.

'I can't. I've got to get home. My sister's coming to visit tomorrow with her kids, and I've got no food in. I'll let you get your beauty sleep. Don't eat all those chocolates, will you? Not when I'm not staying to work the calories off with you.'

'You take them,' I said, smiling sweetly whilst inwardly grimacing at another comment about my weight. 'Then you'll know they're safely out of my reach.'

Tony tilted his head on one side and stared at me for a moment while I continued to smile. 'I don't know if I've said something to piss you off again, but I don't want us to argue so I'm just going to get my stuff and leave.' He walked past the sofa and through the open double-sliding doors into the bedroom.

I leaned on the kitchenette counter and watched him dress for a few moments. 'Tony?'

'Yes.'

'Do you love me?'

'You know I do.' He sat on the bed as he pulled on his socks.

'Why do you love me?'

He crossed the room and wrapped his arms around me, pushing one hand into my robe to cup my breast. 'Because you're young, gorgeous, and amazing in bed. What's not to love?' He kissed my neck then headed into the hall.

'Here's the chocolates.' I passed the part-eaten box to him. 'Save some for your sister.'

'I'll call you,' he said, drawing me in for a kiss. 'Bye.'

Closing the flat door, I sighed. It was twenty past ten and I was far from tired. I gathered the wine glasses from the lounge area and reached for a cold lager from the fridge. Stepping out onto my tiny balcony, I sipped my drink while I leaned against the railing and stared out towards the distant inky sea. The lights of Whitsborough Bay's North Bay twinkled invitingly and, as the late June evening breeze wafted through my hair, I wondered how I'd been so blind. When Tony had first said he loved me, I asked him why, and he'd given me the same answer: because I was young, gorgeous, and amazing in bed. At the time, I'd giggled and shown him just how amazing in bed I was. I'd never for one second imagined he'd been telling the truth. And if that genuinely was his reason, it suggested he probably didn't love me at all; he was just using me for sex. Not good. Not good at all.

3

'I'm not taking no for an answer,' Nick insisted, his voice echoing through the intercom the following morning. 'That's why I turned up instead of phoning.'

'I've got plans.'

'What sort of plans?'

'Erm... cleaning the flat?'

'That's crap and you know it. You might as well buzz me in because you know I'm not leaving. We're going to have a brother and sister day of fun together. It's way overdue.'

I sighed and pressed the entry buzzer then waited in the doorway, listening to him clattering up the two flights of stairs. 'Is Tony here?' he asked, kissing me on the cheek.

I shook my head. 'He left last night. Why do you look so cheerful?'

'It's a gorgeous day and I'm going to spend it on the stunning North Yorkshire Coast with my baby sister. Who wouldn't be cheerful?'

I closed the door and followed him into the living area. 'I hate that you're such a morning person.'

'And I hate that you're not. You have ten minutes to get showered, dressed, and out of the dark mood you're in.'

'Where are you taking me?'

'Today we're going to play at being tourists and do all the things we never do in Whitsborough Bay because they're right on our doorstep.'

'Like what?'

'You want a list?' He grinned at me. 'It might not be in this order, but the day's itinerary includes: a visit to the castle, crabbing in the harbour, crazy golf, jet boat, Ferris wheel, ice-cream, slot machines, sandcastles, doughnuts, an open-top bus ride round The Headland, and fish and chips on the beach.'

I raised my eyebrows. 'Seriously? What are we? Six?'

'Seriously and I guarantee you'll love every second of it. Now get your arse in the shower. You have eight minutes left.'

* * *

Our touristy day turned out to be exactly what I needed. I'd always loved nature and fully appreciated the beauty of living on the North Yorkshire Coast but had stopped making the most of it. I couldn't stop laughing as the jet boat had crashed over the waves, I screeched with excitement when I won a soft toy on the grab machines in the arcades, and I gasped at the magnificence of the views from the top of the Ferris wheel in Pleasureland.

'Thanks, big bruv,' I said as we sat on the sand at about half six that evening with a tray of fish, chips, and mushy peas each.

'For what?'

'For today. How did you know I was down?'

'Facebook.'

'I didn't put anything on Facebook about being down. In fact, I've barely been on it this week.'

Nick leaned over and dipped a chip in my mayonnaise. 'That's how I knew something was wrong. Is it over with Tony?'

I shook my head. 'No. Not yet anyway.' I popped another chip in my mouth. 'Can I ask you a question? You don't have to answer it if you don't want to, but I hope you will.'

'Sounds ominous.'

'You loved Lisa, right?'

Nick breathed in sharply. 'Yes. Why?'

'What did you love about her?'

He shrugged. 'It was eight years ago.'

'I know, but you can't have forgotten. What was it about her that made you want to marry her?'

Nick stabbed his wooden fork into the remnants of his chips and lay the tray down beside him. 'Before she ran off with my best mate? I don't know. Her personality, her sense of humour, our friendship, the good times we had.'

'So you didn't love her because she was young, gorgeous, and great in bed.'

'Callie! No! We were both young. I was twenty-one and Lisa was only nineteen. Yes, she was gorgeous, but looks are only part of the initial attraction, and as for being great in bed, I am absolutely not going to discuss my sex life with my sister. Ever. So eat your chips and shut up.'

I ate a few more chips then lay my nearly empty tray down in the sand. We sat in silence, watching children chasing each other along the beach and couples walking along the shoreline.

'Tony's told you he loves you for those reasons, hasn't he?' Nick said eventually.

'Yep.'

'It's not really the basis for a long-term relationship, is it?'

'Nope.'

'So are you going to end it?'

'Nope.'

'Oh, Callie!' He put his arm round me and I snuggled against his chest. 'What are we going to do with you? Do you love Tony?'

'Yes. Well... I thought I did... but then he threw a strop and walked out on me on Monday for no reason and now I don't know what to think.'

Nick stood up, pulled me to my feet and picked

up the chip trays. 'I'll put these in the bin then we'll go for a beer and you can start from the beginning. Without any reference to your sex life, please.'

'That'll be tricky. Sex is about the only thing we ever do together.'

Nick grimaced. 'Argh! Stop! I can't cover my ears with these in my hands.'

'Okay. I'll try and stick to a PG rating for your delicate ears.'

'Thank you.'

* * *

Nick stopped to chat to someone he knew as we left The Lobster Pot, a cosy two-storey pub by the harbour, a few hours later. I crossed the road onto the esplanade and sat on the sea wall, waiting for him. It had been helpful talking things through with him. The very act of trying to talk about our relationship in PG terms made me realise that it was far from it. Our relationship was purely about sex from that first moment in the laundry room up until last night in my flat. We'd only been out together a handful of times and each of those had been drives down country roads or to remote coves where, you've guessed it, we had sex. We'd never been out for a drink, a meal, a walk along the beach or anything that 'normal' couples did. I'd managed to convince myself that, because we only got to see each other once or twice a week, it was natural that we'd spend a lot of that time in bed. I couldn't convince myself of that anymore, not after nearly a year together.

'Then I put a question to you,' Nick had said. 'What do you want from this relationship? If you're looking for someone who has potential as a future husband, Tony doesn't sound like the one. But if you're only after a bit of no-strings fun, maybe he is.'

It was an interesting point. What did I want? I certainly hadn't gone into any of my other disastrous short-term older-man relationships expecting marriage but Tony was different. Different enough to marry? Different enough to have children with? I wasn't sure.

'Callie!' Nick waved from the other side of the road. I stood up but a long trail of cars meant no chance of crossing. While I waited, I glanced up at the first-floor window of The Lobster Pot and did a double take. Seated in the window seat, all alone, nursing a glass of wine and gazing out to the sea was the She-Devil. As I stared, she lifted her hand and wiped her cheeks, as though wiping tears away, and then she caught my eye.

'Callie! You can cross now.'

I tore my gaze away as Nick called me. When I looked back, the glass of wine was still there, but the She-Devil had gone. Had I imagined it? No. It had definitely been her and she'd recognised me too. She'd looked so very sad. A flicker of sympathy went out to her again.

4

'How was your weekend?' I'd decided to start the week with a new attitude towards the She-Devil, but the shocked look on her face suggested it had been the wrong approach.

'I don't think my weekend has anything to do with the situation with Mr Johnson, does it?' she snapped. 'Do you know anything about his missing money?'

I cringed. 'I don't think it's actually missing.'

'Are you saying that Mr Johnson's family are liars? His son assures me they gave him one hundred pounds cash during their visit last Sunday and it was all gone by yesterday.'

How was I going to tell her without dropping Ruby in it? 'It's still in Bay View. It isn't actually missing. It just... er... doesn't belong to him anymore.'

She fixed a steely stare on me, reminding me of my Year Four teacher who'd terrified me so much that I'd actually wet my pants when she yelled at me one day for talking too much. I hoped I wasn't about to do the same. 'Carolyn Derbyshire, if you value your job here, you'll stop talking in riddles and tell me what you know about the missing money.'

I sighed. 'It's a rumour. I have no facts. Some of the residents like to play cards on an evening.'

She stood up and put her hands on her hips. 'Cards? Yes. I already know that.'

'For money.'

Her grip on her hips tightened and her eyes flashed. 'What did you say?'

'I think that some of them may have graduated from gin rummy for matchsticks to poker for real money and it would appear that Mr Johnson hasn't quite grasped the rules of poker.'

She sank down onto her chair again. 'Oh my! A gambling ring in my care home. Never in my...' She stopped and looked up. 'Who set it up?'

'I don't know.'

'Carolyn!'

'Honestly, I haven't a clue. I haven't done a weekend night shift recently. All I know is the rumour about Mr Johnson.'

The She-Devil ran a hand through her short blonde bob then removed her glasses and left them to dangle on their chain. 'There'll need to be a full investigation. As if I don't have enough to deal with at the moment.' She fixed her evil eye on me again. 'If you know who's involved, it would save us a lot of time and trouble that I really don't need right now.'

'I'd like to help, but I don't know. Sorry.' Bloody Ruby. I'd have to warn her. I turned to leave, but a thought struck me. 'Could you maybe make an announcement instead and say that you're aware of the gambling and that, if any monies won aren't returned by the end of the week, there'll be a full investigation and consequences? If the person who fleeced him hands the cash over anonymously, it would save you the need for an investigation and it would placate Mr Johnson's family.'

She stared at me for a moment then put her

glasses back on her nose. 'I'll think about it. You can leave now.'

'Thank you.' I paused in the doorway. 'Was that you I saw in The Lobster Pot on Saturday night?' Argh! What on earth possessed me to come out with that? Would I ever learn to keep my gob shut?

Her head jerked up and her eyes widened. 'No. Why?'

'I was there with my brother and I could have sworn I saw you in the window.'

'Not me. I wasn't there. I was... actually, it's none of your damn business where I was. What I do on the weekend is nothing to do with my staff. We're finished here. Close the door on your way out.'

I did as instructed and headed down the corridor to find Ruby, kicking myself for pushing the subject with the She-Devil. Ironically, she could have done with lessons from Ruby on what a poker face looked like because I knew, without a shadow of a doubt, that it had been her in the pub on Saturday.

* * *

'My grandson is visiting this Friday,' Ruby said, after I warned her about Mr Johnson and the impending investigation.

'And that's not what we're discussing. You need to take this gambling business seriously, Ruby. You could get evicted.'

'Oh nonsense! Storm in a teacup. Did you hear what I said, Callie, about Rhys coming on Friday? He's such a lovely young man. So kind.'

'Will you stop talking about Rhys and concentrate on what I'm telling you about your gambling racket?'

Ruby laughed. 'I used to make a fortune back in the day. Nobody suspected a woman would be such a great player. I moved in some impressive circles you know. Princes, dukes... fleeced them all.'

'I'll bet you did! But Angus Johnson is neither a prince nor a duke and you need to give him his money back.'

'Spoilsport.'

'I've got work to do,' I said, heading towards the next gambler's room.

'Oh, by the way,' shouted Ruby down the corridor. 'I saw you with your sugar daddy on Friday. He looked familiar. Do I know him?'

'I showed him round here last year and introduced him to some residents. You probably recognise him from then.'

'That must be it. See you later, Callie. I'm off to practise my poker face in the mirror for when the She-Devil tries to confront me.'

I giggled as I continued down the corridor. Gambling with princes and dukes? Nope, that definitely didn't surprise me.

5

I propped myself up on the pillows on Thursday evening. 'Tony?'

'Yes, angel?'

'What are we doing together?'

He grinned mischievously. 'If you don't know that after all this time, I'm not about to explain it.'

I gave him a playful shove. 'Very funny. I mean relationship-wise. What are we doing?'

'Having fun. Aren't we?'

'Yes, but am I the only one with whom you're having fun?'

His eyes widened. 'What are you asking?'

'Are you seeing anyone else?'

'Callie! How could you think that?' He sounded and looked genuinely hurt.

'I'm not saying you *are* seeing someone else, but it struck me that we've never talked about fidelity and I might have made a big assumption that we're both on the same page about it.'

Tony glared at me. 'You think I have a woman in Sheffield and another in Liverpool and—'

'No! I'm not saying that. But we don't have a normal relationship. All we seem to do is have sex. We never go out and...'

I tailed off as he thrust back the duvet, rolled out of bed, and pulled on his boxer shorts. 'Are we really going to do this again?' he snapped.

'Do what?'

He twisted round to face me. 'Have an argument about going out. Because, if that's what you want, I'm leaving.'

I stared at him for a moment, my heart thumping. What did that mean? Leaving the flat or leaving me? All I wanted to do was have a conversation about the future. All of my previous relationships had been short-term, so we'd never got to the future part, but Tony and I were heading towards a year together.

This was long-term. I knew he was divorced, but I had no idea whether he wanted to marry again. I knew he had no children, but I had no idea whether he wanted any. As to where I featured – girlfriend, wife, mother – I genuinely had no idea. And I didn't like being in the dark.

Looking at his raised eyebrows and set jaw, it was clear that tonight wasn't the night for that conversation, but it would have to happen at some point because we couldn't keep drifting like this. I *did* want to marry, I *did* want to have children, and I was reasonably sure I wanted Tony to be the one to give me those things. But if he didn't want to be the one...

Pushing aside my anxieties, I crawled across the bed and wrapped my arms around his back and kissed his neck. 'I don't want an argument and I don't want you to leave. Will you come back to bed? I'll give you a massage.'

His stiff shoulders dropped a bit and I knew I'd got his interest. 'A long one? With oils and everything?'

'Yes.'

'And I won't have to give you one in return?'

As I massaged his back, it struck me that I'd placated him too quickly and he hadn't actually answered my question about what we were doing together. I was still in the dark and I couldn't stay there forever.

Tony stayed the night but left at six in the morning. 'By the way,' he said as he sat on the edge of the bed to kiss me goodbye, 'the purchase of Bay View is back on the cards. I'll be looking round at some point in the next few weeks and would be very interested in checking out that laundry room again.'

'Have any of the other care homes you're looking at got such amazing laundry rooms?'

'Oh yes, but the tour guides don't compare. They're not young, sexy, and bursting out of their uniforms like you.'

I frowned. 'I don't burst out of my uniform.'

Tony laughed. 'Have you not looked at yourself in the mirror lately?'

I self-consciously pulled the duvet over my exposed breasts. 'Are you saying my uniform's too tight?'

'Yes. But I like it like that. I couldn't wait to get my hands on you the minute I met you.' He kissed me again, pulling away when it started to get a bit heated. 'Still can't resist you. But I've got to go. Long drive. I'll see you later.'

I curled up under the duvet, stomach churning, as I listened to Tony moving around the living area then closing the front door. Had he just summed up what our relationship was really all about? Had I been kidding myself all along that we were heading anywhere other than the bedroom?

* * *

'Rhys is coming tonight,' whispered Ruby, startling me as I watered the plants in the residents' lounge the following morning.

'Are you sure?'

'It's Friday, isn't it?'

'Yes, but...'

'Then he's coming tonight. He promised.'

The She-Devil passed the doorway and stopped and stared at me, eyebrows raised. I felt guilty every time she did that, even though I was usually doing nothing wrong.

'Sorry, Ruby,' I muttered as I moved onto the next plant, then the next. When I was certain the coast was clear, I lowered the watering can. 'I'm delighted for you, but I don't want you to get your hopes up. You know how upset you were last time he didn't show.'

'It was my mistake. I'd misread his text message. Rhys would never deliberately let me down.'

'Carolyn!' Damn! The She-Devil was back.

'Yes?'

'Shouldn't you be finished with those plants by now?'

'I'm on my last one.'

'Hurry up. You're paid to work, not to gossip with the residents.'

'Sorry,' hissed Ruby. 'I'm always getting you into trouble.'

'Don't worry about it. If it wasn't you, it would be something else.' I picked up the small bottle of plant feed and the leaf sprayer. 'Actually, Ruby, can I ask you a question? Do you think my uniform's too tight?'

Ruby stepped back and looked me up and down. 'I'd say it fits your curves. If you want to know about tight uniforms, you should have seen some of the outfits I had to wear when I worked in Paris...'

* * *

'Do you think my uniform's too tight?' I asked Maria in the staffroom later that morning.

She shook her head. 'It looks fine. Mine's too tight, though. I've put on a stone since I quit smoking last month. How's that supposed to be good for your health?'

I zoned out as she talked about reaching for snacks when she'd normally have lit-up. It was no good. Tony's comments had really thrown me and I was going to have to ask the She-Devil if I could order some larger tunics.

I crept along the corridor that afternoon whilst the residents were taking afternoon tea. It was only a request for a new uniform. Surely she couldn't tell me off for it. As I got closer to her office, I heard raised voices. Or rather one raised voice: hers.

'I don't want you to do that... There's really no need...' The roller blind was pulled down but it fitted badly and I could see through a gap on one side. She was on her mobile, pacing up and down. I decided to loiter for a short while and tried my hardest not to listen. but her voice was far too loud. 'You're not listening to me... Yes I do... Don't be like that. It's not... Why would you say that? That's not fair... Don't hang up on me... Don't... Shit!' I jumped as she emitted an angry squeal followed by more expletives.

It probably wasn't a good time to ask about my uniform. I took one more quick glance through the gap and jumped again as the She-Devil sobbed loudly. She slumped into her desk chair and dropped her head onto her hands. I held my breath for a moment, watching her shoulders shaking. My natural instinct was to rush into the office and comfort her, but this was the She-Devil. And I was meant to be helping with afternoon tea. If she knew I was skiving as well as witnessing a rare moment of weakness, it would end badly for me.

I didn't see the She-Devil for the rest of the day. As if what I'd seen in her office wasn't worrying enough, I ended my shift to the sight of Ruby, yet again, dressed up to the nines waiting for her grandson, staring towards the door, eyes lighting up every time it opened and shoulders slumping every time it wasn't him. If he was real and he ever did turn up, I'd be having serious words with him for upsetting a wonderful old lady.

6

'I'm worried about the She-Devil,' I said to Maria. She was round at my flat for a pizza and film night a couple of weeks later; something we tried to do every couple of weeks. 'Something's definitely wrong with her.'

Maria helped herself to another slice of pizza. 'Pete says Mr She-Devil has left her. Fact. Couldn't have happened to a nicer person.'

'How does Pete know?'

'His boyfriend works with Mr She-Devil's best mate or something like that.'

'That would explain the mood swings.' Some days she yelled at anyone and everyone. Other days, she looked like too much milk in her tea would cause an emotional breakdown. I thought about the phone call I'd overheard. It would definitely have fitted with her asking her husband not to move out.

I took a swig of my lager. 'I feel sorry for her.'

'What for? She's horrible to you.'

'I know. It's just...' I shrugged. 'I get really upset when I've had a row with Tony but a marriage breakdown must be a million times more stressful.'

Maria nodded. 'I'm sure it is. The difference is that you park the personal stuff while you're at work and she takes it out on her staff. You really shouldn't feel sorry for that woman. Do you think she'd give a damn if the tables were turned?'

She was right. The She-Devil was a bully and I was her favourite target but I still had a sliver of empathy for her, especially when I pictured her in The Lobster Pot all alone or having a meltdown in her office. I hadn't told Maria, Pete, or anyone else about those incidents and I wasn't going to, but they did suggest that the dragon we saw at work might really be an unhappy, lonely woman.

'How's it going with Tony?' Maria asked as I

cleared the pizza boxes away a little later. 'Ditched him yet for having too many man-strops?'

I sighed as I plonked myself back down on the sofa. 'I've only seen him twice in the past fortnight and only for an hour each time. Do you think I'm wasting my time with him?'

She raised her eyebrows. 'Do *you* think you are?'

'I don't know. We've been together for nearly a year so I asked him where the relationship was heading and he evaded the question.'

'Where do you want it to head?' Maria asked.

'I'm not sure. I was thinking marriage and kids, but...'

The shocked expression on Maria's face said it all.

'... but you don't think Tony would be up for that.'

She grimaced. 'If you're after marriage and kids, I'm not sure Tony Sinclair's your man. And do you really want him to be? You're always bickering and you've had a couple of huge bust-ups.'

'We're not always bickering.'

'You are. Nearly every time you see him, you

come into work the next day moaning about something he's said or done.'

I slumped back on the sofa, shaking my head. She was absolutely right.

'I assumed you only put up with it because it wasn't serious,' she continued. 'But if you're looking for a serious relationship...' She shook her head. 'Have you talked to Tony about this?'

'No. I don't know how to broach it.'

'If the relationship was right for you, would you even have to broach it? Wouldn't things have just evolved naturally?'

I sipped my drink, a nervous knot forming in my stomach. She'd hit the nail on the head. Our relationship had certainly started out as a bit of fun and I'd been happy with that but, when he told me he loved me, I'd assumed that meant things were getting serious. Perhaps I had been really naïve there because nothing had evolved and nothing was natural. We definitely needed to have a conversation – soon.

* * *

On Monday evening, Tony came round but only stayed an hour. He was stressed about a proposal at work falling through so it was definitely not the right time for a relationship conversation.

As he dressed to leave, he confirmed that his tour of Bay View Care Home was scheduled for the following afternoon and that a tour of the laundry room was high on his itinerary. He suggested I might like to go commando in preparation. I smiled and said, 'We'll see,' but was he for real? I worked in a care home for the elderly. No way was I going to go about my duties with no pants on. I hoped it was a crass joke but something told me he meant it and I didn't like what that said about him or what he thought of me.

I felt ridiculously nervous the following morning knowing that Tony would be in close proximity all afternoon. One minute, I felt excited at the prospect of being in the laundry room with him but, next minute, I felt annoyed that he seemed more interested in that than doing the job he was paid to do.

'How's that sugar daddy of yours?' Ruby asked during my medication rounds.

'He's fine. He's coming to look round again this afternoon so you might see him later.'

Ruby clapped her hands together. 'How wonderful! Will you introduce him to me?'

I handed over her medication. 'I can try, but I don't think I'll be able to. Denise will want to be in charge of the tour this time.'

Ruby took the cup of water and knocked back her pills. 'I'd love to meet him. I need to suss out the competition.'

'What competition?'

'Tony versus Rhys. As I've told you before, you and my grandson would be perfect for each other.'

The non-existent grandson. I smiled politely. 'I've got to go. I've got extra duties ahead of the visit so I can't stop and chat. Sorry.'

* * *

The She-Devil and Tony appeared in the doorway of the residents' lounge as I was clearing away afternoon tea. I tried to avoid Tony's gaze.

'Where's Maria?' she called.

'Mrs Robinson wasn't feeling very well so Maria's accompanied her back to her room. Can I help?'

'Mr Sinclair here would like to look at the laundry room, but I have another appointment. I was hoping Maria would show him.'

I felt my cheeks redden and I couldn't look Tony in the eye. 'Maybe I could show him what's on offer in the laundry room?'

She tutted and sighed. 'I suppose so. My apologies, Mr Sinclair. As I explained to your office, I already had another appointment booked in about our gardening contract and—'

'It's no problem,' Tony said. 'I believe that this is the same young lady who showed me round last year and, as I recall, she was able to give me exactly what I wanted and a whole lot more.'

I had to fake a sneeze to stop myself giggling. Tony would get me fired if he wasn't careful.

The She-Devil narrowed her eyes at me. 'Yes, well, I'll leave you to it. Carolyn will see you out, Mr Sinclair, but please ring me if you want any more information.' She marched across the room.

'You wanted to see the laundry room, sir?' I asked

when she was out of earshot. 'It's my favourite part of the building.'

'That's a coincidence. It's mine too.'

At that moment, Ruby entered the residents' lounge with Iris, both of them holding paperbacks. Ruby stopped when she saw Tony, then winked. 'Is this him? Is this your sugar daddy, Callie?'

I laughed. 'This is Tony Sinclair. Tony, these are two of our residents, Ruby and Iris.'

Ruby held out a slender hand and Tony made her day by bending down and kissing it instead of shaking it. She giggled. 'Quite the charmer.'

'I try my best,' said Tony, before kissing Iris's hand too.

'Nice to meet you, Tony,' Iris said. 'But please excuse me. I've left my reading glasses in my room.'

Ruby tutted. 'I asked if you had them.'

'I know, but then you distracted me by demanding to know if I had any of my birthday chocolates left. I put my glasses down and forgot to pick them up again.'

'You might as well bring the rest of the chocolates too,' Ruby called after her.

She sat down in her favourite armchair by the

window and stared at Tony. 'I know you from some-where. Have we met before?'

'I don't think so. I'd remember a beautiful lady like you.'

Ruby laughed. 'I can see why young Callie has hung onto you.' She turned to me. 'Callie, darling, I don't suppose there's any tea left in the pot, is there? I fell asleep and missed it.'

'If Tony doesn't mind sitting with you for a few minutes, I'll make you a fresh one, but it will just be a teabag dipped in a mug. I'm not making a pot.'

'Tastes no different to me. It's only that Iris Davies who makes a fuss about having it out of a pot.' She turned to Tony. 'She cheats at dominoes too, you know. And Scrabble.'

'Are you okay if I make Ruby some tea?' I asked Tony.

'I'm fine. Don't take too long, though. I'm des-perate to see that laundry room again.'

I tried to rush back, but I kept slopping Ruby's tea over the edge of the mug and scalding my hand. As I silently approached the residents' lounge in my canvas shoes, I could overhear Ruby and Tony talking in raised voices.

'You're mistaken,' he said.

'I'm not great with names, but I never forget a face.'

'Then I've got a double,' he snapped, arms crossed, staring defiantly at her. 'I don't live in Whitsborough Bay and I never have.'

'You do,' Ruby insisted, nodding vigorously. 'You've got a wife and three little ones, and you live near North Bay.'

'I assure you I don't.'

'Perhaps you're not married to her. Perhaps she's just your... what's the word these days... your partner?'

'Neither. Callie's my partner.'

'And Callie's right here,' I said, marching across the room and handing Ruby her tea, my heart thumping. 'What's going on?'

'Ruby here thinks she knows me,' Tony said. 'But she doesn't, do you?' His emphasis on the last couple of words wasn't lost on me.

Ruby looked up at me, defiance on her face. Then her eyes softened. 'Old age. Gets us all. I'm obviously a bit mixed up. Thanks for the tea, darling.'

Tony stood up.

'Are you still wanting to see the laundry room?' I asked.

'More than ever. Goodbye, Ruby. It was nice chatting to you.'

'Hmm. Goodbye, Mr Sinclair.'

'What on earth did you do to Ruby?' I asked as we walked along the corridor towards the laundry room.

'What do you mean?'

'She was all over you when you arrived and now it's all formal titles and the cold shoulder.'

He shrugged. 'Ironically for my job, I'm not great with the elderly. I get frustrated with people like Ruby who won't accept that sometimes their memory isn't what it used to be.'

'Like when they accuse you of having a wife and three kids?' I stopped and faced him. 'Is there any truth in it?'

'Only in Ruby's head. I had a wife and we divorced eight years ago, as you know. I've never had kids and I don't live in Whitsborough Bay. I have a flat in Sheffield. You know that too. I'd take you there but there's no point. I hate Sheffield and the flat's a dump but it was the first place I viewed when the divorce came through and I was so keen to move out that I stupidly bought it. If you want to believe an old lady's ramblings rather than me, though, we might as well call it a day.'

I looked into Tony's pleading hazel eyes. He was telling the truth. I was sure of it. Ruby was very confused about her grandson and this was clearly another example of that. 'So, about this laundry room...' I said.

7

The She-Devil cast a hard stare around the staffroom a week later, invoking instant silence. 'The Starling Group intend to add Bay View Care Home to their portfolio. They'll be investing in the buildings and grounds and may even expand so I'm not anticipating redundancies. You'll see some branding changes and receive new uniforms but that's it for the moment. I don't have time for questions and I insist that you don't say anything to the residents ahead of my lunchtime announcement or there will be consequences. Do I make myself clear?'

There was a fearful murmur of, 'Yes, Mrs Kimble.'

'Good. You'll notice Mr Tony Sinclair around quite a lot over the next few weeks. Please stay out of his way so he can do his work, but make sure you answer any questions he may have. Back to work, then.'

Something was definitely wrong with the She-Devil. Even though her voice had been strong and scary as always, she looked broken. Her eyes were red and puffy and her hands shook while she spoke. Oh God! What if she knew that we were about to lose our jobs and that's why she'd been crying? Why give us the reassurances, though? Why not say she didn't know what the future held? Unless this Starling Group had told her she had to say that. I'd have to ask Tony. He'd be honest with me. Okay, so he hadn't told me that the sale was confirmed but I understood why. It was business and I knew how these things worked. He wouldn't have been allowed to make the announcement until it was official.

'Callie! Callie! There you are!' Ruby rushed out of the dining room. She'd obviously been waiting for me to pass.

'Morning, Ruby. How are you?'

'I'm brilliant. I've got the most amazing news.'

'Spill.'

'Rhys is moving back to Whitsborough Bay.'

I decided to humour her. 'When's the big event?'

'I'm not sure of the exact details.'

Hardly surprising. How could you be sure of the exact details about something fictional? I smiled. 'I've got to sort out the medication, Ruby. We'll talk some more later.'

I followed the corridor round to the She-Devil's office to collect the key for the medicine room. The blinds were drawn across the internal windows so I lightly tapped on the door. No answer. I knocked a bit louder. She called something. Was it 'come in' or 'coming'? I cringed as I pushed the door open, hoping I'd made the right choice, and gasped. Tablets were strewn across the desk and tears were streaming down her face.

'What are you doing?' she cried. 'I told you to wait.'

'Sorry. Can I help?' I stepped forward to pick up some tablets.

'Hay fever,' she snapped. 'Makes my eyes stream. Spilt the tablets. Stupid caps. Leave it! I'm fine.'

I stepped back.

'You can go.'

'Sorry, but I need the keys to the medicine room.'

She groaned then pointed to a bunch of keys resting in her in-tray. 'Bring them back.'

'I will.' I glanced down at the tablets she was scooping up. I didn't know what they were, but they certainly weren't antihistamines. She clearly didn't want to talk to me, but I hoped she had a friend or family member in whom to confide because something was seriously wrong with her.

8

I squealed as a pair of hands covered my eyes a few days later. 'Happy anniversary.'

'Tony? You didn't say you were coming here today.'

He sat beside me on the bench in the gardens out the back of Bay View. 'I wanted to surprise you.'

'How did you know I'd be here?'

'Your friend Maria said that you had a favourite bench overlooking the sea, so I headed towards the sea and found you. Nice view.'

Perched on a cliff top, there was a sweeping view of the north side of Whitsborough Bay: The Sea Rescue Sanctuary to the far north, the beach, the brightly-painted wooden beach huts, and The Headland bustling with vehicles and pedestrians. To the south, the castle bravely faced the elements from its cliff top position. If I stood up, I could see the River Abbleby separating the two bays as it snaked towards the harbour, although the harbour itself was obliterated by the castle. 'It's perfect on a sunny day like today, but I like it just as much when it's stormy.'

Tony looked around him. 'The gardens are bigger than I thought.'

'They're amazing, but they're not the best for those with limited mobility. We've got a new gardener starting tomorrow who's going to make them more accessible so I nipped out for one last look before everything changes.' I rolled my eyes. 'You probably already knew about the gardener.'

'He's nothing to do with us, but we've given input to the plans because it's pointless him developing where we want to expand.'

'So you *are* expanding?'

'Definitely.'

'And my job's safe?'

Tony took my hand in his. 'I knew you were

moody about something. Is that what's been both-ering you?'

I decided to let the 'moody' accusation go and nodded. 'I didn't like to ask you as I know you'd have to keep certain things secret.'

'You should have just asked, angel, if it's been worrying you. Everyone's jobs should be safe. If any-thing, your boss will be recruiting *more* staff, not laying any off.'

'That's a relief.'

Tony stood up. 'How long have you got left for your lunch break?'

I glanced at my watch. 'About fifteen minutes.'

'And you say the gardener doesn't start until tomorrow?'

I frowned. 'That's right. Why?'

'I'm thinking that last year was the year of the laundry room, but we should start our second year together with a new special place and, on my way to find you, I came across a secluded summerhouse.'

'Tony! We can't. Someone might see us.'

'Who? You just said that the gardens aren't used and there's no gardener until tomorrow.'

I stood up, smiling at his enthusiasm. 'It'll be locked.'

'It isn't. Come on. Race you.'

His enthusiasm was infectious and I couldn't help but run after him, giggling.

Tony was right; the summerhouse was pretty secluded, helped by a scattering of trees and mature shrubs. Yellow gingham curtains covered the windows, which would at least give us some privacy in the rare event that someone did walk past.

Tony's eyes shone as he reached for the door handle. 'What do you reckon?'

It would make a change from my flat. Or his car. 'Go on, then.'

Inside, I wrinkled my nose at the dampness. On one side of the summerhouse, plastic reclining chairs were stacked up and, next to them, a pile of chair cushions. On the other side was a smaller pile of sun-loungers and cushions. At the back, a sturdy-looking wooden table had various plastic plant pots and trays piled on it. Tony swept them to the floor with one swing of his arm, grabbed a lounger cushion, placed it on the table, then turned to me. 'All yours.'

I whipped off my trousers and sat on the table. 'We'll have to be quick.'

'We will be. I'm so ready for you.' He unzipped his trousers and I smiled at exactly how ready he was.

'Happy anniversary to me,' I mumbled as I wrapped my legs round his back, pulling him even closer.

'What the hell are you doing?' yelled a man's voice.

I squealed and leapt back, banging my head on the wall.

'Shit!' cried Tony.

'Get your clothes on and get out.' The door slammed.

Cursing, I pulled my bra into place and zipped my tunic back up, my face flaming. 'I told you it was risky.'

Tony fumbled with his trousers. 'Who was that?'

'I've no idea.' I hadn't seen his face and I didn't recognise the voice. Jumping off the table, I hastily pulled on my trousers and shoes.

'Do you think he's waiting outside?' Tony asked, sounding as nervous as I felt.

'Probably.' I felt queasy at the thought of it. How embarrassing.

The bright sunlight dazzled me when I opened the door and stepped out into the gardens, blinking. For a relief-filled moment, I thought he'd gone, but he stepped out from behind a tall shrub, arms folded, face like thunder. Heart thumping, I surveyed the stranger. He was about the same height as Tony – five foot eleven – but with a larger, more muscular build. Messy dark curly hair ruffled in the light breeze as his bright blue eyes pierced into me.

'Who the hell are you?' he demanded.

I folded my arms too and tried to sound confidant. 'I could ask you the same thing.'

'I'm the new gardener.'

'But I was told you weren't starting until tomorrow.'

He raised an eyebrow. 'So you thought you'd have one last shag in the summerhouse first, did you?'

'It wasn't like that.'

He raised the other eyebrow. Okay, it was *exactly* like that. There was no hiding it.

'Really?' he said. 'Oh! You were doing a stocktake

of the garden furniture ready for my arrival, were you?'

'Sorry, mate,' Tony said. 'It was my fault. It's our anniversary. We both work here. Well, Callie does, and I've been doing a spot of consulting.'

'Is that a euphemism?' Despite his unimpressed tone, his eyes twinkled and I'm sure he was fighting the urge to smile.

'You won't tell the She-... Mrs Kimble, will you?' I begged. 'She'll fire me.'

He stared at me for a while as if debating. My heart thumped until he eventually shook his head. 'I won't tell Mrs Kimble, but only because it would embarrass the hell out of me if I had to describe what I've just seen. Don't let me ever catch you again in the summerhouse, shed, greenhouse, or anywhere else because, regrettably, I can't un-see what I've just seen.'

'Thank you. It won't happen again,' I assured him.

'It had better not.' With a grin, he strode across the garden, whistling.

'Shit!' I cried. 'Do you really think he'll keep it secret?'

Tony shrugged nonchalantly but I could tell by his expression that he was worried about the consequences. 'We'll just have to hope he does. You'd better get going or you'll be in trouble for going over your lunch break.'

I glanced at my watch and sprinted across the lawn, thankful that the She-Devil's office overlooked the front of the building rather than the gardens. How mortifying. That was the end to my lunchtime walks round the garden. There was no way I could face the new gardener again and I suspected he'd seen more than enough of me already.

Tony and I didn't cross paths that afternoon which was just as well because the incident preyed on my mind and I actually felt quite dirty. I should have said no. Urgh. Who was I? I'd always enjoyed sex and liked to spice things up a bit, but what we'd done was disrespectful to the residents and I should never have engaged in any of it. No more. Things were going to have to change. I wouldn't make an issue of it tonight because I didn't want to ruin our anniversary, but we did need to talk.

He was waiting for me outside when my shift finished and, despite having felt irritated with him all afternoon, my heart raced at the thought of the evening ahead. Deciding not to upset things by suggesting we go out to celebrate, I'd spent a small fortune on a special meal and his favourite wine purchased from a super-posh deli in town.

'I can't stay tonight,' he said.

My heart sank. He didn't stay over very often, but I'd stupidly assumed he'd make an exception for our anniversary. There was no point sulking about it so I smiled. 'Okay. I'll make dinner as soon as we get in, then. I've got steaks.'

'Sorry, angel, but I can't stay at all. I'll just have to drop you off and go. Something's cropped up.'

'Like what?'

'A work thing. It's complicated. We'll have to do steaks another night.'

'When?'

We reached the car and he opened the door for me. 'When what?'

'When will we have the steaks?'

'I don't know. I'll text you.'

Seething, I climbed into the passenger side and slammed the door. So much for not sulking. 'They might not keep,' I snarled when he got in his side.

'Then invite your brother round for dinner,' he snapped back. 'I've said I'm sorry and I refuse to have a childish argument about it.'

So we didn't have a childish argument. Instead, I childishly sulked all the way home and gave him a chaste peck on the cheek before exiting the car. *Happy one-year anniversary.*

* * *

'I'm sorry he abandoned you on your anniversary,' Nick said while we waited for the chips to cook.

'So am I. Not that I'm not pleased to see you again, of course.'

Nick nodded. 'Of course. Did you think about what you want from your relationship with Tony?'

'I did.'

'And...?'

'And I decided that I don't see Tony as my future husband or the father of my children, but I like him too much to end it. Except today. I don't like him today.'

'Can't say I blame you.'

I got up and checked on the chips. 'Not all relationships need to be heading for forever, do they?' I asked, closing the oven.

'No, they don't,' Nick agreed. 'However, both parties should still be getting something from the relationship. Are you really getting what you need from Tony? And, before you answer, I'd like to point out that my question has nothing to do with sex.'

I returned to the sofa. 'Five more minutes then I'll start on the steaks. So, am I getting what I need from Tony?' I sighed. 'We're back to the same issue as last time. I enjoy his company and we have fun together, but it doesn't feel right always staying in. I tried to enjoy it for what it was but I kept coming back to the same thing; it's not a normal relationship.'

Nick leaned forward in his chair. 'I want you to be happy, Callie, but I'm not sure Tony's making you happy. You say you love him, yet you don't see him as a forever relationship. You say you enjoy his company, yet you crave more from your relationship. I've never met him and Mum's never met him yet you've been together for a year. That doesn't seem like much of a relationship at all. It sounds more like friends with benefits.'

I slumped back on the sofa, looking at the ceiling as panic gripped me. Although Maria hadn't used that term, she'd alluded to the same thing. 'Oh God! You're so right. That's it, isn't it? We're friends with benefits.'

'Which is absolutely fine... if that's what you really, really want.'

But it wasn't. I wanted marriage and kids. I wanted days out, walks along the beach, and date nights at pubs or restaurants.

The timer on the oven burst into my thoughts and I stood up. 'Medium-rare?'

'Yes please.'

Nick joined me in the kitchenette and dug out plates and cutlery while I cooked the steaks. 'The other thing to think about, Cal, is whether friends with benefits is worth it when the friend in question keeps cancelling or changing plans or storming off in a sulk. I'm not sure I'd want to hang onto a friend who keeps doing that to me. Even if they are amazing in bed.'

I hadn't thought of it like that before. Damn! Was it time to call it a day?

9

'Ooh! Have you seen the new gardener?' Maria fanned her face with her hand as she waited for the kettle to boil at morning break the following day. 'I thought your Tony was hot but he has nothing on this guy.'

I pretended to rummage for something in my bag so she couldn't see my bright red cheeks. 'No. Not seen him.'

'You seriously want to check him out. Marks out of two? I'd give him one.'

'Maria!'

'Well, I would. Tell you what, if anyone's going to

convert you from your old git fetish, that's your man. I'd let him take me in the summerhouse any time.'

I looked up, startled. Did she know something? Thankfully the wistful expression on her face told me she was lost in her own little fantasy and it had been pure coincidence. 'Or the shed. No. Maybe not the shed. Too many spiders. What about—'

'Sorry. Desperate for the loo. I'll see you later.' There was no way I could stay and continue the discussion.

'Oh, Callie! I'm glad I've bumped into you.' I nearly collided with Ruby in my haste to escape to the ladies. 'I wanted to say I'm sorry if I caused problems for your sugar daddy yesterday afternoon.'

'It's okay. Sorry, I'm in a bit of a rush.' I continued along the corridor.

'I wanted to give you the news about my grandson,' she called after me.

'Maybe later?' I shouted back.

Splashing some cold water onto my face, I took a few deep breaths. I grabbed a couple of paper towels and dabbed my face dry, then leaned against the cool white tiles that covered the walls of the staff toilets. It was only when I relaxed that Ruby's words eased their way back into my mind. She'd apologised for causing problems with Tony yesterday, but the discussion I overheard had been the week before. Was she confusing her days, or had she had another confrontation with Tony and, if there had been, was that what had caused him to change his mind about spending our anniversary together? I'd have to ask her about it later.

* * *

'Have a wonderful weekend away with your family,' I said, waving away a taxi for one of our residents at the front of Bay View later that afternoon.

'I nearly didn't recognise you with your clothes on.'

I cringed as I turned to see the new gardener picking weeds out of the raised flowerbeds. I'd avoided the gardens all day, worried about bumping into him after the summerhouse incident, but had hoped I'd be safe out the front. Clearly not. 'You shouldn't sneak up on people like that,' I said, giving him a dirty look.

'I wasn't sneaking. I'm working out here while I

wait for a delivery.' He wiped his muddy hands down his jeans and cocked his head onto one side, grinning. 'No fun in the summerhouse planned for today?'

I put my hands on my hips and glared at him. 'It was a one-off.'

'Shame. I was thinking I could supplement my income by selling tickets.'

'That's disgusting.'

'So is having sex in the garden of an old folks' home. Especially with one of the residents.'

My jaw dropped. 'Tony's not a resident. He's only forty-five.'

'Then he's at about twice your age. And you say I'm the disgusting one.'

I shook my head. 'I'm not having this conversation with you. I don't know who you think you are being rude about my boyfriend like that.'

'*Boy*friend? He's hardly that, is he? The man's old enough to be your dad.'

My throat burned at the mention of my dad. I chewed on my lip, hoping the tears wouldn't flow.

He'd obviously misread the expression on my

face as he laughed. 'Urgh. He's a friend of your dad's, isn't he? Oh, I bet your dad's really proud of you.'

I swallowed hard and willed my voice not to break. 'I wouldn't know. He died when I was six.'

He started to walk towards me, his face pale. 'Shit! I'm sorry. I shouldn't—'

'Riveting as this conversation is, I've got work to do,' I snapped, storming back into the building, head held high, body shaking.

10

A week passed with only text messages from Tony. He apologised for not spending our anniversary together and promised we'd spend some time together the following week when he'd make it up to me. How many times had I heard that? We spoke a couple of times but it was always while he was driving and we invariably got cut off.

I never got the opportunity to catch up with Ruby to ask whether she'd had a second confrontation with Tony. She always seemed to be with Iris and I didn't want to involve another party in my complicated love life and risk a rumour getting back to the

She-Devil that I was seeing Tony. There wasn't a rule against relationships at work but I couldn't imagine her looking on it favourably.

On Friday morning, I walked to the pool for the early bird swimming session. I was the first one pool-side and therefore had the rare privilege of being able to break the surface. I loved doing that. It was like first-footing in fresh snow. Perfect. The moment I dived into the cool water, I felt the stresses and strains of the past weeks ebb away. I glided up and down the pool on my own for five lengths, then was joined by a few regulars, mostly elderly swimmers doing a slow and steady breast-stroke.

I took a moment to rest at the shallow end after thirty-two lengths. Raising my goggles onto my head as I caught my breath, I surveyed the pool. Knitting Lady was on the balcony as always, creating something in a rank shade of mustard. She waved when she saw me looking and I politely waved back. She accompanied Mr Pink Goggles, one of the elderly breast-strokers. Tweety Pie – a man in his mid-thirties with a bald head and a tattoo of Tweety Pie on it – was chatting to one of the lifeguards. I squinted in his direction. I thought I knew all the lifeguards, but I didn't recognise this one. The lifeguard turned and looked in my direction and my heart sank. For God's sake! Was there no escape from him? And how many jobs did one man need? Gardener and lifeguard? That was just greedy. He raised his hand and waved but I pulled my goggles back down and set off again, every muscle tensed.

A mile complete, I looked around, but he wasn't anywhere in sight. Phew! I hauled myself up the steps and made my way towards the changing rooms, but a massive cramp attack in my right leg stopped me in my tracks and I cried out in pain.

'Are you okay?' God knows where he'd sprung from, but he was there by my side in an instant.

'Cramp,' I muttered.

'Hold onto me while you stretch it out.'

'I don't want to hold onto you.'

'I'll just leave you here in agony then, shall I?'

I had no choice. My whole leg was in searing pain. 'Help me to the side, then.' I reluctantly put my arm round his waist while he put his round my wet shoulders and helped me hop to the wall. I leaned against it and tried to stretch my leg out, wincing as I did.

'Do you often get cramp?' he asked.

I bent over and rubbed my leg. 'Never.'

'I'm a first-aider. If you let me massage your leg, it might get some circulation back. It would be easier if we went into the office and you laid down, though.'

I wanted the ground to swallow me up as I lay on the floor of the lifeguard's office a few moments later with the gardener massaging my leg, front and back. A soggy swimming costume and goggle rings round the eyes weren't the most flattering of looks. I felt like a beached whale.

'I'm really sorry about your dad,' he said after a while.

'You weren't to know.'

'I know, but it wasn't a nice thing to say anyway. I'm sorry. Can we start over?'

I sighed then reluctantly muttered, 'I suppose so. You'd better start by telling me your name. I can't call you the gardener or the lifeguard forever.'

'It's Mikey. Pleased to meet you.'

'Callie,' I said.

He stopped massaging my leg. 'How's that?'

'I think I might be able to walk now. Thank you.'

'Pleasure. Drink plenty of water today, and I'll probably see you later.'

'Lucky me,' I said, sarcastically, before limping to the changing room, hoping he wasn't staring at my arse. What a horrendous morning.

11

'What's that in your ear, Callie?'

'I dread to think, Reggie.' I smiled at another of my favourite residents, Reggie Watts, as I poured him a strong cup of tea that afternoon.

He reached out and produced a sherbet lemon from my ear. 'Will you look at that!'

No matter how many times he did the trick, it still made me laugh. 'I don't know where they keep coming from.' I took the wrapped sweet and slipped it into my tunic pocket. 'Thanks, Reggie. Are you feeling any better today?'

'Still not a hundred per cent, my dear, but mustn't grumble.' And he wouldn't. It was one of the things I loved about Reggie. He never had a bad word to say about anyone or anything and always had a smile on his face.

'I'm sure you'll be right as rain for your birthday tomorrow.'

He smiled. 'I'm sure I will. It's not every day you turn ninety.'

'It certainly isn't.' I smiled as he shuffled towards the far window with his drink. He had no idea that the day out with his family was a ruse and they'd really arranged a big party at one of the pubs in Whitsborough Bay. I'd volunteered to chaperone a minibus of residents there and back and was really looking forward to it because his family, who frequently visited, were all as lovely as him.

'My grandson's taking me out for dinner tonight,' Ruby announced, reaching for her drink.

'Are you sure? He hasn't appeared the last few times.'

'That wasn't his fault. He wasn't able to move back to Whitsborough Bay as quickly as he'd hoped, but he's here now. I can't wait to introduce you two. Rhys is such a lovely young man. Good looking too. He takes after my side of the family.'

I smiled. 'If he has your genes, I'm sure he's absolutely gorgeous.'

'He is and I'm so glad he's finally here. You know, Callie, you might have already met him.'

I shook my head. 'I don't think so. He didn't turn up, remember?'

'I know, but he started working—'

A loud smash and a cry from the other end of the residents' lounge sent my pulse racing and my heart thumped as I saw Reggie lying on the floor, convulsing.

'Oh my God!'

Maria dived for the wall to press the panic button and I ran towards Reggie.

'Reggie! Can you hear me?' He was now lying still. Kneeling beside him, I grabbed his wrist and felt for a pulse. Nothing. No!

'Can we all step back to give Callie some space?' Maria's calm but clear commands moved the residents away.

'He's not breathing,' I said, starting CPR.

'Defibrillator,' Maria shouted, presumably to a colleague responding to the panic button.

'Come back, Reggie,' I whispered. 'Don't leave us.'

I felt sick with relief when the second charge of the defibrillator started Reggie's heart. 'Don't you ever scare me like that again,' I said, my voice shaking as I draped a fleecy blanket over him.

'The ambulance is on its way, Reggie,' the She-Devil said, gently placing a cushion under his head.

Reggie grasped my hand. 'Thank you,' he whispered. 'Will you come with me?'

I looked up at the She-Devil and she nodded.

'Of course I will. Now don't you try to speak. That's my job.' I searched my mind for something I could talk about until the ambulance arrived. 'Did I tell you about my day out with my brother?'

'No.'

'It was amazing, Reggie. We pretended we were tourists...'

I caught the She-Devil's eye and she smiled gently and mouthed 'thank you' which nearly broke me.

* * *

Reggie's heart stopped on the way to the hospital and, this time, it wouldn't start again. I held his hand as the ambulance technician pulled a sheet over his face, tears streaming down my cheeks.

'You did your best, Carolyn,' the She-Devil said when I arrived back at Bay View. 'Unfortunately, it was his time.'

I swiped at my tears again, willing myself to act professionally, but it was so hard when my heart was breaking. 'He was such a lovely man. He should have had longer.'

'I know. We'll all miss him.'

I took a deep breath. 'Does his family know?'

She nodded. 'I called them as soon as I heard.'

'How did they take it?'

'They were shocked and upset, as you'd expect. They wanted me to pass on their thanks for everything you did to try and save him.'

My shoulders slumped. 'It didn't work, though.'

'Not in the long-term, no, but you revived him before the ambulance came. That's amazing, Callie. Well done.'

She'd never called me Callie before. She'd never praised or thanked me before, either. I took a deep breath and wiped my cheeks again, trying to compose myself. 'Is there anything I can do to help you? Any paperwork or anything?'

'It's all in hand, but I appreciate the offer. There is something you can do, though. The family want to go ahead with the party tomorrow as a celebration of Reggie's life. If I give you the list of the residents who were going, would you mind asking them if they still want to go? I understand if you'd rather go home early. It's been a tough afternoon.'

'Thank you but, sadly, it's part of the job. I'll stay and speak to them all.'

She nodded and handed me the list. 'Get yourself a cup of tea or coffee first and take a moment. And take your time asking the residents. They might need to talk. Maria or Pete can fill in for you.'

'Thank you.'

'If they want to go, are you still okay to accompany them tomorrow?'

I nodded. 'Yes. Even if none of the residents go, I'll still put in an appearance. I loved Reggie.'

Denise smiled. 'I think his family would appreciate that,' she said gently.

I pulled my bag out of my locker while I waited

for the kettle to boil and rummaged for my phone. I needed a hug. Desperately. I texted Tony:

To Tony
Awful afternoon. One of the residents collapsed. I revived him but he died on his way to hospital. I know we have no plans but I really don't want to be alone tonight. Is there any way you can come round, even if you can't stay for long? xx

My phone beeped with a reply just as I finished my drink:

From Tony
Sorry about your afternoon but I can't come tonight. Sorry. We'll get together next week. I promise. Take care xx

Cheers for that. Tossing my phone back in my bag, I shoved it in the locker and slammed the door shut. What sort of a relationship did I want? I wanted one where I could rely on my boyfriend to be there for me when I really needed him. Like tonight. Surely that wasn't too much to ask.

The door burst open and Maria rushed towards me, arms outstretched. 'I'm so sorry,' she said. 'Are you okay?'

'No.' I gratefully sobbed in her arms. Tony might have been unreliable but at least Maria was always there for me.

'Are you crying?' I asked when I pulled away.

'No.' She wiped her cheeks. 'Maybe a little bit.'

'I thought you never got attached to the residents.'

'I don't but who wouldn't have a soft spot for someone who could pull sherbet lemons out of your ears?'

'You're not as tough as you try to make out.'

Maria smiled. 'Don't you go telling anyone. You'll ruin my reputation.'

When I clocked off shortly after eight, Ruby was waiting in the residents' lounge. She'd told me earlier that Rhys was picking her up at seven. I couldn't bring myself to go in and speak to her. I felt so tightly coiled with emotion after Reggie's death and Tony's rejection that I was likely to snap and tell her exactly what I thought of this unreliable – or fictional – grandson of hers. Thankfully she wasn't alone. A large group had gathered, telling stories about Reggie and toasting his memory.

Flinging my bag across my shoulder, I strode towards the entrance. I heard the noise before I saw it: torrential rain. Just what I needed. And on a day when I had no coat, cardigan or brolly with me. I hesitated under the entrance canopy. Nick would pick me up if I asked him nicely but I remembered him saying he was going out for drinks and a curry with his best friend, Skye. Mum? No. She was having friends round. Taxi? I couldn't afford it. That anniversary meal had set me back a small fortune, especially that damn bottle of wine.

I shook my head at the downpour. There was no way it was going to let up any time soon. If anything, it was getting heavier. I stamped my feet a few times and let out a frustrated cry as I psyched myself up to run for it.

'I hope that isn't cramp again.' I jumped as Mikey appeared round the corner from the car park and lowered a large golf umbrella. He was dressed in dark blue jeans and a white linen shirt rather than his grubby gardening clothes. He scrubbed up pretty well and I could see why Maria had been so enthusiastic about him.

'No. Just crap unpredicted weather. I'm psyching myself up to run home.'

'Run? In this? How far away do you live?'

'It's about a twenty-minute walk. I'm no runner so that's probably a nineteen-and-a-half-minute run.'

Mikey laughed. 'Come on. I'll give you a lift home.'

'Weren't you here to do something?'

'It can wait. It's not often I get to rescue a damsel in distress twice in one day.'

I thrust my shoulders back and glared at him. 'I'm not in distress.'

'That little war dance you just did would suggest otherwise.'

I so desperately wanted to tell him to do one, but I wasn't stupid enough to refuse his offer. I stayed close by his side as he walked me to his van, grateful for the protection of the brolly. He held it over my head while I got in. Chivalrous as well as mildly attractive, eh?

Fastening the seatbelt, I sat back and released a huge sigh.

'Bad day?' Mikey asked as he started the engine.

'The worst. One of our residents died this afternoon.'

'I heard. I'm sorry. Where are we going, by the way?'

'Castle Vale Gardens. Do you know it?'

Mikey nodded. 'Yes. I used to live near there.' He pulled onto the main road. 'I really am sorry about the bereavement today. That must have been tough.'

'It was,' I admitted. 'We all know it comes with the job, but it certainly never gets any easier. Well, not for me, anyway. Reggie was a lovely man. He used to magic sweets out of my ear.'

It wasn't just sweets either. He'd once made me howl with laughter when he produced a whole packet of garibaldi biscuits instead and announced that my ears needed syringing. Cheeky man!

'He'd have been ninety tomorrow and his family had a surprise party planned,' I said. 'They still want to have it as a celebration of his life and all the residents who'd been invited still want to go. I'm not surprised. His family are lovely. They were always visiting him and taking him out. It'll be strange not seeing them anymore.' I jumped as a flash of lightning illuminated the sky, followed by a crash of thunder. 'Wow! Thank you so much for the lift. I'd have been caught in that.'

'Pleasure.'

'You know what really gets me?' I said.

'Unexpected thunderstorms?'

'No. Well, yes they do, but I was going to say something else. What really gets me is that you get these lovely relatives like Reggie's who go out of their way to ensure he still feels part of their family and isn't packed off to wither in a care home, then you get cases like poor Ruby. She's a wonderful lady with a heart of gold, yet she has this absolute waste of space of a grandson who constantly lets her down.'

'In what way?'

'He never turns up when he says he's going to. She gets all ready to see him then he doesn't show. He's done it again tonight. Who'd do that to an old lady? I'm so angry for her. If he ever did turn up, I'd certainly have a few choice words for him.'

Mikey indicated to pull into Castle Vale Gardens. 'How do you know he's not shown tonight?'

'Because she told me earlier that he was due at

seven. It's after eight and she's still waiting. It breaks my heart. Anywhere on the left will do, thanks.'

Mikey stopped the van. 'You should have a little more faith in people. Perhaps this grandson was just running late.'

'I'd like to believe that. I really would. I'm just a little out of faith in people at the moment.' I opened the door. 'Thanks for the lift.'

'Do you want me to walk you across to the door with the brolly?'

'It's fine. I can probably manage to run that far. I hope I haven't made you too late for whatever you were doing this evening.'

He smiled. 'It's fine. I was already running late. Another ten minutes won't have made a huge difference. See you soon.'

Dashing across the car park, trying to avoid the deepest puddles, I unlocked the door to my block as another lightning flash lit the sky. I didn't mind storms, but I didn't like being out in them.

I turned and waved to Mikey as he pulled away. I hated to admit it, but he really had been my knight in shining armour. Twice. Maybe he wasn't so bad after all.

12

Thanks to the thunderstorm, Saturday dawned with clear air and a bright blue sky, which felt fitting for Reggie's party. I stood on my balcony, squinting in the sun. 'Happy Birthday, Reggie,' I whispered, looking up towards the heavens. 'I hope you're partying up there.'

I'd cried myself to sleep last night, thinking about Reggie passing away and the hole it would leave in his wonderfully caring family, Ruby with her seemingly uncaring, unreliable grandson, and my situation with my seemingly uncaring, unreliable boyfriend.

Reggie's party wasn't until three. As I washed up my breakfast dishes, the enormity of yesterday hit me and my chaperoning role suddenly seemed like a huge responsibility. What if one of the residents got upset? What if they all got upset? I always fell to pieces when anyone else cried. Would I be able to hold it together and remain professional? Feeling anxious and emotional, I texted Tony again:

To Tony
Morning! Feeling sad about Reggie and very apprehensive about taking everyone to the party this afternoon. Huge responsibility

He texted back ten minutes later:

From Tony
Don't go to the party, then. You're not being paid for it. They take advantage of you at that place.

My fist tightened around my mobile as I re-read his text. He'd completely missed the point and, once again, he wasn't there for me when I needed him.

Knowing that I'd work myself up into a frenzy if I remained in the flat all morning, I decided to go for a walk. And where better than a walk into town to return that expensive bottle of wine? Unfortunately I could only get a credit note for it but I was sure I'd manage to spend that eventually on delicious treats for me.

I felt much better after returning the wine and decided to walk the long way home around The Headland, psyching myself up to face whatever the afternoon presented me.

Fortunately, everyone seemed in high spirits when I arrived at Bay View at half two. They'd pulled their chairs into a circle in the residents' lounge and were laughing and joking as they reminisced about Reggie again.

A quick headcount revealed one short. 'Where's Ruby?' I asked. 'Still getting ready?'

'No,' Iris said. 'She says she'll see you there. Her grandson's taking her. Apparently he knows some of Reggie's family.'

'Oh. Did he eventually show up last night?'

'Yes. Either that or she has a fancy man she hasn't told us about.'

That was a relief. Not fictional after all. 'You all stay here and I'll go out the front and watch for the minibus.'

Was I finally going to meet the famous Rhys at the party? I'd have to bite my tongue and be on my best behaviour because I wanted to give him a piece of my mind for letting her down so often and a birthday/wake wasn't exactly the appropriate time or place.

* * *

I'd had the opportunity to offer my condolences to most of Reggie's family when I heard her. 'Callie! Darling!' Ruby sashayed towards me in a silver flapper-style dress, arms outstretched. 'Did Iris give you my message?'

I nodded. 'Your grandson's here, then?'

'He's parking, but he'll be along shortly, and I can *finally* introduce you two.'

'So he did turn up last night?'

'He did, but he was running late. Poor boy had a puncture on his way, so he had to change his tyre in that awful downpour, then get showered and changed again because he was soaked through and filthy. Don't look at me like that. He rang me to let me know.'

If this was the truth, things were certainly looking up.

'No sugar daddy today?' she asked.

'No. I didn't ask him, not that he'd have come if I had.'

'His loss is our gain.' She grinned widely as something caught her attention by the door. 'Ah! He's here.'

'Tony?' I spun round, frowning.

'No, dafty. Not Tony. My grandson, Rhys.' She waved towards the door. A few guests had arrived at the same time, but the only person I could see who could possibly be the right age was Mikey. What was he doing here?

'Rhys! Over here!' Ruby called.

Mikey smiled and walked towards us. 'Sorry it took me a while to park, Nanna,' he said. 'I'd forgotten they'd made Chapel Street one-way. 'Hi, Callie.'

'So you *have* met,' declared Ruby. 'I thought you

might have done with Rhys getting the gardening contract.'

I looked from Mikey to Ruby, then back to Mikey again, trying to get my head round things. 'I don't understand. You're Ruby's grandson, Rhys? But you said your name was Mikey.'

'It is. Well, it's what I've always been called. My name's Rhys Michaels.'

'So you lied to me?' I winced at my aggressive tone.

He put his hands up in surrender. 'I wasn't trying to deceive you. Nobody outside my family calls me Rhys.'

I planted my hands on my hips. 'Well, I've got a bone to pick with you, Rhys Michaels. What do you think you've been playing at by telling Ruby you're coming over and then not showing up?' Whoops! So much for biting my tongue.

Ruby clutched my arm. 'Callie, darling, Rhys has never let me down. It was all my fault.'

'You don't have to defend him,' I said. 'I've seen you waiting for him, all alone, on at least two occasions.'

Rhys's eyes widened and he shook his head. 'I don't know where you get your information from, but I have *never* let Nanna down. I was late last night thanks to a puncture, but I phoned her to tell her. Then, because I decided to save you from a drenching, I was even later. I've never left her waiting before, though.'

He looked so incensed that I couldn't help but believe he was telling the truth. I looked at Ruby for affirmation. 'It's true,' she said. 'It really was my fault each time. I misread a text once and thought he was coming during the week when he'd said the weekend. Another time he had to cancel on the day because of a crisis at work. He phoned to tell me, but I hadn't realised my phone was flat, so I didn't pick up the message until bedtime.'

'What sort of person do you think I am?' Rhys asked, then he smiled. 'Actually, don't answer that because I think I know after your rant last night.'

I blushed, feeling very guilty all of a sudden. 'Why didn't you tell me who you were and put me straight last night?' I asked in a gentler tone. 'I said nasty things and you just let me go on and on.'

'It seemed to me like you needed to let off steam and, as you know, I was running ridiculously late to take Nanna out. If I'd taken the time to explain who I was, we'd have been too late for our meal and I really would have been letting her down.'

'Mikey!' One of Reggie's grandsons, Greg, headed towards us, hand outstretched towards Rhys. 'Glad you could come, mate.'

They shook hands. 'I'm really sorry about your granddad,' Rhys said. 'How's your mum doing?'

'Putting on a brave face. Come and say hello.'

Rhys turned to me and grinned. 'You can apologise later if you like,' he said, winking. Then he turned to follow Greg across the room.

Ruby nudged my arm. 'He likes you.'

I rolled my eyes at her. 'Dislikes, you mean. And quite rightly so.'

'We'll see,' she said. 'He'd certainly be a far better choice than that sugar daddy of yours.'

'Right now, Ruby, I think a corpse would be a better choice than Tony.' I clapped my hand across my mouth. 'I can't believe I just said that, given the circumstances.'

Ruby giggled. 'Oh, darling, you do make me laugh. Don't ever change.'

'Can I get you a drink?' I asked, because I could certainly do with one.

'That would be wonderful. Dry sherry. Would you mind if I join the old folk while you get it?'

It always amused me when she referred to the other residents as 'old folk', especially as many of them were younger than her. 'Of course not, Ruby. I'll bring it over.'

* * *

It was a lovely party and a fitting send-off for Reggie. His family had prepared a slideshow of photographs of him from childhood to present day and the overriding impression was how much they all loved him. I could remember him telling me how, when he'd realised he was struggling on his own, he'd been inundated with offers to move in with various family members but had ultimately decided to move to Bay View to be with his friends and maintain an element of independence. He also didn't want to show any favouritism by accepting one offer and not another. He was so thoughtful like that.

I chatted to various members of Reggie's family after the slideshow, sharing stories of things he'd said and done to entertain the residents and me. Greg laughed when I told him the story of the garibaldi biscuits. 'That's very Grandad,' he said. 'He tried to teach me the trick but I was rubbish at it.'

'So how do you know Rhys?' I asked him when we'd finished reminiscing. 'Or is it Mikey to you too?'

He smiled. 'He's always been Mikey to me. I was born in Whitsborough Bay but we moved to York when I was three and I met him at primary school. We lost touch when I moved back here before senior school then reconnected a couple of years ago.' He took a sip of his drink. 'He's a good bloke, you know. You've picked well.'

I frowned, then laughed when I realised what he meant. 'Oh my God, Greg! We're not together.'

He ran his hand through his hair and wrinkled his nose. 'Sorry. He spoke so highly of you and he couldn't take his eyes off you, so I just assumed...'

Fortunately for Greg, his mum saved him from digging the hole deeper by bringing over a relative to say goodbye. 'I'll speak to you later, Callie,' he said. 'Sorry again.'

My glass of wine was empty, so I headed for the bar and ordered another. I rummaged in my purse while the barman poured, praying I had enough money for a large one.

'And a pint of Coke, please,' said a voice.

'Mi... Rhys.'

'I'll get that for you.' He handed over a tenner.

'I should be the one getting you a drink,' I said. 'I owe you an apology.' I hoped he wouldn't take me up on that because I definitely didn't have enough money for two drinks.

'You can get me one next time,' he said. 'Besides, I'd like to buy you it to say thank you for taking such good care of my nanna. She adores you, you know.'

I smiled. 'The feeling's mutual. She's a very special lady.'

'Yes, she is. I'm really glad I found her.' He indicated towards a small table with three chairs near the bar. 'Shall we?'

I glanced around the function room but Ruby and the other residents seemed to be having plenty of fun without me. There was no space left on their table either, so I nodded and sat beside him.

'What did you mean when you said you were glad you found her?' I asked.

'My dad was adopted, but his adoptive parents died when I was quite young, although he wasn't exactly close to them. When my only remaining grandparent on my mum's side of the family died four years ago, I found myself wondering whether I had any biological grandparents left. Dad had never wanted to find his real parents but said I could do what I liked, so I decided to go for it, and I managed to find Nanna.'

'Ruby's told me loads about her life, but she's never talked about being pregnant.'

Rhys nodded. 'I think she finds it difficult to talk about. She fell pregnant towards the end of her dancing days and had an opportunity to take up acting. It would mean constantly being on the road so she decided to give up the baby to do that. Nanna jokes that she'd have been too selfish to be a mum, but I think that's a self-preservation thing. I don't really know anything about my granddad. From what I can gather, he was married.'

'From the way she talks about you, she loves being a grandparent. I bet she'd have been a great mum.'

'I think so too.' Rhys took a sip of his Coke. 'Anyway, it was sheer coincidence that our family had settled in York and Ruby had settled in Whitsborough Bay. When I traced her, it made it so much easier to arrange to visit. I wanted to set up a landscape gardening business and discovered that Whitsborough Bay had very little competition, so I moved over here.'

Her ears must have been burning because Ruby appeared and sat down in the spare seat beside me. She wagged her finger at him. 'Yes, but then you moved away, didn't you?'

Rhys laughed. 'She's never forgiven me for that. I had a chance to work on a huge project back in York so I got one of my team to keep my business ticking over here and moved back to York for a year.'

'But you're back for good, now?' I asked.

'Hopefully. It makes it easier to see Megan.'

My stomach unexpectedly plummeted at the mention of a girl's name. 'Your girlfriend?' I asked tentatively.

'No. My daughter. Izzy and I had already split up and I'd started the contract in York when she discovered she was pregnant. Megan's seven months old now.'

'Show her a photo,' Ruby said.

'I'm sure Callie isn't interested.'

'No. I'd love to see a photo.'

Rhys blushed. 'If you're sure...' He scrolled through his phone to show me several images of a cute baby with dark curly hair.

'She's gorgeous. She's got your hair and eyes.' I looked up at Ruby. 'You never mentioned a great-granddaughter.'

'You thought I was making Rhys up,' she said. 'If I'd thrown a fictional great-granddaughter into the mix, you might have had me carted off.' She smiled and winked, showing that she didn't mind, but how guilty did I feel?

'Do you think you and Izzy will get back together?' I asked Rhys, then bit my lip. Where had that come from? It was none of my business.

'Absolutely no chance.' He shook his head vigorously. 'We've got an amicable relationship and I want to support Megan as much as I can, but that little girl is the only thing that Izzy and I have in common. We only went out a handful of times before it petered out.'

'Is that why you've got two jobs?' Again, it was none of my business, but I found myself wanting to know more about Rhys.

He nodded. 'I should be able to build the gardening business back up to a good level, but I need the lifeguarding money until I do. Plus, it gives me free access to the pool, and I love to swim so it's saving me money too. Do you swim often?'

'Sorry, Callie,' Ruby said before I had a chance to answer. 'I didn't actually come over to eavesdrop on your conversation. Some of the oldies are keen to get home. No staying power. They sent me over to ask if you could call the minibus.'

'Of course. Is everyone ready to go?'

'Iris wants to stay with me. Rhys can drop us both off later.'

I shook my head. 'I'm under strict instructions from the Sh... from Denise to get you all back safely. I know you've made separate arrangements, but I need to take responsibility for Iris.'

Ruby pulled a face. 'But she was at school with

Reggie's brother and they're getting reacquainted. I think love might be in the air, although I'd better warn him that she cheats at dominoes and cards. Oh, and Scrabble.'

I shook my head and sighed. 'I'm sure we can work something out. And stop telling people that Iris is a cheat. They'll start believing you.'

She winked again. 'And so they should.'

13

Ninety minutes later, I left Reggie's party for the second time with a rather tipsy Iris in tow. I'd escorted the others back at Bay View in the mini-bus and Rhys had followed in the car he'd borrowed from a friend. We'd returned to the party to find Iris and Reggie's brother slow-dancing. It seemed Ruby had been right about love being in the air and it warmed my heart.

'She can't hold her drink,' Ruby announced. 'Believe it or not, she's only had two G&Ts all afternoon. Mind you, they were triples. Such a lush.'

I helped Iris with her seatbelt. 'I'm just glad

Denise doesn't work on a weekend or I'd be in serious trouble for bringing her back in this state.'

'It's not your fault,' Rhys said.

'In her eyes, everything's my fault. Although she's been more sad than snappy lately and she was nice to me yesterday after we lost Reggie.'

We pulled out of the pub car park. 'Don't forget I need to drop those cards off,' Ruby called from the back seat.

'I haven't forgotten, Nanna.' Rhys turned to me. 'She wants to hand-deliver some cards to former neighbours. It'll only be a ten-minute detour. Is that okay?'

'Fine by me. I've got no plans.'

Rhys drove us towards North Bay and a 1930s housing estate nestling between the main coast road and the cliff top. We pulled into a tree-lined street filled with large semis.

'It's the one by the red car,' Ruby said, 'but it looks like you'll have to pull up here.'

Rhys stopped the car a few houses from Ruby's former neighbour. 'I'll go with her. Will you be all right for a few minutes?'

Iris was gently snoring. 'We'll be fine,' I said,

winding the window down to let some air in and the alcohol fumes out.

Relaxing back into the passenger seat, I listened to the radio turned on low. I liked the style of houses with their large front gardens and big bay windows top and bottom. Very nice. My whole flat could probably fit four or five times over into a property like that.

The front door opened and a man stepped out, squinted, and put on a pair of sunglasses. I stared at him for a moment as he stretched his arms. My heart raced as I instinctively reached for the door handle. It felt like I was swimming in treacle as I stepped out of the car and glided across the pavement towards the end of the drive.

'Tony?'

His arms dropped from his stretch and his face fell. Removing his sunglasses, he squinted at me. 'What are you doing here?' He stepped off the doorstep and took a couple of paces towards me, then stopped as a woman's voice called his name from inside the house. His panicked look back towards the property told me everything I needed to know. Ruby had been right about recognising him.

He lived on her old street. Which meant... A lump caught in my throat and my eyes stung with tears. 'Your wife?' I whispered.

'Callie, I...' But what could he say?

'Tony!' called the voice again. 'Are you going to help with this buggy or what?'

'Please don't...' He pleaded with his eyes.

'Tony!'

'I'm coming, angel.'

Angel. My stomach lurched at the use of my pet name on someone else. Was that how it worked? Give me the same pet name as his wife and there'd be no danger of him saying the wrong name at a key moment?

Tony stepped back into the hallway and emerged with a double buggy. He placed it on the drive and applied the brake, then looked up at me again. I was completely rooted to the spot. My heart was thumping so fast that I could hear it, my fists kept flexing, and my breathing was rapid, yet I felt I couldn't get enough air into my body. I felt sick and dizzy. Was this what an anxiety attack felt like?

With another panicked look towards me, Tony stepped back inside the house and emerged moments later with a baby dressed in a pink coat in one arm, holding the hand of a boy aged about four. A girl of about six followed them and started skipping round the front garden. Three kids? Just like Ruby had said. Oh. My. God! It took every ounce of control not to scream.

Tony fastened the baby into the buggy then turned to me again. 'Angel...'

I shook my head slowly. 'You lied to me,' I hissed.

He glanced back towards the house. 'I'm sorry.'

'I even asked you about fidelity and you still lied to me.'

'Right! I think that's everything.' A woman in her mid-thirties emerged from the house, holding a toddler dressed in blue. Make that four kids. Two boys, two girls. How absolutely perfect. And the woman was fairly perfect too. Tall, slim, long dark hair pulled back from her face with a simple cream headband, flowery maxi-dress swishing as she moved. She fastened the toddler into the buggy then turned round and jumped as she spotted me at the end of the drive, watching. 'I'm sorry,' she said. 'Can I help you?'

I shook my head, taking in the four children, the

beautiful wife and the absolute git who'd lied and cheated for a year. Much as I wanted to make his life hell, I couldn't do it to his poor family. They'd done nothing wrong. 'I'm fine,' I said to his wife, somehow managing to keep my voice steady. 'I was just waiting for a friend in the car there.' I pointed to where the door to Rhys's borrowed vehicle was still wide open. 'And I thought I knew your husband, so I got out to say hello, but...' I gulped as I stared meaningfully at Tony. 'But it turns out that he's not the person I thought he was.'

She let out a girly laugh. 'He gets that all the time. I think he must have a stack of doubles living in Whitsborough Bay. Come on, kids. Let's go.'

I stepped away from the end of the drive to let them pass. 'Enjoy your walk.'

'Thank you,' she said.

They walked down the road, the woman holding hands with the two older children and Tony pushing the buggy. He turned to me and mouthed, 'Thank you.' I stuck two fingers up at him. I know it was childish, but it was the only thing I could think of. Thank you? THANK YOU? Did he really think I'd done it for him? Was he that bloody clueless? I wanted to run after him and scream the truth, but what was the point? Tony and I were over, but there were another five lives that would fall apart if I confronted him, and I had no right to inflict that pain on them.

Feeling like I was in a dream, I returned to the car. Iris was still asleep so I left the door open and sank onto the grass with my back against the tree, my thoughts whirring. I angrily plucked at blades of grass and chucked them aside. I should have known or at least suspected. For months, I'd been questioning why we never went out and it had never entered my thick skull that the reason was that he might bump into his wife, or his in-laws, or some friends because he actually lived in the same bloody town as me. All those times he'd called or texted me from his grotty flat in Sheffield, he'd actually been less than a mile away from me. He must have been wetting himself laughing that I was such a mug. And all those times when he'd not stayed the night because he'd said he had a long journey to make that evening, he'd obviously climbed straight out of my bed and into his wife's.

A warm, fat tear rolled down my cheek, swiftly

followed by another, then another. A baby. They had a baby. She must have been pregnant for most of the time we were together. With a pregnant wife then a new baby in the house, he probably hadn't been getting much bedroom action at home and I, like the stupid naïve idiot that I was, had been the willing replacement. I pulled my knees up to my chest, wrapped my arms around them, and sobbed.

'Callie! What's happened?'

Through tear-blurry eyes, I looked into Rhys's concerned face as he crouched beside me. Ruby was standing next to him, looking equally worried.

I looked past Rhys and fixed my gaze on Ruby. 'It was Tony. It seems you were right about him, except for one thing. He doesn't have three kids. He has four now.'

She clasped her hand across her mouth, eyes wide. 'You've seen him? Here?'

'He came out of his house with his family just now.' I pointed weakly in the direction of Tony's house.

'Oh, darling! I'm so sorry. I didn't think.'

I wiped my cheeks. 'It's not your fault. You're not the one who betrayed me. You even confronted him about it and I believed him when he said you were mistaken.'

Ruby looked so sad. 'That first time when you introduced him to me, I really thought he was right and that I was mistaken which is why I didn't push it. The second time, I knew it was him but he was so adamant that he had no wife and kids and that he lived in Sheffield. I thought it was me. I thought I was losing it.'

'You weren't losing it,' I said, my voice shaky. 'He's a very convincing liar.'

Rhys reached out a hand to help me to my feet. 'I'm so sorry, Callie. That's such a shitty thing to do to anyone.'

As he pulled me up, I stumbled forward and placed my other hand against his chest, ridiculously aware of how solid he was compared to Tony. 'Sorry. Didn't mean to hurl myself at you.'

'That's okay. How are you feeling?'

'Numb. Used. Stupid.'

'Let's get these two back to Bay View, then I'm all yours if you want to talk about it.'

I shook my head. 'Thank you, but it's been a hell

of a couple of days and I just want to be alone to get my head round things.'

Rhys nodded and pulled a business card out of his pocket. 'Give me a ring if you change your mind.'

Ruby wrapped her slim arms around me. 'He didn't deserve you, my darling. You were far too special for him.'

Far too special? Far too stupid, more like. Far too naïve. Far too much of a mug. Yet again, I'd let an older man into my life, and it had all gone wrong. Horribly wrong.

14

I lay in bed the night of Reggie's party, staring at the ceiling and re-living my encounter with Tony. Had I done the right thing in keeping quiet? Had it been fair to his wife to let her continue in blissful ignorance of his infidelity when I'd had the perfect opportunity to expose him? Perhaps she already knew. Perhaps she was one of those wives who turned a blind eye as long as they were provided for and the kids had a dad. Surely not. Surely nobody would put up with that kind of crap. Yet I'd put up with his crap for a year. Granted, I hadn't known he had a wife and four kids, but I'd pretty much let him use me for sex.

I'd known that staying in all the time wasn't normal or what I desired from a relationship, yet I'd only had the occasional moan or sulk about it. Why hadn't I properly challenged him? Why hadn't I demanded to be treated right? Why hadn't I ended it? Was I really that weak? Or was it that I was needy and I'd rather have someone in my life who didn't treat me with respect than have nobody at all?

I was meant to be going to Mum's for Sunday lunch, but I couldn't face it. I phoned her and said I wasn't feeling very well. Nick obviously didn't buy it. He turned up at the flat after lunch and dragged me out for a walk around The Headland.

'I'm really sorry,' he said when I'd finished my sad tale. 'What a tool.'

'Tell me about it.'

'What happens now?'

We sat on the wall overlooking the sea, staring out at the gentle waves twinkling in the summer sun. 'I pray that Tony finishes whatever he's doing at Bay View really quickly so I don't have to hide from him at work. I'll steer clear of older men from now on and I'll never let myself get duped like that again.'

* * *

Monday morning dawned and I had a sickly nervous feeling in my stomach. I'd planned to go swimming but I'd barely slept all night so, when the alarm went off at half five, I reset it and turned over, longing for ninety more minutes of unbroken sleep. No such luck. Instead, I lay there worrying about the first time I'd see Tony at work. Would it be today? What would he say? What would I say? Would we ignore each other or would it turn nasty?

My eyes were puffy and no amount of concealer was going to cover the dark bags under them. I hoped nobody would notice but knew that was too much to hope for.

'You look like shit!' Maria announced when I walked into the staffroom at the start of the shift.

'It's over with Tony.'

She frowned. 'I thought it was already over.'

'No. What made you think that?'

'My bad. It's just that you were so pissed off with him about the anniversary disaster and you never saw him last week. I assumed...'

I sighed. 'The anniversary disaster probably was the beginning of the end.'

'So what happened to cause the end of the end?'

I shook my head. 'I don't want to talk about it just yet. I'm too angry with him right now and I'm too upset about Reggie.'

'Callie! This is why you need to stay detached,' she said gently. 'Reggie was a day off ninety. It was his time.'

Shoving my bag into my locker, I slammed it closed. I knew it wasn't fair to take my anger at Tony out on Maria but I couldn't help it. 'Honestly, I have no bloody idea why you do this job sometimes. Where's your compassion?' Without waiting for an answer, I stormed out of the staffroom and smacked straight into the She-Devil.

'Is there a fire, Carolyn?' she snapped.

'No, Mrs Kimble. Sorry.'

'What if I'd been one of our frailer residents? I could be on the floor now with a broken hip.'

'I know. I'm really sorry. It won't happen again.' I looked at the floor, willing myself not to cry. It was clearly going to be one of those days where the tiniest thing could set me off.

'I should think not. I was going to ask Maria to do this but I think you can do it instead. The Starling Group have asked us to do a stocktake.' She thrust a clipboard into my hand. 'You can start with the laundry room then move onto the summerhouse. If there's time left before lunch, you can do the residents' lounge too. You'll find the forms self-explanatory.' Without waiting to see if I had any questions, she turned on her heels and strode back towards her office.

Shit! The laundry room and the summerhouse. Of all the places she could have picked, why the hell had she selected those two?

As I counted towels, sheets, and pillowcases in the laundry room I tried my hardest not to think of Tony. It was impossible not to, though. Our relationship had started in that room and I'd never been in there since then without smiling at the fire in his eyes as he'd lifted me onto the vibrating washing machine. At the time, it had been the most daring and most erotic experience of my life, as opposed to the low point I viewed it as now.

* * *

An hour and a half later, I trudged across the gardens towards the summerhouse. A small sit-on lawn-mower stood in the middle of the gardens but there was no sign of Rhys. For a brief moment, I wondered if the She-Devil knew about Tony and was torturing me. No. It would have provided her with the perfect excuse for a formal disciplinary if she'd known.

With a heavy heart and shaky hands, I reached out and pressed the summerhouse door handle. Somebody – presumably Rhys – had put the plant pots back on the table. An image of Tony sweeping them aside sprung to mind and I shuddered. I could do this. I'd held it together in the laundry room and I could hold it together in the summerhouse. And I might have managed if Tony hadn't appeared five minutes later.

'What are you doing in here?' he asked, closing the door behind him, a cheeky twinkle in his eyes.

My pulse raced and I found myself momentarily dumbstruck. I waved the clipboard at him, as if that explained things.

'I saw you crossing the garden,' he said. 'I wondered if you were heading for *our* place, so I thought I'd join you.'

'It's not *our* place. Not anymore. Nothing's *ours* anymore.'

'Don't be like that, angel.' He reached out to touch me, but I stepped back and bashed against the table. 'Don't try to tell me you had no idea about Hazel.'

Hazel? My stomach lurched. Pretty name for a pretty woman.

'Don't look at me like that,' he continued. 'Did you really not have a clue?'

'Yes, Tony, I really didn't have a clue,' I cried. 'And do you know why? Because I believed you when you told me you were divorced, childless, and living in Sheffield. That's what people in relationships do, you know. They trust their partners. They believe what they say.'

'I think you believed what you wanted to believe.' He sounded so cocky, as though it was all my fault and nothing to do with him. I longed to wipe the smug grin off his face.

'What the hell does that mean?' I slammed the clipboard down on the table, knocking a stack of plant pots to the floor. 'I believed what you told me. I didn't make any of that shit up to hide the truth, you tosser.'

Tony's mouth fell open. 'There's no need to resort to name-calling,' he snapped.

'Believe me, tosser is very mild compared to what I want to call you.'

He shook his head. 'I thought you were mature, Callie, but you're really just a naïve, little kid pretending to be a grown-up, aren't you?'

'And you're a sex-obsessed, middle-aged arsehole.'

He flashed his eyes at me. 'Nice. Very nice. I came to see if you wanted to keep seeing each other, but I'm not sure I want to go out with a child.'

'Go out?' I yelled. 'We never bloody went out, remember!'

The door was yanked open. 'What the hell's going on in here?' shouted Rhys.

Relief flowed through me at the sight of him. My knight in shining armour. Yet again. 'Tony was just leaving,' I said.

Rhys squared up to Tony. 'I thought I made it very clear last time that I *never* wanted to see you in my summerhouse again. You need to leave.'

'*She's* in here,' Tony said. 'Are you going to kick her out too?'

'Callie's allowed in here. She's got work to do but you have no business in here. Ever.' He stepped out of the summerhouse and held the door wide. 'I'm waiting.'

Tony glared at me. 'You'll be sorry. We were good together and you know it. You'll be on the phone before the end of the week begging me to come round and give you a damn good seeing to.'

'In your dreams, Tony. In. Your. Dreams.' My voice sounded stronger than I felt.

With one last look of contempt, he stormed out of the summerhouse, deliberately shoving into Rhys on his way out. I closed my eyes when he'd gone and let out a deep breath, my stomach churning.

'Are you okay?' Rhys asked, as he closed the door behind him.

I shook my head as tears welled up. 'I was dreading today. I'd imagined what it would be like to see him, and that was far worse than I thought.' Tears spilled down my cheeks. Next moment, Rhys had his arms round me. Feeling safe and comforted, the emotions intensified, and my body shook with sobs.

'Please don't cry,' soothed Rhys. 'From what I've seen, he's really not worth it, and he didn't deserve you.' He held me tightly, whispering calming reassurances until the tears stopped and I reluctantly pulled away.

'Sorry about that,' I said, wiping at my eyes and sniffing.

'You've nothing to be sorry about. He has.'

I leaned back against the table and put my hands over my face as I shook my head. 'I wish I didn't have to see him at work. I don't know if I can bear it. I might have to leave if he's going to be here long-term.'

'Don't worry. You won't have to see him for much longer.'

I removed my hands from my face and looked at Rhys. 'How do you know? Has his work here finished?'

'Not quite, but Denise has asked for him to be removed from the transfer.'

'What? Why?'

Rhys looked down at his feet, clearly uncomfortable with where the conversation was heading.

'What aren't you telling me?' I asked.

He sighed. 'I caught Tony in the laundry room with another member of staff last week.'

'But he wasn't on site last week.'

'He was. I don't think you were, though.'

My mouth went dry and I closed my eyes again. I'd been away on my first aid refresher on Tuesday and Tony had never breathed a word about coming to Bay View. Probably because he had other plans. 'Who was he with?'

'Does it matter?'

I opened my eyes and nodded. 'My boyfriend has betrayed me, and I'd like to know whether one of my friends has too.'

He nodded slowly. 'Okay. I think her name's Marie or Mary or something like that.'

I slumped against the table, feeling sick. No! She wouldn't. She couldn't.

'Are you sure?' I asked. 'Long dark hair? Hispanic?'

'That's the one.'

'That's Maria. My alleged best friend.'

I sighed as I shook my head. I hadn't had a clue and yet so many things suddenly made sense. Maria had never hidden her attraction towards Tony but I'd been flattered rather than worried. She'd often questioned me about our encounter in the laundry room and had shared how much she'd like to do the same thing. I just hadn't realised she meant with my boyfriend. And how many times had she suggested he wasn't right for me? I thought she was looking out for me, but it was obvious she was really looking out for herself. What was that she'd said this morning about thinking we'd split up after the anniversary disaster? She certainly hadn't wasted her time.

'I'm not a very good judge of character, am I?'

Rhys grimaced.

'What did you say to the She-Devil? I mean, Denise. Does she know about Tony and me?'

He shook his head. 'No. I kept you out of it, although I can't guarantee Maria won't say anything.'

'I think she'll keep quiet. I caught her smoking pot on the premises a few months back and I think they'd view that a bit more seriously than a bit of a grope in the laundry room. Could be the difference between a warning and a dismissal. And please don't tell me if it was more than a grope. I really don't want to know.' I bit my lip, butterflies going crazy in my stomach. 'Was it more than a grope?'

'I thought you didn't want me to tell you.'

'I don't. But I do too. Was it?'

Rhys shrugged. 'I didn't stick around long enough to be certain. But...'

Who was I kidding? This was Tony. There was no way it had just been a grope. The man was insatiable. 'Would you have told me about Tony and Maria?' I asked.

Rhys held my gaze and nodded. 'Sort of. My plan was to catch Tony next time he was on site and try to convince him to confess, but he hasn't been on site till today. Then, of course, you found out about his lies on Saturday and you ended it anyway. I didn't see the need to add to your pain by telling you then. I hope I did the right thing.'

I twisted round and picked up my clipboard. 'Thanks, Rhys. You did do the right thing. Look, I'd better get this stocktake done. I don't need to add a bollocking from the She-Devil to my morning of gloom. Oh, God, don't tell her I call her that.'

He smiled. 'Don't worry, I won't. It's funny, though.'

'I'm glad something is.'

He said goodbye and I returned to my stocktake feeling quite numb. Tony and Maria. I was actually more hurt by her than him. I'd never in a million years have expected her to do something like that to me.

15

I received a text from Tony that evening:

✉ **From Tony**
Thanks for getting me sacked from the
job. Bitch.

I couldn't resist responding:

✉ **To Tony**
You got yourself sacked for shagging
my best mate at work. Karma.

He didn't respond to that one. Feeling smug, I texted Maria:

✉ To Maria
Sloppy seconds is your style, is it? You're welcome to him. Did he tell you he's married with 4 kids? Not that it would bother you. If you can shag your best friend's boyfriend, you'd hardly care about a stranger

A reply came back immediately:

✉ From Maria
I've been suspended thanks to that pretty-boy gardener. I might tell the She-Devil about you and Tony. You won't be so sarcastic then, will you?

I knew I should be the bigger person and rise above it, but what the heck:

✉ To Maria

Be my guest. You'll only get a warning
for your indiscretion but throw in
smoking pot on the premises and it'll
be a completely different outcome. Do
you want to take that risk?

From her silence, I suspected not.

* * *

Tony didn't return to Bay View and neither did
Maria, except to attend a disciplinary hearing on the
Thursday. Pete accompanied her and he re-appeared
in the staffroom, ashen-faced, while I was having my
afternoon break.

'What happened?' I asked, although it was obvious from his expression and the absence of Maria
it wasn't good.

'She's been sacked.' He started to empty her
locker into a carrier bag.

'Oh my God! Why?'

He shook his head. 'I'm not allowed to say.'

'But surely an indiscretion with Tony would have
got a warning instead.'

He closed the locker door and shrugged. 'Maybe it would but there was something else. Sorry, Callie. It's not worth the risk to my job if I—'

'It's fine. Sorry. I'm not going to push. Tell her I'm sorry.'

'Will do. See you later.'

With another sigh, he left the staffroom and I slumped back in my seat. Poor Maria. She wasn't exactly my favourite person for what she'd done with Tony, but she hadn't deserved to lose her job. What else could have come to light? I found out that evening:

✉ From Maria
Thanks for getting me sacked. Great friend you turned out to be

✉ To Maria
How am I supposed to have done that? As for your last comment, that's the pot calling the kettle black

✉ From Maria
You told them about me smoking pot

✉ To Maria
No I didn't

✉ From Maria
Well someone did and you were the
only one who knew. I've got a text
threat from you and you told Pete to
tell me you were sorry. Pretty con-
clusive evidence

✉ To Maria
I swear it wasn't me! The threat
wasn't an actual threat. I was angry
about you and Tony and letting off
steam. And as for asking Pete to tell
you I was sorry, I genuinely am… that
you got sacked. Not that I ratted on
you and got you the sack because I
didn't do that!

✉ From Maria
And you expect me to believe that?
Stop texting me. I can do without
'friends' like you

✉ To Maria
Same here. Good luck job hunting and
good luck with Tony. You're welcome
to him

* * *

With each passing day, I missed Maria more. At
work, I missed the way she made me laugh, especially after a run-in with the She-Devil, of whom she
could do a scarily accurate impersonation. I missed
the seamless routines we'd adopted for all our joint
tasks and felt frustrated when everything seemed to
take twice as long with other colleagues. And I
missed her out of work. We'd spent so much of our
spare time together wandering round the shops in
Whitsborough Bay, fantasising about what we'd buy
if we weren't always skint, walking around The
Headland, and our film and pizza nights at each other's flats. I missed having someone to talk to. Nick
and Mum were there for me but it wasn't the same.
Boyfriend-stealing aside, Maria had been a great
friend. The best.

With each passing day, I became more aware that

I didn't miss Tony. I loved having the freedom to make plans with Nick or Mum instead of worrying that I'd schedule something for one of the rare days Tony wanted to see me. I loved no longer treading on eggshells. I loved being able to eat what I wanted without snide comments about weight-gain. What I didn't love was Tony and I started to wonder whether I ever had or whether I'd just been swept away by it lasting longer than any of my previous relationships.

Ruby continued to sing Rhys's praises and I couldn't help but agree with her. He'd taken to joining me for lunch on my favourite bench and I found him to be sensitive, funny and kind. How wrong my first impressions had been. Mind you, I'd hardly given him a great first impression of me.

I remained seriously concerned about the She-Devil. She'd lost so much weight that she looked gaunt. Her eyes held a haunted look and she often stared into space when she was meant to be giving the staff a briefing for the day. I knew my colleagues loved the behaviour change because it meant they weren't always in trouble, but I actually found myself wishing the old She-Devil would return. I couldn't bear seeing someone so strong become a shadow of her former self. She wouldn't let me in, though, and what right did I have to push? I was only an employee.

The following Tuesday was Reggie's funeral, ten days after his death. The weekend manager, Gillian, was a friend of Reggie's family, so she was attending the funeral alongside the same residents who'd attended Reggie's party, leaving the She-Devil to manage Bay View. With Maria no longer on the payroll, I thought she might object to me attending the funeral, but Gillian had convinced her that I would be more helpful supporting the dozen or so attending the funeral than staying at work. I was relieved because I wanted to pay my final respects to a wonderful man.

The residents were split across taxis and Gillian's car. Rhys borrowed his friend's car once more and drove Ruby, Iris and me.

At the wake, Iris went overboard on the G&Ts again whilst engaging in some shameless flirting with Reggie's brother. When we returned to Bay View, Rhys took Ruby into the residents' lounge for a game of cards and I accompanied Iris back to her room.

'I might have a bath,' Iris announced. 'A lovely relaxing bubble bath before bedtime.'

'I don't know about that. You've been drinking. What if you fall asleep in there?'

She laughed. 'Reggie's brother's gorgeous. He was my sweetheart when I was seven. Did you know that?'

'Yes, Iris. You told us earlier. Several times.'

She laughed again. 'He was the first boy I kissed, you know. A girl never forgets her first kiss.'

I unlocked her door for her and steered her towards her bedroom. 'Would you like a drink of water?'

'Yes please.'

When I returned with her drink, she'd kicked off her shoes and was sitting on the side of her bed, grinning, no doubt thinking about her first kiss with Reggie's brother. I moved to place the glass on the cabinet, but she reached out to grab it at the same time. The glass tipped onto the bed, sloshing water over her pillows and sheet.

'Whoops! It's missed your duvet but I'm going to have to strip the rest of the bed.'

I helped Iris over to a tub chair in the corner of

the room, then peeled back the duvet, removed the sheet, and grabbed the pillows. 'I'll get you some fresh bedding.'

My heart thumped as I hesitated outside the laundry room. Not only did it hold memories for Tony and me, it was now tainted with his and Maria's deception. I closed my eyes for a moment and concentrated on pushing my emotions aside. Taking a deep breath, I pushed down on the handle. Locked. How strange. I knocked on the door and listened. Silence. 'Hello? Anyone in there?' Silence again. I rattled the handle, but it was definitely locked.

I poked my head round the door of the residents' lounge as I passed. 'Water spillage,' I called to Ruby and Rhys who were sitting by the window, engrossed in their game. 'I'm getting Iris some fresh bedding but the laundry room's locked. Won't be long.'

Retrieving the key, I dashed back round the corridor, opened the laundry room door, and flicked on the light. The room seemed to spin around me and I felt like I was in a vortex as I launched myself to my knees beside her still body.

'Denise!' I grabbed her cold arm and, with shaking hands, felt for a pulse. 'Denise!' An empty bottle of pills lay on the floor beside her. 'Shit, Denise! What have you taken?' I could feel a pulse, but it was weak. I pushed a strand of hair away from her face and flinched at the coolness of her cheeks. Shit! Shit! Shit! I needed an ambulance. I didn't want to leave her but I had no choice. She was already on her side so I quickly moved her into the recovery position before racing along the corridor. Entering the residents' lounge, I tried to apply a poker face so I didn't scare anyone. Where the hell were the staff? 'Rhys. Can I borrow you for a second?'

'Is everything okay?' asked Ruby, frowning. Poker face obviously hadn't worked.

'Fine. One of the washing machines is leaking so I just wanted Rhys's help. Men stuff, you know?'

Rhys smiled and ambled over. As soon as we'd passed the windows, I grabbed his hand and broke into a run. 'Can you call an ambulance?'

'What? Is Iris okay?'

'It's not Iris.' I pushed open the door to the laundry room.

'Shit! Is that...?'

'I think she's taken an overdose.' I crouched down beside her as Rhys dialled 999.

'Is she breathing?' he asked.

'Yes, but her pulse is faint.'

'Hi, yes, ambulance... yes, that's right... Rhys Michaels... just my mobile... yes... we've just found our manager on the floor unconscious and we think she might have overdosed... yes, female, early forties...'

Heart thumping, I held onto Denise's cold hand and stroked her hair back from her face while Rhys spoke to the operator, reading out the name on the bottle of tablets and outlining the circumstances around finding her. He hung up. 'All we can do is keep her in the recovery position and wait for the ambulance.'

'Did they say how long?'

'Ten minutes. Do you want me to wait out the front?'

I shook my head. 'Can you stay with Denise? I need to see if Gillian's back and I'd better check on Iris.' I grabbed a bag containing two new pillows, two pillowcases, and a sheet off the shelf and hurried to the front of the building. Reception was empty. So were the offices. As I made my way back past reception, one of my older colleagues, Sally, wandered in from outside, wafting a cloud of cigarette smoke away.

She stopped when she saw me. 'You're back!'

'Is Gillian back?'

'I saw her about five minutes ago. How was the funeral?'

'Sorry, Sal, but I need to find Gillian urgently.'

'She's in the staffroom, I think. Are you okay?'

'Can you get these to Iris?' I thrust the bedding at her then sped off down the corridor towards the staffroom.

'Callie!' Gillian exclaimed when I burst into the room. 'What's wrong?'

'Denise...' I turned and ran back along the corridor with Gillian hot on my heels.

'On my God! What happened?' she cried as I opened the door to the laundry room.

'An overdose by the looks of it. The ambulance is on its way.'

Rhys stood up. 'I'll go out the front and wait for it.' He caught my hand as he passed and gave it a gentle squeeze. 'I'm sure she'll be fine. You've done everything you can.'

'Denise! Can you hear me?' Gillian bent down and lightly tapped her face. 'Denise!'

* * *

A pair of paramedics appeared and lifted Denise onto a stretcher. I recognised them as the same pair from the day Reggie died. Moving Denise to the recovery position could have kept her alive, but what if lightning struck twice? What if she died in the ambulance just like Reggie, despite my intervention? My throat felt like it was encased with razor blades. I sagged against Rhys's side and he put a comforting arm round me.

'I can't get hold of Ian and I can't leave the site,' Gillian said as the paramedics wheeled the stretcher towards the entrance. Ian was our relief manager.

'I'll go with her,' I said, unable to bear the thought of her being all alone. 'Will you ring her husband?'

'Of course. Thanks, Callie. Will you let me know how she's doing?'

'They might not tell me anything with me not being family, but I'll ring you later either way.'

'I'll follow the ambulance,' Rhys said.

'You don't have to...' But as I said the words, I knew I desperately wanted him to.

'No arguments. You've had a shock. I'm staying with you.'

* * *

Pacing up and down in the waiting room was agony. After forty minutes or so with no news, a man in his mid-to-late forties marched into the room. I recognised him immediately from a photo on Denise's desk. 'Mr Kimble?' I asked.

He nodded. 'I'm looking for my wife.'

'I'm Callie. This is Rhys. We work with her. I'm the one who found her.'

'What happened?'

I bit my lip. 'It looks like she might have taken too many tablets.' I couldn't bring myself to say the words 'overdose' or, even worse, 'suicide' to him. It could have been an accident. It wasn't up to me to speculate about what had happened.

'Christ! Stupid woman! Where is she?'

'In surgery, I think.'

He rubbed his hand over his stubble then sat down heavily on one of the plastic chairs. 'I should have seen it coming.' He looked up at me. 'You work with her, you say?'

I nodded.

'Is she as horrendous to work with as she is to live with?' He shook his head. 'Don't answer that. Actually, the expression on your face already has. Did she tell you we're getting divorced?'

So Pete had been right. 'Not directly. I'm sorry to hear that.'

He sighed. 'I knew she was struggling, but I had no idea she'd do anything like this. Christ! Denise! What was she thinking?'

'She maybe wasn't thinking. She's been pretty upset recently.' I cringed. Had I said too much? Thankfully he nodded.

A doctor appeared a few moments later, breaking the awkward silence. 'Kimble family?' he asked, looking round the waiting room.

'I'm Denise's husband, Gavin. Is she okay?'

'She should be. We've pumped her stomach and she's regained consciousness.'

'Can I see her?'

'Give us five more minutes.'

'Would you like us to give you some space?' Rhys asked. I could have hugged him for asking the question that I was struggling to phrase as anything other than, 'Please can we go?'

Gavin nodded. 'Yes, that would be good. Thanks for staying with her.'

I stood up, my legs feeling quite shaky, tears pricking my eyes. 'Please can you give her our best wishes when you see her?'

'I will.'

Rhys took hold of my hand as we left the waiting room. Feeling very unsteady on my feet, I was so grateful to have him to cling onto. He drove us back to my flat in silence. I didn't need to invite him in. He didn't need to ask. It just felt like the right thing to do.

As soon as we stepped into the lounge, I crumbled. 'There was one pill left in that bottle. One pill. What if that was the difference between her living and...?' My voice cracked.

'Hey. You can't think like that,' he said, gently placing his hands on my shoulders. 'We'll never know, and the important thing is you found her and raised the alarm. You saved her.'

'What was she was she thinking of doing something like that at work? Why did she...?'

'I don't know. Hoping she'd be found? A cry for help? Maybe whatever is hurting her simply became too much to cope with today.'

'But if Iris hadn't split her water, we might never have...'

Rhys wrapped his arms around me and held me close as tears rained down my cheeks and my body shook. As he stroked my back and hair, whispering reassurances, my thoughts drifted to how Tony would have responded in these circumstances. From past experience, it was obvious that he wouldn't have been there to comfort me when I needed him and, if by some miracle he had come round and hugged me, he'd have made a move and made it all about sex as usual. Yet here was Rhys, a virtual stranger with whom I hadn't had the best of starts, simply being there for me when I needed him, and doing it without being asked. To think that, only a few weeks back, I'd thought that I loved Tony and hated Rhys.

'I've soaked your T-shirt,' I said when I finally pulled away.

'It'll soon dry. How are you feeling?'

'Like I've just had the worst day ever. Actually, make that the worst month ever.'

He pushed a strand of hair behind my ear, butterflies doing an unexpected swoop in my stomach at his tender touch. 'I think that might be an understatement. Can I make you a drink? Tea? Coffee? Something stronger.'

'There's some lagers in the fridge. I think we've both earned one. Ooh! I promised I'd ring Gillian.'

'You do that, and I'll sort the drinks.'

* * *

'Do you want to talk about Denise? Reggie? Tony? All three?' he asked, handing me a bottle and sitting beside me on the sofa after I'd updated Gillian. 'Or would you rather watch some mindless TV and sink a few of these?'

I smiled weakly. 'The latter? For the moment, anyway. I feel so drained that I don't think I could actually have a coherent conversation. You don't have other plans tonight? A hot date or anything?' I wasn't sure why I'd added the last part, but it suddenly felt important to know the answer.

He laughed. 'Between the house move and work, I can't remember the last time I had one of those. You?'

'God, no! I'm still licking my wounds after Tony.'

'I hope there aren't too many wounds,' he said, his expression sympathetic.

'No. My pride was hurt the most, I think.'

Rhys smiled at me and butterflies fluttered in my stomach again. 'Are you hungry?' he asked.

I shook my head. 'I was starving earlier but my appetite's completely gone now. I can't stop thinking about Denise and hoping she's going to be okay, not just now, but long-term.'

'I know. Me too.'

Handing Rhys the remote control, I stood up. 'I smell of the hospital. Do you mind if I put my PJs on while you pick out a film?'

'No problem. I'm thinking a comedy or a rom-com?'

'Yes please.'

* * *

Halfway through the film, Rhys announced that we needed to eat something to soak up the lager, so he made cheese on toast.

'Why do you keep smiling at the cheese?' he asked.

I blushed. 'I didn't realise I was. Sorry. I was just thinking how nice it is to tuck into a pile of cheese without someone wittering on about the high calorie count.'

Rhys frowned. 'Tony did that?'

'Regularly.'

'Why would he do that?'

'To stop me getting any fatter.' I stuffed the final piece into my mouth.

Rhys put his empty plate down on the coffee table and shuffled round to face me. 'Any fatter? That would imply that you're fat in the first place, which you're not.'

'I'm hardly skinny like his wife.'

'Callie, you're gorgeous. I've seen you in a swimming costume, remember.' He laughed at my shocked face. 'Sorry, was that too full on?'

I hung my head, cheeks burning, partly out of embarrassment, but partly from the unexpected compliment. He really thought I was gorgeous? 'I'm mortified about that,' I muttered.

'Don't be. You have an amazing body and if that stupid twat couldn't see that... well, he didn't deserve you and I'm glad it's over.' He ran his hand through his curls and shook his head.

'Thank you. That's the nicest thing anyone's said to me in a long time.'

'I mean every word,' he said. 'Can I ask you a question? Why did you stay with Tony if he treated you like that?'

I shrugged. 'That's a very good question. Without a very good answer.'

Sipping on my drink, I told him all about my ill-advised year with Tony and he told me all about his relationship with his daughter's mum, Izzy. They'd only been together for a couple of months and he admitted even that was probably six weeks too long. After the initial attraction faded, he realised they had very little in common so ended it. He was shocked to discover she was pregnant as he thought they'd both taken precautions. It turned out that Izzy wasn't really on the pill and had deliberately placed pin pricks in the condoms. Her sole objective had been to have a baby so that she could pack in the job she hated and live off benefits as a single mum instead. Seriously. What sort of woman does that? The respect I'd initially felt for her for raising Megan on her own was replaced with disgust and contempt. It appeared that being devious was a shared trait amongst our exes.

I gazed into those cornflower-blue eyes of his that sparkled as he talked about his daughter and realised that I'd enjoyed the last week-and-a-half in Rhys's company more than I'd enjoyed a whole year in Tony's. He properly listened when I spoke, seeming genuinely interested in what I had to say. In return, he was fascinating to listen to, but it made me realise how little Tony and I had talked about things. Conversation had always been superficial and cut short by sex. It turned out that Rhys and I loved the same music, films, food, and doing the same things. Had Tony and I had anything in common outside the bedroom?

'I can't believe Tony never took you out anywhere. What a nob.'

I nodded. 'Now that I know about the wife and kids, I know why. The worst thing is that he kept promising me we would go out, then he'd change his mind and say he was tired from work. Idiot here believed him.'

'If you had gone out, what would have been your idea of a perfect date?'

'After a year of not going on one, absolutely anything. It could be a meal, the cinema, the pub or just a walk along the beach. Anything other than being stuck in my flat. What about you? What's your idea of the perfect date?'

'Glamping.'

I laughed. 'Glamping? Well, it's certainly different.'

'I have this mate, Kev, whose parents own a campsite just outside Whitsborough Bay. It's got this glamping field with a mixture of Bedouin tents and wigwams. About a dozen of us stayed there on Kev's twenty-first birthday. There's this amazing view and you can see the sun setting over the moors and Kittrig Forest. It's so romantic, or it would be with someone special and not a load of lairy, drunk lads.

I've never been out with anyone I'd consider special enough to take there, though.'

It sounded like the most perfect date ever. Even if Tony had taken me out, I suspected he'd never have thought of anything romantic like that. A trip to the pub and a grope in the park on the way home would likely have been his idea of a good time. An image filled my mind of Rhys and me sat on a hilltop watching the sun set, his arm round me, my head resting on his shoulder. I liked that image. 'I hope you find that special person.'

'I'm working on it.' He held my gaze as butterflies danced in my stomach again. Then I ruined it. I tried so hard to stifle it, but a huge yawn escaped. It was shortly after one in the morning and, much as I was loving Rhys's company, I really was drained.

He leaned forward and put his empty bottle down on the coffee table. 'I think that's my cue to leave. You looked shattered when we got back from the hospital and I've selfishly kept you up talking. I'll call a taxi and pick my van up in the morning and—'

'Stay.' I reached out to touch the back of his hand, a zing of electricity zipping up my arm. 'I don't want to be alone. Not after everything that's happened today. Unless you have to get back for something. It wasn't an order. It's just that...'

He turned his hand over so that it was holding mine. 'I'll stay.'

'Thank you.' Was he going to kiss me? He didn't move, but neither did I. I didn't want to misread his kindness and embarrass us both, especially when I'd have to keep bumping into him at work. Plus, I was beat. I reluctantly let go of his hand and heaved myself up off the sofa. 'I'll tidy this lot away if you want to use the bathroom. There should be a spare toothbrush under the sink.'

I headed into the bathroom after him, but clearly took far too long. When I returned to the living area, Rhys was laid on the two-seater sofa, legs dangling over the arm, a fluffy turquoise cushion behind his head, fast asleep. I whispered his name. Silence. I stood over him for a while, but I could tell from his deep breathing that he was gone. Wandering into the bedroom, I found a soft throw, which I gently laid over him.

'Good night, Rhys,' I whispered. 'Thank you for today.'

16

It was 7.30 a.m. when I opened my eyes to the sound of the alarm. Sunlight flooded through a gap in my curtains, warming my face. Rhys! I sat upright, pulled back the duvet, and padded into the living area, but he was gone. Resting on top of the neatly folded throw was a note:

So sorry to run. I didn't like to wake you. I'm life-guarding first thing or I'd definitely have stayed and made you breakfast. I'm not at Bay View for the rest of the week – got a contract elsewhere to finish – but are you free on Saturday night? I'll pick you up at 7 p.m. and take you out for dinner. Text me if you have

other plans, although I'm hoping you don't. Scribbled
my number below in case you've lost my business
card. Rhys xx

I smiled as I read the note again and again. He
wanted to take me out. Out! I'd almost forgotten
what that felt like.

✉ To Rhys
`Sorry I missed you. Saturday sounds`
`great xx`

* * *

Gillian was waiting for me in the entrance at Bay
View. 'I meant to call you to tell you not to come in
today, but I'm afraid I lost track of time. How are
you?'

'Still a bit shaken, but I slept well. How's Denise?
Have you heard anything?'

'Gavin rang earlier. She's doing really well, but
they'd like to keep her in another night for observa-
tion. She's been asking after you.'

I gasped. 'Me? Why?'

'Because you saved her life. I want you to go home and rest then, if you don't mind, I'd really appreciate if you could visit her this afternoon.'

'But I can't just take the day off.'

'Yes you can. And I'll make sure you get paid for it. You've had a hell of a fortnight with Reggie's death and finding Denise yesterday. You need a break. She's on Ocean Ward and visiting starts at half one. Bye.' She literally shooed me away.

Crap! The She-Devil wanted to see me? Gillian had put a positive spin on it, but what if she wanted to tell me off for interfering? If she really had wanted to end her life, I'd scuppered her plans and she might not thank me for it. I looked at my watch. Five hours to go. By the time I walked home, then caught the bus to hospital, I probably had four hours. What the hell would I do with four hours when everyone I knew would be at work? I needed a distraction, or I'd worry myself into a right state. Cleaning. That would have to do.

* * *

Four hours later, the flat was gleaming and I had eight binbags full of clothes, books and oddments to take to a charity shop. I changed my T-shirt and walked round the corner to wait for the bus.

✉ To Rhys
Denise wants to see me. On my way to hospital. Really nervous in case she's angry with me for finding her!

✉ From Rhys
I've been thinking about this and I'm convinced that, if she didn't want to be found, she wouldn't have done it at work. I bet she wants to thank you for saving her life. You were amazing yesterday. Good luck xx

Arriving at the hospital, I took a few deep breaths to try and calm my nerves. 'Denise Kimble?' I said to the nurse at the entrance to Ocean Ward.

'Bed eight at the far end,' she said.

Denise's eyes were closed when I approached.

Her face was grey, her blonde bob was dishevelled, and she looked more like a woman in her late fifties than early forties. My nerves stepped aside and all I could feel for her was compassion. I cleared my throat slightly. 'Mrs Kimble?'

She opened her eyes and turned her head towards me. 'Callie,' she whispered. 'I'm glad you came.' She indicated the chair beside her bed and I tentatively perched on the edge.

'Please call me Denise.' She pointed to her throat. 'Can't speak properly from the tube.'

I nodded. 'How are you feeling?'

'Embarrassed. Relieved. Thankful. You saved my life.'

'I thought you might be angry with me, if you really wanted to... you know.' I bit my lip as she stared at me and my heart thumped while I waited for her to speak.

'I've been very tough on you since I started at Bay View. I've been hard on all the staff, but you especially.' She paused and I wondered if she wanted me to say it was all right, but I couldn't. It wasn't all right. She'd been a bully. She'd reduced me to tears on several occasions and I'd lost count of how many times

I'd decided to hand in my notice because of her, but I hadn't been able to bear the thought of saying goodbye to the wonderful residents, so I'd put a brave face on it.

'Do you know what I admire most about you, Callie?'

My eyes widened. I didn't think she admired *anything* about me, never mind enough things to have a 'most admired' quality amongst them. I shook my head.

'Your loyalty and your discretion. You knew who was in that gambling ring, but you avoided trouble and found a way to resolve it. You didn't tell anyone when you found me in the office with all those pills or when you saw me in The Lobster Pot.' She smiled weakly. 'Yes, it *was* me you saw that day. I know from Gillian that you handled yesterday discreetly too. You have the trust and respect of all the staff and residents. I should have given you credit for that sooner.'

'I don't see what there is to gain by spreading rumours and gossip. There's always another side to the story.'

She nodded. 'There is to mine, but it's no excuse

for how I've treated you. Gavin and I are getting divorced. I can't have children. He knew that when we met and said he wasn't bothered, but he's struggled over the years to deal with it and it's torn us apart. He's met someone else. I found out yesterday that she's pregnant.' A solitary tear trickled down her right cheek. 'I've recently been diagnosed with depression, and I'm afraid the pregnancy news was a little too overwhelming for me.'

Tears welled in my eyes. 'Did you mean to...?'

She clasped her hands together across her stomach. 'I don't know. I think so. But I'm glad I'm still here. I'm getting some help. It might be a while before I'm back at work.'

'I'm so sorry, Denise. Is there anything I can do?'

'There is actually. The Starling Group are expanding which means more staff. We need some team leaders. I want you to go for one of those jobs and show everyone what you're made of.'

I shook my head in disbelief. 'You really think I could do that?'

Her hand reached out and grasped mine. 'I do. I think you'll be great at it. I'll give you a glowing reference.'

'Thank you.' Then my smile slipped. Was she bribing me? Had she just been flattering me with all that stuff about me being trustworthy and discreet? 'Is this because of yesterday? You don't have to. I won't tell anyone about it.'

She gripped my hand more tightly. 'I know you won't, but the reference has nothing to do with yesterday. I've already recommended you. I put your name forward after the way you handled Reggie's death.' She released my hand as her eyes flicked past me and she sighed. 'Gavin's here.'

I stood up, hoisting my bag onto my shoulder. 'I'd better leave you to it, then. I'm so relieved you're okay and that you're not mad at me. I can't thank you enough for putting me forward for the promotion. If I get it, I promise I won't let you down.'

'I know. And I can't thank you enough for saving my life. You're an amazing young woman, Callie Derbyshire.' The tears glistening in her eyes were mirrored in my own.

Gavin appeared by the bed, shook my hand and thanked me again for yesterday. All I could do was nod and smile. If I'd opened my mouth to speak, a sob would have escaped and I'd probably not have been able to stop there.

By the time I made it back to the flat forty minutes later the sobs had started again, and I felt lost without Rhys's comforting arms around me.

17

The buzzer sounded at about 6.50 p.m. on Saturday. Rhys was early. Not that it mattered because I'd been ready for the last hour, anxiously pacing up and down. 'Do you want me to buzz you in or shall I come straight down?' I said into the intercom.

'Buzz me up.'

My stomach lurched. 'Tony?'

'It's okay. Someone's letting me in.'

Shit! I stood in my doorway, fists flexing, teeth grinding, while I waited for him to climb the two flights of stairs. 'What the hell do you want?'

'I miss you.'

'You miss the sex, you mean. I doubt you get much at home with a baby and three kids around.'

'Come on, angel,' he said seductively. 'I bet you miss it too.'

'Don't call me that. And, funnily enough, I don't. What I miss is what I've been missing all year – a normal relationship where the couple go out and do things together.'

He grinned at me. 'That's bollocks and you know it. You were never really bothered about going out. You preferred staying in bed.' He reached out to stroke my cheek, but I leapt back, crying out in pain as I smacked my head on the doorframe.

'Don't you dare touch me!' I snapped.

He laughed. 'That's not what you used to say.'

At that moment, I smelt it. 'Are you drunk?

'I've had a few.'

'Then I suggest you go home to bed and sleep it off.'

'I'd rather go to bed with you and work it off.' He took another step closer. 'You look gorgeous tonight.'

'That's because I'm going out. On a date. Like normal people.' As soon the words were out, I knew I shouldn't have said anything.

Tony's eyes narrowed and his lips curled into a snarl. 'You little slapper. Didn't waste your time finding your next lay, did you?'

'It isn't like that.'

As he moved closer, I stepped back into the flat and grabbed the door, but he had his foot and hand jammed against it and it wouldn't budge. Oh my God! My heart thumped. I'd never been scared of Tony, even when he'd confronted me in the summerhouse, but I was now.

'Please go.'

'Not until I've got what I came for.' He lunged forward and grabbed me, crushing his lips against mine before I had a chance to scream. He pushed me back against the wall, cracking my head on the corner of the intercom, pinning my arms by my side. The intercom buzzed. Tony moved his mouth from mine and onto my neck and I seized my opportunity. Banging my head back against the intercom, praying I'd catch the button, I yelled, 'Rhys! Help!'

Tony stopped slobbering on my neck. 'Who's Rhys?'

'Let go of me. You're hurting me.' I tried to

squirm free but, at five feet four, I was no match for
his height and strength.

'I said, who the fuck is Rhys?'

'I am!'

I sank to the floor, gasping, as Rhys hauled Tony
off me.

'The gardener?' cried Tony. 'You're screwing the
gardener?'

'She asked you to leave,' Rhys shouted. 'Get out!
Now!'

Tony laughed – a bitter and cruel sound. 'I'm not
taking orders off a slapper or the gardener.' He
sneered at Rhys. 'Liked what you saw when you
found us in the summerhouse? Fancied a bit yourself, did you?'

Clinging onto the door handle, I managed to
haul myself to my feet. 'Please just go, Tony.'

'I'm not going anywhere. Or at least not until I've
done this.'

Rhys stood no chance. He was looking at me,
eyes full of concern, when Tony's fist caught him on
the cheek, splitting it open, sending him straight to
the floor.

'Tony! Stop it!' I screamed, dropping to the floor beside a dazed Rhys. 'He's bleeding.'

'You're not worth it,' Tony spat. Then he clattered down the stairs, out of the building and, with any luck, out of our lives.

* * *

'This wasn't quite how I envisaged our first date,' I said as we walked across the floodlit hospital car park towards Rhys's van a few hours later. He'd had his cheek glued and I'd needed six stitches in the back of my head where I'd struck the corner of the intercom. 'Assuming it was meant to be a date, and not just a night out as friends.'

Rhys took my hand. 'It was meant to be a date. If you wanted it to be, that is.'

I nodded. 'I did. Sorry I messed it up.'

Rhys stopped walking and turned to face me, still holding my hand. 'You didn't mess anything up. Tony did. And not just with you. I think his whole life's going to get pretty messy when the police catch up with him.'

I'd felt so sorry for Tony's wife and children, but

there was no way I could let him get away with assaulting us both like that. If Rhys hadn't shown up, we could have been facing attempted rape, or even... I shuddered at the thought.

'I never imagined that Tony could be violent like that,' I said. 'Then again, I never thought he had a wife or kids. I guess I didn't know him at all. I think I know you better after two weeks than I know him after a year.' I smiled at Rhys and added, shyly, 'I look forward to getting to know you even better.'

'Same here. There's something I'd like to know about you right now, though.'

'What's that?'

'How it feels to kiss you.'

I smiled as I tilted my head towards his. 'Like this.'

Rhys lowered his head until his lips met mine. I closed my eyes as they lightly brushed against mine then parted to kiss me properly. Every part of my body felt on fire at his touch – a sensation I'd never felt before. So this was what real chemistry felt like rather than lust. I liked it. A lot. Rhys moved his hands into my hair and I touched his face at the same time. We both winced and pulled away, laughing. Then we both winced at the laughter, because that hurt too.

'Come on,' Rhys said, 'let's get you home.'

'A quick question before we do. Where were you going to take me tonight?'

Rhys smiled. 'Moor View Farm.'

I grinned. 'Is that your mate Kev's place?'

He nodded. 'The sunset would have been pretty spectacular tonight, but I'll take you another time.'

'I thought you said that you'd only take someone special there.'

'That's right.'

'So that would mean...' Despite the pain in my head, I couldn't stop smiling. 'That would mean you think I'm special.'

Rhys grinned too. 'I think you might be.'

As he bent down and kissed me gently again, I had a feeling he might be pretty special too. Thank goodness it had been his cheek rather than his mouth that Tony had hit.

18

THREE MONTHS LATER

'Callie Derbyshire, are you staring at my grandson's bottom again?' Ruby asked, feigning shock.

I turned round from the window of the residents' lounge, giggling. 'Busted. But it's so tempting when he's bent down like that.' I couldn't help myself. The last three months with Rhys had been so amazing. He'd shown me what a relationship should be like: a partnership with kindness and respect.

I nodded in the direction of Brenda Simkins who, despite her winsome claims at frailty, had somehow managed to turn one of the rather large armchairs to an angle where she could enjoy the perfect view. 'It seems I'm not the only one,' I whispered to Ruby.

'Oi, Brenda! Enjoying the view?' Ruby called.

Brenda shuffled awkwardly in her chair. 'I was trying to work out what the young man was planting,' she said.

Ruby laughed. 'If you could manage to raise your gaze from my grandson's posterior, I think you'll find that he's weeding, not planting.'

Brenda squirmed again and pretended to drink from her empty cup of tea.

'You're a wicked tease,' I told Ruby.

'I've got to get my kicks somewhere. That darned Iris Davies is spending far too much time in Reggie's brother's company, so I've got nobody else to torment.' Ruby helped herself to another chocolate Hobnob from the tea trolley and settled into her favourite armchair. 'I can't bear the sight of those two together, fawning over each other. It's quite disgusting at their age.'

'Ruby! How can you say that? Love knows no age. I think it's really romantic. Childhood sweethearts finding each other again in their seventies.'

'Childhood sweethearts? Pah!' She waved her hand and shook her head. 'They were in the same class at school when they were seven. That's hardly the same as being childhood sweethearts, is it?'

I picked up the last few dirty cups and saucers off the coffee table and added them to the pile on the trolley. 'That's not the way Iris tells it.'

'Yes, well, she's a liar, isn't she? And she cheats at dominoes. And cards. Not quite as innocent as she looks, you know.' She tapped her nose, knowingly.

'You're becoming very cynical, Ruby. Anyone would think you didn't believe in love, which clearly isn't the case given how supportive you are of Rhys and me.'

'That's different. You two were made for each other. Anyone can see that.'

'And I think that Iris and William were made for each other.' I was thrilled that something beautiful had grown from Reggie's passing.

'Piffle!'

'Not piffle! What's more, I reckon there'll be wedding bells before spring is over.'

Ruby sat forward, her pale liver-spotted hands gripping onto the arms of the chair. 'Do you really think so, Callie?'

'I'm pretty certain of it. Reggie's death was a

shock to us all and a reminder to grasp every moment as you never know when there'll be no moments left to grasp.'

Ruby released her grip on the chair arms and slumped back, staring out of the window. 'I suppose you're right.'

I bit my lip. She suddenly looked very frail and quite lost in the huge chair. Had my reminder of the fragility of life been inappropriate for a woman of Ruby's years? She was such a lively, vibrant individual, so full of crude comments and fascinating anecdotes, that it was easy to think of her as one of my besties rather than a woman rapidly approaching eighty-five.

As if reading my thoughts, she looked up and smiled brightly. 'I used to grasp more than my fair share of moments back in the day. And other things. Did I tell you about the time when I was caught in a rather compromising position with Lord Finton Kingsley...?'

And she was back in the room. Phew! But as I cleared the pots away, the expression on Ruby's face haunted me. Although she liked to make out that she didn't care for Iris's company and 'tolerated' rather than liked her, I was certain it was a front. Over the years, she'd recounted many stories of life in the circus, followed by dancing then acting, but all the tales featured men. I couldn't recall any stories about female friends. With her stunning looks and risqué career choices, I wondered if she'd struggled to earn the trust or respect of other females. Perhaps they'd viewed her as a threat. Or perhaps she was one of those women who simply didn't find joy in the company of other females. However, I'd seen her deep in conversation or in peals of laughter with Iris on far too many occasions to believe that theirs wasn't a genuine friendship. I was convinced that Iris was the first proper female friend in Ruby's life, and that the real reason she turned her nose up at the idea of Iris finding love with William was because she was terrified of her friend moving out of Bay View. Poor Ruby. I couldn't bear the thought of such a wonderful woman feeling lonely like that. If only there was something I could do.

19

'What do you think? Is it straight?'

I took a few paces back and surveyed the eight-foot Christmas tree standing proudly in the middle bay window of the residents' lounge. 'I think so.'

He joined me and nodded. 'Looks good. I chose well.'

I nudged him in the ribs. '*Who* chose well?'

'Okay, okay, *you* chose well.' He put his arm round me and gave me a gentle squeeze. 'I suppose you'll want my help decorating it.'

'Only the high bits. And you can only place the baubles where I tell you.'

Rhys laughed. 'Really? Is this where it starts?'

'Where what starts?'

'The revelation about the *real* Callie Derbyshire? Am I about to discover that you've lulled me into a false sense of security over the past few months, making me believe you're all relaxed and lovely when you're actually a control freak who insists on symmetry on the tree and combs the pine needles?'

'Combing pine needles? No! Is that a thing?'

Rhys shrugged. 'I bet someone out there does it. Nowt so queer as folk, as they say. Nice avoidance of my question, though.'

I gave him another playful nudge. 'I promise I'm not a control freak. I just like the tree to look pretty and it doesn't if you don't distribute the colours and styles of bauble.'

Rhys raised an eyebrow. 'Yes, I was right. It's starting...'

'Ha ha. We'll decorate it when my shift ends. Is that okay? You aren't seeing Megan tonight, are you?' I hoped I'd managed to keep the tension out of my voice as I said her name. It didn't bother me that Rhys had a daughter; we both had relationship histories. What bothered me was that I'd never met her. Izzy had created a 'rule' around not introducing new partners to Megan unless it was 'really serious' in case it confused her. Megan wasn't even a year old yet. How confused could a baby get? Rhys agreed it was silly, but he was terrified that Izzy might start restricting his access if he challenged it, so he kept quiet. What did 'really serious' mean anyway? Together for over a year? Living together? Married? I dreaded to think. It made things difficult for Rhys and me, though, creating the only tension in an otherwise amazing relationship.

'Not tonight. I'm all yours tonight.' Rhys gave me a playful wink.

'Then we'll have to be quick with the decorations so I can make the most of you.'

* * *

'Oh my goodness! That's stunning.' Ruby clapped her hands together later that evening before sitting in one of the armchairs. 'Best tree ever.'

'Thank you,' I said, placing some empty bauble packets into a plastic crate. 'My assistant had a few dodgy bauble placement moments, but I think I managed to re-educate him.'

'Ooh! That's pretty.' Iris appeared and took a seat opposite Ruby. 'You've done well.'

Ruby looked Iris up and down. 'To what do we owe this pleasure? I do believe we had your company last night too. No hot date tonight?'

'Not tonight. He's away visiting his sister and won't be back until tomorrow, as you're perfectly aware. I don't see William every night, you know.'

'Wouldn't bother me if you did.'

'Wouldn't bother me if it bothered you,' Iris retaliated in an unusual display of feistiness.

I half-expected Ruby to respond with something ridiculous like, 'wouldn't bother me if it bothered you that it didn't bother me', so I was relieved when she straightened her crocheted silver cardigan instead and uttered one word: 'Poker?'

Iris smiled. 'I'll get the cards.'

'For matchsticks or pennies,' I reminded Ruby. 'You know what happened last time.'

'Silly Angus should have—'

But she didn't get to finish her sentence because Iris squealed like a little girl from the other side of the lounge. 'William! You're back!'

He kissed her on the cheek then handed her a

bunch of flowers. 'I couldn't bear two nights in a row without my darling girl, so I came back early.'

Iris sniffed the flowers then they hugged. So sweet. A gentle sigh beside me made me turn round to look at Ruby. Was it my imagination or were there tears in her eyes? She looked up at me and cleared her throat. 'Looks like poker's off the agenda this evening. Just as well. I'm tired and an early night beckons. You wouldn't be a darling and make me a cup of tea, would you?'

'Of course.' I pointed to the plastic crates. 'I'll need to put these away before anyone trips over them. Shall I bring a cuppa to your room?'

'Yes please.'

'I can make your tea, Nanna,' Rhys said.

Ruby shook her head vigorously. 'My darling boy, I love you very, very much, but I'm not so enamoured by your tea-making attempts.'

Laughing, Rhys said, 'In that case, I'll walk you to your room instead.'

Ruby smiled. 'I'd like that. Thank you.'

* * *

'I'm worried about Ruby,' I said as I snuggled up to Rhys in bed back at my flat that evening. 'She's been really quiet lately. I think she's lonely.'

'Nanna? Quiet? Lonely? I don't think she knows the meaning of those words. How can she be lonely? She's got loads of friends at Bay View.'

'You can be surrounded by people and still be lonely.'

'True. But I don't think that's the case with Nanna. Is this because Iris abandoned her tonight?'

'Partly.'

'You don't need to worry about that. She told me she was relieved that William had arrived because Iris had kept her up until the small hours of this morning playing poker and she'd nearly nodded off in her soup at teatime.'

'And you believed her?'

'Of course I did.' He squeezed me and kissed the top of my head. 'I love that you worry about her, but I really don't think you need to. If she's been quiet, it's because she's tired. She'll be fine after a good night's sleep. Plus, you know how much she loves Christmas. Now that the tree's up, she'll be so excitable that you'll long for her to be quiet again.'

'I hope so.'

'I know so. Night, night.'

But I struggled to get to sleep. I wasn't imagining it. Something had definitely changed with Ruby since things started to get serious between Iris and William and I didn't like it.

20

'What are you doing out here?' Rhys stood up and removed his heavy-duty gloves a few days later. He tossed them on top of the overflowing wheelbarrow next to him and wiped the sweat off his forehead. 'It's freezing.'

'I'm on my break and I thought you might like a drink.' I handed him the mug of coffee, then pulled my coat tightly around me, trying to shield myself against the biting wind.

'Not that I'm not grateful, but you don't normally bring me a cuppa, so I'm guessing there's something on your mind.'

'I wanted to see my gorgeous boyfriend and bring

him a hot drink on an icy cold day.'

'Callie! Spit it out.'

Damn! He knew me far too well already. 'Okay. So, I've been thinking...'

'Yes...?'

'It's about Christmas. I know it's still five weeks away, but with us putting the tree up this week...'

'Yes...?'

'My Christmas Day shift finishes at two and I wanted to check you're still okay to spend the rest of the day with me.'

'Yes. I'm looking forward to our first Christmas together.' He cocked his head onto one side and smiled. 'But you already knew that. What else?'

'Well, I was wondering if you could ask Izzy if we can see Megan at some point during the afternoon. I know Izzy's got her stupid rules, but we'll have been together for four months by then. Surely that's long enough for her to see it's not just some casual fling that's going to "confuse" Megan.'

Rhys sighed, as if to say, *Not this again!*

'I'm only thinking of you,' I said, rubbing my icy hands together. 'It's not fair that you don't get to see your daughter on Christmas Day, especially when it's her first Christmas.' Rhys spent every other Sunday with Megan, occasional Saturdays if he wasn't working, and random days during the week which Izzy usually dropped on him last minute, often putting paid to plans that Rhys and I had for time together. Although Christmas would fall on Sunday, it wasn't his Sunday to have her.

'Who says I won't get to see her?' Rhys asked.

'It's not your Sunday for her. I just assumed...' I bit my lip as I tailed off. Something about Rhys's expression told me I wasn't going to like what he said next.

'Izzy invited me round to be with Megan when she opens her presents.'

My stomach churned as I imagined the pair of them laughing together while their baby daughter ripped up shiny wrapping paper, like a perfect family. 'Oh! When was this discussed?' I tried to sound positive.

'When I saw her last night.'

'And you were going to tell me when exactly?'

Rhys shrugged. 'Probably tonight.'

I knew that the right thing to do was to smile

brightly, tell him I was thrilled that he was going to spend Christmas morning with his daughter, kiss him and head back to work. But my gob was in overdrive as usual and I just couldn't seem to shut up. 'You didn't think to tell me when I saw you this morning?'

'We didn't have time to talk, and we weren't alone.'

True. We'd only seen each other briefly whilst making a drink in the staffroom and he'd been called away for a delivery so he genuinely hadn't had an opportunity to tell me. Didn't stop me being pissed off at the news, though.

'How cosy. Mummy, Daddy, and baby playing happy families together on Christmas morning.' I winced at my sarcastic tone.

'Don't be like that,' Rhys called as I turned and tramped back up to the building, tears pricking my eyes.

I stopped and spun round. 'What do you expect, Rhys? I'm not allowed to meet your daughter and your selfish cow of an ex has you at her beck and call. How do you expect me to react?'

'You're being daft. What do you expect me to do?

Turn down a chance to spend my daughter's first ever Christmas with her?'

'No! I'm glad you're spending Christmas with her. You *should* spend Christmas with her. But I expect you to tell Izzy that you're serious about me and insist that it's time I met Megan. Unless you're not serious about me after all. Is that it?'

'Of course not.'

'Then tell her.'

I waited for him to give me some sort of reassurance that he'd raise the subject, but he just stood there, frowning. With an exasperated shrug in his direction, I stormed back to the building, muttering under my breath and refusing to give in to the tears.

'He's told you then?' I jumped as Ruby appeared whilst I was aggressively wiping my feet at the back entrance. She must have been watching us from the residents' lounge.

'Told me what?' I said, refusing to catch her eye. 'I was just taking him a drink, but it was freezing so I came back in.'

Ruby wrapped her slender fingers round my arm and waited until I looked at her. 'Callie, darling, I was an actress. I've studied human behaviour. He told me earlier that he's seeing Megan on Christmas morning and now he's told you, hasn't he?'

'He might have done,' I muttered.

'He loves you, you know. So very, very much. Izzy's no threat.'

I looked into her pale eyes. Were my fears that transparent?

'I know,' I whispered. 'It's just that...'

'It's just that they've got something to bind them together forever, that you don't currently have?'

I nodded.

'You'll have your own family in time, darling. But only if you don't let the green-eyed monster control you like that again.' She patted my arm then wandered off down the corridor.

I turned to look out of the door again, hoping to give Rhys a wave, but there was no sign of him or the wheelbarrow. Crap! I'd never been jealous of anyone before, but there was absolutely no escaping that jealousy was the emotion I felt. Ruby was right; if I didn't get it in check, it would eat away at our relationship and I could lose him. I wasn't prepared to risk that.

I didn't see Rhys for the rest of the day, but only

because I was snowed under with my new role – not because I was deliberately avoiding him. My colleague, Pete, and I had both secured team leader positions on the back of Denise's recommendations. A third team leader, Odette, had been recruited externally. We had processes to put in place and plans for recruitment and training, working closely with the weekend manager, Gillian, and our relief manager, Ian, who was covering in Denise's absence. I'd never been busier.

Rhys finished work a few hours before my shift ended, when it turned dark, so usually went back to his place – a rented room in a friend's house – to shower and change, before returning in his van to pick me up. We were meant to be having dinner at my flat that evening then going into Whitsborough Bay for a few drinks. As my shift ended, I wasn't sure whether he would be waiting for me thanks to my stroppy behaviour. Butterflies flitted in my stomach as I grabbed my bag from my locker and made my way to the entrance. *Please be there.* The sliding doors opened and I stepped outside but there was no sign of him.

I waited for ten excruciatingly slow minutes,

smiling politely as various colleagues left, wishing them a great Friday evening and pretending nothing was wrong. He wasn't coming. I reluctantly pulled my bag onto my shoulder, wrapped my scarf a little more tightly around my neck, and set off on foot in the direction of home.

Halfway home, I became aware of a vehicle slowing down beside me. Rhys?

But it wasn't him.

'Well, well, well,' said a male voice. 'It's the home-wrecker who likes to get people sacked.'

My pulse raced and a wave of nausea hit me. Tony.

'What do you want?' I demanded, continuing to walk.

'An apology.'

'From me?'

'Do you see any other homewreckers around here?'

I stopped and stared at him, hands on my hips. I knew that even Tony wasn't stupid enough to get out of the car and try something on whilst we were on a well-lit busy road, but it didn't stop my heart hammering. 'Yes,' I said. 'I'm looking at one. Now are you going to piss off and leave me alone, or do you want to get arrested for kerb-crawling?'

'You and gardening boy would love that, wouldn't you? Getting me into more trouble with the police.'

'We didn't get you into trouble. You did that yourself.'

I set off walking again, but he kept the car in pace beside me.

'I owe you one for what you did to me,' he snarled. 'I'd watch my back if I were you.'

'Is that a threat?'

'It's a promise.'

I stopped walking and gave him the stoniest stare I could manage, trying to exude confidence whilst my legs shook uncontrollably. 'It sounds like a threat to me. I think the police would be very interested to hear that you've breached your restraining order *and* you've been threatening me.'

He stared at me for a moment before hissing, 'Fat bitch,' then flooring the accelerator.

The shaking had moved from my legs into my whole body and I slumped down on a nearby garden wall the moment he disappeared from view, gulping in cold air, trying to steady my racing heart.

I jumped as my mobile rang. Rhys! Thank goodness for that. 'I'm so glad it's—'

'Where are you?' he demanded, cutting me short and instantly putting me on edge again.

'Where do you think I am?' I retorted.

'I don't know. That's why I'm phoning you.'

'You didn't show up, so I waited for ten minutes then set off walking. I know you were annoyed with me earlier, but you could have let me know you wouldn't be picking me up.'

'I am picking you up. I'm at Bay View right now.'

'You weren't when I finished my shift.'

'I was. I got here ten minutes early.'

'You did not!'

'Did you check the car park?'

I paused. 'No. But you always meet me at the entrance.'

'My mum phoned and I didn't realise the time.' His voice softened. 'Do you really think I'd just not show up?'

'I suppose not,' I muttered.

'Where are you?'

'Sat on the wall of one of the terraces on Whitby Road, opposite the chippy.'

'I'll be there in five. Don't go anywhere.'

I wasn't sure I could move even if I wanted to.

Five minutes later, Rhys's van mounted the pavement. 'Hey pretty lady,' he called. 'Can I interest you in dinner, drinks and some make-up sex?'

I couldn't help smiling. 'In that order?'

He grinned. 'I can be very flexible, depending on what pleases you.'

* * *

'I'm sorry if I upset you,' Rhys said as we snuggled in bed that evening after a lovely night out together. 'I wasn't keeping secrets. I'd never keep secrets from you, especially after what Tony did to you.'

I winced at the mention of his name. 'I know. I over-reacted. I was just a bit surprised and a bit jealous.'

'You know that Izzy means nothing to me, don't you? She never did. I know that sounds awful, especially when we have a child together. If it wasn't for Megan, we wouldn't have kept in touch. She'll never be anything to me other than the mother of my child.'

'I know. I'm being stupid. I just don't want you feeling like you've drawn the short straw by having to leave your daughter to spend the afternoon with me.'

'Callie, you could *never* be the short straw. Spending the morning with Izzy is the short straw, but it's the only way I'm going to get to spend Megan's first Christmas with her.'

I stiffened. 'Does that mean you're not going to ask her about Megan spending the afternoon with us?'

Rhys gently stroked my arm. 'It means I'm not going to ask her *now*. I'm surprised at the invite myself and, with Christmas still being weeks away, I don't want to do anything to risk a retraction. It doesn't mean I won't ask at a later date. If the timing's right.'

There was no point in pushing it. Rhys was stuck between a rock and a hard place. Izzy was an awkward little madam who needed to grow up and step into the real world.

'There's something you're not saying,' Rhys said after several minutes of silence. 'You're thinking I should push about Christmas?'

'No,' I said. 'I get why you're not and, knowing

how awkward Izzy is, I think you're right.'

'So what is it?'

'I saw Tony earlier.'

Rhys tightened his arms around me. 'When?'

'When I was walking home. He slowed the car down, called me names, and threatened me.'

'Are you okay?'

'I was shaken. That's why I was sitting on the wall when you found me.'

Rhys kissed the top of my head. 'He can't do anything to you, you know.'

'I thought that last time.'

'What's he playing at? He's got a restraining order.'

'I know. Didn't stop him, though.'

'It's my fault. I shouldn't have lost track of time.'

'And I should have thought to check the car park instead of assuming you were in a strop with me and had done a no-show.'

Rhys and I lay in silence holding each other, lost in our thoughts. We'd had such a lovely evening planned yet our exes, Tony and Izzy, had managed to put a dampener on it. It wasn't fair. Why did they still have power over us?

21

'Morning, gorgeous,' Rhys said as I emerged from the bedroom the following morning, rubbing my eyes, stomach rumbling at the enticing aroma of bacon.

'What time is it?'

'Seven. Sorry. I know it's early for a Saturday, but I wanted to make you breakfast before I left for my shift at the pool. You can always go back to bed if you're still tired.'

I shuffled over to him for a kiss. 'No. It's good that I'm up. I've got a few things to do before I go Christmas shopping with Mum. Did your parents enjoy their cruise, by the way?' I asked, realising Rhys hadn't told me about his conversation with his mum. I hadn't met his parents yet because they'd been away for three months. Rhys's dad had sold his construction company for a hefty sum and his mum had taken early retirement so they could travel.

'Loved it. They're already planning their next one. They want to tell me – us – all about it so they've invited us over to York for lunch tomorrow. I know it's short notice, but do you feel up to meeting the parents? I can't wait to show you off.'

'Ooh, I think so.' I might not be permitted to meet his daughter, but meeting his parents at the first possible opportunity was pretty special, even if it was a little terrifying. 'Do you think they'll like me?'

'They'll love you.'

'Did they like Izzy?' It slipped out before I could stop myself. 'Sorry. You don't need to answer that.'

Rhys grabbed a pair of tongs and placed the bacon onto slices of bread. 'They never actually met her, or at least not while we were together. Obviously they've met her since Megan was born.' He handed me a plate and we moved to the sofa.

'They know about Izzy's deception,' he continued. 'My dad can be very opinionated and very tunnel-visioned. There's only one correct viewpoint on everything and it's his. If you do something he doesn't agree with, he never shuts up about it. As soon as I told them she was pregnant, Dad went off on one, as I expected, about how irresponsible I was for not practising safe sex in this day and age and what an idiot I was for ruining a young girl's life. I didn't see why I should take the flack so I set him straight'

'I bet he was impressed with that.'

'Let's just say that Mum and Dad both tolerate Izzy because she's Megan's mum, but they aren't exactly fans, particularly Dad.'

It was naughty of me, but I felt rather smug about it. It would have been horrendous if Rhys's parents adored Izzy and believed that Rhys should be with her because of Megan. I'd have hated feeling like it was a competition.

When we finished eating, Rhys reached for my empty plate. 'I'm going to have to love you and leave you with the washing up,' he said, wrinkling his nose. 'Sorry.'

'I think I can forgive you seeing as you make the best bacon butties in the world.'

He gave me a gentle kiss. 'Have a lovely day with

your mum. Make sure she buys me an enormous and very expensive present.'

I giggled. 'She probably will do without the prompt. If your parents like me even a quarter as much as my mum likes you, I'll be a happy bunny.'

'They will. I guarantee it. I'll pick you up at about half ten.'

* * *

The buzzer to my flat sounded shortly after nine the next morning. Ever since Tony had pushed his way in, I'd been wary of unexpected visitors. Pulse racing, I pressed the intercom. 'Hello?'

'It's only me. Don't sound so scared.'

I relaxed at the sound of Rhys's voice. Then panic set in. 'I thought you said you'd pick me up at half ten. I was about to have a shower. I'm nowhere near ready!'

'I did say half ten, but I missed you. I wanted to spend some time with my gorgeous girlfriend first. Is that okay?'

I smiled. 'Flattery will get you everywhere.'

'Will it get me inside your flat, then, because I'm freezing my bollocks off out here talking to you?'

Laughing, I buzzed him up. I kept meaning to get a spare set of keys cut for Rhys but it always slipped my mind when I was in town.

Hearing footsteps on the stairs, I leaned seductively against my open doorway. I was wearing a pair of tartan PJs with the jacket open except for one button just below my breasts, although it wasn't successfully hiding anything.

His eyes widened appreciatively as he stopped on the landing and took in my attire. 'Nice PJs.' He ran up the final set of stairs and gently took hold of the tartan material. 'I think you've missed a button, though,' he said, pulling me against him and kissing me. He tasted minty and smelled of pine forests. Delicious.

'I'm not very good with buttons,' I whispered as he trailed kisses round my neck. 'I might need some help.'

He swiftly unfastened the remaining button and slowly slid his hands over my exposed breasts. I gasped at the cold and at the pleasure of his touch.

My body arched against the doorframe as he kissed my neck again, then trailed kisses down my body.

'I think we'd better move this inside,' he whispered between kisses, 'before we get arrested for indecent exposure.'

I didn't want to move and pause the ripples of pleasure running through me, but I knew he was right. One of my neighbours could open their door at any point, although I wondered if that element of risk was part of the reason I was responding even more passionately than usual to Rhys's touch.

We reluctantly pulled apart. As I went to close the door, my next-door neighbour stepped into the corridor, chatting to someone on her phone.

Giggling, I slammed the door shut. 'That was close! Now, where were we?' I wriggled my PJ bottoms to the floor. 'Oops! How did that happen?'

Rhys quickly removed his jacket, pulled his shirt off over his head, kicked off his shoes, and slipped out of his jeans. 'Must be contagious,' he said grinning at me. 'I could still do with warming up, though. Did you say you were about to take a shower?'

I nodded. Still holding his gaze, I eased off my PJs top. 'Care to join me?'

My bathroom wasn't big enough for a bath, but it was big enough for a large shower, perfect for two. It was just as well that my neighbour had gone out because my bathroom wall bordered her flat and we were a little bit noisy. Okay, a lot noisy. Sex with Tony had been great, much as I hated to admit it given how much I despised the man now, but sex with Rhys was on a whole new level. It was as though our bodies had been designed to fit together. And he was so strong. Years of lugging sacks of soil and bags of rubble meant he could lift me with ease, holding me securely with my back against the tiles, legs wrapped round him.

By the time we'd finished in the shower, we were both exhausted.

'A quick snuggle on the bed, then get dressed?' Rhys suggested.

I gave my hair a rub with the towel, then dived under the cover to cuddle up to him.

* * *

The sound of my mobile ringing made me snap my eyes open. I focused on the clock on the wall oppo-

site the bed. No! Sitting upright, I shook Rhys franti-
cally. 'It's ten past eleven!'

'Shit! We're late!' He threw back the covers and
ran through the flat, retrieving his clothes.

I dived for the bathroom. My hair lay flat in parts
and stuck up at peculiar angles in others – classic
slept-on wet hair look. Shaking my head in despair, I
squirted on some deodorant and perfume. I could
apply make-up in the van, but there was sod all I
could do with my hair except hope that it looked a
bit less post-sex-in-the-shower after I'd run a brush
through it. Why today?

'I've texted Dad to say we're stuck in traffic,' Rhys
said. 'How long do you need?'

'An hour to re-shower and sort out this mess,' I
said, pointing at my hair. His panicked expression
suggested jokes weren't appropriate. 'Three minutes
to get dressed?'

Rhys pulled his jeans up and fastened the belt.
'Good. I don't mean to rush you. It's just—'

'I know. It'll be fine.' I hoped it would be. Rhys
didn't say a lot about his parents. From the little he'd
told me, his mum sounded lovely, but I wasn't too
sure about his dad. Rhys's jaw seemed to clench on

the rare occasion he mentioned him and I suspected they weren't the best of mates. Hopefully I'd be able to charm his dad. I was pretty good at handling older men, after all.

* * *

The journey through to York was, thankfully, a smooth one with little traffic on the roads. Even so, we were over an hour late. Rhys barely spoke, seeming nervous and twitchy every time I asked if he was okay.

'This is it,' he said as he stopped the van opposite a large, immaculate, double-fronted property. 'Better late than never.' He smiled as he took my hand. 'You look amazing, by the way. I should have said so earlier.'

'My hair's still sticking up, but it'll have to do.' I grabbed the flowers I'd bought the day before.

A shiny, silver Mercedes was parked on the drive alongside a sporty-looking two-seater. Looking up at the house again, I whistled. 'Your parents must be loaded. It's huge.'

'It's pointlessly huge,' he muttered. 'It used to

have three bedrooms, but Dad built the extension on the right to make it five.'

'I thought you only had one sister.'

'I do. Debbie. Yeah, I know. Why the five beds?' He sighed. 'It's a status thing. My dad's like that. Always wants the biggest house on the street, the newest cars, the brightest kids in the best jobs. Hands up who let him down on that one.' Rhys raised his right hand in the air.

I frowned. 'But you've got an amazing job.'

'*I* think so, but I'm *just* a gardener to him.'

'And he was *just* a builder, wasn't he?'

Rhys laughed as he hugged me. 'Don't let him hear you say that.'

'Why didn't you park on the drive?' I asked as we crossed the road. There was enough space to accommodate several more vehicles.

'It lowers the tone apparently. If he had his own way, I'd park round the corner and walk, but I like to rebel occasionally.'

'Surely he had a work van before he retired.'

'He did. But his was new and clean, not old and rusty like mine.'

I squeezed Rhys's hand. Clearly there was history

between him and his dad that I'd need to explore at some point. Perhaps that was the reason for the silence on the way. I now felt like I was about to walk into the lion's den. It therefore seemed fitting that the doorknocker was in the shape of a lion's head.

The door flung open to reveal a tall well-built man with salt and pepper hair, bright blue eyes just like Rhys's, and an impressive tan. He stared at Rhys, expressionless. Taking in his expensive-looking dark grey suit, I felt very under-dressed in a jersey dress, leggings and boots.

'Hi, Dad. Sorry we're late. This is—'

'So you finally decided to grace us with your presence,' he interrupted, barely glancing at me.

'I *did* text to say we were stuck in traffic,' Rhys said.

'Ah yes, the text. The thing is, I spoke with Giles Thomas earlier. Remember Giles? His son runs the travel desk for Radio York. He says the roads have been clear all morning. So what have you been doing?'

Shiiiiiit! I gave a sideways glance to Rhys who held his dad's gaze.

'I told you. We got stuck in traffic.'

It was like watching a staring contest. Who was going to blink or look away first? My money was on Rhys's dad to win. What a scary bloke. I gave an awkward cough and they both looked at me. Oops. Maybe I shouldn't have done that.

'Er, hi Mr Michaels. I'm Callie.' I added a stupid little wave to the greeting. What a muppet! 'Thanks so much for inviting us for lunch.'

He stared at me for a moment, then smiled, transforming his face from terrifying to quite charming.

'Welcome, Callie. It's lovely to meet you at last. Please come in. And it's Ed.'

'Thank you, Ed.' I stepped into a grand entrance hall with a polished parquet floor and feature cornicing. Wow! 'You have a beautiful home.'

'That's very kind of you, Callie. We try our best.'

After hanging up our coats, he led us to an enormous kitchen-diner at the back of the property. I tried not to gasp. You could fit my whole flat into their kitchen. Twice. The unmistakable aroma of roast lamb and mint sauce wafted towards me and my stomach grumbled appreciatively.

'Jenny! Our guests have *finally* arrived.'

A petite woman with short, dark, curly hair and red cheeks turned round from an impressively large range cooker and smiled warmly.

'Rhys!' She hugged her son. 'And you must be Callie.' She hugged me too, helping dissipate the rising nerves thanks to Ed's not-so-warm welcome. 'I've heard so much about you. It's lovely to meet you.'

'These are for you,' I said, handing her the flowers.

She looked genuinely touched. 'That's so thoughtful of you. Thank you.' She sniffed the bouquet. 'Gorgeous. I'll pop them in some water for now and arrange them properly later, if that's okay. Ed, can you put these in the sink and get our guests a drink? I need to mash the potatoes.'

He took the flowers from her without a word, although I swear his lip curled up as he clocked the Aldi label. Snob.

* * *

After the shaky start, Ed was charming throughout the meal. He and Jenny spoke with passion about their cruise: the ship, the people they'd met, the places they visited. However, if I hadn't already been aware of his interest in all things materialistic, I certainly would have been by the time we finished dessert. Crikey! Thank God Rhys was nothing like that or he'd never have picked a poorly paid shift-working care-home employee who lived in a tiny rented flat and whose only mode of transport was a knackered old bicycle.

After lunch, Jenny headed into the kitchen to load the dishwasher and make some coffee. She refused my help, but Rhys wouldn't let her clear up on her own and followed her into the kitchen, leaving me alone with Ed. My stomach did a nervous flip as he invited me to join him in the lounge. What if Mr Nasty returned?

The lounge was as impressive as the rest of the house. Light streamed through the huge bay windows and, because the top panels were colourful stained glass, it was like a rainbow bursting into the room. Sitting down on the smaller of two sofas, I smiled at Ed. 'Beautiful lounge.'

'Thank you. We think so.' He placed his glass of wine on a coaster and sat on a high-backed armchair.

'Rhys tells me you work in a care home. I can't imagine that pays very well.' *And Mr Nasty is back in the room.*

'It's not the best, but I don't do it for the money. I do it because I love my job.'

'Running round after old people all day, cleaning their rooms and wiping their backsides?'

Keep smiling. 'Most of our residents are completely independent so I don't need to do anything like that.'

'What do you do then?'

'Run errands, organise activities, help them make their rooms feel homely, distribute medication... It varies every day. And I'm a team leader now so my role's changing.'

Ed looked bored. 'You can dress it up however you like, but it sounds to me like you run after old people all day, cleaning their rooms and wiping their backsides.'

Yes, well, it would, wouldn't it? Rhys had said his dad had tunnel-vision so it was pointless trying to change his mind about a job he clearly knew nothing about.

'Rhys has some amazing plans for landscaping

the gardens there,' I said, keen to change the subject. 'He's so talented.'

Ed gave a snort. 'He's a gardener. That hardly takes much talent, does it? Not like his sister, Debbie, who's a barrister. Now that takes talent. That's a career to be proud of. Anyone can dig a few holes or push a lawnmower.'

What an absolute git! I didn't mind him criticising me, but I wasn't going to stand by and let him belittle the man I loved. 'Yes, they probably can, but could they redesign five acres of sloping land to make it accessible for those with mobility issues? That takes *real* talent, and your son has that in spades. You should be very proud of him.' It was my turn to play the staring game. 'Didn't you start off as a labourer?' I asked, my tone as smooth as honey. Ed blinked. *Ha! Gotcha!*

'Yes, we all have to start somewhere, but then I developed the business into something spectacular.'

'By the time you were Rhys's age?'

'No. These things take time.'

'Yes, they do.' I nodded as I held his gaze. I was pretty sure he realised he'd just made my point for me and I longed to stick my tongue out at him and say, 'so ner'.

'Coffee!' announced Jenny, bursting through the door. Rhys followed her holding a tray of mugs, cream, and a plate of wafer-thin mint chocolates. Posh ones.

'What have you two been talking about?' she asked, taking a seat on the larger sofa as Rhys sat down beside me.

I wasn't sure how to respond, but Ed beat me to it. 'Callie was just telling me all about her job and the wonderful work our son is doing in the gardens there.' Ooh, sarcasm!

'Oh! How lovely! We must visit Bay View and see the gardens when they're finished,' Jenny gushed.

'We'll do no such thing,' Ed snapped. 'Not while *she's* living there. I have no intention of *ever* meeting that woman.'

'You mean Ruby?' It was out of my mouth before I could stop myself.

All heads turned towards me.

'It's none of your business,' Ed growled.

'But she's a wonderful lady. I know she had you adopted, but I really think that—'

Ed leapt to his feet and turned to Rhys. 'Hadn't you better be setting off back home? Wouldn't want to be stuck in horrendous traffic like you were on the way here, would you?'

I hadn't touched my coffee and I really wanted some of those chocolates.

'I'm sorry,' I said. 'It's just that she's so lovely, and if you got to know her, you'd—'

'Enough!' Ed bellowed. 'You don't know me, young lady, so don't you dare to presume that you do.'

'It's just—'

Rhys put his hand on my knee. 'Leave it, Cal,' he whispered. 'It's not worth it.' He stood up and indicated with a slight movement of his head that I should too.

'Mum, that was an amazing lunch as always. Thank you. I'll see you soon.' He gave her a hug and a kiss on the cheek. She nodded and tried to smile, but I could see the pain of the confrontation on her face and in the tears glistening in her eyes.

'Goodbye, son.'

'Thanks, Jenny,' I said. 'I'm really sorry. I shouldn't have—'

She shook her head. 'It was lovely to meet you, Callie. I mean that.'

'I'll see you to the door.' Ed might as well have said, 'I'll escort you off the premises and don't ever come back', because that was clearly what he meant.

In the hall, Ed thrust our coats at us without a word.

'Dad,' Rhys said, by way of a goodbye.

'Rhys,' he replied.

I said nothing, not wanting to thank him as he'd clearly done nothing to prepare the meal and unwilling to apologise again because he'd been rude about my job, his son and Ruby, so *he* was the one in the wrong. I only hoped that Rhys wasn't mad at me.

Ed opened the door before we had a chance to fasten our coats. An icy draft enveloped me, but it wasn't nearly as cold as the atmosphere inside the house.

22

'I'm sorry, Rhys,' I whispered when we were seated in the van. 'I didn't mean to stir things up.'

'I know. It wasn't you. I should have warned you about him. I thought... hoped... he'd be on his best behaviour.' He fastened his seatbelt. 'I know it's cold and it'll be dark soon, but do you fancy a walk round the city walls rather than heading straight back?'

'Sounds good. Unless you're planning to push me off the walls for upsetting your dad.'

Rhys laughed. 'No. But it's tempting to take my dad and push him off.'

'You're sure you're not mad with me?'

'I'm not mad with you.'

'Want to talk about it?'

He started the engine. 'When we get to the walls.'

* * *

'We have one of those difficult father-son relation-ships you hear about,' Rhys said as we set off along the ancient stone walls surrounding York City Cen-tre. 'I don't really know why.'

'You haven't had a fallout or anything?'

'No. He's always been off with me, even when I was a young kid. It's weird because Mum said he was desperate for a son when Debbie was born, yet she's always been the clear favourite and I've been the one who can never do anything right.'

'He doesn't think much of your career choice, does he?'

'Why? Did he say something while I was in the kitchen?'

I told him about my conversation with Ed.

'I'm sorry he had a go at your job,' Rhys said when I'd finished. 'It wasn't about you. It was more about me.'

'I don't understand. Why's he so down on your

career when he started out as a labourer?'

'I don't think I'll ever understand him. I've given up trying to impress him because I'll never succeed. The way he tells it, you'd think he was a company director from the start, but it took years to get to that point. He was in his late thirties when he made it.'

'But you're only twenty-five. What does he expect?'

'Something that makes a lot of money, like Debbie.'

We continued along the city walls, up and down steps. Dusk fell and so did a blanket of freezing fog so we retreated to a pub and settled in front of a roaring fire.

'Was your dad funny about you finding Ruby?' I asked.

'Not funny. Dismissive. He said I could do what the hell I liked as long as I didn't expect him to meet her if I found her. I think he expected me to fail. He'd make snide comments each time I hit a dead end but I tracked her down after about eight months. When I told him she was living in Whitsborough Bay, you should have seen his face. He stormed out of the house and didn't speak to me for weeks.'

'Why do you think he wants nothing to do with Ruby?'

Rhys shrugged. 'He won't talk about it. Debbie and I assume it's a self-preservation thing. In his mind, his mum didn't want him so he doesn't want her either. Easier to blank her out than find her and face rejection again. We could be wrong. As I said, I've given up trying to understand the man.'

'And you've no idea who your grandad is?'

'No. I hunted for Dad's birth certificate when he was away once, but it says father unknown. Ruby's the only one who can tell us who my granddad is, but she won't, and I have to respect her for that.'

'Would you like to know?'

'I'd *love* to know. I'd love to meet him if he's still around. I suspect he doesn't know he has a son, though. I get the impression that Ruby never told him she was pregnant.'

I sipped on my lager, my mind whirring. Even though Rhys didn't agree with me, I was still convinced Ruby was lonely. What if Ed's dad had been the love of her life? Iris and William had found love again after six or seven decades apart. Could Ruby? Assuming Ed's dad was single. And alive.

23

'Oh my God! You scared the life out of me!' I dramatically clutched my chest as I crossed the residents' lounge a little after 6 a.m. a few days later.

Ruby continued to stare out the window into the darkness. 'Sorry, darling.'

'What are you doing in here so early?'

'I couldn't sleep.'

Her coral-coloured twenties-style dress was rumpled, her hair was dishevelled and dark bags hung below her bloodshot eyes.

'Are you okay? Do you need a doctor?'

She smiled. 'Do I really look that terrible? No, darling, I'm well. Just a bit tired.'

'Can I get you a cup of tea?'

'You're such a good girl,' she said. 'Thank you.'

When I returned with her drink, she was still staring out the window. 'Did you hear the news?' she asked without turning her head.

'No. What news?' My heart thumped. Perhaps another resident had passed away during the night. I hoped not.

She fiddled with the lacy hem of her dress. 'Reggie's brother only went and proposed to that dippy Iris Davies last night. Stupid woman said yes.'

'Really? That's amazing news.'

'Do you think so, Callie?'

'Of course it is! I take it you don't.'

She finally looked at me. 'They've only known each other for five minutes.'

'They knew each other at—'

'Don't you dare say they knew each other at primary school. They're in their seventies. That was a long time ago and they'll both have changed beyond recognition since then. Five minutes. That's all.'

'Sometimes that's all it takes to know you want to spend the rest of your life with someone. Look at Rhys and me.'

'That's different, darling.'

'How?'

Ruby stared at me for a moment, then turned back to the window. 'It just is. Haven't you got some work to do?'

'Yes. But my main responsibility is making sure our residents are happy so, right now, speaking to you is top of my task list.'

'I can assure you that I'm fine. Why wouldn't I be?' She stood up. 'I'm going back to my room for a lie-down before breakfast. I'll see you later.'

There was no point in protesting. I didn't like it, though. Ruby was far from okay and her reaction reaffirmed my belief that she was lonely. If Iris and William were getting married, Iris would probably move out and Ruby would miss her friend, no matter how much she protested that they weren't close. I also couldn't help thinking that Ruby wished she had someone special in her life, and I was determined to do something about it.

* * *

I was sorting out some paperwork in the office that afternoon when there was a knock on the open door. I looked up to see Ruby loitering in the doorway. She'd changed her clothes, pinned up her hair and carefully applied her make-up. This was the Ruby I knew and loved: strong, confident and immaculate.

'Have you got a moment, Callie, darling?'

'Of course. Grab a seat.'

Ruby sat down opposite me. 'I'm sorry about this morning. I'm always grumpy after a sleepless night.'

'Same here,' I said. 'You'll still see her, you know.'

'Who?'

'I know you know who I mean. I saw Iris earlier. She says they're getting married on Christmas Eve.'

'So she tells me. Who gets married on Christmas Eve? People are far too busy to attend a wedding then. So selfish.'

I smiled. 'I think it's a lovely idea. I understand you've been asked to be matron of honour.'

'Yes, well, the stupid woman hasn't got any other friends to ask.'

'Oh! So you admit that you're friends.'

'Fiddle faddle. We're no such thing.'

My smile widened. 'You keep convincing yourself that, Ruby. So, if you're not friends, I assume you turned her down.'

'She promised me a new dress in the style of my choosing, so I decided to go along with the charade. Just for the free dress, mind you.'

'Of course. Just for the dress. What other reason could there possibly be?'

Ruby raised her eyebrows at me. 'Has she invited you?'

'Yes. And Rhys.'

'Are you going?'

'Yes. I'm not on the rota for that day and, even if I had been, I'd have swapped.'

'Good. It might be bearable if my two favourite people are there.' She stood up. 'I'd better go and see what she's up to. She was looking at wedding dresses on that interweb thingy earlier. I wouldn't put it past her to order a huge white meringue designed for someone a quarter her age. I need to make sure she doesn't do anything stupid because, free dress or not, I won't stand next to a meringue.'

Ruby left the office. Thank goodness she was

back to her usual self, but I still maintained that she was lonely, and I wanted to do something about it. Very soon.

24

The moment Rhys's mobile rang early on Friday morning, I knew who it was and I knew exactly what she was going to say. I sighed and snuggled under the duvet, not even bothering to tune into Rhys's half of the conversation as he paced around in the living area. We were meant to be catching the train to York for a spot of Christmas shopping. I'd fantasised about wandering through the cobbled streets, dipping in and out of all the little independent gift shops, our arms laden with exciting purchases. We'd have a boozy lunch and perhaps even look in a few jewellery shop windows... But Rhys had told Izzy our plans and I could have put money on her sabotaging things.

'Don't tell me,' I said as he returned to the bedroom with guilt written all over his face. 'Izzy needs you to look after Megan today.'

He nodded. 'She says she's got a job interview.'

I shuffled onto my elbows and looked at him. 'And they phoned her at half seven to let her know?'

'No. She knew a couple of days ago, but her best friend, Jess, was meant to be having Megan and she's come down with a stomach bug.'

'Megan will have to come Christmas shopping with us then. Only Izzy's told you she can't, hasn't she?' I tried to keep the sarcastic tone out of my voice, but I failed abysmally. It wasn't fair.

Rhys sighed. 'She says Megan's got a temperature and needs to stay inside.'

I didn't want to cry because it wasn't fair on Rhys, but I was so damn frustrated by the whole situation. She kept pulling this sort of crap on us. What had I ever done to deserve it? They'd split up long before I came on the scene so why keep causing us problems like this?

'You'd better go, then,' I said, trying not to sound annoyed. 'I hope Megan's okay.'

Rhys sat beside me. 'I'm angry with her too, you know.'

'Don't be nice to me,' I whispered as a tear escaped.

'I'll make it up to you. I promise.'

'You don't owe me anything. It's Izzy that's the problem. Will you come round tonight?'

He nodded then kissed me gently, before dressing and abandoning me to go to her. Again.

I tried to get back to sleep but I couldn't switch off. I didn't believe for one minute that Izzy had a job interview, given that she'd had a baby specifically so she could live off benefits. Tempting as it was to stay under the duvet, seething, I wasn't going to let her ruin my whole day. I texted Nick to see if he was free for lunch. He replied saying he could do a late lunch in town, his treat. Perfect.

I took a long shower, dressed slowly, and took what felt like ages over my breakfast, flicking through the morning breakfast programmes on the TV, yet it still wasn't even 9 a.m. Could I be any more bored? I looked around the room for inspiration but the flat was clean and tidy. Rhys had been round on Tuesday night for all of fifteen minutes before being summoned to Izzy's. Allegedly someone had tried the handle on her front door: *Ooh, help me, I'm so scared. I'm all alone with our baby. What if he comes back?* Somehow the damsel in distress had convinced Rhys to spend the night on her sofa. I trusted him implicitly, but I didn't trust her, so I'd spent the evening in a rage-fuelled cleaning frenzy.

With nothing else to do, I hauled my artificial Christmas tree out of the garage and put a Christmas film on. Even decorating the tree – a task I usually relished – didn't cheer me up.

* * *

'You look tired,' Nick said, when we'd taken our seats in The Chocolate Pot, my favourite café in a lovely cobbled street called Castle Street off Whitsborough Bay's main shopping precinct.

'I am. I met Rhys's parents last weekend. Disaster. And Izzy has stepped up her plans for being crowned 'Awkward Ex of the Year' this week so I've had a few unsettled nights. I'll tell you about it when we've ordered.' I picked up the menu. 'Actually, you look tired too. Been on lots of hot dates this week?' Nick had recently signed up to an online dating site.

'One date, and hot would not be the description. She turned up drunk then spent the evening telling me how much she still loved her ex and was hoping to get back with him.'

'Ouch!'

'Tell me about it. She'd only put her profile online to make him jealous. I sent her home in a taxi after an hour.'

'That's crap. But it was only one date. It hasn't put you off, has it?'

Nick shrugged. 'Not yet, but another couple of experiences like it will.'

A petite blonde waitress came over and took our orders.

'Crap! I forgot to tell her not to put tomato in my panini,' I said shortly after she'd left. I twisted round in my seat but couldn't see her. Another waitress was nearby, cleaning a table. She had very dark hair, scraped back tightly and piled high on her head in a tumble of curls. I frowned for a moment. I couldn't see her face, but there was something familiar about that hairstyle. She looked like... no, it couldn't be. This woman was clearly pregnant and there was no way...

'Excuse me,' I said. No response. I cleared my throat and said, 'Excuse me,' again, a bit louder this time.

The pregnant brunette turned round and dropped her cloth on the floor. 'Shit! Callie?'

It *was* her. I'd thought about her so often over the past few months. 'Oh my God! Maria?'

She tried to cover her baby bump with her arms, but it was too late. I couldn't take my eyes off her stomach.

'Tony's?' I whispered.

She didn't need to answer that. Guilt was written all over her face. I swallowed hard. 'How long?'

'Nearly seven months.'

I flinched. The laundry room obviously hadn't been a one-off. 'You're still together?' I asked.

She lowered her eyes. 'Yes. Well, sort of.'

'What does "sort of" mean? Is he still with his wife?'

She lowered her head even further and her shoulders slumped.

'Are you okay?' I asked, wondering whether I should get her to sit down or perhaps give her a hug. Tony had put me through hell, and I suspected he'd done the same to her given her hesitancy about whether they were on or off. Instead of feeling angry or hurt about the baby, I just felt compassion. 'You know what he's like. You're better off without him.'

She looked up and stared at me for a moment. I thought she was going to accept. Then her eyes narrowed and she planted her hands on her hips. 'Did you actually want something or are you here to cause a scene and get me sacked from yet another job?'

'I didn't get you—' I stopped. Not worth it. 'I wanted to ask for no tomatoes in my panini, please.'

'I'll pass it on.' She retrieved her cloth and headed towards the counter.

'Wow! That was fun,' Nick said. 'No wonder she didn't return any of your calls.'

'Yep. No wonder. Looks like Tony had three of us on the go at once. How stupid do I feel?'

Nick patted my arm reassuringly. 'He's out of your life now and you've got Rhys.'

'Diet Coke and a cappuccino?' Our blonde waitress reappeared and placed a glass in front of me and a large cup in front of Nick.

'Did you get the change to my order?' I asked, not convinced that Maria would have passed it on.

'Yes, I did, thanks. Your paninis will be out in about five minutes.'

'Thank you.'

'I thought Maria wasn't going to sort it out for you,' Nick said when our waitress was out of earshot.

'Me too. Maybe she isn't as spiteful as I thought.'

But when our paninis were delivered five minutes later, my stomach churned.

'What's this?' I asked, pointing at my sandwich.

Our waitress smiled. 'Extra tomato as requested. Enjoy your lunch.'

25

Despite my protests that we needed to save for Christmas, Rhys insisted on a pub crawl along South Bay that evening. We made a pact not to talk about any of the things that had caused us stress recently – Izzy and Megan, Tony and Maria, Rhys's parents – and it worked wonders. I hadn't laughed so much in ages.

'I love you so much,' Rhys slurred as we staggered along the promenade. 'I'm sorry that Izzy's trying to come between us.'

'Ssshhh!' I whispered, placing my finger across his lips. 'It's illegal to talk about her tonight, remember?'

'I know, but—'

I silenced him with a kiss, my heart racing as the passion between us intensified.

'You glad we came out?' Rhys asked when we broke apart.

'Very.'

We leaned against the railings, looking out towards the sea.

'There's someone down there,' I whispered, spotting a couple on the beach below. Their voices drifted up to us.

'Quit moaning,' the man growled. 'You're putting me off.'

'But I'm not comfortable,' whined the woman. 'My back hurts.'

'That's your fault for being pregnant.'

'My fault? It takes two, Tony.'

'For God's sake, Maria! Stop wittering. You're the one who called me and begged me to meet you.'

'Not for sex! I wanted to talk.'

Rhys tugged on my arm. 'Come on. Let's get a taxi home.'

Feeling very sober all of a sudden, I let him lead me away.

'He's using her,' I said.

'I know. That's what blokes like him do.'

'I bet he wants nothing to do with the baby.'

Rhys put his arm round me. 'I hate to agree, but I bet you're right. Tony's an arse. He's never going to change.'

'Poor Maria. She could probably use a friend right now.'

'And I'm sure she has plenty of friends she can turn to.'

'But I was her best friend and you know I miss her.'

'Callie! Don't forget the part she played in all this. If you get involved, it'll only end in tears. For you.'

He was probably right, but I kept picturing her in The Chocolate Pot with her head hung low and her shoulders slumped. Rhys was wrong. She didn't have plenty of friends to turn to. Part of the reason we'd become so close was that I didn't have many friends either. I'd gradually pushed my friends out of my life when they'd disapproved of my choices of older men. It turned out they'd been right, but I hadn't appreciated that back then and by the time I did, the damage was done. My only friends now were my brother, my mum, and the elderly residents at work.

Despite Rhys's concerns, we both knew I was going to reach out to Maria again.

26

Ruby rushed up to me during my morning break the following day. 'Callie, darling! Thank goodness you're here. That Iris Davies has only gone and ordered a white dress for her wedding. A white dress, I tell you. At her age. You've got to stop her.'

'A *big* white dress?' I asked, surprised. A slim and attractive woman, Iris's style was twinsets and shift dresses and she always looked classy.

Ruby nodded vigorously, looking genuinely concerned. 'It's enormous. Frills and everything. It's strapless with a low back. You *have* to say something to her, darling. She's going to make a fool of herself.'

'Okay. I'll ask her to show me a picture later and see what I can do.'

* * *

'Oh!' I said, taking in the image on Iris's iPad a little later. 'That's... er... quite a dress.' Crap! With a tight bodice, the dress flared out into what could only be described as toilet-roll-holder-chic. Yards and yards of net and organza swirled in puffy craziness. Peering closer, it appeared that the net had been sculpted into a few hundred roses.

'Gorgeous, isn't it?' Iris gushed. 'I love big dresses.'

'It's... er... certainly very big. What does William think?'

'Callie! Surely you know that it's bad luck for the groom to see what the bride is wearing until she joins him at the altar.'

'Of course it is. Silly me! So you've already ordered it?'

She was grinning from ear to ear and excitement emanated from her. I couldn't say anything. Besides, what right did I have to say what was hideous and what was beautiful, or what was more appropriate on a younger woman than someone of advancing years? It was her day and she deserved to wear whatever she wanted. Oh, but why did she have to pick the loo-roll holder?

'I spent hours searching for the right dress,' she said, chuckling. 'The one that would be absolutely perfect... for winding up Ruby.'

I looked up. 'You mean this isn't the wedding dress of your dreams?'

She smiled widely. 'I would like to think it isn't the wedding dress of *anyone's* dreams. It's the most ostentatiously vile creation I've ever seen. Do you know what it brings to mind? Those repulsive toilet roll covers that Nancy Emerson insists on knitting.'

'Oh my God, Iris! I thought the same, but I didn't like to say anything in case I upset you.' I let out an exaggerated sigh of relief. 'So have you really chosen the perfect dress or are you still looking?'

Iris touched a few buttons on her iPad. 'This is what I'll be wearing.'

I gasped, feeling suddenly quite emotional at the classy, cream lace dress. 'It's stunning.'

'Thank you. I told Ruby she could pick her own

dress but what do you think of this?' It's very her, isn't it?'

I smiled as she showed me another dress – a green A-line dress with lacy capped sleeves and rose detailing at the waist. 'It's beautiful. I reckon she'll love it.'

'I thought we could have simple white bouquets with trailing ivy.'

I nodded. 'Sounds perfect. When do you think you'll tell her that you're winding her up?'

'I'd love to string it out for weeks, but we don't have that long. I need to order her dress, so I'll probably continue my ruse over the weekend, then confess.'

I stood up. 'I'd better get on. You're a cheeky little monkey, Iris Davies. I didn't know you had it in you.'

'I used to be very mischievous, but I think I let growing old knock it out of me. Then I met William, and I feel like a teenager again, so my mischievous streak has returned.'

It was lovely to see her with so much energy and enthusiasm. It was amazing what love could do to someone. If only Ruby had someone to love. I kicked myself for still not having broached the subject of

Rhys's grandfather. Maybe I'd stay back after my shift and ask her tonight.

I didn't get a chance to, though. Iris, the little minx, had obviously decided to take the wind-up a step further. When I called round to Ruby's room after my shift, she was in a right state, telling me that Iris had ordered her 'a revolting shiny cerise satin eighties-style frilly beast of a dress'. She claimed that the clowns had worn more tasteful outfits when she'd been in the circus and she'd rather wear a clown costume than what Iris had selected. I eventually managed to calm her down, but there was no point in raising the subject I wanted to because she'd only get het up again and I was starting to worry for her blood pressure. It would have to keep for another day.

27

I was at a loose end on Sunday. It was Rhys's Sunday with Megan, Mum was out with some friends, and Nick needed to work. Not for the first time, I wished I hadn't let my friendships slip. I picked up my phone and started a text to Maria, but I couldn't find the right words, so I tossed it on the sofa and sulked.

Shortly after lunch, Ruby texted me:

✉ From Ruby
That cheating woman has been winding me up. She's wearing a surprisingly classy and dignified dress and has suggested a dress for me which I ac-

tually love. Wonders will never
cease! Feeling like this charade
won't be quite as ridiculous as initially expected and I might finally
have a good night's sleep xx

✉ To Ruby
Rhys is with Megan and I've got
nothing to do. It's a gorgeous day.
Fancy a stroll around Hearnshaw
Park?

* * *

We met at the entrance at 2 p.m. Ruby kissed me on
the cheek, then slipped her arm through mine as we
set off into the park. 'I'm glad you got in touch, darling. I was at a bit of a loose end myself.'

'Is Iris with William?'

'She spends most of her time with him these
days.'

'Well, they have got a wedding to plan. Things
will be back to normal after that.'

Ruby sighed. 'Only they won't be, will they? She's

moving in with William after their honeymoon and...'

'And what?' I asked after she tailed off.

'And I'm going to miss my friend,' she said, softly.

I knew it! I knew she saw Iris as a friend, despite the bravado. 'I'm sure you'll still see each other.'

'She says so, but people in love can get so wrapped up in each other that they lose track of their other friendships.'

I couldn't offer her any encouragement on that one. I was living, breathing proof of how easily that could happen. 'You've always got Rhys. And you've got me too.'

Ruby patted my arm. 'I know, darling, and I count myself very lucky.'

We arrived at the ice-cream kiosk by the boating lake which, in the winter, sold hot drinks. 'Cup of tea?' I asked.

'Perfect. And perhaps a little packet of short-bread,' Ruby said, eyeing up the wicker basket brimming with homemade treats.

Purchases made, we sat in silence on one of the green metal benches. The red and green dragon-shaped boats had been stored for the winter so the only ripples on the lake were from ducks, geese and the occasional swan gliding through the water. Soggy clumps of bread kissed the edge of the lake.

'I'm sorry that things are going to change for you, but it's lovely seeing Iris and William so much in love, don't you think?' I asked, looking for a way in.

'I suppose so.' She shook her head. 'I'm being mean-spirited. Yes, it is lovely, darling. I've never seen Iris so happy. I swear the woman looks ten years younger since they got together. You could almost pass her for a woman in her seventies.'

I laughed. Iris was in her seventies and Ruby knew it. 'Have you ever been in love?' I asked.

'Loads of times, darling.'

'Really? Then you must have been very lucky. I've always believed that love – true love, that is – only comes along once.'

Ruby's shoulders slumped. 'Twice,' she whispered. 'It was twice for me. A very long time ago, but I lost them both.'

'Was one of them Rhys's grandfather?'

She nodded.

'Why don't you ever talk about him?'

'Too painful.'

'Did he die?'

Ruby looked towards the waterfall cascading from the island in the middle of the lake, and I wondered whether I'd already pushed too far. Eventually, she turned to me. 'You're not going to rest until you know all about it, are you?'

'I don't want to force you,' I assured her.

She shrugged. 'It's been so very long, but I remember every moment of my time with both of them like it was yesterday. In fact, I remember it better than I remember what I had for breakfast this morning, or for dinner last night.' She took a sip of her tea. 'Teddy and George. You really want to know my sad story?'

I nodded, my heart racing. Finally I was going to hear about Rhys's heritage and something told me it was going to be worth waiting for.

'Teddy was first,' Ruby said. 'Teddy Latimer. We met in Paris when I was nineteen.' She fell silent for a few minutes. I didn't dare speak in case she changed her mind about confiding in me. Eventually she sighed. 'I told you I was an exotic dancer, didn't I?'

'Yes.'

'Teddy came to the show for his twenty-first birthday. His friends had arranged for a special back-stage pass to meet the girls. We were paid to give him special attention.' She laughed at my agape mouth. 'Oh, Callie, darling! Not *that* sort of attention. I wasn't a prostitute! And just so you're clear, exotic dancing back then was nothing like I'd imagine it is these days.'

She gently slapped my leg when I giggled. I have to admit, I'd tried to avoid thinking about what her exotic dancing had involved.

'We were asked to flatter Teddy and fuss over him,' she continued. 'That's all! The other dancers were, quite literally, all over him and poor Teddy looked absolutely terrified. I said I wasn't a prostitute but some of the other girls... Let's say they weren't averse to earning some extra money. One of them whispered that he could go the whole way with her for a small fee. Teddy leapt out of his chair and dashed for the door, muttering something about needing some air. His so-called friends seemed un-concerned by his absence. I suppose it meant more attention for them, but I felt sorry for the birthday boy, so clearly out of his depth. I grabbed my robe and went to find him to make sure all was well.'

She paused and smiled at the memory. 'I couldn't find him at first but then I heard the music. Oh, it was exquisite. I followed it and found Teddy in the concert hall, playing the piano. Chopin's "Héroique" Polonaise in A Flat Major. Do you know it, darling?'

I had to stop myself from laughing. As if! 'Er, no. Can't say I do.'

'You should seek it out. It's beautiful. Perry Como had a song called "Till the End of Time" in the hit parade a few years earlier. It featured in a wonderful film of the same name and was based on Chopin's piece.'

I decided not to mention that I had no idea who Perry Como was either.

'I can still hear the music now,' Ruby continued. 'And I can still picture Teddy poised at the piano. Such an accomplished pianist. Even though he was a couple of years older than me, he looked so much younger with only a shaft of light from the moon illuminating him. I lost my heart to him at that very moment.'

'What happened next?' I asked when Ruby showed no sign of elaborating.

Ruby looked at me as though she was surprised to see me there. I imagined that she'd been back in that concert hall, reliving that moment.

'I watched and listened for ages, mesmerised by both Teddy and the music. He eventually saw me and asked me to join him. I apologised for the behaviour of the other dancers, but he smiled and said that he needed to apologise for the behaviour of his friends and that, when they'd been drinking, they tended to forget how to behave like decent English gentlemen.'

'He was English, then?' I asked.

'A proper English gentleman in every sense of the word. He came from wealth. His father was a Lord and his family owned a grand estate in Northumberland. We were from entirely different worlds, but it didn't seem to bother Teddy. We talked all night. He was the first man I'd ever met who was genuinely interested in me as a person. Teddy walked me home and asked if he could take me to dinner the following night. It was a Sunday so there was no performance. I genuinely didn't expect him to turn up but he did and we had a wonderful evening. We dined in the most incredible restaurant in the Champs-Élysées then walked along the Seine. He kissed me for the first time in the shadow of the Eiffel Tower. It was heaven.'

Ruby closed her eyes for a moment, clearly lost in the memories again. It sounded so romantic. Questions whirred in my mind, but I sensed she needed to tell the story in her own time. If I fired questions at her, she might stop talking.

'We were touring Europe. I only had one more week in Paris, but I spent every spare moment with Teddy. He told me that he couldn't bear to be separated from me, so was going to travel to Italy and follow the tour. It all seemed to be too perfect so, of course, something had to go wrong. Teddy's grandmother took ill and he was called back to England. Even though Teddy said he loved me and wanted to spend the rest of his life with me, I was a realist. He was the heir to a grand estate and there was no way his family would let him throw that away for a dancer. The only way I'd be able to stay in his life was if he took me as his mistress and I knew I couldn't do that. I couldn't share him.'

'So what happened?' I asked, completely capti-vated by their story.

'It was a year before I saw him again. We were in America and I was about to leave the theatre one evening when I spotted him outside. I was angry with him for staying away for so long yet I knew the absence had only deepened my feelings. I hid be-hind the door, shaking, not daring to step outside. Somehow, I knew that my reaction to him could change my life. I took a deep breath, straightened my shoulders, and walked down the steps smiling. I said something stupid like, "Good evening, Lord La-timer, what brings you to America?" He smiled and said, "The most beautiful woman in the world." He asked if we could take a walk so that he could ex-plain his absence. It turned out that his grand-mother *had* died but not immediately. She hung on for another three months. Then his mother took ill although, thankfully, she recovered. He'd started making plans to find me when there was a fire on the estate. His father needed to go away on business so Teddy had to take care of the reconstruction. It seemed like one thing after the other was keeping us apart. He wrote regularly. I never received the letters but we moved around frequently so that was hardly surprising.'

'What was it like seeing him after a year?' I asked.

'Oh, Callie, it was as though we'd spent no time apart. I knew it couldn't last, though. Teddy had been promised since birth to Gabriella Allerston, the daughter of another wealthy landowner. He told his father that he had no intention of marrying her and that he was in love with someone else but his father wouldn't hear of it. He told Teddy that he had until he was twenty-five to get it out of his system and then he needed to settle down and marry Gabriella.' She shook her head slowly. 'It was a terrible position for him to be in but I knew his family wouldn't accept me. I was determined to make the most of the time we had left. He joined the tour for the next three years. We told people we were married. It was fun imagining that I was his wife, but the bubble was always going to burst. Tensions arose as his twenty-fifth birthday approached. If he refused to marry Gabriella, he'd be disinherited and the estate would pass to his unreliable cousin who'd likely squander it all, leaving Teddy's mother and five sisters destitute. He loved me and wanted to be with me, but what choice did he have? I told him he had to forget about me and return to England, but he refused to leave.' Ruby stretched and stood up. 'Shall we walk, darling? I'm getting a little stiff sitting here.'

We set off walking around the lake in silence. The temperature had dropped and the breeze had picked up, chilling my cheeks and sending red and golden curled leaves scuttling across the path towards the water.

'I thought about running away,' Ruby said when we were about a quarter of the way round the lake, 'but I knew he'd find me. The only way to get him to leave and marry Gabriella was for me to convince him that I didn't love him. And, sadly, the only way I was going to be able to do that convincingly was if I moved onto someone else.'

I could hear the regret in Ruby's voice and had a feeling I knew where this was heading.

'I was the principal dancer at this point, with my own dressing room, and dedicated fans. George Hetherington-Smythe was one of them. He was in his fifties and his wife had died young. Poor man yearned for companionship. George knew I was seeing Teddy and that we weren't really married. He made it clear that he was interested and I only had to say the word. I arranged for George to come to my dressing room after the show one evening, a fortnight before Teddy's twenty-fifth birthday. I told Teddy that I had a meeting immediately after the show and he should come to my dressing room an hour later. I was honest with George about what I wanted him to do and why. He was happy to be used as long as I promised him at least three dinner dates afterwards. I had to admire George for his persistence and commitment. I'd handed myself to him on a plate with no strings attached yet he still wanted to woo me.' Ruby stopped walking. She rested her hands on a wooden fence and stared out at the lake in silence.

'It was the hardest thing I've ever done,' she said eventually. 'I'd been faithful to Teddy from the day I met him, even during that year when I had no idea whether I'd ever see him again, so being with another man and letting Teddy witness it absolutely broke my heart.'

'You mean you...?'

Ruby nodded. 'A kiss would never have been enough to convince Teddy that I didn't love him anymore.' She closed her eyes and shook her head. 'I can't tell you... His face, Callie... Devastated doesn't even begin to describe it. I said some cruel things to him about only ever wanting him for his money and, because being with him would mean he had no money, I'd found myself someone who had a fortune and who could keep it if he married me. I was a good actress. Too good. Teddy returned to England, married Gabriella Allerston and she produced an heir. The estate was saved. And I married George.'

'Oh my God! Really? I thought you'd never married.'

'Nobody knows. Not even Rhys. I owed George three dinners and I got to know him during that time. He'd been devoted to his wife but she was unable to bear any children. She'd died ten years earlier and he'd never remarried. Every woman he met seemed to be after his money and he didn't like being used.'

'Wasn't he worried about that being the case for you too?' I cringed, hoping she wouldn't take offence.

Ruby laughed as we set off walking again. 'I love the way you just come out with what you're thinking, darling. It's so refreshing. No, George wasn't worried.

He knew that Teddy could afford to lavish me with expensive jewellery and fine clothes, but that I refused. He knew that Teddy could set me up in an apartment and I'd never have to work again, but I refused that too. He knew it was never about the money for me.'

'So what happened to George?' I asked.

'We had a happy marriage and, over the few years we had together, I learned to love him. George knew it was Teddy who truly held my heart forever, but he knew that I had space in my heart for him too and he was content with that. I gave him the companionship he yearned for. We made each other laugh so much. We really were the best of friends and, if I could have loved him as deeply and passionately as I loved Teddy, I would have done. We can't control our hearts, though. They choose whomever they want. Dear George died six years later and, to this day, I still miss that wonderful man.'

We were halfway round the lake now, by the wishing well.

'Fancy throwing in a coin?' I asked.

Ruby stared at the well, as though weighing up whether to go for it. Eventually she shook her head. 'No, darling. I have everything I could wish for. If you'd like to make a wish, though, I'll sit over there.' Without waiting for my response, she made her way to the nearest bench, next to a giant wooden carving of an owl.

I removed a handful of change from my purse and threw one coin at a time towards the bell. There were so many wishes I could make: for Izzy to stop playing games, to never encounter Tony again, for Rhys's dad to have a personality transplant. But, at that very moment, there was really only one wish I could make. With each successful strike on the bell, I made the same wish: *I wish for Ruby to find love again.* Kissing my fingers, I lightly touched them on the side of the well. 'Please make my wish come true,' I whispered, before joining Ruby on the bench.

'How are you feeling?' I asked. She looked quite shell-shocked, her eyes wide and her face pale.

'I don't quite know.' She pressed her fingers to her lips and shook her head, then dropped her hand loosely into her lap. 'I've kept that story hidden for over half a century, darling. I never thought I'd tell it to anyone.' She released a shaky breath but then she smiled. 'Happy memories.'

I squeezed her hand, wincing at how icy it was. I'd kept her out for far too long. 'It'll be dark soon. I think we should get you home and warmed up.'

'Yes, I think that would be sensible. Just give me five more minutes, then we'll go.'

While I waited for her to do whatever she was doing – thinking, praying, reminiscing – I did some rough calculations in my head. If Ruby was coming up to eighty-five and Rhys's dad was in his mid-fifties, she must have been about thirty when she had him, so Teddy couldn't be the father. She'd ended things before Teddy turned twenty-five and she said she was a couple of years younger than him. Therefore, George had to be Ed's father. If he'd died when she was pregnant or just after Ed was born, the dates would work. Unless Teddy came back into her life...?

A few minutes later, Ruby rose to her feet. 'Time to go. Thank you for listening, darling. Surprisingly, it feels good to talk about it.'

'Thank you for confiding in me.' I linked my arm through hers as we made our way out of the park. 'It's an amazing story.'

We exited Hearnshaw Park and started the ten-minute walk back to Bay View.

Ruby squeezed my arm. 'I sense there's a question, young Callie. You want to know whether George was Rhys's grandfather, don't you?'

I laughed. 'You read my mind.'

'Well, darling, unless you can read my mind, then you're not going to find out just yet. I'm feeling very tired all of a sudden. I can manage the walk, but I can't manage the next chapter of my story. Another day?'

'Of course. Would you like me to call a taxi?'

Ruby shook her head. 'That's very good of you but it's too cold to wait for one.'

We steadily made our way back to Bay View as the curtain of darkness lowered. I ran Ruby a hot bubble bath while she relaxed in her favourite armchair, listening to Radio Four. She had that frailty about her again that I'd seen the morning after William proposed to Iris. I couldn't bear to see her looking so small and vulnerable. It scared me that she wasn't the tower of strength she usually pretended to be.

28

Back at my flat an hour later, I changed into my PJs, switched on the fairy lights, lit some scented candles and curled up on the sofa. Wrapped in a soft throw, I replayed Ruby's revelations. She'd made me promise not to say anything to Rhys about his ancestry, then had laughed when she realised that I didn't know who the father was so couldn't exactly do a big reveal even if I wanted to. My head told me that Rhys's grandfather was George, but my heart told me it was Teddy. Why tell me their story if it wasn't him? She promised to tell me the rest of the details soon.

'How was Megan?' I asked as Rhys curled up on the sofa beside me that evening.

'Grizzly. She's teething at the moment. I had to take her on a long walk to get her settled. How was your day?'

'Ruby's a bit down about Iris's wedding. It hasn't helped that Iris has been winding her up about what they'll both be wearing. I thought it would be good for her to get out of Bay View for a bit so we went for a walk round Hearnshaw Park, which was lovely but a bit on the chilly side.'

'I wish I'd known. I could have walked Megan round the park instead.'

'As if Izzy would have let you do that. It might have confused her if she'd met me, remember?' I hated the sound of my voice, dripping with sarcasm.

Rhys got up and put the kettle on. 'I spoke to her, you know. About Christmas.'

I twisted around on the sofa to face him. 'Really?' I didn't need to ask what she'd said. His expression told me.

'Sorry,' he said. 'I'll try again nearer the time.'

'Don't bother. She won't change her mind. She—'

Rhys's mobile rang and my heart sank. It would be her.

'Hi Izzy... Yes... How high? And you've given her

Calpol...? Yes... Yes... I don't know what you want me to do. Babies get temperatures when they're teething. No... Of course I care... No... Don't cry.'

I marched over to the kitchenette and grabbed his phone. 'He's on his way, Izzy,' I spat into it, then hung up and thrust the phone back at Rhys.

'Callie! She's only teething.'

'And Izzy's only going to pester us all evening if you don't go round.'

Rhys hugged me. 'I'll be back as soon as I can.'

I kissed him tenderly to show that I wasn't angry with him. I didn't want to fall out again over Izzy and her demands. 'Text me to let me know Megan's okay and it is just Izzy being a pain as usual.'

With Rhys gone, I flicked through the TV channels but nothing could hold my interest and I felt too tired to start on a film. Switching the TV off, I heard my mobile bleep. That would be the text from Rhys telling me there was absolutely nothing wrong with Megan and that Izzy had ruined our evening for no reason, yet again.

Only the text wasn't from Rhys:

From Tony
I hear you told Maria she's better off without me. Still meddling in other people's lives, eh? Think you're so bloody perfect, don't you? Well, you're not. You're flawed. And so is gardening boy

I knew I should ignore Tony's text, but I couldn't take my eyes off his last sentence. With trembling hands I typed in:

To Tony
What's that supposed to mean?

My stomach churned as I stared at the phone, waiting for a reply. After a few minutes, a message flashed up, making my heart thump:

From Tony
Ha ha. That's for me to know and you to find out

29

A couple of weeks passed. I was dying to know the second half of Ruby's story. Although she assured me she wouldn't leave me hanging, she said it had stirred so many memories that she needed some space first. I could certainly understand that. There were no more texts from Tony, and I tried, but abandoned, several texts to Maria. Izzy continued to be awkward. I joked that she'd had my flat bugged because it seemed that, every time Rhys was round, she phoned with some sort of crisis.

* * *

At the start of the following week, Ruby asked if I'd be willing to spend my day off on Thursday accompanying her to York. When I agreed, she confirmed that the second part of her story would be forthcoming. I was so excited that I could hardly sleep the night before and was relieved, for once, when Izzy called Rhys away because it was hard to act all casual around him.

Ruby and I caught an early train out of Whitsborough Bay station, slipping into a pair of seats either side of a small table in first class; Ruby's treat.

'How lovely to have single seats,' she declared. 'Nobody spreading into our space or listening to our private conversation.'

'Perfect opportunity for the next chapter,' I said, expecting her to tell me to wait until we were in York.

She was silent for a moment, then she smiled. 'You've waited patiently for long enough. What are you dying to know?'

'Who Rhys's grandfather is. Was it George? I think it probably was, but I feel like I want it to be Teddy.'

Ruby laughed and clapped her hands together. 'I

didn't mean to make it into a huge mystery, darling. It wasn't George. We tried for a family, but it turned out that the reason why George and his wife couldn't have children was down to him. Teddy is Edward's father. Teddy. Ted. Edward. I thought the name would have given it away, darling.'

Of course! How dense was I? 'But if my calculations are right, you hadn't seen him for six or seven years when Ed was born.'

'You have been giving this a lot of thought, haven't you? You're right. I didn't see him after the incident in my dressing room, although I thought about him every single day. He was absolutely the last person I expected to bump into when I went for a walk through Regent's Park the day after George's funeral.'

'No! I bet that was a shock.'

'Just a bit. We're jumping ahead, though. Let me go back to George. As I said, he was a rich widower with no children, but he had a sister, Frances. Her poor husband lost his life at those dreadful Normandy landings, leaving her with four young children. She'd married for love rather than money so

George did everything he could to make life comfortable for them. I loved Frances and those little ones. She'd always been kind to me, welcoming me into the family, whereas some of George's friends and relatives had sneered at him for marrying a dancer, accusing me of being after his money.'

'That's a bit harsh.'

Ruby shrugged. 'Yes, but it was the reaction I expected and it was a reasonable assumption because so many women from my background did it. Frances, thank goodness, took the time to get to know me and draw her own conclusions. George, God rest his soul, contracted TB. He wanted to leave everything to me, so long as I continued to support Frances and her family. I insisted he left his full estate to them and said I wouldn't hold his hand at the end unless he did. It was cruel of me because I knew he feared being alone, but the tactic worked. He called his solicitor to the house to make the final changes to his will. When he died, most of his estate went to Frances and the children but he left me a large lump sum and a cottage in Devon. When I say cottage, I'm not talking your basic two-up two-down. Country pile is probably a more accurate description.'

'Oh my goodness, Ruby. What did you do?'

'Tried to give it to Frances but she believed I should have been bequeathed his entire estate. She insisted on me staying at George's London residence until the funeral and for as long as I wanted to afterwards. I was grateful because it gave me time to think. On the day following dear George's funeral, I decided that a change of scenery may help me gather my thoughts so I took a walk alone through Regent's Park. Clearly Frances was not going to accept the cottage, so I had four choices. I could live there myself, sell it, lease it, or give it away. I'd had an offer of acting work via one of my former contacts and it was tempting. I'd continued to dance when George and I first married. I'd also tried a little acting and loved it.'

Ruby stared out of the window for a moment, a slight smile on her lips. 'I'd been so lost in my thoughts as I walked through the park that I tripped over a gentleman who'd bent down to retrieve his glove. That gentleman turned out to be Teddy. I'm not sure who was the most shocked. I swear we just stared at each other for about five minutes, both too astonished to speak.'

I sighed softly. How romantic, bumping into the

man she loved after so many years apart. Fate had obviously been determined to reunite them.

'He looked exactly the same,' Ruby continued, 'and I felt exactly the same as I'd felt six years previously. He still held the biggest piece of my heart. Teddy was running late for an important meeting, but he begged me to meet him for dinner that evening. I told him that I wouldn't turn up, but we both knew that I would. There was much to say.'

'You did turn up?' I prompted, when Ruby fell silent again.

'I couldn't not. I'd pushed him away twice already and I owed him an apology for the set-up with George. He said he hadn't believed that I didn't love him, but he understood why I did it because he knew that I was never going to let him walk away from his family and his responsibilities. He did marry Gabriella, which I already knew, but their marriage was a farce. His father died two years after they wed, so Teddy had the family estate and businesses to run which frequently took him to London. While he was away, Gabriella entertained a steady stream of men and didn't even try to hide it. Her argument was that he'd given his heart to another before they wed so she could give her body to whomever she wanted.'

I shook my head. 'She sounds delightful.'

'Doesn't she just? Gabriella had three children, although Teddy wasn't convinced they were all his. His first son and heir definitely was, but he was doubtful about the other two. Being Teddy, though, he still adored them and treated them as though they were his own.'

'Poor Teddy,' I said.

Ruby nodded. 'I didn't want to cause him further pain. I tried not to get involved, but I couldn't resist that man. I couldn't push him away for a third time so I prolonged my stay in London and met Teddy whenever he was down, which became more and more frequent. Then I discovered that I was pregnant.'

She fell silent again, her finger lightly tapping on her train ticket.

'You didn't tell him about the baby, did you?' I said.

Ruby slowly shook her head. 'He'd have given up everything for us and it would have ruined his family. I had no sympathy for his despicable wife but I felt for the children, his mother and his sisters. We shared one more incredible weekend together and then, as far as he was concerned, I disappeared into the wind. Where I really went was the Devon cottage where I read scripts and learned parts. Edward was born and adopted and I moved to Europe, changed my name and became an actress. I donated the cottage to a charity and I never saw Teddy again.'

I swallowed hard on the lump in my throat as I watched Ruby's eyes fill with tears and her bottom lip tremble. Reaching across the table, I took her hand in mine.

'Surely he looked for you? Didn't he ask Frances where you were?'

'Many times, but I told her the full story, pregnancy and all, and she promised to keep my whereabouts secret. Because George had bought the cottage only days before he died, none of his friends or business contacts knew of its existence and I had the deeds for the property changed into my new identity before I gave it away. I did keep my real name on Edward's birth certificate just in case... well, you never know, do you? Teddy could search as much as he wanted but he wouldn't find anything. I have to say, though, giving up my baby – Teddy's baby – was the hardest thing I've ever done.' A tear slipped down her cheek at this point and she swiped at it. 'Goodness me, darling. Who gets upset over something that happened more than fifty years ago?'

'Anyone with a heart as big as yours,' I whispered.

30

Ruby remained silent for the rest of the journey to York and I gazed out the window. There'd been heavy rainfall over the past week and the River Derwent had broken its banks. Looking at the flooded fields and rapidly flowing water, a million questions whirred around in my mind, the most important one being whether Teddy was still alive. If he wasn't, surely Ruby would have said. Or perhaps she'd avoided finding out anything about him, for fear of what she'd discover.

'Is Ruby Miller your real name or your acting name?' I asked, as we walked from the train station into York City Centre.

'My real name although I was, of course, Ruby Hetherington-Smythe for six years. Damned long name, that one. Ruby Miller is the name on Edward's birth certificate. He was approaching eighteen when I retired from acting in my late forties so I changed my name back in case he wanted to find his biological mother.' She laughed. 'Silly me. Edward has never wanted anything to do with me.'

I'd heard that straight from the horse's mouth, but I wasn't going to let on. 'But Rhys found you years later instead.'

'This is true and that young man is my world. As are you, my darling.'

I wanted to ask her more about Teddy, but I suspected the train journey had been pretty emotional and that it was best to stick to the lighter subjects for the moment.

'What was your acting name?' I asked.

'Promise you won't laugh.'

'Of course I won't.'

'I wanted something that sounded sophisticated and that linked me to Teddy and to my past life. You are looking at the actress formally known as Theodora Sapphire.'

'Oh wow! Theodora Sapphire. I absolutely love it. What sort of acting did you do? Plays? Films?'

'Mainly plays, but I was an extra and had a small part in some films too...'

* * *

We had a lovely morning, wandering around the cobbled streets of York while Ruby regaled me with fascinating stories from her days as an actress. We had tea and a scone in a tearoom during late morning and skipped lunch to avoid ruining our appetite for afternoon tea at Betty's Tea Rooms.

'Go on, then,' she said, as we slowly edged our way along the side of Betty's that afternoon, still many tables away from being seated. 'Ask me the question you're dying to ask me.'

'Is Teddy still alive?'

'Yes.'

I grasped her arm. 'Oh my God! Really? Are you sure? How do you know?'

'Callie Derbyshire! How do you think I know? I thought you young people lived your lives on social media.'

'He's on Facebook?'

'Facebook, Twitter, that Instant-thingy...'

'Instagram?'

'That's the one. Well, he isn't personally on there, but the estate is and there are pictures of him and comments about him.'

'Has he changed much?'

'He's still got most of his hair, although it's pure white now. Very distinguished. Wrinkles and glasses like the rest of us, but he's still my Teddy.'

'And the despicable wife?'

'Not in any family photos so I'm not sure. Divorced? Dead? I don't really care. That woman doesn't deserve a moment of my time.'

We shuffled forward in the queue.

'So how long have you been cyber-stalking your ex?'

Ruby nudged me playfully. 'Goodness me, darling, is that what they call it? Cyber-stalking? I've been doing no such thing. After our walk round the park the other day, I couldn't stop thinking about him so curiosity got the better of me and I searched for him. I only did it once and I haven't looked since.'

'You haven't made contact, then?'

'Of course not. And I'm not going to.'

'Why not?'

'Do you even need to ask?' She lowered her voice to a whisper, although she didn't need to. The people queuing either side of us were engrossed in their own conversations in other languages so there was no danger of them over-hearing. 'I pushed that man out of my life three times, then had his baby fifty-four years ago and didn't tell him. I can hardly chirp him with a "hello, remember me?" message, can I?'

'Chirp him?' I frowned. 'Ah, you mean tweet him.'

'That's the one. Tweet. I can hardly do that. It's been too long, darling. We had three opportunities and none of them worked out. Our time has passed.'

'They only didn't work out because you wouldn't let them. It sounds to me like he'd have moved heaven and earth to be with you.'

'He would have but, as I said, it was—'

'Yeah, I know. It was a different time back then. It's the twenty-first century now, though, and any-thing's possible. Do you still love him?'

'Darling, I don't know him anymore.'

'That's not what I asked.'

'How can you love someone you don't know?' Ruby protested.

'Also not what I asked.'

'I don't want to have this conversation anymore, Callie.' Ruby linked my arm and patted my hand as though I was a small child. 'It's been liberating to share my secret, and I *will* tell my wonderful grandson about his heritage at some point, but, until I tell you that I'm ready to do that, I'd like to close the book on the story of my life. As for writing an epilogue, that's not going to happen. If you care for me, you'll respect my wishes. I am *not* going to get in touch with Teddy and I don't want you to do so either.'

'But—'

'No, Callie. This isn't about you. This is about what I want and I want to leave the past in the past. I'm too old and tired to do it all again.'

I felt like a petulant child, dragging my feet and pouting as we shuffled closer to the front of the queue. She couldn't be more wrong with her decision. She'd opened up after more than fifty years so what was the point in closing the conversation again? And the love of her life was still alive. Why wouldn't she want to get in touch, especially if Gabriella was out of the picture, which surely she had to be, given how bad their marriage had been?

I glanced at her set jaw and narrowed lips. 'Okay. It's your life. I won't do anything you don't want me to do.'

'Is that a promise?'

'It's a promise.'

'Good. Now it's time to change the subject. Let's talk about you and Rhys. What are your Christmas plans?'

I answered Ruby's question, trying to sound enthusiastic, but my mind was picturing a romantic reunion between Teddy and Ruby, a speedy wedding, and a happy ever after for as many years as they had left. I felt sure that it would happen. I'd promised Ruby that I wouldn't do anything she didn't want me to do, though, and I wasn't one to break promises. The thing was, I was absolutely convinced that she really *did* want to be reunited with Teddy and was scared of either her or me making the move in case he wasn't interested. If I thought she really *did* want me to make contact, even though she said she didn't, then I wasn't breaking my promise, was I? I was doing something that she really wanted me to do, even if she hadn't voiced it.

31

As soon as I got home from our trip to York, I Googled Teddy Latimer. He definitely looked distinguished with thick white hair, warm dark eyes, and a sharp suit. Curiosity nudging me, I read about his estate, Burghfield Hall, his charity work, his businesses and his family. I discovered that Gabriella and Teddy had divorced about a year after Ruby last saw him. Two divorces and a bereavement later, she passed away eight years ago. Definitely out of the picture, then.

I found the Chopin music that Ruby said Teddy had been playing when she fell in love with him and the Perry Como track she'd mentioned. How had I not heard of Perry Como before? What a voice! I found myself playing a live version of the song over and over on YouTube, captivated by his silky smooth, effortless tone. The lyrics were quite beautiful too, talking about everlasting love. I closed my eyes and imagined Ruby and Teddy swaying to the music, Teddy singing along to the lyrics. Whatever Ruby said about not wanting to get in touch, I was convinced that theirs was an everlasting love, just like in the song.

Rhys, who was on a night out with friends, texted me shortly after 11 p.m.

✉ From Rhys
Missing you. Hope you've had a relaxing evening. Saw Maria in The Old
Theatre. If looks could kill! No sign
of Tony, though xx

I nibbled on my thumbnail. Maria. It was almost three weeks since I'd seen her in The Chocolate Pot and I still hadn't found a way of reaching out. I pictured her on the beach with Tony and shuddered.

Why hadn't I seen him for what he was? Why couldn't she?

I missed Maria's friendship so much and felt sure she had to miss mine because she didn't have any other friends and wasn't in touch with her family. Her dad had walked out when she was eight, leaving her mum with five girls. It turned out that her mum wasn't very good at being on her own, working her way through a string of loser boyfriends and leaving Maria to bring up her sisters. When Maria was fifteen, the latest boyfriend indecently exposed himself to her and her two eldest sisters. She called the police, social services got involved and the already dysfunctional family fell apart. Her mother stood by the boyfriend and disowned Maria – something I've never been able to get my head around. Her two younger sisters never forgave her for causing their separation from their mother. The next two were old enough to understand but took the opportunity to put as much distance between them and their childhoods as they could, one emigrating to New Zealand and the other to Canada, leaving Maria with nobody. And now the only person in her life was Tony. It didn't get much worse than that.

I picked up my phone and started typing a text:

✉ To Maria
Hi Maria, I'm worried about you

No, too direct. Try again.

✉ To Maria
Hi Maria, how are things going with
the baby?

Argh! Too chatty.

✉ To Maria
Hi Maria, I just wanted to check
you're OK. I saw you on the beach
with Tony and...

I shook my head. Completely inappropriate. It sounded like I was stalking her and, given what she was doing with Tony on the beach, that was not a good opening line.

✉ To Maria

Hi Maria, I know that things didn't
end well between us but it doesn't
mean I don't care. I'm here if you
need someone to listen x

I re-read the text a dozen or so times. It wasn't
perfect, but it was the best I could think of. Pressing
send, I suspected she wouldn't get in touch – unless
it was to hurl some insults – but I'd reached out with
the olive branch and it was up to Maria whether she
accepted it or not.

✉ From Maria
You cared so much you got me sacked

✉ To Maria
It wasn't me! I don't know who it was
but I swear I didn't drop you in it

✉ From Maria
As if I'm going to believe that. Sod
off, Callie. I don't need you trying
to fix me

I poised my fingers ready to reply, then sighed and put the phone down. Enough. The offer was there. If Maria didn't want to take it, then that was her decision and I wasn't going to beg. I was, however, going to do some digging. Somebody had dropped Maria in it and I was determined to find out whom. No way was I going to let her think it was me in some desperate act of revenge.

32

'Aren't you having breakfast this morning?' I asked Ruby, surprised to find her all alone in the residents' lounge first thing on Monday.

'Ruby?' I prompted when she didn't answer. 'Ruby?'

She turned her head and seemed to take a few moments to register where she was. 'Oh, it's you, darling. Did you ask something?'

'I asked whether you were skipping breakfast this morning.'

'I'm not really hungry.'

I bent down by the Christmas tree and switched the fairy lights on. 'You've got to eat. You'll be nothing but a bag of bones in that gorgeous brides-maid dress if you start skipping meals.'

'That Iris Davies is getting me a yoghurt. If she remembers, that is. She's so giddy these days, I wouldn't be surprised if she brought me a used teabag instead.' Even though she'd cracked a joke, Ruby didn't smile. Instead she turned and gazed out the window again.

'You look like you could do with some fresh air. Should I get your coat for a wander round the garden?'

'I don't want to keep you from your work and get you into trouble.'

'Keep me from my work? What do I always say my number one priority is?'

Ruby smiled at last. It was a weak one, but it was a starting point. 'Making the residents happy.'

'Exactly. And right now, my favourite resident doesn't look happy, but Rhys has made something for the garden that I know will make you smile. Shall I get your coat and boots?'

* * *

I linked arms with Ruby as we set off down the pathway. Rhys and his team had made great progress in the gardens, creating gentle slopes with wooden handrails to help the residents who weren't so steady on their feet, with seating at regular intervals. He'd carefully chosen colours, smells and textures to facilitate a journey for the senses.

'So, are you going to tell me what's going on?' I asked after we'd walked down the first slope in silence.

'I don't regret telling you about Teddy but it's churned up so many memories and I suppose the upshot is that I want to see him.'

I nearly squealed with excitement. 'Teddy?'

'For goodness' sake, Callie. Did you not listen to a word I said in York? Teddy's in the past. Done. Forgotten. Well, not forgotten, obviously, but definitely in the past.'

'Then who...?'

'Edward. I want to see my son.'

I stopped walking. 'Really? But...'

'I know, darling. You don't have to say it. He hates me and never wants to see me.'

I thought back to Ed's aggression when Rhys and

I had visited, culminating in our swift ejection from his home. 'Maybe Rhys could ask him again?' I could hear the doubt in my voice.

Ruby indicated that we should carry on walking. 'No. I can't ask him to do that.'

'I'm sure he wouldn't mind.'

She shook her head. 'He doesn't say much about his father, but I've been on this planet long enough to pick things up. I can tell that their relationship is strained. I'm not going to do ask him to do anything to damage it further.'

'So what's your plan?'

Ruby sighed. 'That's what I was trying to work out when you found me in the lounge just now. I'm thinking I might write to Edward. He'll probably tear it up, but I feel I need to try. If I do write, will you read it before I send it?'

'If you'd like me to.'

'I would.' She patted my hand. 'You're a good girl, Callie. Now what did you want to show me in the garden?'

I smiled at Ruby's way of changing the conversation, making a very firm statement that the original subject matter was closed. For now, anyway. 'It's at the bottom, overlooking the sea.'

We made our way down to a wooden bench, lovingly crafted by Rhys from driftwood. I led Ruby to the front so she could see the dedication. Reggie's name was carved into the middle of the backrest, above a heart-shaped cut-out, and the names of his closest friends at Bay View were carved across the rest of the backrest in smaller letters.

Ruby gasped and her hand went to her mouth. 'Oh my goodness. That's... that's... oh, it's so beautiful.'

I remained silent, watching the emotions flicker across her face.

'Oh my goodness,' she said again. 'Did Rhys really make this?'

I nodded. 'The driftwood came from local beaches and he's been working on it for weeks. He toyed with a grand unveiling but we decided that it would be more meaningful for the residents if we spread the word and let them visit in their own time with their own thoughts.'

'I think that's a good decision, darling.' Ruby perched on the bench and ran her fingers along the names, then looked up at me, a warm smile finally lighting her face. 'Reggie would have loved this. And it's in his favourite spot.'

I sat beside her. 'I know. Mine too. When I think of him, it's always to picture him either producing sherbet lemons out of my ears or sitting down here with his crossword puzzle and never getting more than two or three clues completed because he couldn't stop gazing at the view.' And who could blame him? It really was stunning.

The wind whipped my hair and I noticed Ruby shivering. 'I don't think the weather's quite as nice as the view today. Time to retreat?'

I helped Ruby to her feet and we made our way back inside.

'Ah! There you are.' Iris held up two yoghurts. 'You said raspberry but they had vanilla too. I know how much you love vanilla and they hardly ever have it so I brought you both.'

Not a used teabag in sight, then. I raised an eyebrow at Ruby who smiled.

'Thank you, Iris. That's very kind of you. Would you like to join me in the lounge for a cup of tea while I eat them?'

'That would be lovely.'

'Is William coming over?' Ruby asked.

'Not until this afternoon.'

'Do you think he could come over this morning? There's something in the garden that I'd like to show you both.' Ruby turned to me. 'Can we keep it quiet until they've seen it?'

'Of course. I'll leave you ladies to it.'

I headed towards the office feeling warm and fuzzy. It had definitely been a good decision not to make a big thing about the bench. How lovely that Ruby wanted to personally show it to Iris and William. Hopefully that would keep her mind occupied and that smile on her face for the morning at least, because writing to Rhys's dad was guaranteed to make that smile slip.

33

'Argh!' Iris crumpled up a piece of paper and tossed it towards the bin the following afternoon.

I poured her a cup of tea and made my way to the large table in the corner of the residents' lounge, which we used for games and activities. 'I'm pretty certain you can buy confetti,' I said, nodding towards the balls of paper on the table and floor. 'You don't have to create your own, you know.'

Iris took the cup of tea and sighed. 'I was only nineteen when I married my Walter. I'd forgotten how much goes into organising the big day.'

I sat beside her. 'What are you trying to do?'

'The place cards. I bought some scented

pinecones and I want to slot each guest's name into the top of one to make the place settings a bit more festive.'

'Sounds lovely.'

'It would be if my writing wasn't worse than a small child's. I used to have beautiful handwriting, but the arthritis makes it hard to hold a pen.' She picked up a packet of cream cardboard rectangles with scalloped edges. 'Just as well I decided to practise on paper first or I'd have wasted all of these.'

'I can do calligraphy,' I said. 'I don't mind writing them, unless you're particularly wanting to do them yourself.'

Iris grasped my hand. 'Goodness, no. I'm more than happy to delegate. I had no idea you could do that.'

I shrugged. 'I haven't done any for ages so I might need a few practice goes, but I'm sure it'll soon come back. My brother bought me a kit for Christmas when I was fifteen and it became an obsession for a while.'

'Are you sure you have the time?'

'Hand them over. It'll be a pleasure. I'll need

some new ink but I can nip into town when I finish at four and start on them tonight.'

'That would be a godsend. Thank you so much.' She handed me the cards and a list of names. 'I'll give you some money for the ink before you go.'

I shook my head. 'You'll do no such thing. I won't do them if you try to pay me so you can stop shaking your head right now. Would you like black ink or would you like me to do a colour? Perhaps a forest-green to be Christmassy?'

'Forest-green would be wonderful. Thank you so much.'

Standing up, I slipped the packet of cards into the pocket of my tabard. 'Where's Ruby, by the way? She's usually down here well before the tea trolley arrives.'

'In her room writing a letter, I think.'

My stomach did a somersault. 'Did she say who she was writing to?'

'I don't think so, but I did think it a bit odd. Ruby *never* writes letters.'

The door opened and the residents started filing in for their afternoon tea. I returned to the trolley to serve them but my mind was on Ruby and her difficult letter to Ed. Sadly, I expected she was right and it would go straight into the bin or on the fire and the words she'd likely have agonised over for hours would go un-read.

* * *

When I finished my shift shortly after four, I slipped out of the building and caught the bus into town. I finally remembered to nip into the cobbler's to get a set of keys cut for Rhys then headed for Bay Books on Castle Street.

At closing time, I left the bookshop, with three paperbacks and two pots of ink. Peering into my bag, I smiled. I couldn't wait to get started on the place settings and maybe delve into one of the paperbacks before bedtime.

'Careful!'

I stopped just in time to avoid colliding with a heavily pregnant woman.

'Maria?'

'Jesus!' she cried. 'You're everywhere. Leave me alone.'

'I'm not stalking you. I needed to get some things

from the bookshop.' I lifted my branded paper bag to prove it although we were right by the door so she had to have seen me coming out. 'How's it going? How's the baby?'

'Like you care.'

'I *do* care.'

With a shake of her head, she turned and strode towards the main precinct.

'Maria! Wait.'

She stopped and spun round to face me. 'Seriously, Callie, just leave it. We've got nothing to say to each other anymore. I know I hurt you but you could have destroyed my life. You got me sacked and I came this close to being evicted.'

'I swear it wasn't me. I just—'

'You just want to interfere, like always,' boomed a male voice.

Crap! Tony.

'What are you doing with *her*?' Tony demanded of Maria. 'Don't tell me you're best friends again?'

'Not after what she did. And what are you doing here? I thought you were meant to be in Liverpool.'

Liverpool? Very likely a lie. Squirming, I tightened my grip on my bag and started to move round them but Tony stepped into my path.

'Move!' I demanded, trying to sidestep him.

'I'm glad I bumped into you,' he said. 'So you and gardening boy are over, then?'

My stomach somersaulted. 'No, not that it's any of your business.'

'You're still together? Interesting. Well, I suppose women are often attracted to a certain type. Obviously your type isn't monogamous.' He laughed as he grabbed Maria's arm. 'Come on. I'm starving.'

'What's that supposed to mean?' I called after them, finally finding my voice.

Tony turned round, a sickly grin on his face. 'Long blonde hair? Cracking figure? Baby girl?'

Izzy. A wave of nausea hit me and I had to lean against a shop window to stop myself from slumping to the ground. I gulped the cold air. Blurred figures with armfuls of shopping bags drifted past me, revealing glimpses of fairy lights in the shop windows opposite, like a kaleidoscope of colour in my darkening world. No. Tony was lying. It was his way of getting revenge on me for messing up his life, despite the fact that it was him who'd done that spectacularly without my help. Rhys was nothing like Tony. I trusted him implicitly. Thing was, I didn't trust Izzy and I wouldn't have put it past her to try something on with Rhys. Tony had obviously seen them together to be able to describe her and to know she had a baby. Maybe he'd seen Izzy making a move. Or maybe he'd simply seen them together and decided it was the perfect way to wind me up.

Catching the bus home ten minutes later, I still felt shaky. I hated that Tony continued to have power over me. At least Rhys would be at the flat when I got back. I'd tell him about my confrontation and he'd reassure me that Tony was the liar that I knew he was, and everything would be fine.

The flat was in complete darkness. Where was Rhys? Why hadn't he called? I took out my phone. On silent. Three missed calls and a voicemail. I dialled into my messages: 'Hi Callie, it's me. I didn't want to leave a message but I can't get hold of you. Izzy's not feeling well. She says she's not up to looking after Megan on her own and has asked me to stay over. I'm really sorry. I love you.'

Tossing my phone onto the sofa, I clenched my fists. No way was she ill. It was another of her ridiculous games. What was wrong with the woman? I dashed around the room, flicking on all the fairy lights in an effort to cheer myself up, then changed into my fleecy PJs and flung myself onto the sofa. My stomach rumbled and I groaned. Rhys was supposed to be picking up something for dinner.

Rolling off the sofa, I opened the kitchen cupboard and curled my lip at the empty shelves. Anyone for pasta? I had shells, bows, spirals and spaghetti, but nothing to accompany them.

I pushed my bowl aside fifteen minutes later. Urgh. Pasta with baked beans was definitely *not* a taste sensation.

My phone started ringing. It was so tempting to ignore Rhys and continue to sulk, but it wasn't his fault I'd had an encounter with Tony and it wasn't his fault he'd had one with Izzy.

'Oh, thank God!' he said when I answered. 'I was beginning to think you'd been kidnapped by aliens.'

'I switched my phone to silent earlier and forgot to switch it back. I got your message. *Is* she ill?'

He lowered his voice. 'She looks a bit pale and she's quieter than usual.'

'Not ill, though?'

'I ... well, I couldn't be sure. She says she was sick before I got here.'

'And you believe her?'

'I *want* to believe her.' That was so like Rhys, wanting to see the best in people, but it also told me that he didn't believe her because he'd have told me outright if he did. I wanted to tell him about Tony and Maria but was that fair? He was committed to staying at Izzy's and I was going to place him in a difficult position if I insisted on him coming home to comfort me. And what if she really was ill? I was ninety-nine per cent certain she wasn't, but that nagging one per cent was enough to keep my mouth shut.

'It's probably just as well you're not here,' I said, brightening my voice. 'I've volunteered to write some place cards for Iris's wedding so I wouldn't have been much company.' What I really meant was that I was glad I had a distraction from thinking about him and Izzy, alone together, all night. I trusted Rhys. I did. Yet I'd trusted Tony too and look how that had turned out.

34

I barely slept. Every time I closed my eyes, I either pictured Rhys with Izzy or imagined Tony cornering me. Lying in the darkness in the early hours, every creak of the building had me flicking on the light, scrambling out of bed to check the locks, and peering nervously into dark corners.

I hated that Tony made me feel unsafe in my lovely flat. Maybe it was time to move. He could still track me down at work but at least he wouldn't know where I lived. Where would I go, though? Moving in with Rhys was the obvious choice, but he rented a room off a friend who was always polite but managed to slip in little comments that made it clear that it was *his* house and overnight visitors were tolerated occasionally but certainly not welcomed or appreciated. Mind you, if Rhys was cheating on me with Izzy, then moving in with him wouldn't be an option anyway because we wouldn't be together; there was no way I'd tolerate infidelity. I shook my head to dislodge the thought. Rhys was *not* cheating on me. He'd never do that.

I wondered whether to call the police and tell them about Tony, but what could I say? Bumping into him outside Bay Books had been pure coincidence. Other than that, there'd been one text and a kerb-crawling incident in the space of a month. It didn't exactly spell out a pattern of him harassing me, did it?

At about 4.30 a.m., I gave up on sleep and curled up on the sofa with a cup of tea and a documentary about the increasing popularity of knitting; anything to take my mind off Rhys and Izzy, Tony, and Maria. I must have drifted off eventually because I woke up a couple of hours later with a crick in my neck, icy-cold feet, and a nervous feeling in the pit of my stomach that one or both of the situations was about to come to a head.

My shift wasn't due to start until two that after-noon but I decided to go in an hour early to give Iris the place cards and to see if I could catch up with Rhys. Iris and Ruby were coming out of the dining room, arm in arm, as I entered the building.

'Did you manage to get some ink last night?' Iris asked after we'd exchanged greetings.

'I did one better than that.' I indicated that we should go into the residents' lounge and pulled an envelope out of my bag when they'd both sat down. 'All done.'

'All of them?' Iris opened the envelope. 'Oh my goodness, they're beautiful. Such accomplished pen-manship.' She showed them to Ruby and they both gushed about how talented I was.

'Thank you so very much, my dear,' Iris said. 'But I wasn't expecting you to drop everything and do them all last night. Didn't you have plans with your young man?'

'We did, but his evil bitch of an ex decided to in-terfere yet again and, of course, Rhys put her first like he always does.' I flinched at their shocked expres-sions and no wonder. I'd never heard such venom in my voice before.

'I'm sorry,' I muttered. 'I should *not* have said that. Sorry.' I hurried across the room, my cheeks burning, ignoring Ruby calling my name. Dashing into the staff toilets, I locked myself in one of the two cubicles and slumped down on the seat with my head in my hands as anguished sobs shook my body.

I flushed my soggy tissues down the toilet and unlocked the door, reluctantly peering at my reflection in the mirror. What a sight! I grabbed some more loo roll from the cubicle and wet it, dabbing at my puffy eyes.

Making my way to the back of the building, I wandered around the gardens until I found Rhys near the bottom, emptying a sack of shingle round the base of a water feature.

As though aware of being watched, he turned round and smiled. 'Hi, you.'

'That's looking good,' I said.

'It's taken me all morning to get the damn thing to work, but I'm pleased with it.' He tossed the empty sack and his gloves towards the base of his wheelbarrow and walked towards me. 'I wasn't sure if you'd still be speaking to me today.'

My heart raced as he took hold of both of my

hands in his and fixed his eyes on mine. 'I'm not speaking to Izzy,' I said. 'She's definitely off my Christmas card list.'

Rhys laughed. 'Somehow I suspect she was never on it in the first place.'

'She wasn't ill, was she?'

He shook his head. 'The enormous takeaway pizza she rammed down her neck was a bit of a giveaway.'

I let go of his hands. 'She ordered pizza? So why didn't you come home?'

He wrinkled his nose. 'I'd had a few drinks so I couldn't drive.'

Rhys reached for my hands again but I snatched them away. 'Thanks a lot. So I lay awake all night thinking Tony might...' Damn! I lowered my eyes.

'Tony? Has he been to the flat?'

I shook my head. 'I had to go into town and I bumped into Maria. I didn't plan to before you say anything about me interfering. I came out of Bay Books and she happened to be leaving work at the same time. We exchanged unpleasantries then Tony appeared, stirring things up.'

'Between you and Maria?'

I lowered my eyes again.

'Callie?' Rhys gently lifted my chin so I had to make eye contact. 'Complete honesty, remember?'

My shoulders sagged. 'He made some comment about you and I splitting up and, when I said we hadn't, he said I obviously liked the unfaithful type because he'd seen you looking cosy with another woman who matched Izzy's description.'

Rhys hugged me, but frustration prevented me from hugging him back. After a moment, he let me go and tugged on my hand. 'Come with me.'

Reluctantly, I followed him into his tool shed. He cleared some rubble sacks off an old wooden chair so I could sit down, then crouched by my side. 'Start from the beginning.'

'You didn't believe him, did you?' Rhys asked when I'd explained in full. 'Callie?'

'No, but I don't trust Izzy. Can't you see what she's doing? Every time we're together, she's on the phone to you and you go running. I get that you have re-sponsibilities to Megan, but you owe Izzy nothing.'

Rhys was silent and my heart thumped. I'd said too much and pushed him too far. He couldn't shut Izzy out completely, but surely he could stand up to her from time to time instead of pandering to her every whim. Eventually he sighed. 'You're right. I'll speak to her about it. I promise.'

'Thank you. I'm not trying to be awkward about—'

'I know.' He kissed my hand. 'It's Izzy who's being awkward. I'll sort it.'

Ruffling his hair, I sighed. 'Maybe you could leave it until after Christmas, eh? Knowing how she operates, I wouldn't put it past her to cancel your Christmas morning with Megan if you say anything before then.'

He stood up and gently pulled me to my feet and kissed me. My heart raced at his touch, but my stomach rolled as though I was on a big dipper and I had a horrible feeling that this was far from over.

35

Shrieks of laughter from the residents' lounge drew me out of the team leaders' office on Friday afternoon. Small groups were set up around the lounge working on different tasks, some slotting the name cards I'd written into pinecones and others working on what looked like wedding favours. Another group including Iris and Ruby were creating buttonholes at the main table, surrounded by foliage, berries, and flowers. Bottles of champagne and sherry had been opened and, judging by the red cheeks and the volume of chatter, I suspected the bottles had already made several rounds.

'Callie, darling!' Ruby cried, waving me over.

'Look what I've been making.' She held up a bunch of mistletoe and berries tied together with red gingham ribbon.

'Very beautiful.'

'May I?' she asked, waving it in front of me.

'Of course.' I bent forward so she could give me a kiss on the cheek.

'Are you excited?' I asked Iris.

'Oh, my dear, I'm beside myself. When I married Walter, it was so different. We both wore our Sunday best and we had a few sandwiches and a pork pie in the church hall with family and a few close friends. It was how it was done back then.' She swept her arm round the room taking in the various creative groups. 'I might have gone a bit over the top but William never married and I never had the big party so we thought, what the heck, let's splurge. We don't know how long we have left so let's spend our money and enjoy ourselves.'

'You do right, Iris. Can't take it with you when you're gone, can you?'

I left them to it and made my way back to the office. I'd only been in there about ten minutes when there was a light tap on the open door. I looked up expecting either a resident or one of my colleagues but did a double-take when I saw Rhys, brow furrowed, looking more anxious than I'd ever seen him. Oh crap. Izzy? Megan? Both?

'I can come back later if you're busy,' he said.

'No. Come in. Shut the door. I'm guessing this isn't a social call.'

Rhys sat down on the other side of the desk. 'I'm really sorry to do this, especially so close to Christmas.'

My breath caught in my throat and tears stung in my eyes. Oh my God! He was going to dump me. At work. On Christmas Eve's Eve. No!

'Bad news?' I asked. 'Obviously it's bad news with an expression like that.'

He nodded. 'I'm sorry. I didn't want to do this. Not yet, anyway. I thought maybe after Christmas but...' He rubbed the back of his neck as though he was building up to delivering a crushing blow.

Stay strong. Don't cry. Don't crumble.

'... but they've already booked the table and there's no stopping my dad when he's made his mind up. I could probably tell them you're ill or you've been called into work if you want to give it a miss, but I'm going to have to go myself which screws up our plans yet again.'

'What are you talking about?'

'Dinner with my parents. Tonight.'

'What?' I wasn't dumped? I felt dizzy with relief as I slumped back in the chair.

'They're coming over to Whitsborough Bay to drop off presents and take us out for dinner. Mum mentioned the idea a couple of weeks ago, but I didn't realise it was a definite arrangement. Apparently it was. As I said, I can probably wangle you a get-out-of-jail-free card, although I could do with you by my side to...' He stopped and frowned. 'Why are you crying?'

I put my hands up to my cheeks and wiped at my tears.

'I know the prospect of dinner with my dad isn't the stuff of dreams, but I wasn't expecting tears.'

'I thought you were going to dump me,' I whispered.

'Why would I do something stupid like that?' He stood up and came round to my side of the desk so that he could hug me. 'Is this because of Izzy?'

'I don't know. Probably.'

'I'm not about to dump you and if I was, which I'm not, I certainly wouldn't do it at work two days before Christmas. What do you take me for? I'd do it by text on Christmas Day instead.'

I laughed, sending snot bubbles down my nose and onto his overalls.

'I have to say, Cal, you've never looked sexier, and I think I'm rocking the snot-daubed gardener look.' I giggled again as I grabbed a tissue from the box on the desk, wiped him down, and blew my nose.

'Shall I tell Mum it'll just be me?' Rhys asked when we'd both stopped laughing.

'No. I'll be there to hold your hand, although I can't promise I'll be able to hold my tongue if he has a go at you again. Or my job. Or Ruby.'

'Hopefully he'll be on his best behaviour. At least he can't throw us out of the restaurant. He'll probably try, though.'

When Rhys left, I sat back in the chair and thought about Ruby's wish to see her son. Would the meal be a good time to broach the subject again? I'd asked Ruby about the letter a couple of days ago but she said she'd decided to leave it until the New Year, not wanting Ed to add an accusation of ruining

Christmas to his list of reasons to hate her. Could I do the legwork for her instead? Was I brave enough?

I glanced over at a cream envelope resting in front of the mailing tray to my right. I'd already done enough interfering. Practising writing the place cards had turned into writing 'Ruby loves Teddy', which had turned into writing a letter to Teddy telling him I was a friend of Ruby's, that she was in good health and, if he was interested in knowing more about her, he should get in touch. It was short and factual, with no mention of Ed and no suggestion that Ruby still loved him, although maybe he'd pick that up if he read between the lines. I'd addressed it and placed a stamp on the envelope, but I'd chickened out of posting it. For the past couple of days, it had been resting by the mailing tray with a bright orange Post-it note stuck to it stating: DO NOT POST! I wanted to post it. I really did. But Ruby had made me promise not to make contact and I was still having the debate as to whether she really, truly, genuinely one hundred per cent meant that.

* * *

'Sidney's is that posh place on Ocean Ravine, yeah?' I asked Rhys as I pushed hangers back and forth on the rail in my wardrobe after work.

'Yes. I'm looking at the menu now. What's seared fois gras with a Cabernet balsamic berry reduction?'

'Buggered if I know. I hope they've got something normal on the menu like gammon and chips or we might be visiting the kebab shop on the way home.' I tutted loudly. 'I know this sounds like such a girly thing to say, but I genuinely have nothing to wear, or rather nothing suitable for somewhere posh like Sidney's.'

Rhys wrapped his arms round me from behind and kissed my neck. 'You look amazing in whatever you wear. Or in nothing at all.' He pulled open the press-studs on my tabard and slipped his hand inside, brushing it over the lace on my bra.

I moaned softly as my body immediately responded to his touch. 'What time do we need to meet them?'

'Table's booked for eight, and it's only six now. Plenty of time to show you how sorry I am for what happened on Tuesday.'

'It'll take a pretty big apology.'

'I think we can safely say it's pretty big,' Rhys said, laughing.

* * *

Amazing as it was, a spot of hot, frantic sex with Rhys had not resolved my wardrobe crisis. He packed me off to the shower telling me he had an idea but needed to go out for a bit. When I reappeared later, wrapped in a towel, Rhys was back and sitting on the bed with a carrier bag in front of him.

'I might be able to solve your wardrobe crisis but it means getting some of your Christmas gifts early. Would you like them?'

I grinned. 'If that's okay with you.'

'If it makes you happy, it's more than okay with me.' He handed me a gift and grimaced. 'I can handle the most delicate of plants but give me some paper and Sellotape and, well, you can see for your-self.' The paper was crumpled, there were rips in it, and scrunched up bits of Sellotape barely held the edges together.

'No wonder you wanted me to wrap Megan's presents for you.'

It was pointless me delicately peeling back the Sellotape so I ripped the paper open and removed the gift. 'Oh, wow! It's gorgeous.' I held up a short, flared navy-blue dress covered in red hearts.

'I know you don't wear many dresses but I thought it was really you.'

'It is. I love it. Thank you.'

'That's not all.' He handed me a smaller yet equally battered package and a soft red fitted cardigan tumbled out.

'It's a perfect match,' I said, holding the cardigan against the dress.

'I'd like to take credit but the computer suggested they matched. I chose this one myself, though.'

He handed me a much smaller package this time. Inside was a glass heart-shaped necklace on a leather thong. The red heart seemed to have threads of silver and gold running through it. Silently, Rhys took it from me and fastened it around my neck. I looked down and gently stroked the glass.

'I gave you my heart shortly after we met and it's yours forever, but I've let you down lately and made you doubt how important you are to me. If you ever doubt me again, just look at this and know that my heart is – and always will be – yours.'

I didn't care about annoying Ed by being late again as I dropped my towel and, this time, made love to Rhys slowly and tenderly. That tiny weeny seed of doubt that Tony had planted evaporated. Rhys loved me and only me and I wouldn't let either of our exes do anything to jeopardise that.

36

'Your dad is going to be so pissed off with us,' I whispered, gripping onto Rhys's hand as we walked towards Sidney's, fifteen minutes late.

'When isn't my dad pissed off?' he answered. 'If I could turn back time, I wouldn't change a thing.' He stopped and kissed me so slowly and gently that my legs felt like they were made of liquid and I could melt into a pool right there on the pavement. I'd never felt so close to him as I had done in the last few hours, as though our relationship had just stepped up to a new level.

'We'd better get inside,' I said, even though I'd

happily have climbed back into his van and headed home.

'Whatever he says or does, remember that I take after Mum, not him.'

Sidney's was small, with seating for about thirty diners. It was contemporary with white walls and lots of chrome. White flowers and swathes of ivy softened what could have been a clinical feel. The minimal acknowledgement to Christmas came from white fairy lights strung across the wooden beams on the ceiling and across a driftwood tree in the corner. Whoever made the design decisions clearly wasn't a fan of colour.

A waiter smiled in welcome, but we could already see Ed and Jenny at a table for four. Jenny beamed at us and stood up ready for hugs, but Ed remained seated. He looked at his watch and raised his eyebrows. It was going to be a fun evening.

'So good to see you both,' Jenny gushed, hugging Rhys then me.

'Timekeeping impeccable as always,' Ed said.

'Great to see you too,' Rhys replied, defiantly holding out his hand to Ed.

For a heart-stopping moment, I thought Ed was

going to refuse to shake it. I actually think he might have done if Jenny hadn't cleared her throat in a way that clearly meant, 'Shake your son's hand or I will stab you with my salad fork, you wanker.' Or at least I'd like to think that's what it meant.

Our waiter held my chair out for me and I sat down gratefully, a sudden attack of nerves making me feel quite nauseous.

Ed seemed to remember his manners and acknowledged me with a stiff smile. 'You look lovely this evening, Callie.'

'Thank you. My outfit's an early Christmas present from Rhys. He's got brilliant taste.'

Ed simply raised his eyebrows. Pig.

'That necklace is beautiful,' Jenny said. 'Is that from Rhys too? I'd love one like that myself.'

'I bought you a ruby necklace on a gold chain,' Ed said. 'Why would you want something plastic on a piece of string instead?'

Callie nil: Ed two.

I felt my nails digging into my clenched fists and didn't dare look at Rhys. Thankfully the waiter reappeared with menus and asked if we wanted any drinks. Yes. Wine. Lots of it! I hadn't planned on drinking anything but I wasn't sure I could face the evening without alcohol so gratefully accepted Jenny's suggestion that we share a bottle of white.

The problem with having a bottle of wine in one of those posh silver ice buckets is that, every time a waiter passes, they top up your drink and you have no way of keeping track of how much you've had. At some point during our main course, I realised that we were on our second bottle and that I'd probably had the lion's share of the first one because I was suddenly very, very drunk. And being drunk made me even more outspoken than normal, which meant that I couldn't politely ignore any more of Ed's thinly veiled insults.

'A Christmas Eve wedding?' Jenny said after I'd told her about Iris and William's wedding the following day. 'How romantic.'

'Bloody inconvenient if you ask me,' Ed said, shovelling a large chunk of rare steak into his mouth.

'I didn't ask you.'

Rhys squeezed my thigh under the table, as though to say, 'leave it'.

'I beg your pardon.' Ed flashed his eyes at me.

Rhys squeezed my thigh again, a little harder this

time, but I couldn't help myself. 'You said, "bloody inconvenient if you ask me," and I said, "I didn't ask you". A wonderful lady who I care very much about is getting married tomorrow and I'm sure that the friends and family who care about her as much as I do see it as a double celebration instead of an inconvenience.' Oh my goodness. I couldn't seem to stop the words spilling out. 'You're not invited so it's not inconveniencing you in any way, so why did you feel the need to share your unwelcome opinion?'

Rhys laughed awkwardly. 'Lovely meal, wasn't it?'

'Oh yes,' Jenny agreed. 'Quite delicious. Don't you think Ed?'

But Ed just stared at me, open-mouthed, and I wondered for a moment whether anyone had ever dared answer him back. I caught Jenny smirking and quickly covering it by pretending to dab her mouth with her napkin.

'So, Jenny,' I continued, 'I agree that it's very romantic. Iris lost her husband when she was in her early forties and she never expected to find love again, especially in her mature years. They decided to seize the moment and marry sooner rather than later, because you never know what might happen if you don't. It's amazing how time can race by just like that.' I clicked my fingers to emphasise my point. 'You can keep putting things off such as thinking that you'll have that conversation or make that apology another day, but people don't live forever, you know.' I stared pointedly at Ed.

'You're not seriously bringing up the subject of *that* woman again,' Ed hissed, angry red spots burning on his cheeks.

'What woman?' I asked innocently.

'Ruby.'

Rhys cleared his throat as he squeezed my thigh again. 'I'm not sure I can manage a dessert. Mum?'

Jenny didn't respond. She was too busy starting at her husband's face turning from red to purple.

'I didn't say a word about Ruby,' I said, calmly, 'but now that you've mentioned her, why is it that you're so adamant that you want nothing to do with her?'

Ed stared at me across the table. I could feel sweat pooling under my arms under his scrutiny but I defiantly held eye contact.

He wiped his mouth with his napkin then

dropped it onto his plate. 'Don't mess with what you don't understand, young lady.'

'What's there to not understand?'

'Callie!' Rhys said, firmly. 'Please forget it.'

'No. This is important. What's there not to understand, Ed? She gave you up for adoption because she couldn't be with your father who, by the way, she loved very much and still does. Unfortunately having a baby with Ruby would have ruined him and his family so she didn't have much choice. She was only doing what was best for you and your dad. If you let her explain about—'

'You know who my granddad is?' Rhys said, clear astonishment in his tone.

'Er... no?'

'You do! She's told you about her past, hasn't she?'

Damn you, white wine and your truth-inducing abilities. I screwed my nose up at Rhys. 'She might have done, but she begged me to keep it quiet. She wanted to tell you in her own time.'

'What happened to absolute honesty about everything?' Rhys's voice was low but the anger in it was unmistakable. He stood up and tossed his napkin onto his plate. 'Thanks a lot, Callie. Excuse me.'

'Rhys!' I pushed my chair back.

Rhys stopped and turned round, his eyes filled with hurt. 'Please, Callie. I need a moment.' The anger was still there.

I pulled my chair back in and glugged down the remnants of my wine, cursing myself for being so stupid.

'Seems Rhys has a type.' Ed made a snorting noise. 'Girlfriends who lie and deceive. First Izzy, now you.'

'Ed!' Jenny hissed. 'Callie's nothing like Izzy.'

'Really? From what I've seen so far, she's a manipulative liar with a crap job who's trying to bleed our son dry. Have I got that wrong?'

I slammed my glass down on the table. *You asked for it.* 'Do you know what I see, Ed? I see a man who likes to conveniently forget that he started his own career at the very bottom, who refuses to acknowledge his son for the exceptionally talented individual he is, who dishes out insults and barbed comments instead of love and pride, and who is too damn selfish and self-centred to even hear what an old lady has to say.' I've no idea how I managed to sound so confident.

'Have you quite finished?' he snapped.

'No, I'm not. She's eighty-four. *Eighty-four.* She might have another ten, fifteen or twenty years in her yet. But she might only have ten, fifteen or twenty weeks. Ruby wants to see you, you know. She told me. She wants to apologise and explain, but you won't even give her that courtesy. She's not expecting anything from you but surely you can let her tell you why she couldn't keep you, and who your father is, before it's too late.'

I glanced across at Jenny. From the glisten in her eyes, I could tell that my words had touched her, but Ed's eyes simply flashed with anger. 'We're done here.'

'But—'

'I said we're done here.' He emphasised every single word.

I opened my mouth to protest again but caught sight of Jenny, wide-eyed and shaking her head vigorously, and closed my mouth again. I'd already told Ed exactly what I thought of him so there wasn't much to add. Probably not my finest moment.

Jenny stood up and put her hand out towards Ed. 'If you give me the car keys, I'll get the presents out of the boot and meet you outside in a bit.'

Wordlessly, Ed handed her the keys.

I picked up my bag. 'Thank you for the meal,' I muttered. 'Happy Christmas.'

If he'd had the manners to look at me, I'd have apologised, but he deliberately and childishly kept his head turned away from me. Fine. We'd leave it there.

Our waiter helped me into my coat then helped Jenny into hers. As we made our way outside, she took my hand and squeezed it. 'Ed's a complicated man. Always has been.'

'I'm so sorry for causing a scene. I shouldn't have drunk so much. I'm not used to wine. I should have kept my big trap shut.'

'This may sound strange but I'm glad you spoke up. He needed to hear that.'

'But it was so rude of me, Jenny.'

'And he was being rude to you and Rhys throughout the meal and you both smiled politely and did your best not to rise to it. One of you was going to snap eventually and I'm glad it was you because you'll have opened Ed's eyes to how he treats Rhys. I bring it up when I'm feeling brave and Rhys's sister, Debbie, has made comments but Ed doesn't listen to us. He'll have heard and digested every word you said, though, and it'll have had a greater impact than anything any of us have ever or could ever say.'

'You're just saying that to make me feel better.'

She linked her arm through mine as we walked towards her car. 'I assure you I'm not.'

There was no sign of Rhys outside. Presumably he was in his van or walking round the block.

'I don't want you to feel bad about tonight,' Jenny said. 'Ed will snarl and grump about it all the way home, but he'll have taken it all in and I wouldn't be surprised if he doesn't agree to see Ruby at some point in the New Year just to prove you wrong, the stubborn fool.'

We reached their car and she popped the boot open.

'Do you know why he refuses to speak to Ruby?' I asked. 'Is there something I don't know?'

Jenny took a deep breath. 'There was an incident while he was at school. That, and a few other things, shaped him into the person he is today. I can't betray him by going into the details, but let's just say that he has to be the one in control and he has to be a success at everything he does. He can't control his adoption in terms of un-doing it and the impact it had on him, so he controls it in the only way he can. Avoidance.'

'But he could be missing out on so much.'

'We all are. From what Rhys says, Ruby sounds wonderful. I lost my own mother a few years ago and would love to have a mother-in-law. Debbie wants to know her too, but she's a daddy's girl, as I'm sure you've picked up, and doesn't want to hurt Ed by meeting Ruby. Ed struggled to deal with Rhys finding her.' Jenny sighed and shook her head. 'It is what it is and we keep hoping that, one day, he'll change his mind.'

She reached into the boot and lifted out several large gift bags and a bin bag. 'I'd better give you these and say goodbye before Ed appears.' She closed the boot. 'They're mainly for Megan but there's something in there for you and Rhys too.'

'Thank you. That's very kind. We've got something for you in the back of the van too so we can do swapsies. If he's in the van, that is.'

As we made our way towards Rhys's van with the gifts, he emerged from a side street and stopped, looking shocked to see us there.

'There you are!' Jenny said. 'Perfect timing. Can you open the van for these?'

I hoped to catch Rhys's eye but he wouldn't look at me while he loaded the gifts into the van. The fresh air and the walk obviously hadn't calmed him down. I'd never seen him riled like this before.

'These are for you and him.' Rhys picked up a cardboard box containing presents and a couple of bottles of wine in sparkly gift bags.

'There's far too much,' Jenny protested. 'You shouldn't have.'

'We wanted to. You deserve to be spoilt. Not sure about him, though.' Rhys nodded in the direction of Sidney's. 'What are you doing out here anyway? I thought you'd be having coffee and dessert.'

'The evening ended a little prematurely,' Jenny said as we made our way back to her car, Rhys carrying the box.

'It was my fault,' I admitted. 'I told him what I thought of him. I'm sorry.'

Rhys stopped walking and finally turned to look

at me. 'For God's sake, Callie. What did you say this time?'

'She was amazing.' Jenny put her arm round my shoulder and pulled me to her side. 'She told him a few home truths.'

'Great. As if I don't have a difficult enough relationship with him already.' If the expression on his face hadn't conveyed his disgust with me, the tone of his voice certainly did. 'I don't know what you were playing at, baiting him like that. It was so embarrassing and completely unnecessary.'

Rhys disappeared round to the back of Ed's car with the box. Tears pooled in my eyes from the sting of his words. How had we gone from being so close to being so far apart in the space of a couple of hours? I turned my face away from Jenny and wiped at the tears before they trailed down my cheeks.

'I'd better head home,' I said to her. 'Thanks for this evening and I really am sorry. That's twice I've met you and twice I've screwed up. Maybe Ed was right about me.'

'No, Callie, don't—'

I shook my head, cutting her off. I had to get away from Rhys before he said anything else.

Grateful that I was wearing flat boots, I turned and ran down the street that Rhys had emerged from moments earlier, then up a dark alley. I thought I could hear Rhys calling my name, but it could have been my imagination. My phone rang but I ignored it as I aimlessly ran up unfamiliar streets of terraced houses and along alleyways, my pounding footsteps echoing in the darkness until a stitch pierced my side. I slowed down, wincing at the stitch and gulping for air.

Turning into another unfamiliar street, laughter and loud music hit me. There was obviously a party going on, with a group of smokers huddled in the front yard, swigging from bottles of lager between drags on their cigarettes or e-cigs. I crossed the road so I didn't have to pass too close to the laughter and excitement – the exact opposite of how I felt right then.

The street curved in front of me and I couldn't help noticing that pretty much every single one of the bay windows had a tree displayed in it. Red lights, white lights, blue ones and multi-coloured flashing sets all screamed that Christmas was nearly here. I'd been so excited about my first Christmas with Rhys and now I wasn't sure if we were even in a relationship. Why had he stormed out like that when he found out that I knew about his grandfather? Couldn't he see that it wasn't my story to tell? It wasn't *my* secret. It wasn't *my* past. I'd never been anything but completely honest with him. And his dad. Maybe I should have left that one alone but Ed had been horrible and I didn't regret telling him what I thought. All I regretted was any pain I'd caused Rhys or Jenny.

My mobile burst into song again and I ignored it once more, unable to bear an argument or, even worse, news that I was dumped.

Turning a few more corners, the streets started to take on a familiarity. Nick lived near here. Could I? I glanced at my watch. 10.15 p.m. My brother was a night owl so would still be up. I only hoped he didn't have company because that could be awkward. The last time I'd spoken to him, he'd met a woman called Lindsay online who seemed 'nice and normal' so they'd been on a few dates.

I soon found myself at the top of Fountain Street where Nick lived. My mobile rang again. This time, I took it out of my bag and switched it to silent, not even checking to see whether it was Rhys calling. I wasn't in the mood for a lecture. Let him stew and hopefully calm down.

As I neared Nick's house, his front door opened and he stepped out, mobile phone pressed to his ear. He locked the door and headed down the street away from me.

'Nick!' I called.

He turned round, looking shocked. 'How did you get here so quickly?'

'What?'

Nick walked towards me. 'You picked up my voicemail?'

I shook my head. 'What's going on?'

'Don't panic, but Mum's had a fall. We need to get to the hospital.'

37

It was gone 3 a.m. by the time we left the hospital on Christmas Eve with Mum hobbling on crutches. Thankfully it was only a hairline fracture which would heal within six to eight weeks, although she wasn't best pleased to be wearing a plaster cast, unable to drive anywhere over the Christmas period. I'd struggled not to laugh when she told me she'd done it playing silly wine-fuelled party games with her friends.

'You don't have to stay with me,' Mum said after we'd helped her into her house and lowered her onto the large sofa in the lounge. 'Nick can drive you home.'

'I don't like the thought of you being on your own so I'm staying.'

'Honestly, sweetheart, there's no need. Besides, don't you need to be at work early to get everyone sorted for the wedding?'

Crap! The wedding had completely gone out of my head. 'I need to be there for seven. Half past at a push. It'll have to be you staying, Nick.'

Twenty minutes later, I unlocked the door to my flat. 'Rhys?' I called out, hopefully, but I knew he wasn't there without looking. Somehow the flat felt completely empty.

In the bedroom, I removed my gorgeous new outfit and carefully hung it up on my wardrobe door next to my dress for the wedding. Pulling on my PJs, I clambered under the duvet and took my phone out of my bag: four missed calls – two from Rhys and two from Nick – plus two voicemails and three texts. Yawning, I dialled into the voicemails, but they were both from Nick, as were the texts. My stomach churned. Why hadn't Rhys left a message or texted? Clearly he'd been really worried about me walking home in the dark on my own... not. Grinding my teeth, I jabbed at the keys on my phone:

✉ **To Rhys**
```
Just got back from hospital. Mum
broke her leg tonight. Thanks for
checking I made it home safely.
```

Setting my alarm for six, I settled down for a couple of hours' sleep, my left hand wrapped around the heart on my necklace, praying he'd meant what he'd said when he gave me it; that his heart was mine forever.

It seemed as though I'd only just closed my eyes when my alarm sounded. I rolled over, hoping that the disastrous evening would turn out to have been a dream, but Rhys's side of the bed was empty and the flat was in silence and darkness.

Much as I wanted to crawl back under my duvet and sleep until my Christmas Day shift tomorrow, I couldn't let Iris down. She'd booked Bay View's regular hairdresser to wash and style her hair and Ruby's, and our beautician to do their make-up and nails, but I'd volunteered to do the nails and hair for several of the residents and to help Iris and Ruby get dressed. I was then responsible for herding everyone into taxis and minibuses.

With my own relationship in tatters, the last thing I wanted to do was spend the day at a wedding, but I'd put on a brave face for the people I loved and try to remain focused on them instead of thinking about Rhys.

Yawning, I cycled to work, a backpack and the bike basket overloaded with everything I needed for the day ahead. There was no sign of Rhys's van in the car park, not that I'd expected there to be.

My first plan of action was to retrieve that letter to Teddy from in front of the mailing tray. If Rhys discovering that I knew about Ruby's past had caused such a negative reaction, I dreaded to think what would happen if he found out I'd tried to make contact with his grandfather behind his back too, especially as that would expressly have gone against Ruby's wishes as well.

I unlocked the office and flicked on the light. Placing my bags by the desk and draping the suit carrier containing my dress over the chair, I made my way towards the mail tray on the cabinet by the printer and... oh crap! It wasn't there. It had been sitting in front of the mailing tray for the best part of the week and neither Odette nor Pete, the other team leaders, had ignored the instruction on the Post-it note so why now? Dashing back to my bag, I rummaged for my phone.

✉ **To Pete**

Sorry to pester you when you've probably only just got home. Did you post that letter with the Post-it on it?

✉ **From Pete**

Yes, but the Post-it note was gone so I assumed it needed sending. Did I mess up?

Argh! I dashed to the cabinet and looked around and behind it. Nestling amongst the dust and cables, there it was. A bright orange Post-it note, staring at me.

Breathe. Just breathe. There was nothing I could do now except reassure Pete it was fine to post the letter because it was me who'd messed up. I should never have written the letter and I certainly shouldn't have left it next to the mailing tray.

✉ To Pete
The Post-it came off but it's absolutely fine. Just checking it hadn't
got lost. Have a great Christmas x

I pulled the chair out and slumped in it, not caring that I was probably putting creases in my dress.

'Callie! Thank God it's you. Thought we had an intruder.'

I looked up to see Odette standing over the desk, holding a mug of coffee in one hand and a yoghurt in the other.

'Sorry, I needed to collect something before I commence with nail-painting duties.'

Odette grinned. 'You should see Iris this morning. She's glowing. It's so adorable.' She dumped her mug down on the desk, slopping coffee, and peeled the lid off her yoghurt, spattering that onto the desk too.

My hands twitched but I managed to resist the urge to grab the antiseptic wipes from the drawer. 'I'd better go and see her, then.'

'Promise me you'll take lots of photos so I can experience it vicariously.' Odette had only started at Bay View a couple of months ago so she didn't know any of the residents that well yet, which was just as well because we could hardly all take the day off to attend the wedding.

'I promise.' I grabbed my dress and bags and left her to it. My stomach churned at the thought of the letter winging its way to Teddy but what could I do? Absolutely nothing. I'd already done the damage when I'd written it and I'd known the risks when I'd added the address and stamp and placed it by the mailing tray. Had I secretly hoped that this would happen, taking the decision to post it out of my hands? If I was honest, I probably had.

But that had been before last night.

I hung my dress up on one of the coat pegs in the staffroom and shoved my bag in my locker. With one last look at my mobile, I dropped it into my bag and closed the door. It was better out of sight than me checking every five minutes to see if Rhys had been in touch.

Ten minutes later, I was all set up in the residents' lounge ready for my first makeover. Ruby and Iris appeared moments later and I hugged them both. Odette was right; Iris's eyes shone and pink tinges in her cheeks transformed her.

'Have you heard from William this morning?' I asked.

'Not directly, but he gave me a card and a gift with strict instructions that I wasn't to open them until this morning.' She thrust her hand out, showing me a silver bracelet with an oval setting containing a delicate purple iris. 'Isn't it beautiful? I'm going to wear it today.'

'It's lovely. The man has taste, although we already knew that because he chose you.'

'Oh, bless you, my dear.' Iris hugged me once more. 'You'll start me crying again.'

'She was a wreck when I called for her this morning,' Ruby said. 'Although I admit that what he'd written in the card was quite touching. It even brought a tear to my eye.'

Iris nudged her. 'It did more than that, you little liar.'

'No, I told you, I had an eyelash irritating me.'

Iris rolled her eyes. 'You cried and it's nothing to be ashamed of.'

'Piffle!'

The next few hours flew by with a steady flow of residents dropping by for a spot of beautifying. Just as well, as the constant chat kept my mind away from Rhys and last night. Odette appeared mid-morning holding a silver gift bag. I expected her to hand it to Iris but she came straight to me. 'This was dropped off at reception for you.'

'Who by?'

'I didn't ask.'

I continued painting Maggie Dennison's nails, even though I was dying to dive in and see if it was from Rhys.

'Aren't you going to open it?' Odette asked.

'I'm busy.'

'Nonsense,' Maggie said, retracting her hands. 'Get it opened.'

I screwed the brush back into the bottle, rolling my eyes at them both. There was a card and a gift wrapped in lilac tissue paper. I unwrapped the tissue and took out a framed picture of the most adorable and sorry-looking Pug underneath the caption: *I'm sorry. I pugged up.*

'That is *so* cute,' Odette said. 'What did he do?'

I glanced across the room but Ruby wasn't there. Even so, I lowered my voice, 'He found out that I knew something that he thought I should have told him even though it wasn't my information to tell.'

Maggie and Odette both stared at me, eyebrows raised. 'Well, I'm glad we cleared that up,' Odette said, shaking her head. 'I'd best get back to it. See you later.'

I turned to Maggie. 'Sorry, Maggie, but I can't—'

'I understand.' She placed her hands flat on the table again. 'Consider the subject dropped.'

When I'd finished Maggie's nails, I apologised to my next 'customer' and headed to the staffroom with my card and picture. Opening the card, I smiled at the cartoon drawings of various cacti amongst the words, 'I've been a prick'. Inside, he'd written:

Dear Callie
The front of the card says it all. I shouldn't have re-acted like that. It's really Ruby I'm angry at. I've asked

her so many times about my granddad and it hurt to know she confided in you instead of me, but you were right not to tell me because it wasn't your secret to tell. I was wrong to walk out. I'd probably have been fine if it hadn't been for Dad's digs and snide comments all night. The news about Ruby was a push too far.

For some reason, I've never been able to stand up to my dad and wish I'd been there when you gave him what-for. Mum thinks you're amazing and I do too. I should have told you that last night. Please forgive me.

Rhys xxx

PS Please meet me by Reggie's bench at noon

Noon was forty minutes away so I returned to my duties in the residents' lounge, setting an alarm on my mobile for five to. There was no question of me not meeting him and I wasn't going to play games by being late, but I wasn't going to make it easy for him when I did see him. I wanted to know why he hadn't phoned or texted and his excuse had better be a damn good one.

My breath hung in the air and I shivered, zipping my coat up to the top, as I made my way across the gardens shortly before noon. Fret had rolled in from the sea and hung in wide ribbons, giving the gardens an ethereal look.

Rhys turned round and stood up as I approached. 'I wasn't sure if you'd come. I'd have understood if you didn't.'

'Why didn't you text me last night?' I asked.

He handed me his mobile and I gasped. 'Oh my God! What happened?' The screen was badly smashed and the side of the phone was scratched and dented.

'I ran after you. I was really worried about you but I couldn't find you. I called you a couple of times but you didn't answer then, as I was running, I managed to trip over something, drop my phone, then stand on it. As you can see, it didn't survive. Completely dead.'

'Were you hurt?'

Rhys shook his head. 'No. I didn't actually fall. My bank account's hurt, though. I had to go into town this morning for this.' He lifted a new phone out of his jeans pocket. 'So I finally got your text. How's your mum?'

'In pain and very embarrassed, but she's fine. I'll

give you a laugh by telling you how she did it later.' I shrugged. 'I thought you didn't care.'

'How could you think that? When I couldn't find you on foot, I drove around in the van. Luckily enough, I ended up on Nick's street in time to see you get into his car so I knew you were safe. I figured he was dropping you home so went to the flat to wait for you. I waited for two hours but you didn't come home. I assumed you'd gone for a drink with Nick then stayed at his so I went home for some sleep. Obviously I now know that you were at the hospital. I'm so sorry, Cal. As that picture said, I pugged up.'

He opened his arms and I ran into his embrace. 'I thought it was over.'

Rhys stroked my hair. 'That's the second time you've thought I was ending things with you. Do you want it to be over?' he whispered.

I stepped back, shocked. 'Of course not! I love you. I want to be with you forever.'

'Good.' He cupped my face in his hand and tilted it towards his, giving me the most tender, gentle kiss that took my breath away. Then he took hold of my hand. 'Come with me. I've got something to show you.'

Hand in hand, we made our way across the cliff top, through the fret, and emerged at the water feature he'd been working on earlier in the week. The large three-tier pond feature was clearly still a work in progress but there was another stone water feature beside it with a small trickle of water dripping from its base onto the surrounding pebbles. The feature itself consisted of two contemporary figures curved towards each other, joining hands, their bodies and arms creating a heart shape.

'Do you like it?' Rhys asked.

'I love it.'

'The bench is my homage to Reggie and this is for you, in the gardens where we first met. A constant reminder of you and how much I love you.'

I squeezed his hand and leaned against him, a whirlpool of emotions preventing me from speaking.

'I'm worried I might have to send it back, though,' he said.

'Why?'

'It's not working properly. You see where the water is? It should be bubbling up between the figures instead of trickling like that. It was working properly earlier so hopefully it's something blocking the water flow, like a leaf, rather than a fault with the whole thing.'

I bent down to look, poking my finger into the icy water. 'Ooh! There *is* something in here but I don't think it's a leaf.' I plucked the object out with my fingers and frowned at it. It was a sparkly silver child's plastic heart-shaped ring. 'How did that get in there?' I turned round to show it to Rhys and nearly dropped it at the sight of him on one knee, holding a ring box towards me.

'Fancy swapping it for the real thing?'

Mouth open, I stared at the heart-shaped diamond on a platinum band. *Oh my God!*

'I hope the silence is surprise rather than a no. Some would say it's too soon but, when you know, you know. I spoke to Nanna this morning. I know the story. She's lived all these years without the love of her life. I don't want to spend another moment without mine. Callie Derbyshire, will you marry me?'

I took a step closer to him and held out my shaking left hand. 'Yes!' I squealed.

Rhys slipped the ring on my finger, then stood up and kissed me. As we stood there enveloped in sea fret, the water feature bubbling beside us, all of our problems – Izzy, Tony, Ed – paled into insignificance. What was important was that we loved each other and Rhys had just proved to me that he'd always be by my side no matter what challenges the three of them threw at us.

38

'I now pronounce you husband and wife.' The vicar turned to William. 'You may kiss your bride.'

Rhys squeezed my hand. I looked into his bright blue eyes and knew he was thinking the same as me: that would be us soon. We'd decided I wouldn't wear the ring for the wedding or share our news because it didn't seem right to take the attention away from Iris and William. I'd placed the plastic ring on my right hand instead and had the real one safely stored in the ring box in my bag.

Iris looked stunning in her cream lacy dress, as did Ruby in her pale green vintage-inspired frock. William had opted for a smart suit rather than a morning suit and looked very dapper and festive with his shiny shoes and Christmas-themed buttonhole.

When they took to the dance floor later that evening for their first dance as husband and wife, I looked at Ruby across the table. That faraway look was on her face again and I was convinced she was either remembering her past with Teddy or thinking about how life might be if she hadn't pushed him away that final time.

I nudged Rhys and nodded towards his nanna. 'You still think she isn't lonely, now that you know about Teddy?'

He shook his head. 'I see it now. You were right.'

'I usually am.'

Rhys laughed. 'Would you mind if I asked Nanna to dance?'

'I think that's a lovely idea.'

I smiled as Ruby shook her head, pointing to me, but Rhys led her to the dance floor to join the newlyweds and several other guests.

After a couple of dances, Ruby led Rhys over to me. 'I need to catch my breath, so it's your turn now.'

On the dance floor, Rhys made me giggle as he

spun me around then pulled me close. 'I know that Nanna's refusing to make contact with my granddad, but do you think we should ignore her and do something?' He laughed as I stiffened. 'You've already made contact, haven't you?'

'Don't be mad at me.'

'I'm not mad. Have you spoken to him?'

'Nothing like that.' I explained what had happened.

'That's going to be an unexpected late Christmas present,' Rhys said.

'Looks like it. I didn't give any details of how to find Ruby so he would have to ring me if he wants more information. Obviously Ruby doesn't know I've made contact so she'll never know if he decides to leave the past in the past.'

'Did you give him your mobile number or your work one?' Rhys asked.

'Both. Why?'

'Then it's very possible he'll find her himself. All he needs to do is Google your work number and he'll find Bay View and likely assume she's a resident.'

I pondered on that for a moment. 'Would that be such a bad thing?'

'Probably not.' Rhys flung me into another twirl, making me giggle again.

'When do you want to get married?' he asked when he pulled me back to his side.

'I'd love to say next year, but I don't know if we'll be able to afford to.'

'Maybe the year after?' he suggested. 'Just think, next time I twirl you round a dance floor, it could be at our wedding.'

'Or it could be at Ruby and Teddy's. That's my Christmas wish.'

Rhys held me close. 'I would love that, but please don't pin your hopes on it. So much has happened since then. If they do meet up, which is a very big if, they might not even like each other anymore.'

'Or they might still love each other and the years will simply melt away.'

A crowd gathered in the hotel lobby to wave the newlyweds goodbye. They were spending two nights in York then catching a train to Edinburgh, returning in time for Bay View's annual New Year's Eve party.

Iris looked like a movie star in a pale blue winter coat over her dress, and a soft cream scarf. 'Thank you so much for celebrating with us today,' she said to the guests. 'We've loved every single moment. Who's next? Are you ready to catch the bouquet?' Iris caught my eye and gave me a wink as I moved towards the front of the group, as we'd planned.

Ruby, who'd been standing beside me, shuffled off to the side. Iris caught my eye again and smiled, then turned and tossed the bouquet in Ruby's direction. Everyone clapped and laughed at Ruby's astonished expression as she stared at the flowers in her hands.

With shouts of 'Merry Christmas,' Iris and William headed out for their lift and everyone else moved back into the function room.

'*You* can have this,' Ruby muttered, thrusting the bridal bouquet into my hands. 'I should have known that stupid woman would try a trick like that. As if I'll be the next to get married. She'd better come back with the best Scottish shortbread or I will *never* forgive her for this.' With a humph, she stormed off towards the toilets.

'Stranger things have happened,' I whispered,

inhaling the faint scent of pine from the bouquet. 'Especially at Christmas when wishes can come true.'

* * *

'You do realise that you've had most of your Christmas presents already, don't you?' Rhys asked as I slipped my gorgeous new engagement ring onto my finger after everyone was safely back at Bay View and we were on our way back to my flat.

'I'm slightly embarrassed by the box of Maltesers and pair of socks I've got for you.'

Rhys laughed. 'Maltesers, good. Socks, essential. I've already got the best Christmas present ever. I've got you.'

'When did you become so mushy? Not that I'm complaining.'

'It's Nanna's fault. She's hidden her true feelings for most of her life and, whilst the circumstances were completely different, it made me realise that I don't tell you enough how much you mean to me. With the problems Izzy and Tony have caused, I should have been reassuring you more than ever.'

My heart sank at the mention of their names. 'What time's she expecting you?' Although I didn't like it, I knew it made sense for Rhys to stay at Izzy's again so that he was there when Megan awoke. If he didn't, Izzy was likely to awaken her early and open the gifts without Rhys, just to spite him.

'I told her that the wedding finished at one rather than midnight and that I had to see the residents back safely so I'd be there at about two. She refused to give me a spare key, insisting on waiting up.'

'That's a bit daft.'

'I think it's her way of making sure I'm no later than that.'

I pushed down my evil thoughts and focused on my ring, glinting as we drove under each streetlight. 'So I have you for at least an hour and a half. Hmm. Wonder what we can possibly do during that time.'

Rhys pressed his foot down on the accelerator a little harder.

39

'I'm so sorry about posting that letter,' Pete said as soon as I poked my head round the team leaders' office door on Christmas morning. 'I wasn't meant to, was I?'

'No, but please don't worry. I think it might have been serendipitous.'

'So, how was the wedding?'

I grinned. 'Lovely. I have photos if you have time.'

'Always.'

I handed over my phone so he could scroll through them, ooh-ing and aah-ing at each shot. 'They look so happy,' he said.

'They were. They are.' I reached for my phone

with my left hand then leapt when Pete released a high-pitched shriek.

He grabbed my hand. 'Callie Derbyshire, you kept that quiet.'

I retraced my hand and swiftly removed my ring. 'I was meant to take that off this morning.'

'Why? Is it a secret? I love secrets.'

'Yes and no. I don't want Ruby to see it yet. Rhys proposed yesterday before the wedding but we didn't want to steal Iris and William's thunder so we kept it quiet. He's meeting me after my shift so we can tell Ruby together. Will you promise not to say anything in the meantime?'

Pete made a zipping motion across his mouth and smiled.

'Thanks, Pete. You can tell anyone you want from tonight onwards, but Ruby needs to be the first to know this afternoon and that has to come from Rhys and me.'

'Can I tell Maria?'

I smiled weakly. 'If you want. I don't think she'll rush to congratulate me, though.'

'I hate that you two aren't friends anymore.'

'Me too. I've tried.'

He nodded. 'I know. Anyway, congratulations from me. He's quite a catch, your young man. If only I'd been younger and had seen him first...'

'As if you'd ever be with anyone except Lars.'

'True. But Rhys is dreamy. Congratulations again.'

I always felt really guilty at Christmas time because, everywhere I went, residents pushed gifts into my hands with a whispered comment such as, 'Don't tell the others, but you're my favourite.' I seemed to be constantly traipsing back to my locker with boxes of chocolates, bottle bags and wrapped gifts that would likely be a mixture of smellies, stationery and jewellery. There was absolutely no need for them to be spending their money on me, but it was touching that they wanted to. I felt quite choked up that what I saw as doing the job I loved, they saw as going over and above. They weren't simply residents to me; they were fascinating people with stories to tell and I was happy to be the person to listen.

Everyone crowded around the piano in the residents' lounge for post-lunch carols and songs. We were midway through a raucous rendition of 'The Twelve Days of Christmas' when I felt Rhys's arms slip around my waist.

'Happy Christmas,' he whispered, nuzzling my neck.

'And to you.'

Placing my song sheet on one of the tables, I followed him into the corridor. 'How was Megan?'

'I'll tell you in a minute but, first, I need to do this.' Rhys wrapped his arms around me and kissed me. 'I've been counting down the hours all day till I could see you to do that. Have you had a good shift?'

'It's been lovely, actually. You won't believe the stack of presents I've got from the residents. They've spoilt me so much.'

'You deserve to be spoilt.'

'So...? Megan...?'

He smiled. 'It was good. She didn't have a clue what was going on, of course. It took me and Izzy ages to open everything for her and then all she wanted was her favourite bunny rather than any of the new stuff.'

'I suppose that was inevitable. And how was Izzy?' I felt I ought to make some effort towards her.

'A bit weird, actually.'

'In what way?'

'Really hyper one minute and crying the next. I asked her what was going on but she said it was just the emotion of Megan's first Christmas. I'm not convinced, but she didn't want to talk to me about it. She's round at her mum's now. Maybe she'll open up to her.'

'Maybe. Speaking of opening up, is it time to share the news with Ruby?'

'Definitely.'

Ten minutes later, we were settled into the lounge area of Ruby's accommodation with a cup of tea.

'Sorry to drag you away from the carols, Nanna, but we wanted to give you your Christmas present before we leave.'

Ruby tutted as Rhys passed her a large gift bag with a fat Robin on the front. 'I told you I have everything I need.'

'We've bought you something you don't need, but which we think you'll love,' I said, hoping we had.

Ruby had never expressed an interest in anything like it before, but it had seemed like the perfect idea when I'd walked past the window of Bear's Pad, the specialist teddy bear shop on Castle Street.

Ruby lifted out the jointed mohair teddy bear, a look of confusion on her face, then she smiled. 'She's dressed like me.' The bear wore a dusky pink silk and lace skirt, crocheted top, silver tiara and sparkly brooch. 'She's gorgeous. Thank you. I've never owned a teddy bear before.' She stroked the fabric of the bear's outfit, seemingly captivated.

'She's actually a musical bear,' I said. 'There's a key in her back.'

'How delightful.' Ruby found the key and wound her up. Tears pricked her eyes as she listened to the tune. Holding her hand against her heart, she looked over at us. 'It's... Oh my goodness. This is... You do know what tune this is, don't you?'

I nodded. 'I'm hoping it's the Chopin piece that Teddy was playing the day you met him and I'm guessing by your reaction that it is.'

Ruby reached in her pocket for a lacy handkerchief and dabbed her eyes. 'I can't believe you found a bear that dresses like me and plays our song.'

'Callie had it made especially,' Rhys said. 'She saw one similar in the window of Bear's Pad in town and asked if they could make a musical version dressed like you. And of course, it's a teddy like Teddy.'

'Oh, darling. It's the most wonderful, thoughtful gift I've ever received. Thank you so much.' Still holding the tinkling bear, Ruby reached out her hand to me and drew me closer for a hug.

'You're welcome. Obviously Rhys didn't know the relevance of Teddy or the music when we ordered it. I told him it was because the bear looked like you.'

'And there's something else,' Rhys said after Ruby had hugged him too.

'I hope not, darling. This gorgeous teddy bear is more than enough.' The music had finished and I suspected that Ruby was dying to wind her up again.

'It's less of a gift and more a piece of news,' Rhys continued.

Ruby's head snapped up and I knew from the smile lighting her face that she'd guessed what he was about to say.

'I asked Callie to marry me and the crazy girl only went and said yes.'

Ruby pressed her fingers across her mouth, tears glistening in her eyes again. 'Oh my goodness, you two. When did this happen?'

'Yesterday before the wedding, but we wanted to wait until today to announce it.' I held out my hand so she could admire the ring, which I'd placed back on my finger after Rhys arrived. 'We wanted you to be the first to know.'

She stood up this time to hug me, then Rhys, then dabbed her eyes with her handkerchief again. 'What did your parents say?' She looked from Rhys to me.

'You genuinely were the first, Nanna,' he said. 'We're seeing Callie's mum and brother this evening so we'll tell them then. As for Mum and Dad... well, I'm not exactly on speaking terms with him, but I'll ring Mum later and tell her.'

We stayed with Ruby for another half an hour then headed back to my flat to exchange gifts. I might already have had an engagement ring, dress, cardigan and necklace, but there were still plenty more gifts from Rhys. I laughed when I opened a heavy package and a selection of bridal magazines tumbled out along with a wedding planner. I couldn't wait to start filling it out.

'You should phone your mum,' I said when the presents were all unwrapped. 'You could always ring her on her mobile if you're worried about your dad answering.'

He kissed me gently. 'Not just a pretty face.'

Jenny was obviously delighted by the news because I could hear her excited squealing down the phone. She insisted on speaking to me so she could officially welcome me to the family.

'Thank you, although I suspect there's one person who won't share your enthusiasm. Did I ruin your Christmas?'

The phone went quiet and I could hear her opening and closing doors. 'Sorry about that. Just moving away from prying ears. No, you didn't ruin Christmas. He sulked all the way home on Friday, he was like a bear with a sore head yesterday, and he's coming round today, exactly as I predicted. He even suggested coming across to the coast at New Year. I predict big changes.'

'Let's hope so.'

I said my goodbyes then handed the phone back

to Rhys, flicking through one of my bridal magazines as he chatted to her. My phone beeped with a text. Why hadn't I had the sense to block him?

From Tony
Happy Christmas! I hear you and gardening boy are engaged. Good luck with that. Check your emails.

He'd added the crying with laughter emoji three times. How the hell did he know Rhys and I were engaged? Then I remembered Pete asking if he could tell Maria. News spread fast.

My fingers fumbled as I clicked into my emails. The title of Tony's message was 'Gardening boy gets his hose out.' As I clicked on each image, my heart thumped faster. Taken in Hearnshaw Park, they depicted a cosy sequence of Izzy and Rhys pushing Megan in her buggy, laughing as Izzy threaded her arm through Rhys's, Izzy touching his face, Rhys with his arms around her, and several pictures of them kissing.

Looking up from the photos and watching Rhys laughing as he chatted to Jenny, I thought about his apology card and picture, his proposal, and everything he'd said to me since. I touched my beautiful engagement ring, then reached for the glass heart on my necklace, recalling his words when he'd given me it: 'If you ever doubt me again, just look at this and know that my heart is – and always will be – yours.' And I knew.

Rhys ended the call. 'Mum's so excited about the wedding. She's dying to meet your mum.'

'I'm sure that can be arranged.' I sighed. 'I've got something to show you.' I passed him my phone and watched his eyes widen as he scrolled through the photos, shaking his head. 'This isn't what it looks like. I know that's a cliché said by men who've been caught cheating, but I swear that—'

I silenced him with a kiss. 'I know. I trust you.' I took my phone back and clicked on one of the photos that was clearly meant to show them kissing. 'I don't know what's really happening here but, if you had been kissing, Tony could have captured your faces easily. He'd have been dying to rub my face in that but obviously he couldn't because it was innocent.'

Rhys rubbed his hands across his eyes. 'Izzy said her necklace was caught in her hair.'

'And the one of her touching your face?'

'She said I had some mud on my cheek.' He took my phone and scrolled through to the one of Izzy with her arm threaded through his. 'She'd tripped over trying to avoid some swan poo and grabbed my arm, then she managed to stand in another pile. It was funny.'

'Do you think Izzy and Tony know each other?' I ventured. 'It seems very staged.'

'How would they know each other?'

I shrugged. 'I'm not sure. Maybe they don't. Maybe she has nothing to do with it and it's just been about Tony stalking you and trying to cause trouble.'

'He's a tosser. That's all. I know she's been a pain recently but I don't think even Izzy would pull a stunt like this. Although.... Shit! She wouldn't...' He picked up his phone and clicked on a few buttons. 'The little... ooh, I could kill her.'

'What's she done?'

'She kept going on about having a 'family selfie' this morning.' He made quote marks with his fingers. 'I didn't want to. I told her we weren't a family so she dropped the family bit but insisted it would be nice for Megan to have a photo of us all together on her first Christmas. I couldn't see the harm in that. Izzy took a couple of photos of the three of us, then she said something... I can't even remember what... but I remember turning my head to look at her and she kissed me and took a photo. I went mad with her and she tried to make out it had been a joke and she'd delete the photo. She's only gone and posted it on Facebook and tagged me in which means you'll get to see it.'

He handed me his phone and I grimaced at the caption:

Merry Christmas from me, my man, and my munchkin xx

Even if Rhys hadn't had his eyes wide open, clearly startled at the kiss, I'd have believed him. As soon as I'd discovered Tony's infidelity, it seemed so blindingly obvious and I couldn't believe I hadn't seen the signs. With Rhys, it was blindingly obvious that he was innocent and the guilty parties were Izzy and Tony. Whether they were doing it jointly or separately, I had no idea, but it was time it ended. Right now.

I handed Rhys his phone back. 'Fancy going out to spread a little Christmas cheer?'

He eyed me suspiciously. 'What are you thinking?'

'A couple of home visits. Izzy's at her mum's, yeah?'

'Yeah.'

'And you know where her mum lives?'

'Yeah.'

I wandered into the kitchenette and looked into the various bottle bags I'd been given at work. Selecting a couple of bags containing bottles of red wine, which neither Rhys nor I liked, I grinned at Rhys. 'We'll pay Tony a visit first and it would be rude to turn up on Christmas Day without a gift.'

40

We sat in Rhys's van outside Tony's house. I wasn't sure whether he was still living with his wife but I was pretty certain he'd be spending Christmas Day there even if she'd kicked him out. She didn't seem like the sort of woman who'd keep a father away from his kids. Whether they were a couple or not, how would she react if she knew about Maria and the baby?

✉ To Tony
Thanks for your Christmas gift.
You're too kind. I've got something
for you. I'm outside now ☺

It didn't take long for him to reply:

✉ From Tony
Outside where?

✉ To Tony
Outside your house. Or is it just
your wife's house now? You have one
minute

Rhys and I stepped out of the van and both leaned against the side, looking at Tony's house.

✉ From Tony
Sod off. It's not funny

✉ To Tony
Neither were those photos. Time's up

We marched up the drive to the right of the property and rang the bell.

'I'll get it!' I heard a woman shout. Next minute, the door opened revealing Hazel, a green paper hat jauntily angled on her head. I'd only seen her once before, the day I'd discovered Tony was really married with four kids. Back then, I'd been struck by how stunning she was and had been at a loss to understand why Tony had turned to me. The same thought popped into my head now.

'Hi,' she said, beaming at us.

"Hello. I'm Callie,' I said, wondering if she'd remember me from our brief encounter on the day I discovered the truth about Tony, or whether my name would be familiar, but there was no flicker of recognition, so I continued. 'This is my fiancé, Rhys. We're friends of Tony's. We wanted to drop round with a bottle of wine to say Happy Christmas and thanks to Tony for some photos he took of us recently.'

'Oh, how lovely.' Hazel took the bag from me. 'Tony's nipped out for a bit but he should be back soon. Do you want to come in and wait?'

I hesitated. Much as I'd love to see Tony squirming, it wasn't fair to Hazel and their kids to have us in their home. 'No. But I would like you to give Tony a message.' I bit my lip. I hated doing this, but Tony hadn't given me much choice. 'I lied when I said we were Tony's friends.'

'Oh. Then who are you?'

'We're the ones he assaulted in August. I promise we're not here to cause any trouble. It's just that Tony has—'

The lounge door burst open and a couple of kids came running out shouting, 'Mummy!'

Hazel turned around. 'Back in the lounge and stay there please. I'll be with you soon, but you must leave Mummy in peace for the moment to talk to these visitors. Understand?' Giggling, they chased each other back into the lounge. When the door had closed, Hazel turned back to Rhys and me and sighed.

'What's he done now?' she asked, her voice weary. 'Another affair? Punched someone else?' She leaned against the doorframe, looking completely defeated. 'You and Tony aren't...?'

I shook my head vigorously. 'God, no! I actually hoped I'd never have to see him again but he's broken the terms of his restraining order several times and he's been following Rhys, taking photos of him with his ex, and trying to make out there's something going on between them. I haven't been to the police yet, but that doesn't mean that I won't if it doesn't stop.'

Hazel gasped at the mention of the police and glanced back towards the lounge from where I could hear her children giggling. My heart went out to the poor woman and everything she must have put up with over the past months.

'I don't want to cause any more pain for you or your family,' I said, softly. 'You've been through enough already and I'm sure you want to move on. The thing is, I do too, but Tony seems intent on stopping me from doing so. Will you tell Tony that I don't appreciate his interference and, if he doesn't leave us alone, I'm sure the police will be very interested to hear what he's been up to?'

Hazel nodded. 'You're sure you're not...?'

'Seriously, I wouldn't touch him with a bargepole after discovering that he lies and cheats and hits people, and I can't believe you've let...' I stopped, holding my hands up. 'Sorry. I know nothing about your relationship and I get that it's more complicated because you've got kids. If you could just pass on that message, we'd be grateful.' I turned to head back down the drive.

'For all his many, many, faults, he's a good dad,' she said. 'When he's around.'

I turned round again. 'But is he a good husband? He can still be a good dad, even if he's not your husband.'

'You think I should leave him?'

'No. Make *him* do the leaving. If he thinks he's got away with it once, can you ever be sure that he's being completely—?' But I didn't have a chance to finish the sentence. The sound of a car horn followed by a screech of tyres announced Tony's return.

Leaving the car running, he leapt out of the car and slammed the door, taking a couple of strides towards us.

'What the hell do you think you're playing at?' he yelled.

Rhys stood up taller. 'We could say the same to you, stalking me, stalking Callie, sending her lies.'

'You deserved it. You ruined my life so now it's my turn to ruin yours.'

'I did *not* ruin your life,' I cried. 'You did that all by yourself. Why can't you see that?'

Jaw grinding, he looked towards Hazel. 'Why are you talking to them? You do know who they are?'

'Of course I know who they are,' she snapped. 'And Callie's right. Yes, she had an affair with you but she thought you were single.' She pushed back her shoulders and stepped out onto the drive. 'You hurt her and you hit him. That was all you, Tony. When will you ever grow up and take responsibility for your screw-ups? Speaking of which, who are you screwing now?'

'You bitch! You told her!' Tony lunged towards me but Rhys pushed him back and in an impressive manoeuvre, pinned Tony's arm behind his back and pushed his face down onto the bonnet of his car.

'Get off me!' Tony yelled, trying to wriggle free.

Hazel crouched down beside him. 'What's the matter, Tony?' she said in a sing-song voice. 'Does it hurt?'

'Yes! Bloody gardener's gone mad.'

'Good,' she snapped. 'I'm glad it hurts.' She gave him a shove. 'Because you've hurt me and you've hurt our kids and you've hurt Callie and Rhys and yet you *still* think it's everyone else's fault. Even now, you're blaming Callie for your latest sordid affair. But she didn't tell me. It was you who told me just now. So who is she?'

'Nobody.'

Rhys twisted Tony's arm even further and he cried out.

'Liar!' Hazel yelled. 'Who is she?'

'The stupid woman's obsessed with me and won't accept it's over.'

'*Who is she?*'

'Okay, okay, it's Maria. She worked with Callie.'

Hazel looked towards me. 'You knew her?'

'She was my friend. I only discovered he'd been seeing her after I found out about you and ended it. And I only recently found out about the...' I stopped myself just in time, but it hadn't gone unnoticed.

'You useless piece of shit,' Hazel spat, shoving him again.

'Ow!'

'Let him go, Rhys,' she said, shaking her head. 'He's not worth it.'

Tony staggered about, grimacing as he rubbed his arms and shoulders.

Hazel crossed her arms and scowled at Tony. 'I want you gone. Go on! Sod off back to your girlfriend and baby.'

'What baby?'

'Don't you dare. Don't you bloody dare. I'm not stupid so don't treat me as though I am. I had my suspicions before today so don't you go blaming any of this on them. Once again, Tony, it's all your fault.'

'But it's over.'

'No, it's not! This Maria woman is having your baby. How's that over?'

'It might not be mine. She's a right slag.'

Hazel stamped her feet and released a frustrated squeal. 'Jesus, Tony! Listen to yourself! Lying, blaming someone else and refusing to accept responsibility for your actions yet again. What's the matter with you?'

'I made a mistake. Two mistakes. Callie and Maria meant nothing to me. It's you I love. Always has been, always will be.'

'Is that meant to impress me? Am I meant to rush into your arms and tell you I love you too? Where's your respect for women? Look at her.' She pointed to me. 'Look at that beautiful woman. She's a human being with feelings, not a piece of rubbish for you to toss aside. I bet you told her you loved her too, yet you were busy getting her best friend pregnant while your wife was pregnant with your fourth child. How many others were there?'

'None.'

'I don't believe you.' She turned to Rhys and me. 'Do you believe him?'

I grimaced. 'Probably not.'

She turned back to Tony. 'I'll leave a suitcase of your stuff outside after the kids have gone to bed. You will not knock, ring, or do anything to try and get our attention. My solicitor will be in touch in the New Year.'

'And what if I refuse to leave?'

'Then I will insist that Callie and Rhys go to the police with the evidence that you've been stalking them. I think your new employer would be very interested to hear about the ABH charges too.'

'You wouldn't dare...'

Hazel folded her arms and stared at him. 'Oh, I would. And when you hear from my solicitor, you'll discover that I'm not the forgiving little wifey that you had me pegged as. You're going to pay for this.'

'Then you'll have a fight on your hands,' Tony growled as he got in the car and slammed the door shut.

'I can't wait.'

With a wheel spin, the car sped off the drive, screeching down the street.

The lounge window opened. 'Mummy! Liberty's got a piece of Lego stuck up her nose,' shouted one of the kids before slamming the window shut again.

Hazel took a deep breath. 'From one pleasant task to another, eh?'

'I'm so sorry,' I said. 'We probably shouldn't have come. I didn't want to cause trouble. All I wanted was for Tony to leave us alone.'

She smiled as she shook her head. 'It's fine. You simply gave me more reasons to be strong about it and not take any more of his bullshit excuses.'

The window opened again and another child poked their head out. 'It's okay. She's sneezed it out.'

Hazel laughed. 'Crisis averted, although now I have the pleasure of washing snot off a piece of Lego. Who'd have kids, eh?'

'We'd better leave you to it,' I said. 'I'm still sorry though.'

She shrugged. 'I'm sorry for what he's put you through. If you see this Maria, will you tell her she can do better and not to be scared about being on her own with a baby? I'm about to be on my own and, if I can do it with four kids under the age of seven, she can certainly do it with one.'

I nodded, although I doubted we'd be in touch unless it was for Maria to tear a strip off me for interfering again, as she saw it.

Hazel headed back towards the house as Rhys and I set off down the drive.

'Oh, Callie,' she called. 'Thanks for the wine. I think I'll be very grateful for that tonight. I hope you have some more at home as I think you might be in need of a stiff drink too.'

'I do. Enjoy it. And good luck.'

She smiled, waved, then closed the door. Rhys pulled me to his side and kissed the top of my head. 'Does it make me a bad person for enjoying that? The way Hazel kicked ass, that is, not what he's put her through.'

I squeezed him around the waist. 'If it does make you a bad person, then that's two of us off Santa's list next year. Ready for round two?'

'Bring it on.'

41

It had taken a lengthy text exchange with Rhys, but Izzy finally opened the door of her mum's house and stepped outside. Wearing skinny jeans tucked into Ugg boots and a sparkly silver top, she pulled on a puffer jacket. Rhys got out and walked around the van to lean against the side next to my door. I wound down the window, my heart thumping.

'What do you want?' she snapped, giving Rhys a filthy look.

So that was Izzy. She was very pretty, with expertly applied make-up and long blonde hair twisted into spiral curls.

'A few things,' Rhys said, 'but first I'd like to introduce you to my fiancée, Callie.'

Her eyes widened and her jaw tightened, but she blatantly refused to look at me. 'Your what?'

'My fiancée. I proposed yesterday.'

'Hi Izzy,' I said, cheerfully. 'It's nice to finally meet you.'

She looked in the other direction and I half expected her to say 'whatever', the petulant little brat. What had Rhys seen in her?

'Secondly, your little games are going to stop right now.'

'What games?'

'That family selfie this morning. What were you thinking of, kissing me then posting it on Facebook when I specifically asked you to delete it?'

'You were the one who kissed me.' She turned to me, grinning. 'Proper snog with tongues and everything.'

'Wow! You're a real class act, aren't you?' I shook my head, stunned at her audacity. 'Your mother must be so proud of you.'

'Meaning?'

'Let me see. There's how you got pregnant, using

your daughter like a bargaining chip, the fake selfie on Facebook, and paying my ex to take photos of you and Rhys in the park together.' I had no idea whether she had anything to do with it but calling her bluff was worth a try.

'Is that what he told you? The wanker still owes me the money.'

'You're friends with Tony?' I asked.

She screwed up her face. 'As if. Creepy old git.'

'How do you know him?' Rhys asked.

Izzy sighed. 'He'd followed you to the house one day so he knew where I lived. He said he needed revenge on Callie and did I want to help him for £100? Except he reckoned the photos weren't good enough so he wasn't going to cough up.'

'Yeah, well, I'd say goodbye to that money because Tony has other more pressing financial priorities now,' I said.

Izzy pouted. 'I knew I should have made him give me the money first. He said I could trust him.'

I laughed. 'Believe me, Tony is the last man on earth you can trust.'

'Are we done?' she asked, rolling her eyes.

'No,' Rhys said, 'we're not. Here's what's going to

happen. The constant phone calls and texts are going to stop. From now on, I only want to hear from you regarding arrangements to see Megan or if there's something genuinely wrong with her, which doesn't mean she's teething and needs Calpol. We'll also have regular access, we being Callie and me.'

'No way.' Izzy shook her head vigorously, narrowing her eyes at me.

'Yes, way,' Rhys continued.

'Good luck with that.' Izzy threw me a filthy look, then turned and started walking towards her mum's house.

'I'd hoped we could resolve this informally,' Rhys called. 'But have it your way. I'll call Social Services next week.'

Izzy stormed back towards him and jabbed him in the chest. 'You'd seriously take *my* baby away from me?'

'I have no intention of taking *our* daughter away from you but if you're not going to play fair with visiting rights, then I'll have no choice but to go down an official route and, while I'm at it, we'll sort out payments too. You and I both know I'm paying way more than I need to.'

'You're bluffing.'

'You think so?' Rhys shook his head. 'By the way, did you ever tell your family about how Megan was conceived? I'm sure they'd be fascinated to discover I'm not really the bad guy you've no doubt led them to think I am.' He turned to me. 'Where's that other bottle of wine?'

I handed him the second gift bag and he smiled at Izzy. 'Shall we go and wish your family a Merry Christmas?'

She grabbed the bag off him. 'You can have Megan tomorrow if you want.'

'Just me?' Rhys asked.

She scowled again. 'Both of you.'

Rhys grinned at her. 'That wasn't so difficult, was it? Merry Christmas, Izzy.'

'Piss off.' She stormed back to her mum's house, giving us the finger.

'Well, isn't she a delight?' I said when Rhys clambered back into the van.

He exhaled and his shoulders slumped. 'Not that I'm trying to defend her, but I've never seen her that bad. She can behave like a spoilt kid sometimes but the aggression was a new thing.'

I gently squeezed his thigh. 'Do you think it's over with them both?'

He shook his head. 'I'd love to say yes. You?'

'Same here. I think they've heard the message and they're scared, but I have a feeling this isn't over yet.'

Rhys started the engine. 'It's over for today, though. What time are we due at your mum's?'

'Not till six.'

'Then we have a couple of hours to make it a memorable Christmas for good reasons. Let's get out of here.'

* * *

Our final visit of the day couldn't have been more different. Nick answered the door, hugged me, and shook Rhys's hand.

'Nice apron,' I said, smiling at the Mrs Santa design.

'Argh! I forgot I was still wearing that.' He swiftly untied it and dropped it onto the floor.

'Happy Christmas!' Mum said as I bent down to

hug her. Seated in an armchair with her leg up on a footstool, the plaster-cast was wrapped in tinsel.

'Very festive.'

She smiled. 'The plain white was far too boring.'

Rhys hugged her then sat beside me on the sofa.

'So, how was your first Christmas together?' Mum asked.

Rhys and I exchanged smiles. 'Amazing,' I said. 'Rhys asked me to marry him.'

There were high-pitched squeals of excitement from Mum and slightly more manly ones from Nick, more hugs, and photos. Nick disappeared into the kitchen and returned with glasses of bubbly to toast our happy news.

As I relayed the story of Rhys's proposal, I tried not to think about the reaction Ed might be having to the news, or about the earlier confrontations with Tony and Izzy. Ruby, Jenny, Mum and Nick were all thrilled at the news and hopefully Jenny was right about Ed and change was afoot.

Nick had to head off early in the evening to exchange gifts with his girlfriend so I walked him to the door.

'I'm so chuffed for you both,' he said, hugging me again. 'And I think Rhys will make you really happy.'

'So do I. What about you and Lindsay? Going well?'

He shrugged. 'I like her but I'm approaching it cautiously. I'm taking it as a good sign that she wants to see me on Christmas Day when I know she usually spends the day with family.'

'And you're going out on New Year's Eve.'

He grimaced. 'To a toga party. What's that all about?'

'You'll have fun. I think. Never been to one myself.'

'There's probably a good reason for that.'

We hugged again and I waved him off then returned to the lounge where Mum was laughing at something Rhys was telling her. The affection she felt towards him was obvious. I watched them for a moment with a smile on my face. Would Ed ever be like that with me? I suspected not but I'd happily accept a polite truce. Something else to wish for...

42

'How are you feeling?' Rhys asked as we pulled up outside Izzy's house after lunch on Boxing Day.

'Ridiculously nervous. What if she doesn't like me?'

'She'll love you.'

It was a cold day but very still so we'd decided to take Megan for a walk down to South Bay.

Izzy was waiting outside her tiny two-bed terrace rocking Megan in her buggy. Bundled up in a snow-suit, she was fast asleep. What a stunning little girl, with pudgy pink cheeks, dark curly hair, and long thick eyelashes. I couldn't wait to see her awake.

'You're late,' Izzy snapped.

Rhys looked at his watch. 'By one minute.'

'You're still late. Bring her back by four at the latest.'

'We'll bring her back somewhere between four and five,' Rhys said, taking hold of the buggy.

With a tut, Izzy stepped back into the house and slammed the door. She hadn't looked at me in the whole of that time. Great.

* * *

Megan woke up shortly after we arrived on the seafront. She grinned when she spotted her daddy and giggled as he blew a raspberry on her cheek. Reaching for one of his dark curls, she yanked on it and giggled. Untangling himself, Rhys turned Megan round to face me. 'This is Callie, sweetie. Say hello.' He swooped her towards me, making her giggle again.

I loved watching Rhys with Megan. He seemed so relaxed and comfortable in the role of dad and, thankfully, he didn't laugh at me when it was obvious I had no idea how to hold a child. 'Do I have to support her head?'

'Not at this age. Only when they're babies but she's nearly one now. You need a firm hold, though, as she's like a wriggly snake.'

We had such a lovely afternoon together. Megan was the complete opposite to her mum: warm, affectionate and full of giggles.

'She's beautiful, Rhys,' I said as we walked back towards Izzy's house a couple of hours later. 'Do you think she could be a flower girl at our wedding?'

'I'd love that. I can't guarantee she'd do what she's meant to, but she'd definitely look cute.'

When we arrived back at Izzy's, she answered the door in her dressing gown. Megan put out her arms and started squirming in her buggy. 'Hi, precious. Have you missed me?' Izzy bent down and picked her up, cuddling her close. 'I've missed you so much. Did you have a lovely time with Daddy?'

Watching her with her daughter, I saw a different side to Izzy. The sulky brat was gone and she seemed normal. And nice.

* * *

On the way home, a text arrived. 'It's from Maria.'

'A mouthful of abuse?' Rhys asked.

'No, it's... oh my God!'

✉ From Maria
Thought you might be interested to
know that you were wrong about Tony.
He's left his wife and moved in
with me. He can't wait for the baby
to arrive so we can be a proper
family

'Will that man ever stop lying?' I said to Rhys.

✉ To Maria
When did this happen?

✉ From Maria
Not that it's any of your business
but he moved in this afternoon. Said
he didn't think it was fair to tell
her he wanted a divorce on Christmas
Day

I bit my lip. 'So if he only moved in this afternoon, where do you think he was last night and this morning?'

Rhys glanced at me; eyebrows raised. 'Do you really need to ask?'

'Should I tell her?'

'I think you should stay out of it. She's made her bed.'

'But she's having his baby.'

We'd arrived back at my flat so Rhys pulled into a parking space and we headed into the flat before continuing the conversation.

'I know she was your friend,' Rhys said as we plonked ourselves down on the sofa, 'and I know you still care about her, but she did the dirty on you and now Tony's very likely doing the same to her. I can't help thinking it's karma.'

I ran my fingers through my hair and released a frustrated squeal. 'I know but I can't help thinking about that poor little baby. And Maria is really vulnerable, despite making out that she isn't.'

'I'll never tell you what to do but my very strong advice would be to leave it alone. Send her a text wishing her well, then cease contact.'

I scrolled through the texts from her, wincing at

the aggression in them. Rhys was right, but my conscience wouldn't let me leave it completely alone.

✉ **To Maria**
I hope you know what you're doing because, if you ask me, leopards don't change their spots. Be careful xx

✉ **From Maria**
I didn't ask you so you know where you can stick your unwanted opinions

'Maybe you should introduce her to Izzy,' Rhys said when I showed him Maria's response. 'They're like peas in a pod.' He took my hand and squeezed it. 'You're a good friend to Maria, even if she doesn't deserve it. And you were amazing with Megan today. She loved you.'

'Do you think so? I'm used to being round people at the other end of the path of life. I don't know anyone with kids.'

'You were a natural. You'll be a brilliant mum when we have our own... assuming this afternoon hasn't put you off having kids.'

I changed position so that I could gently kiss Rhys. 'Definitely not. If anything, being around Megan has made me a bit broody.' I kissed him again. 'I'm not quite ready for kids yet, but I'm not averse to practising making them.'

As I lifted my T-shirt off, then pulled Rhys's over his head, I closed my mind to Maria. She was making a mistake but that was her choice and I'd done everything I could to warn her. From now on, my focus was on my gorgeous fiancé.

43

I spotted Ruby shortly before my shift ended the following day and my stomach lurched. Postal deliveries would resume in a couple of days' time so Teddy would receive my letter. Should I warn Ruby? What good would it do, though? I was a nervous wreck thinking about Teddy receiving the letter, so imagine the state Ruby could get in if she knew I'd made contact. I also felt guilty as hell. Lies. Deceit. But my intentions were honourable.

'Are you all right, my darling?' Ruby asked. 'You look a bit pale.'

'Just tired. There's been a lot going on.'

'You youngsters, you've got no staying power

these days. I used to perform until late, go out dancing until the small hours and be fresh as a daisy the next day.'

'With Teddy?'

'Yes, with Teddy,' she said wistfully, then straightened up. 'And with other suitors before him. Teddy and I... well, I wasn't the one he was meant to find.'

'But he did find you and he loved you.'

'Yes, darling, but that's in the past. I'm more interested in the future so sit down and tell me more about your wedding plans.'

And the subject was changed. Again.

* * *

Rhys was waiting for me under the covered entrance at the end of my shift, pacing up and down, scowling into his phone.

'What's she done now?' I asked. When I'd seen him at lunchtime, Rhys told me that Izzy had phoned asking if he could babysit Megan that evening. Apparently she had a last minute opportunity to go to a gig with her best friend, Jess. Rhys said no because we were going out for a meal at a potential wedding venue. Why had he been so honest? It was the sort of plan she loved to mess up for us.

'She's at it again. Supposedly Megan's got a rash and she's terrified it's meningitis.'

'Has she called the NHS Helpline?' I asked.

'I don't think so.'

'Has she rolled a glass over it?'

Rhys looked at me blankly and I shook my head. 'Come on. We'll go there now. If she has got meningitis, which I very much doubt, then we need to get her to hospital. We can quickly confirm it, though.'

* * *

'What are *you* doing here?' Izzy snarled at me when she opened the door.

'Callie's a first-aider and she knows what she's looking for,' Rhys said.

Izzy's eyes widened, then she looked down at her arm, scratching her nail over the sleeve of her hoodie as though removing a piece of muck. Imaginary muck. 'I think I might have over-reacted. She seems okay now. Thanks for checking.'

She tried to close the door but I wasn't having

any of it and pushed past her. 'I'd rather take a look, just to be on the safe side. You can't be too careful where little ones are concerned.'

Megan was seated on a colourful play mat in the middle of the small lounge, poking brightly-coloured wooden shapes into a holder. She looked over at me and waved her arms in the air as though she wanted me to pick her up.

'Hello, sweetheart,' I said, unwinding my scarf and slipping off my coat as I sat down beside her. She handed me a purple triangle covered in slobber. 'Is that for me? How kind are you?' I held the back of my hand against her forehead. It was a little clammy but no more than I'd have expected considering how warm Izzy had the room. Megan's cheeks were pink but that was also expected because she was teething again.

'Has she been sick?' I asked, turning to Izzy.

'She brought up some of her dinner.'

'Has she eaten since and kept it down?'

Izzy shrugged.

'Has she?' Rhys snapped.

'Yes. She's kept it down. Happy?'

'There is nothing about this situation right now

that makes either of us very happy,' I said. 'But you called Rhys in a panic and mentioned meningitis. Either you are genuinely worried about her or you're making it up and causing trouble again.'

Izzy glared at me. 'She does have a rash.'

'Where?'

'On her tummy.'

'Then I'd like you to fetch me a glass.'

'What? Why?'

'A glass. Now. Ideally one with a smooth edge to it.'

Muttering under her breath, Izzy stormed out of the room. Rhys and I exchanged exasperated looks.

'Right, sweetie,' I said, turning back to Megan. 'Let's have a look at your tummy.' I gently laid her on her back and unfastened her clothes. No rash. *Quelle surprise!*

Izzy reappeared and thrust a glass at me. 'It's under her nappy.'

I undid the tags on either side of her nappy expecting to find nothing but there actually was a rash. I slowly rolled the glass across the redness, holding my breath. Phew! 'It's not meningitis.'

'How do you know?' Rhys asked.

'Not everyone with meningitis gets a rash but, if they do, one of the tests is to roll a glass over it. If you can still see the rash where the glass is pressing, then we need to be worried. If you can't see the rash where the glass is pressing, then it's not meningitis and, as you can see, the rash disappears when I press the glass on it.' I showed them both, then looked up at Izzy. 'Her nappy's wet. Do you have a fresh one?'

'Of course I do.' She disappeared for a moment and returned with supplies. I reached out for the items but she glowered at me. 'She's *my* daughter. *I'll* change her.'

'Be my guest.' I moved to one side. 'I think it's nappy rash,' I said as I watched Izzy deftly change Megan. 'But you knew that, didn't you?'

Izzy paused for a couple of seconds then resumed what she was doing.

'For God's sake, Izzy,' Rhys said. 'You're like the boy who cried wolf. What if she's really ill one day? I'm not going to believe you, am I?'

'It *could* have been meningitis,' she muttered.

Rhys helped me to my feet. 'We're going out now. And while we're out, I suggest you think very carefully about what I said on Christmas day.'

Nappy changed and clothes back in place, Izzy picked up Megan and kissed her cheek, holding her close. 'Are you threatening me?'

'No. It's not a threat,' Rhys said. 'It's a promise.'

* * *

Rhys reached for my hand as we returned to his van, but I snatched it away.

'What's wrong?' he asked.

'Her. Again. Is she always going to be like this?'

'I've tried talking to her. You've seen what she's like. You've seen how selfish and self-centred she is. She doesn't listen to me. The only one she ever listens to is her friend, Jess.'

'Then tell this Jess to have a word.' I clambered into the van and slammed the door shut.

'Callie!' Rhys ran round to his side and got in beside me. 'I barely know Jess and I'm not dragging anyone else into this. I'll keep trying with Izzy. Something will get through to her eventually.'

'You think so?' I clicked my seatbelt on. 'I hope you're right because I don't think she'll ever change. What the bloody hell did you ever see in her?'

Rhys started the ignition. 'I could say the same about you and Tony but you don't hear me going on and on about it, do you?'

We drove home in silence and I had this terrible fear of this argument playing on continuous repeat for the rest of our lives.

When we arrived back at my flat, I sighed. 'Sorry, Rhys, but I'm not in the mood for going out tonight. Will you phone them and cancel?'

'If that's what you want,' he said.

'No, it's not, but I'm too wound up to enjoy it so I think we'd better cancel otherwise that's a potential wedding venue tainted by Izzy and her games.'

He reached out for a hug and I cuddled against him telling myself that it wasn't his fault, but it was all so exhausting and the thought that there'd never be an end to it absolutely terrified me.

44

'No! Don't do this to me.' I slammed the mouse on the desk the following day and pounded the wheel a little too aggressively as I scrolled up and down the spreadsheet I'd spent the last couple of hours updating. Except my updates weren't there. 'Argh! I hate you.'

'Is that how you greet all your visitors these days?'

I looked up, startled to hear the voice of my former boss. 'Denise! I wasn't expecting to see you today.' We'd stayed in touch after her attempted suicide, even meeting for coffee on a few occasions. She'd been eager to apologise for how she'd treated me and I'd been happy to draw a line in the sand and do what I could to help her move forward.

'Bringing belated Christmas gifts.' She held up her arms, laden with bags. 'Is this a bad time?'

'No. Please come in. Actually your timing couldn't be better. The computer was close to being thrown out the window.' She sat down opposite me and I picked up a pen. 'So, tell me why you think you're a good candidate for a position at Bay View?'

Denise laughed. 'Sitting across the desk like this, it does feel like I'm being interviewed. My palms are starting to sweat. I'm appalling at interviews. I still don't know how I secured the role here.'

'How are you holding up?' I asked.

Denise took a deep breath and nodded. 'Good days and bad days. Mainly good, though.'

'We missed you at Iris's wedding. She says you were poorly.'

'A little white lie. My ex-husband's new girlfriend had their baby on the twenty-third.'

'Ooh. That must have been tough.'

'The ridiculous thing is that I had four months to get my head around Gavin's new life and prepare for the baby arriving. I even knew it was a boy and that they were going to call him Freddie, yet the birth announcement absolutely floored me.'

'You didn't...?'

She shook her head. 'But I'd be lying if I said it never crossed my mind. I phoned my counsellor and she calmed me down and helped me focus on all the great things I have to live for next year. My little sister, Ellen, is expecting her first baby in June and I've decided that it may not be my destiny to be a mother myself but I can make sure I'm a damn good auntie and help out Ellen whenever she needs me. And I'm moving out of *the marital home.*' She said those words as though they were dirty ones. 'It's a family home – that's why we bought it – but the family never came. I don't think rattling round on my own in all that space was doing me any good so Gavin's buying me out. They're moving in and I'm buying a two-bed cottage in Great Sandby.' Her eyes lit up as she talked about her new home and the knot in my stomach loosened. She was going to be okay.

'It sounds lovely. I trust I'll be invited to the housewarming.'

'If it wasn't for you, there'd be no house to warm

because there'd be no me. I still owe you my life. Literally.'

Tears pricked my eyes and I tried to block out the image of her collapsed on the floor in the laundry room, an empty bottle of pills beside her. There wasn't anything I could say. 'You're welcome' or 'any time' didn't seem like appropriate responses so I simply smiled.

'Oh. And guess what?' she added. 'I'm coming back.'

'To work?'

She nodded. 'It'll be a phased return starting mid-January. Only a couple of half-days at first but we'll build it up over time and the hope is that I'll be back full-time by the end of March.'

'That's wonderful news. It'll be great to have you back.'

'I've missed this place so much,' Denise said. 'And... oh my goodness, I've just spotted something sparkly on your left hand and can't believe I didn't notice it sooner. Congratulations! When? How?'

Denise and I chatted for another twenty minutes or so before she announced she'd better leave me to it. She lifted up a gift bag. 'This is for you and I want no arguments and no guilt that you haven't got me anything. It's a sort of thank-you gift for everything you've done for me. It's something very relevant to me right now and it makes me cry, but it's something everyone needs to think about as we can all... you know... have dark days.' She stopped and shook her head. 'Listen to me. You haven't even opened it and I'm a gibbering wreck.' She placed the bag on the desk and gently pushed it towards me.

'Denise, you shouldn't—'

'What did I just say? No arguments.'

'Thank you, then. But there really was no need.'

The office phone rang.

'I'll pop in to say goodbye before I go,' Denise said, picking up the rest of her bags and heading for the door. I nodded and waved before picking up the phone.

The gift bag beckoned me as soon as the call ended and I lifted out a photo frame made from driftwood. Instead of a picture it contained a quote on cream textured paper: *Life is not about waiting for the storm to pass. It's about learning to dance in the rain.* I read the words over and over. Yes, they were perfect for Denise and her daily battle with her mental health, but she was right that they could be relevant to anyone and, for the last four months, very apt for me. I'd let that storm hang over me with Tony, Izzy, Rhys's dad and even Ruby's situation with Teddy. I hadn't been my usual optimistic self, yet Rhys had stuck by my side every step of the way. He'd never moaned once about how stressed I'd become by the whole thing, yet how had I treated him? I'd had yet another go at him about Izzy's latest trick after he'd tried his best to resolve things. If I wanted Rhys in my life, I was going to have to accept that, because Megan was part of the deal, so was Izzy. I needed to find a way to rise above it.

Propping up the frame on my desk, I smiled. Yes, I *was* going to learn to dance in the rain and hopefully the rain would stop one day.

During my break an hour later, I found Rhys in the tool shed sawing a piece of wood, headphones in his ears, singing along to something on his phone. I loved hearing him sing, although sing was perhaps not the right word for it. Caterwaul perhaps?

He finished sawing the wood at the point the song finished, reaching some sort of unrecognisable high-pitched crescendo and punching his hand in the air. His smile dropped when he spotted me. 'How long have you been there?'

I grinned. 'Long enough, Freddie Mercury.'

He put the saw down on the workbench. 'Let's not mention this again, eh? Is that for me?'

Nodding, I handed him a mug of coffee, from which he took a couple of eager gulps. 'I needed that. Thanks. Could have done with an Irish one, though.'

'Bad morning?'

'She's been at it again.'

'Izzy? You're joking. Megan again?'

'No. Izzy this time. She reckons she's really ill. Stomach cramps, feeling sick, headache. Wants me to go round and look after Megan.'

'You're not going, are you?'

'What do you think? After last night, I don't believe a word she says. She'll either have a hangover, period pains or bullshititis.'

I laughed. 'I suspect the last one.'

'Me too.'

Rhys hugged me. 'I'm sorry about all the crap she's been putting us through. I want to say I wish I'd never met her but that's not true because that would mean no Megan. I do wish she wasn't so high-maintenance, though.'

'You have nothing to apologise for. It's me who needs to say sorry for being so awkward about things. I know it's not your fault she's how she is and I shouldn't be taking it out on you, especially when I brought Tony into our lives and he's someone I *do* regret meeting.'

He kissed me gently. 'From now on, we won't let them get us down. We—'

But he was interrupted by his phone ringing. 'Sorry, Cal... Izzy? What now? No... Because I don't believe you. I'm taking Callie out for a meal tonight after you ruined our plans last night... Then ask Jess... Seriously, Izzy, stop calling me. If you're that ill, call an ambulance.' Then he hung up.

'She certainly scores ten out of ten for persistence,' I said. 'How many times has she called?'

'Four or five.' He shrugged. 'Maybe six times.'

My stomach tightened and alarm bells started ringing in my head. I hadn't been able to hear the exact words Izzy said but I'd certainly been able to pick up on the tone and she'd sounded quite desperate. Could that have been part of the act? 'She's never pestered you that much before.'

'That's because I've always rushed to her aid. This is obviously the new tactic to keep ringing until I drop everything.'

I nodded slowly. 'Perhaps. Oh well, I'd best get back to work.'

Rhys kissed me again before I opened the shed door to leave. But something was niggling me. 'You mentioned tonight. Was she wanting you to babysit?'

'No. Get this, right. She wanted us to have Megan overnight.'

'Us as in you and me? Don't you think that's a bit strange going from me not being allowed to see Megan to letting me have her overnight?'

'Very. Maybe it's part of her latest twisted game.'

'Or maybe she is genuinely ill this time.'

'You think so?'

I shrugged. 'I don't know. Something about this time feels different. And she doesn't normally pester you at work either.'

Rhys dialled her back. I could hear the phone ringing out at Izzy's end but not connecting.

'Try again,' I urged when he hung up, but the same thing happened.

'You'd better go,' I said. 'I'll lock up. Hopefully it's nothing.'

* * *

Forty minutes later Rhys called. 'I'm at the hospital. She'd collapsed.'

'On my God. Is she okay?'

'I hope so. It's a burst appendix. The paramedic said she was in a bad way but they think they got to her in time.' There was a pause. 'What if she hadn't phoned while you were there? I'd never have gone round. She could have—'

'Stop it. You can't think like that. She's the one who cried wolf too many times. She's to blame. Not you. You saved her life.'

'*You* saved her life.'

'*We* saved her life. Where's Megan?'

'With me. She was asleep at the time. I'm going to find out how Izzy is, then I'll go back to the house with Megan.'

'Do you want me to come round when I've finished?'

'Yes please.' Rhys sounded exhausted.

'I can ask to leave now. I'm sure Ian would understand.'

'No. There's no point. There's nothing you can do here but I appreciate it. I love you.'

'I love you too.'

I hung up and went to find Ruby to put her in the picture. It touched me to hear the musical teddy bear playing when she led me into the lounge area. 'It's a beautiful piece,' I said.

'If I close my eyes, I'm back in the concert hall listening to Teddy playing it on the piano.' She shook her head as though trying to dislodge the memory. 'What can I do for you, darling?'

Sighing, I explained what had been going on with Izzy and her demands on Rhys, culminating in the latest genuine cry for help, which was very nearly ignored.

'Why didn't she call anyone else?' Ruby asked.

'Rhys said her mum and sister went to Spain on Boxing Day to stay with her grandma who emigrated over there, and her best friend is away too. I'm not sure she has anyone else.'

'How sad. I always got the impression she had lots of friends but maybe that changed after Megan was born. Well, I hope she gets well soon, but she's a very silly little girl and I hope this is a terrifying wake-up call for her to grow up and take some responsibility for herself.'

'Did you see much of her when she and Rhys were together?'

'Only a couple of times. He brought her round to the house before I moved in here. She seemed like a pleasant enough young woman so I'd never have expected this sort of shenanigans from her. I didn't think she was right for Rhys, mind.'

'Why?'

'Something about how they were together. They were awkward in each other's company, like two people with very little in common who'd been set up on a blind date. I was always surprised it lasted a couple of months instead of a couple of weeks.'

'Having met her twice now, I can't see why it even lasted a couple of hours, although I'm sure Rhys probably thinks the same about Tony. Each to their own, eh?'

'Don't keep punishing yourself about Tony. He was a charming man. He had everyone fooled.'

'Except you.'

'That's because I recognised him from where I used to live, darling. That Iris Davies thought he was wonderful and many of the others who met him did too.'

Ruby stood up and wandered over to the window. She had an amazing view over the gardens and North Bay beyond. Looking out the window, with her back to me, she said, 'Before I moved to Devon, dear George's sister, Frances, challenged me about walking out of Teddy's life. She'd seen Teddy and Gabriella together once and had been astonished when somebody told her they were married. She described them as "uncomfortable strangers" just like Rhys and Izzy. She said George and I were "extremely comfortable companions" and that Teddy and I were "two halves of the same person".' She turned to me. 'I'm not sure where I'd classify you and Tony because, other than that horrible day when you found out about his wife, I never saw you together outside of work. You and Rhys, though, are definitely two halves of the same person.'

'Like you and Teddy.'

She nodded.

'Then why don't you make contact with him? Gabriella's dead and...' I stopped when I saw Ruby's eyes widen. Crap! I'd given myself away.

'You looked him up?'

'I'm sorry. I couldn't resist. He's still pretty yummy.'

I thought Ruby was going to tell me off, but her expression softened. 'Yes, he still has it.' She sat down in her chair again. 'Gabriella's dead?'

'Eight years ago. But they'd divorced long before that. She married three more times after Teddy.'

'And Teddy? He remarried?'

'Not as far as I could tell.'

Ruby leaned back in her chair and closed her eyes. She breathed in deeply, exhaled, then repeated that before opening her eyes again. 'I keep saying it's too late and our time has passed, but you don't think it's too late, do you, darling?'

I took her hand in mine and squeezed it. 'It's never too late.'

She squeezed my hand back. 'Let's get this New Year's Eve party out of the way and then I'll think about it.'

'For Teddy *and* for Ed?'

'Goodness me, you are persistent.'

I stood up and smiled at her. 'What do I always say is my number one priority?'

'Making the residents happy.'

'And I know that getting in touch with your soulmate and your son will ultimately make you happy so I'm going to keep nagging.'

45

'Izzy wants to see you,' Rhys said when I arrived at the hospital after my shift.

'Me? Why?'

He shrugged as he took over from me, gently pushing Megan's buggy back and forth in the hospital corridor.

Taking a deep breath, I headed down the corridor towards Chestnut Ward. Looking so pale that her face appeared almost transparent, Izzy was dozing as I approached her bed. I hesitated. Should I wake her? We weren't friends so it didn't seem appropriate to sit beside her while she was sleeping. The decision was taken out of my hands when a patient on another bed coughed loudly. Izzy opened her eyes, looked momentarily disorientated, then spotted me hovering near the end of her bed. Her lips were dry and cracked and she started coughing as soon as she tried to speak. Dashing forward, I grabbed the jug of water on her bedside cabinet and poured her a cup as she pressed the button to raise the top half of her bed. I held the drink to her mouth and she took a few sips.

'Thank you.'

'How are you feeling?' I asked, lowering myself onto the bedside chair.

'Sore and tired.'

'I'm not surprised. Sounds nasty.'

'It was... I was lucky... Have you to thank.' She was clearly exhausted, struggling to speak in full sentences. 'Rhys told me... He wouldn't have...'

'It wasn't his fault, though.' I grimaced. I'd just implied that it was her fault. Although it was.

'Been stupid... So sorry...' A tear ran down her cheek. 'Could've left my baby with no mum.'

Noticing a box of tissues by the water jug, I pulled one out and passed it to her.

'Don't think like that,' I assured her. 'Consider it a

tough lesson learned. It happens to all of us. Maybe not with such a dramatic outcome, but we all make mistakes. It's what makes us human.'

Izzy wiped her eyes and blew her nose. Lying back on her pillow, she stared at the ceiling. 'Thought I had it all worked out. Perfect life planned... baby... house. Only needed the man.' She coughed. 'Saw Rhys and it had to be him.' She smiled as though fondly recalling the evening they'd met. 'That hair... those eyes... He's gorgeous. Our baby would be too.'

My jaw tightened, listening to her talking about my fiancé in that way. I dreaded to know where this was going, but I stayed quiet and let her continue.

Izzy sighed. 'Never thought of the impact on him. Changed his life because it suited me.' She shook her head. 'Had no right to make that decision. Can't regret it cos I love Megan. Don't love Rhys. Lovely guy. Gorgeous. Doesn't do it for me, though.'

'Just as well you're not engaged to him, then, isn't it?' I bit my lip again. Why couldn't I just think things?

Izzy turned her head towards me again. 'You're funny. You say what you think. My sister does that.'

'I sometimes wish I didn't.'

'Not trying to steal Rhys. Not that I could, even if I wanted to.'

'Then why did you kiss him? Why did you keep calling him round on nights you knew he was with me? It doesn't make sense.'

She coughed and I handed her some water to sip again.

'Thought I'd be happy,' she continued. 'Thought this was the life I wanted but...' She paused. 'It's hard work on my own. Most friends ditched me... Go out drinking, but I'm the boring one with the baby. My best mate, Jess, loves Megan but she's with Lee. Barely see her. Got jealous of Rhys and his freedom. Didn't want to be with him but didn't want anyone else to be. Wanted Megan and me to be his main priority.' She looked at me again and another tear rolled down her cheek. 'I panicked when you were serious. What if you had babies and he didn't want Megan anymore?'

'You must know that he'd never abandon Megan, even if he had a dozen kids with me.'

She seemed to sink further into the mattress. 'I

do. But when you're alone with a crying baby at three in the morning... Too much thinking time.'

Izzy's eyelids kept flickering and I could tell she was struggling to stay awake. 'You'd better get some sleep.'

'I'm a nice person really... I'll show you I am. So sorry...' And then she was gone.

I pressed the button to lower the bed and tucked her arms under the covers. However selfish and misguided her actions with Rhys had been around Megan's conception, the result had been a gorgeous little girl and nobody could ever regret that happening. Everything since then had been the actions of a lonely young woman who clearly hadn't considered the consequences. It was time to draw a line in the sand and move on.

* * *

'I keep thinking about Maria,' I said as I snuggled up to Rhys on the sofa at Izzy's house late that evening. Megan was settled in her cot, although for how long was anyone's guess. Apparently she was going through a particularly unsettled period, tending to wake in the early hours.

Rhys shifted position so he could look at me. 'I thought you'd decided that she wasn't worth it.'

'I had, but what Izzy said got me thinking. I reckon Maria's lonely too. I told you about her family, didn't I? She never seemed to have many friends, either. Pete and I were the only ones she was close to at work. I know Pete still sees her but I don't think she has anyone else.'

'She's got Tony.'

I nudged him. 'That's probably worse than having nobody.'

We fell silent for a while. 'Why don't you call her?' Rhys suggested eventually. 'Not now, obviously, but maybe in the New Year? Give her one more chance. But if she gives you a mouthful again, can you promise me you'll let it go? I hate seeing you so worried about it all. You can't keep pushing against a closed door, you know. Sometimes it'll never open.'

I laughed. 'That sounds very wise and profound, Mr Michaels.'

'I'd like to take credit, but it's something Mum

used to say about me trying to convince Dad to meet with Ruby.'

'I suppose you're both right. Although sometimes it does just take that one final push for the door to open.' I kissed him. 'Thank you for understanding about Maria and I promise I'll let it go after this final push.'

* * *

I woke up, heart thumping. What the hell was that noise? Then I registered where I was.

'I'll go,' Rhys mumbled.

Pressing my phone beside the bed, I frowned. 1.18 a.m. Urgh. We'd only been asleep for about an hour. A streetlight outside Izzy's house cast a faint glow into the room so I lay back in the semi-darkness, cringing as I listened to Megan squawking. She'd cried a little when we'd been out with her on Boxing Day, but this was something else. How could something so small create such a hideous racket? I picked up my phone again and Googled '*How to stop a baby from crying*'.

Fifteen minutes later, Rhys reappeared, with a

screaming Megan squirming in his arms, all red cheeks and flailing fists. 'I'm out of ideas.' He looked at me helplessly. 'I've changed her and tried her with a bottle but nothing works.'

'I've Googled it and it's a minefield. The only sensible suggestion I can find for now is to take her for a drive. Worth a try?'

'I'm up for anything.'

Rhys disappeared to start the engine and get the heating going as we didn't want to add freezing van to her list of woes, which left me to wrestle her into a fleecy sleepsuit. And I mean wrestle. I actually had sweat trickling into my eyes by the time I'd finished.

The drive from Izzy's to North Bay was fraught. Megan's fists continued to flail and her legs kicked as she let the whole world know about her displeasure. The roads were deserted and rightly so. Who in their right mind would be driving around in the early hours of a Thursday morning?

North Bay and South Bay are connected by The Headland – a road that runs the entire two-and-a-half miles from Hearnshaw Park in the north to the site of the old lido in the south, passing over the river and harbour below Whitsborough Bay Castle roughly halfway. With roundabouts at either end, it provided the ideal loop to hopefully lull Megan back to sleep.

Megan's sobs started to decrease in intensity as we approached the roundabout at South Bay on our first pass along the seafront. By the time we'd made it to the castle on the return journey, she was sound asleep.

'You're a genius, Cal,' Rhys said, glancing down at his peaceful daughter. 'That was the worst noise in the world.'

'I know! I thought my ears were going to start bleeding. Respect to Izzy if she's been putting up with that.'

'I need to give her more help. I had no idea.'

'Why would you?' I said. 'She never told you. And it hasn't always been like this, has it?'

'True. Izzy doesn't have a car, though. I wonder how the hell she settles her.'

After rounding The Headland, we passed a small car park; a popular spot for couples. I gasped as I clocked the unmistakable private registration plate of one of the cars parked there.

'That's Tony's car,' I said. 'Why would he bring

Maria here now that he's living with her?' Even as I said the words, I knew the answer, and Rhys's sympathetic sideways glance confirmed it. 'Except that won't be Maria he's with, will it? God, Rhys, will that man ever learn to keep it in his pants?'

'Maybe you should make that final push on the door tomorrow?' he suggested.

'And tell her about this?'

'I don't know. Maybe. Wouldn't you rather have known?'

We completed the lap and set off on our second one, then our third. My stomach churned each time we passed the car park and Tony's car was still there. The streetlights were too dim for me to see inside the car. I hoped that it was my imagination that had it rocking, but suspected it wasn't.

On our fourth lap, with Megan completely zonked out beside me, I whispered to Rhys to slow down. A couple were leaning against Tony's car. The headlights from Rhys's van briefly illuminated his face and the back of her hair. Her auburn hair. Definitely not Maria, then.

46

We'd been worried that Megan wouldn't settle in her nursery and we'd have to strap her back into the van and drive up and down the seafront all morning. Thankfully it seemed that the drive had soothed her into a deep sleep because she didn't even stir as I slipped her out of her sleepsuit and laid her back in her cot.

Rhys was up again for work a couple of hours later. Feeling drained after he left, I lay back and closed my eyes, only to be woken five minutes later by Megan grizzling. I prepared myself for high-pitched wailing again but picking her up for a cuddle instantly placated her. Phew!

It was my day off although I suspected that a day with Megan, when I hadn't a clue what I was doing, was going to be far more demanding than the toughest of days at work.

Despite Izzy's apology the evening before, I wasn't exactly comfortable about turning up at hospital with Megan but no Rhys. I wasn't exactly comfortable in her house on my own either. Feeling like an intruder, I was grateful that the mugs and teabags were on display because I wouldn't have felt right riffling through her cupboards to find them.

I felt much more relaxed in Megan's nursery. It was beautifully decorated with a lilac and purple owl-theme contrasting against the white furniture. One of the walls contained a large decal of cute cartoon owls in a tree and there were various soft owls and owl-themed cushions around the room. Picking out an outfit for Megan to wear was great fun. Despite limited income, Izzy certainly made sure Megan wanted for nothing with a wardrobe and drawers bursting with clothes. I eventually settled on a cute purple cord pinafore with an applique owl on the front, over a pink top and striped tights. Lifting

Megan off her changing mat and holding her pudgy cheek against mine, I felt broody again. Last night had been horrendous but it was worth it for the cuddles.

After feeding her, I sat Megan on her play mat with a selection of colourful wooden blocks and some plastic stacking cups. 'Auntie Callie is going to make a phone call and then we'll get the bus to the hospital to see your mummy,' I told her. 'Would you like that?'

Megan grinned at me as she knocked over the pile of cups I'd just stacked. I sat on the floor beside her and stacked them again as I waited for the call to connect to Maria's mobile. I wasn't sure if she was still working at The Chocolate Pot or whether she'd have finished at Christmas, being heavily pregnant at that point. After ringing out for ages, it connected to voicemail. Knowing I'd make a mess of it, I decided not to leave a message.

'Let's stack these for you again,' I said to Megan, but the little monkey swiped at them, giggling, before I'd even managed to build half the tower. 'Cheat!'

I gave it another ten minutes then tried Maria again. This time it cut off before reaching voicemail, suggesting she'd disconnected the call herself.

As I pushed Megan's buggy up the street towards the bus stop, I tried one more time. This time, Maria answered.

'If a person doesn't answer, don't you think that's a pretty big clue that they're not interested in speaking to you?' She sounded exhausted rather than angry.

'I know, but I'm worried about you. I wanted to check you're okay and that Tony's...' I paused. How could I phrase it? 'That Tony's treating you well.'

'When will you get it through to your thick skull that we're not friends anymore and therefore it's not up to you to worry about me?'

'I know, but I still care, and it's just that—'

'It's just that you have to fix people, don't you? You want everyone to be happy and for life to be perfect but, do you know what? It isn't like that. Ever. Life is full of liars, cheats, and people who let you down and it's about time you accepted that instead of childishly believing you can change people and help them live happily ever after.'

'Has Tony done something to you?'

'Like what? Tony loves me. He left his wife for me and we're going to get married after the baby's born.'

'But I thought... well, you talked about liars and cheats and I wondered if...' I couldn't say it. I couldn't even hint at it. How useless was I?

'What is it with you and Tony?' she snapped. 'Is gardening boy not man enough for you? You can't have Tony back, you know.'

I recoiled. As if I'd want him back after what he did. But there was nothing to be gained by slagging him off. 'I'm really pleased it's all working out for you and I won't call again, but I wanted you to know that, if anything happens in the future... anything at all... and you need a friend, you can still call me.' There was silence for a moment and I wondered if I'd been cut off. 'Hello? Maria? Are you still there?'

'I'm still here,' she said, sighing. 'Right. I need you to listen carefully and don't interrupt. Got that?'

'Got it.' We'd arrived at the bus stop so I stopped walking and gently rocked the buggy back and forth.

'We are *not* friends anymore and I don't need you in my life. I have Tony and I'll admit that it's not perfect but it's good enough for me because, as far as I'm concerned, happy ever afters don't exist.'

'They can. They—'

'You're interrupting,' she cried. 'Shut up for once. I'm *not* your pet project and I *don't* need you to fix me. You're always interfering in other people's lives. Concentrate on your own instead. There's only one thing I need from you from now on and that's for you to leave me alone. Is that clear?'

'Yes, but—' But she'd already hung up.

'Well, that went well,' I said to Megan. 'Oh well, ball's in her court now. What she said was spectacularly unfair, though. I don't interfere with people's lives. I don't make them my pet projects and I certainly don't try to fix people.' Even as I said the words, I felt my resolve crumbling. Ruby and Teddy were my latest pet project and, before that, I'd tried to interfere with Denise's life and fix her. The thing was, Denise *had* needed me and, judging from yesterday's conversation, Ruby needed me too. Maria was wrong. I wasn't interfering in peoples' lives. No. I was supporting those in need and, like it or not, Maria was in need. And having seen Tony with that redhead on the seafront, she might need me sooner rather than later.

* * *

Izzy looked a lot brighter and was delighted to see Megan, showering her with kisses and making the little girl giggle helplessly. Although the operation had gone well, her blood pressure was on the high side so they wanted to keep her in for another night. She was understandably gutted but a little relieved at having another day to heal.

My original plan for my day off had been to spend the afternoon with Mum. I couldn't decide whether Izzy genuinely didn't mind me taking Megan to Mum's or whether she was just pretending it was fine because, right now, she needed my help. Either way, permission was granted. Mum got a bit emotional when it struck her that Megan would be her step-granddaughter when Rhys and I married. I think Mum would have been happy to spend all afternoon cuddling her, but Megan was captivated by the plaster-cast and seemed to want to sit on the floor instead, where she could stare at it and stroke it.

Rhys came straight to Mum's after work, made us some dinner, then we returned to Izzy's for the night.

Shortly before 9 p.m., my phone rang, flashing up Maria's name.

'Hello?'

Silence.

'Maria? Are you there?'

Signalling to Rhys to mute the TV, I switched the phone to speaker mode.

'Maria?'

Turning to Rhys, I whispered, 'Can you hear crying?' He nodded.

'Maria?' I called. 'Speak to me. Please.'

'Help me.'

'Are you hurt?'

'Baby's coming.'

'Okay. Keep calm. Have you called an ambulance?'

'None free. Crash on A64. Argh!'

'We're on our way.'

Rhys was already sprinting up the stairs to fetch Megan. I pulled my boots on as I spoke. 'Don't hang up. Keep talking to me. Where's Tony?'

'Gone. Phone's off.'

'Have your waters broken?'

'Yeah.'

'Regular contractions?'

'About four minutes apart. Argh!'

For obvious reasons, first-aid training focusing on the elderly hadn't covered childbirth. I was aware that I sounded like I knew what I was asking, but the reality was I'd got it all from TV programmes. Four minutes? I had no idea what that signified but suspected it might mean the baby's arrival was imminent.

'We're in the van,' I said into the phone a few minutes later. 'You're in the same flat, yeah?'

'Yeah.'

'How will we get in?'

'Buzz number two. Roger. Tell him I'm having the baby. He's never out.'

'Okay. Hang on.' I gave the address to Rhys. 'We'll be about five or six minutes. Where are you?'

'Kitchen. Floor's wet.'

'Don't you have a number for a midwife or something?'

'Lost it. Hurry. Argh!'

Rhys accelerated as we headed across town towards Maria's flat.

'We're nearly there,' I told her, trying my hardest to keep the panic out of my voice. Perhaps I'd have felt calmer if the baby was actually due around now but, as far as I was aware, Maria was only eight months pregnant.

47

Maria's baby arrived kicking and screaming at 9.37 p.m. on Thursday the 29th of December. I delivered a baby. I actually delivered a baby! Rhys held onto Maria's hand while I knelt on the floor taking telephone guidance from a midwife contacted through the NHS Helpline.

It was far from the most dignified of births, on the wet kitchen floor, surrounded by all the towels and sheets we could find, yet it was the most movingly beautiful thing I'd ever experienced.

'It's a girl, Maria,' I sobbed, checking her mouth was clear before wrapping her in a towel and handing her over. 'She's so beautiful.'

I looked at Rhys who opened his mouth, but no words came out. Eyes sparkling, he simply nodded and wrapped a towel around Maria's shoulders.

'Have you thought of a name?'

Maria nodded. 'Sofia.'

'That's lovely. It suits her.'

'Sofia Callie Fernández,' she said, fixing her eyes on mine. 'After the best friend I ever had but didn't deserve.'

I lost it at that point, only managing to pull myself together when the midwife on the helpline reminded me I still had the placenta to deliver. Until that point, I hadn't realised this was something that actually had to be delivered although I'm not sure what I thought happened to it. Thankfully the paramedics arrived so they were able to take over.

It turned out that Maria had been a little over thirty-seven weeks pregnant so there weren't too many risks. Sofia seemed to be a good size and we later found out that she was 5lb 11oz.

'My bag,' Maria said as they took her out to the ambulance. 'It's in the lounge.'

Rhys grabbed it for her, checking on Megan at

the same time. How she'd slept through the drama, I'll never know.

Finally lying on a stretcher in the ambulance with Sofia enjoying skin-to-skin contact under a blanket, Maria reached out and took my hand, her eyes wide with fear. 'Will you come with me?'

I smiled. 'If that's what you want.'

Tears filled her eyes. 'It is. I'm scared. I think I might need you after all.'

Rhys picked me up from hospital a little after midnight. He'd cleaned up the kitchen, bundled the soiled towels and sheets into a couple of bin bags and taken them back to Izzy's where he put them through the wash. Exhausted, I hadn't relished going back to Maria's to clean up so was thrilled to discover he'd already tackled it.

We'd no sooner settled into bed than Megan's screams awoke us again and we were back out for an early hours drive along the seafront.

I was on a two-till-ten shift on the Friday and Rhys had a day off so we headed up to the hospital in the morning and then went our separate ways. Rhys to Izzy and me to Maria.

My heart thumped as I made my way along the hospital corridor towards the maternity ward. Maria had been very emotional the night before, understandably, but what if she'd woken up hating me again? What if she regretted naming her daughter after me? What if she thought I was interfering and told me where to go? She'd called me for help, though. That had to mean something.

My footsteps slowed. What if Tony was there? He was the father and he had every right to be. Or did he? His repeated infidelity and disrespect of the mothers of his children certainly didn't suggest so. I tentatively approached the ward, clutching onto the new baby balloon and soft pink teddy I'd picked up that morning during a quick dash into town. Then I froze.

Maria was out of bed, fully dressed, and packing a few items into her hospital bag. Tony was sitting on the bedside chair but he wasn't holding Sofia, which struck me as strange, although maybe she was asleep and they hadn't wanted to disturb her.

I hesitated but Maria looked up and smiled at

me. Taking a deep breath, I made my way over to them.

'Happy new baby.' I handed over the balloon and teddy.

'Thank you.' She took the teddy and gave it a cuddle before placing it in the crib beside her sleeping baby. 'Look, Sofia. Your first presents and guess who they're from? Daddy, you say? Don't be daft. They're from Auntie Callie. Daddy was too busy screwing around to be there for your birth so he's hardly going to have made it to the shops, is he?'

My stomach flipped. So she knew. How? I sneaked a sideways glance at Tony.

'It was a one-off,' he muttered, eyes narrowed at her. 'I told you it didn't mean anything.'

Maria took the balloon from me with a smile and tied it to the baby carrier resting on the bed. She turned to Tony again. 'I bet you say that to all the girls.'

Tony's eyes narrowed, but he didn't respond. Instead he nodded in my direction. 'What's *she* doing here anyway?'

'*She's* Sofia's godmother.'

'Over my dead body.'

'Don't tempt me, Tony.' Maria zipped her bag shut and stared at him. 'Oh. I forgot to tell you Sofia's middle name, didn't I?'

'We agreed on Grace.'

She planted her hands on her hips. 'Funny that, because we agreed that I'd be the only woman in your life, but I came home early from work to find you in *my* bed with your dick in some blonde tart's mouth.'

I gasped. Poor Maria. And, even worse than that, the woman I'd seen him with on the seafront had been a redhead. How many women did one man need at a time?

Tony stood up, eyes flicking round the ward, clearly conscious that the women in the beds either side and their visitors were listening to the exchange and not even trying to hide their interest.

'Can't we discuss this at home?' he hissed.

Maria ignored him, looking like she was relishing the opportunity to humiliate him in public. Good for her.

'Callie tried so hard to warn me that leopards don't change their spots and would I listen to her? Would I heck. Here was me thinking that you *gen-*

uinely loved me and wanted to spend the rest of your life with me. Only with me. So, come on, fess up. How many? Two, three, five, ten, twenty? Am I getting warm?'

Tony shook his head. 'I'm not doing this,' he growled.

She turned to me, her voice gentle. 'You know something, don't you? That's why you kept warning me.'

Ground swallow me up. Now. I nodded slowly. 'I saw him with a redhead in the early hours of Thursday morning and I know for a fact that his wife kicked him out on Christmas Day, not Boxing Day, because we were there when she did it. He must have been with someone else that night before he came crawling to you on Boxing Day making out that he was the one who'd demanded the divorce.'

Maria took a deep breath and nodded, then turned back to Tony. 'The great thing about Callie is she never lies. Just yesterday, I had a real go at her for interfering with other people's lives but that's not what she does. What she does is care and try to stop people from getting hurt. Even when people treat her like crap and betray her in the worst possible way.

Even when they don't deserve her friendship or compassion. Even when they keep pushing her away, she's there waving her olive branch and letting them know she'll always be there for them, no matter what.'

'She ruined my life,' Tony shouted.

'Grow up! You're forty-five, for God's sake. Start behaving like it and take some responsibility for your actions. *You* ruined your life. You. Not Callie, not your wife, not me. You. You're toxic and I don't need someone like you in my life.' She glanced towards the cot. 'And neither does Sofia.'

'You can't stop me seeing her.'

'If I thought you actually gave a shit about her, I'd be happy for you to see her, but you were the one who wanted the pregnancy terminated. You've done nothing but moan about me being pregnant and the inconvenience of having another baby and, since you got here, you haven't touched her. You've barely even looked at her. So I think I'm doing you a favour, aren't I?' When he didn't respond, she said. 'You can come back tonight for your stuff.'

'You're kicking me out?'

'Er, yeah. Obviously.'

'You can't do that. I've got a key.'

'And Pete's boyfriend is a locksmith. He's at the flat right now.'

'You bitch.'

'Perhaps. But you made me this way. I'll be in touch about maintenance payments. See ya.'

Tony shot her a filthy look then shoved past me. 'I wish I'd never met you. Either of you.' He turned to walk off the ward.

'That makes two of us,' Maria hissed.

'Three of us,' I added.

Tony shook his head and stormed towards the exit.

'By the way,' Maria called after him. 'Sofia's middle name? It's Callie. Sofia Callie Fernández.'

Tony stopped but didn't turn round.

'Yes, you heard me right. Fernández, not Sinclair. *Never* Sinclair.'

Tony shook his head then left. *Wow! Go Maria!*

I watched with concern as she appeared to deflate before my eyes and slump onto the bed. Dashing round to her side, I crouched down beside her. 'Are you okay?'

She had one hand pressed across her mouth and her face was pale.

'Do you feel sick? Faint? Should I call someone?'

'Water.'

Grabbing the jug, I poured her a cup, wishing my hands would stop shaking.

'Thank you,' she said, gulping it down. Then she looked up at me and her lips started to curve into a smile. 'How did it feel when you dumped him?'

I thought for a moment. 'Weirdly, I felt relieved. I was devastated by what he'd done but I remembered all the times he'd let me down or put me down and, to be honest, I was glad to be shot of him.'

'Relieved,' she repeated. 'Yeah, I get that. I actually feel like a huge weight has been lifted from me.' The tentative smile disappeared again. 'I'm scared, though. I'm on my own now. I've got no income, no family, no friends...'

Sitting on the bed beside her, I took her hand. 'I can't help with the income but I know a man who can. He can afford it and he owes you. As for family, that little girl right there is your family and I know you were probably calling me auntie and godmother just to wind Tony up, but you've got honorary family right here in a friend who never stopped caring because, despite the boyfriend-stealing, I know you're a lovely person. I just think you've got a bit lost lately, not helped by Tony's bad influence.'

A tear dripped onto our joined hands, quickly followed by another.

'What if I'm just like my mother?'

I put my other arm round her and cuddled her to my side. 'You are nothing like your mother. Do you hear me? Nothing like her. And that little girl over there is your chance to prove that.'

Maria wiped her eyes with her sleeve. 'Do you think you can fix me?'

'Do you want me to?'

She nodded.

'I think you've already taken your first step by kicking him out, but I can only help you if you stay strong and keep him out of your life.' I remembered what Tony's wife had said on her driveway. 'Hazel knows about you and she said that, if I ever saw you, I had to tell you that you can do better and not to be scared about being on your own with a baby because it will be fine.'

'His wife said that?'

'She did. So can you promise not to let him back in, no matter how charming he is or how scared you feel?'

'I promise. He's gone and he's not coming back.'

'Good. Let's get you home, then.'

I wasn't sure how we were going to manage the logistics of getting two patients, two babies, Rhys and me home in a three-seater van but we'd sort something. The most important thing was that Izzy was on the mend, Sofia was healthy, the old Maria was on her way back and Tony was gone. We could manage any other minor complications.

48

The only way to fight the fatigue at work that after-noon was to drink lots of coffee to the point I could almost hear it sloshing around inside me. I worked like a woman possessed that shift, moving through my to-do list at a cracking pace, knowing that a short break or a moment of procrastination would make me want to slump forward in my chair and sleep. With everything that had been going on, I'd actually forgotten that Iris and William were due back from their honeymoon early that evening.

'Mr and Mrs Watts,' I exclaimed when they knocked on the office door. 'Where has the past week gone?'

We exchanged hugs and kisses on the cheek.

'We've had such a wonderful time,' Iris gushed. 'Some of the residents have gathered in the lounge. They say it's to hear about our trip, but we know it's because we've got shortbread, don't we, William?' They both laughed. 'Would you have a moment to join us?'

Five minutes later, I perched on the arm of one of the sofas and listened to a brief overview of their honeymoon. Iris's iPad was passed around and I was relieved to see that they'd already edited the photos, selecting about twenty of the best. If there'd been hundreds, I might have keeled over with exhaustion.

Iris and William were buzzing. Anyone who didn't know them would be forgiven for believing they'd been away celebrating their golden wedding anniversary rather than their honeymoon after only a few months as a couple. There was something about them that suggested they'd always been together. They finished off each other's sentences and kept catching each other's eyes as they talked about a memory that seemed particularly special to them. I was captivated watching them until I noticed Ruby sitting quietly, slowly flicking through the photos, that wistful expression on her face again. *Please get in touch, Teddy. Please.*

Ruby poked her head round the office door shortly after I returned to my work. 'You look deep in thought, darling. Is it a bad time?'

'It's fine. Come in.'

She closed the door and sat down. 'Iris and William are moving into one of those luxury retirement apartments on Sea Cliff.'

'Oh. I'm sorry.'

'I never thought I'd say this but I've really missed that silly woman this past week.'

'Of course you have. She's your best friend.'

'Yes, I suppose she is. I've never had a best friend before. Well, not a female one. I suppose I was close to Frances, but she was family and we lost touch after I had Edward. My fault, of course.'

'When's Iris moving out?'

'The flat will be ready at the end of January, but she'll be staying with William in the meantime. Ian already has someone wanting her rooms so she's moving her things out next week.'

'You'll still see her, you know.'

Ruby sighed. 'I know. I'm not one for regrets, but

I wish I'd appreciated her more while she was here. It's true what they say: you don't know what you've got until it's gone.'

'Like Teddy?' I ventured.

She nodded. 'Like Teddy. I'm going to get in touch in the New Year.'

'Really?'

'Yes, although he'll probably want nothing to do with me and who can blame him after what I did?'

I hugged her. 'It's a good decision, Ruby. I'm so pleased for you. And Ed?'

'He's Teddy's son. I can hardly make contact with one and not the other. I don't think either of them will respond, but I need to try.'

* * *

'Ruby's going to get in touch with Teddy and your dad,' I told Rhys as we lay in bed that night.

He propped himself up on his arm, facing me. 'Really?'

'She told me tonight. Have you spoken to your dad since I made a mess of things?'

'How many times do I need to reassure you that

you didn't make a mess of anything? But, no, I haven't spoken to him since then. Mum reckons things are back to normal, though. She's convinced he'll want to meet Ruby soon.'

'It would be amazing if he made contact first. I think she's more nervous about getting in touch with him than she is about Teddy.'

Rhys gazed at me, a slight smile playing on his lips.

I propped myself up on my elbow too. 'What?'

'You. Do you realise how amazing you are?'

'Me? What have I done?'

Rhys laughed. 'In the past couple of weeks, you've saved Izzy's life, delivered Maria's baby, stood up to my dad, started the ball rolling to reunite Nanna with her son and her soulmate, got my daughter and ex-girlfriend to fall in love with you, been there for Maria while she dumps Tony, helped your mum cope with a broken leg... and all this on top of your regular job and Christmas.'

No wonder I felt drained. 'You really think Megan and Izzy like me?'

He shook his head. 'I said love you. Izzy's not shut up about you all day and you only have to look at

Megan's face when you're around to see how much she loves you already.'

I grinned. 'When you put it like that... although give Izzy a couple of weeks and I'm sure the snide comments will be back.'

'As long as the stupid games aren't.'

'I'd like to think she's learned her lesson there,' I said. 'Do you think you can cope with being married to so much awesomeness?'

Rhys grinned. 'I can't wait. In the meantime, I've been thinking. How would you feel if I gave notice at my place and moved in here?'

I squealed as I launched myself into his arms.

'I gather that's a yes,' he asked as I kissed his neck.

'Yes. A very big yes.'

49

I was working another two-till-ten shift on New Year's Eve. The plan was to stay back for a few drinks with the residents, see the New Year in with them, then go back to the flat with Rhys. I'd be present throughout the earlier part of the party, though, as I was responsible for the entertainment.

The morning flew by with back-to-back visits starting with Izzy and Megan. Izzy had colour in her cheeks, which was great to see, but she seemed to have contracted a severe case of verbal diarrhoea. I barely got a word in edgeways and felt quite exhausted by the time I left, having been talked at non-stop for over an hour. Granted, Hyper Izzy was better than Stroppy Izzy, but I found both approaches pretty uncomfortable. Hopefully the real Izzy Hemsworth would reveal herself at some point.

A visit to Mum's was much more relaxing and fun. Nick was there too so it was good to catch up with him. His relationship with Lindsay had ended a couple of days before. For Christmas, he'd given her a bracelet, some perfume and a few other bits and pieces and said he had a feeling the end was approaching when Lindsay had given him a tub of chocolates – the sort that all the supermarkets offer for a fiver in the run-up to Christmas. Awk-ward!

'The right one's out there,' I assured him. 'Plus you don't have to do the toga party now.'

'Silver linings,' he said, smiling. 'I'm fine about it. I knew Lindsay wasn't going to be long-term, but I thought it might last a bit longer. I can't help thinking she was only in it for the Christmas gifts.'

I'd have loved to assure him that nobody was that calculated, but Izzy had opened my mind as to exactly how devious some women could be.

* * *

Everyone dressed up in posh frocks and suits for New Year's Eve – a bit of a tradition at Bay View. Ruby looked stunning in a cream twenties-inspired gown with green trim, a red and green floral design round the skirt, and a green crocheted cardigan.

'I know I said it earlier but you really do look incredible this evening,' I said when my shift finished and I managed to get Ruby alone in the corridor.

She gave me a twirl.

'I absolutely love that dress,' I said. 'They knew how to dress back then.' Ruby had been born in the late-twenties so had been too young to enjoy the style first time round, but she'd always maintained that it was her favourite era for fashion. I couldn't imagine her dressed any differently.

'Thank you, darling. It's very similar to the dress I wore the last time I ever saw Teddy. It felt appropriate to see in the New Year wearing it.'

We sat down in a pair of armchairs nestling in an alcove.

'You haven't changed your mind about contacting him?' I asked.

'No. Iris and I were looking at photos of him online this afternoon and... oh, darling, this is probably going to sound ridiculous and it may well be the champagne talking...'

'Go on...' I encouraged when she fell silent, frowning.

'It's just that I had this overwhelming feeling that he was calling to me.' She laughed. 'It does sound silly when I say it aloud.'

I shook my head. 'It sounds romantic. I take it you've told Iris about Teddy?'

'Yes. We had a lovely afternoon together. She asked if I'd help her pack up some of her things, but I think it was a ruse to spend some time together drinking G&Ts and reminiscing. I think she's sad about leaving Bay View. She has so many friends here. Me included, before you say anything.'

I held my hands up in a surrender position and smiled. 'As if I'd ever comment on such a thing. You're right, though. She *will* miss being here but she's only the other side of town so it's not like you're not going to see her regularly. Unless, of course, Teddy whisks you away to Burghfield Hall to live out your days as Lady of the Manor.'

'You read too many romance novels, young Callie Derbyshire. Exotic dancer turned actress becomes a

Lady? I don't think so. Even in these more liberal times, something like that simply won't happen.'

'Then I'm confused. Why...?'

'Why am I getting in touch with Teddy? To say sorry, hopelessly inadequate as that will be, especially when I tell him about the son that I gave away.'

'But I thought that you were hoping to rekindle something. I thought you still loved him.'

'Oh, darling, I do. My love for that man is deeper than the ocean, higher than...' She paused, frowning again.

'What's the matter?'

Ruby shook her head. 'Nothing. A moment of déjà vu. Just something that Teddy and I used to say to each other.'

'What was it? Deeper than the ocean and...?'

She waved her hand dismissively and shook her head. 'It was nothing. Silly really.'

I was dying to know the rest but I knew her well enough to know that she'd clam shut again if I pushed. 'If you love him that much, surely—'

'No. It could never be back then and it still can't be, but I do want to see him so I can explain, just as I want to see Edward so I can explain to him. Selfishly,

I want to shuffle off this mortal coil with a clear con-science.'

My stomach dropped to the floor. 'Oh my God, Ruby. You're not ill, are you?'

'Oh, darling, no. Or, if I am, I'm not aware of it. It's just a turn of phrase. I've hopefully got many years left in me because there's so much to look for-ward to with your wedding and more great-grand-children. There's no way I'm going to miss all of that.'

I exhaled loudly. 'You had me scared for a mo-ment. Don't do that to me. And I think you're wrong about Teddy. From what you've told me, I think he'd move heaven and earth to be with you. I really do.'

'We'll see.' She patted my knee. 'Let's get back to the party. I do believe your shift has finished which means you need to get a glass of bubbly in your hand so we can toast your engagement properly. So far, we've only done that with a cup of tea which simply won't do.'

'Nanna! There you are.' Rhys appeared round the bend in the corridor. 'Something's just arrived for you.'

I looked at Rhys questioningly, but he shrugged.

'What is it?' Ruby asked, accepting Rhys's hand as she stood up.

'It's wrapped up so I don't know.'

A wave of heat and noise hit us as we returned to the residents' lounge. Iris stepped forward holding a large cardboard box wrapped in a ruby red ribbon.

'It's heavy,' she said, handing it to Ruby.

'It's from you?' Ruby asked.

Iris shook her head. 'We don't know who it's from. There's no label.'

Ruby sat down and placed the box on a side table, carefully untying the ribbon as a small audience gathered round. She lifted the lid and removed wads of scrunched up red tissue paper.

'Oh my goodness,' she whispered.

'What is it?' I peered over her shoulder. A small wooden grand piano sat in the box.

'It's a musical box,' Ruby said, turning the key underneath it.

Despite it competing with Frank Sinatra crooning about luck being a lady, I immediately recognised the Chopin piece. A flap on the top of the piano opened and a dancer in a long red gown appeared, twirling to the music.

Ruby put her hands to her mouth. 'I was wearing a dress just like that the night I met Teddy.'

Was he here? I looked around the room but there was nobody unfamiliar there; just residents, staff and a few friends and family members.

'Do you know who delivered it?' I asked Iris.

She shook her head.

'It was a woman,' said Odette. 'Late thirties, brunette, nice clothes, posh voice. She asked if I could give it to Ruby, then left.'

Ruby appeared mesmerised, watching the dancer twirling.

'Teddy?' I asked.

No answer.

The party continued around us, the residents quickly losing interest in the mysterious musical box. Only Iris, Rhys and I stayed with Ruby as she repeatedly wound it up. After seven or eight listens, she straightened up and looked at me.

'Callie, darling, would you be an angel and package that up and put it in my room? I don't want to risk damaging it.'

'Of course.'

'And Rhys, would you mind getting me a gin and tonic. Without the tonic.'

'Yes, Nanna.'

On my way back from Ruby's accommodation, I checked the entrance but there was nobody loitering outside and no cars parked in the visitors' spaces. I couldn't see the large car park at the side, but it was too cold and dark to go exploring. Reception was only staffed until 10 p.m., after which time the building was locked up. Visitors needed to press a bell, which buzzed through to a pager allocated to the team leader on shift.

Returning to the party, I found Ruby still in the same chair, nursing a tumbler of gin, although I was pleased to see that Rhys had added ice which, given the warmth in the room, would hopefully melt quickly and dilute the neat alcohol.

* * *

Shortly after 11 p.m., Odette appeared, holding another package, wrapped in brown paper and tied with a ruby red bow again. 'The same woman dropped it off,' she said, handing the package to

Ruby. 'I asked her who it was from. I even invited her in, but she just smiled and left.'

Ruby ripped open the packaging and pulled out a wooden picture frame with space to mount three A4-sized images, but the mounts were all empty. She turned the frame over but there was nothing written on or attached to the back.

I picked up the packaging but there was no writing on it and no card.

'Do you know what it is?' I asked.

'It's a picture frame, darling. I'd have thought that much was obvious.'

'Hilarious,' I said. 'I mean why. The musical box I get but why would Teddy send you an empty picture frame?'

'Because it probably wasn't Teddy who sent the gifts although I wish that whomever had sent them had included their name.' Ruby propped the frame up beside her chair.

'It has to be Teddy,' I insisted. 'I don't understand the picture frame, but the musical box is too personal to be from anyone else.'

'Then it's from you and Rhys,' she suggested.

'Sorry, Nanna,' Rhys said. 'It's not us. I'm with Cal. It must be from my granddad.'

'But how? How would he have found me and why now? I don't under...' She stopped and narrowed her eyes at me. 'Callie? What did you do?'

Busted! 'Er... I might have written to him.'

She clapped her hand across her mouth. 'Oh my goodness. When?'

'Just before Christmas. But, in my defence, I didn't post it because you didn't want me to make contact.'

'Then how does he know?'

I bit my lip and screwed up my nose. 'Because somebody else might have posted it by mistake.'

'Callie! I specifically ordered you not to...' She shook her head and took a gulp of her gin. 'I should be angry with you for interfering when I explicitly told you not to.'

'But you're not, are you, Nanna?' Rhys said. 'Callie did a good thing. Do you want me to go outside and see if there's anyone in the car park?'

'Oh, would you? You're such a good boy, Rhys. Unlike your meddling fiancée here.'

'I'm sorry, Ruby,' I said when Rhys left. 'I thought

I was doing the right thing and I didn't mean for the letter to get posted.'

'How many times? This isn't a romance novel. This is real life. I said I didn't want to get in touch but you knew best, didn't you? I told you that Teddy and I are in the past but you couldn't just accept that. Oh no. You had to go and try and fix it. It wasn't your situation to fix.' She sounded really annoyed with me. I'd never heard her take that tone before.

'But you've decided to meet him now, so I did the right thing.' I knew I was pushing it, but I couldn't bear the thought of her hating me.

'That was my decision to make, not yours. Goodness knows what you've told him about me. I hope you haven't told him that I want us to get back together.'

'Of course not. I was very vague in my letter.'

'I hope so.' She held out her empty glass with a raise of her eyebrow. 'No tonic.'

Obediently, I headed over to the drinks table to top it up. My fingers twitched against the bottle of tonic, but she'd know and I didn't want to give her further ammunition.

Ruby was deep in conversation with Brenda

Simkins when I returned with her gin, which sent a loud and clear message that she didn't want to speak to me, given how much she couldn't abide Brenda.

Rhys returned with nothing to report. There were plenty of cars in the car park but there was nobody in any of them. He'd even walked up and down the street but there was nobody waiting there either.

Fifteen minutes later, Odette handed Ruby an A4-sized envelope. 'The doorbell rang but there was nobody there this time. This was on the mat.'

It was one of those stiff cardboard-backed envelopes with 'do not bend' stamped on it. Ruby removed an A4 photograph of a stunning pink and purple coral reef. She stared at the photo for a moment, then flipped it over. Written on the back were the words: *Deeper than the ocean.* That was the first part of the phrase that Ruby had mentioned earlier.

Silently, she put the photograph back in the envelope, picked up the frame and packaging, then made her way to the lounge door.

'Should we go after her?' I asked Rhys.

He shook his head. 'She obviously wants some alone time. Leave her be.'

'I've messed up,' I said, gratefully accepting his

hug. 'Maria was right the other day. I interfere. I made Ruby and Teddy one of my "pet projects" thinking I could fix the past.'

'Give her time,' he said. 'I think it's all a bit over-whelming and emotional for her right now. I think you did the right thing and Nanna will realise that when she's had time to process it.'

I hoped so, but I was worried. I'd foolishly as-sumed that, if she wanted to get in touch with Teddy, it would be to try again; not just to explain and apol-ogise then part ways once more like she'd suggested earlier. Teddy's gifts – and they had to be from him – suggested to me that he still loved her and he wanted to rekindle things. Even though I'd taken care in my letter to avoid any suggestion Ruby was still in love with him and wanted to try again, had the very act of sending the letter made that very clear? Had I set them both up for heartache again?

It was ten to midnight when Ruby returned to the party. Two more envelopes were waiting for her. From the first, she removed a photo of bright blue sky broken up by some fluffy white clouds with the sun's rays bursting from behind them.

'Higher than the sky,' I whispered when she

turned the photo over to read the message on the back.

She placed the image and envelope on the table and opened the other one, which came out back first.

'Longer than time,' I said under my breath.

Ruby turned it over to reveal a photo of an opened pocket watch resting on a beach, with the ocean and the sky in the background.

'I love you deeper than the ocean, higher than the sky, and longer than time,' she said, looking up at the sea of puzzled faces around her. 'Teddy and I used to say it to each other.'

'He must be here,' I said. 'Not in the room, obviously, but in Whitsborough Bay.'

Without speaking, she picked up her tumbler and downed the rest of her drink.

'Less than five minutes until New Year,' she said. 'What do you think he'll do next? Proposal at midnight? He'd better not. I can't think of anything more humiliating.'

The residents joined hands with the staff and counted down to midnight. Streamers were thrown and party poppers pulled. Ruby looked as though she was fully in the moment, celebrating with the others, but I kept seeing her glance towards the door. I had to give it to her: she was a great actress, but she didn't fool me.

Five past midnight came, then ten past, and still nothing. I asked Odette to check her pager to see if we'd missed anyone at the door, but there was nothing. No more envelopes, no more gifts, nobody there.

At half past midnight, the party thinned out. Residents bid each other a Happy New Year and steadily dispersed to their rooms. Shortly before one, Ruby stood up, stretched, and announced that she needed her beauty sleep.

'Walk me to my room, will you Rhys?' she asked.

I thought she was going to completely blank me but, at the last minute, she turned and said, 'Happy New Year, Callie.'

'Happy New Year, Ruby.' There was no point adding that I was sorry. Again.

'She'll come round,' Iris said, placing her hand on my shoulder. 'For what it's worth, I think you did the right thing. Deep down, I guarantee you that Ruby knows that too. She may have dismissed the idea, but I'm pretty certain she was disappointed that there wasn't a proposal at midnight.' She patted my shoulder. 'Good night, my dear, and Happy New Year.'

I looked around the messy room after Iris and William left. Some of my colleagues were collecting glasses and crockery. 'Pass me one of those bin bags,' I said to Odette. 'I might as well make myself useful.' I billowed it open and started to fill it with streamers and deflated balloons. Deflated. Exactly how I felt.

50

December had been such a crazy busy month that I could really have done with a relaxing New Year's Day lounging around the flat, eating junk food, and watching films. No such luck. Rhys was spending the morning with Megan and Izzy and had offered to do some washing and cleaning. Much as I wanted to spend time with Megan, I'd arranged to visit Maria. I was then meeting Mum and Nick at the cemetery late morning and, after lunch with them, would briefly nip to Izzy's before going to Bay View to see Ruby. Assuming she'd forgiven me and was willing to see me.

Sofia was fast asleep in a Moses basket when I

arrived at Maria's flat, her rosebud lips pouting, one hand resting against her cheek.

'She's so cute,' I said, admiring the mass of dark hair. 'She's got your colouring.'

'Good. Wouldn't want her to take after her wanker father.'

I took the cup of tea that Maria handed me and sat on the sofa. 'Have you heard from him?'

'Only when he collected his stuff but Pete and Lars were here to make sure it didn't turn nasty. He tried to give me a sob story about having nowhere to live and how much he loved me. It might even have worked if he hadn't got his latest shag waiting for him in the car. Lars spotted them all over each other before he buzzed.'

'I'm sorry it didn't work out for you.'

Maria raised an eyebrow. 'Pull the other one.'

'Seriously, I am. You really loved him, didn't you?'

Tears filled her eyes and she sighed. 'More than life itself. You know what, Callie? Men have treated me like crap all my life and I genuinely thought Tony was different. Looking back, I'm buggered if I know what made me think that.' She shrugged. 'I wasn't seeing him the whole time you were together, you know.'

'It doesn't matter.'

'It does. I was a crap friend but maybe not as crap as you think. I'll admit I fancied him from the start but he was your boyfriend so no way was I going to make a play for him. Then the two of you split up in April and I couldn't help myself. I called it off as soon as you got back together. He bombarded me with texts and phone calls begging me to have him back but I stayed strong, even when I found out I was pregnant. I didn't tell him about the baby at first because I wasn't sure how he'd react. When you and I had our pizza night and I said I didn't see Tony as a marriage and kids kind of guy, I meant it. Of course, like you, I didn't know he was already married with four kids. Having him working back at Bay View was so hard. He kept telling me he loved me and wanted me back but I refused while he was seeing you. Then your one-year anniversary went wrong and you were so angry with him, I managed to convince myself that it was over for good. Tony came to Bay View the following week while you were on your first aid course. You two were barely even on speaking terms and I knew you weren't expecting him in Whitsborough Bay which suggested it was over for him too.'

'Is that when Rhys found you in the laundry room?'

She lowered her eyes. 'I decided I'd better tell him about the baby before I started showing and it became obvious, so I took him into the laundry room, away from prying ears. When he kissed me, I tried to push him off but I couldn't do it. I wanted him so badly. Because I was only expecting to talk, I hadn't locked the door and... well, you know the rest.' She sighed. 'Then I found out about the wife and kids but I was in too deep by then as well as being an emotional wreck because of the job situation. I needed him. He kept promising he'd leave her and just needed to find the right time. I genuinely thought he loved me and only me. Turns out that, if he'd been wearing a sign round his neck with "I'm a cheating git who'll break your heart" written on it, it couldn't have been more obvious that he was a wrong 'un.'

'We all make mistakes,' I said gently. 'He fooled me and his wife.'

'And God knows how many others,' Maria added.

'Lesson learned. From now on it's me and Sofia against the world, isn't it baby girl?'

On cue, Sofia released a few little cries. Maria stood up and in an impressively speedy and confident move, lifted Sofia onto her shoulder, instantly silencing her.

'You're a baby whisperer,' I said, awestruck.

She smiled. 'No. Just used to it. I had to be mum to my little sisters, Luna and Violeta, when they were babies. Didn't stop them turning on me, though, and it didn't stop Jazmin and Elisa from leaving me either.'

'You're still in touch with Jazmin and Elisa, though?'

'We're Facebook friends but I don't think the occasional like on a post constitutes sisterly love. So it really is just me and Sofia against the world and, do you know what? I think we'll be just fine that way.' She settled Sofia back in the basket then returned to the sofa. 'I'm really sorry for everything I did and said to hurt you. If you want to have a go at me, feel free. I deserve it.'

I shook my head. 'I'd be lying if I said the air wasn't blue when I found out although I really appreciate you telling me the truth. When I discovered you were pregnant, I assumed you'd been together for months.'

'No. I couldn't have done that to you. Although I didn't know you were definitely over that day in the laundry room.'

'If it makes you feel any better, you can assume we were.' I sipped on my tea while I digested the information. There was so much about the scenario that made me squirm: Maria getting together with Tony the moment we'd separated or she thought we'd separated, him chasing her while we were together, and her being in love with him all that time. I tried to imagine myself in the same situation. I'd like to think that I'd have seen the man as off-limits even if he was the ex of my best friend, but love could do funny things to people. Who could say how I'd have reacted if I'd been in that situation? What if Rhys had been Maria's ex? Would I have been able to ignore my feelings for him?

'We need to talk about your disciplinary,' I said. 'I didn't tell anyone about you smoking pot that time. I know I was angry when I texted you, but I swear it wasn't me.'

Maria smiled weakly. 'I know.'

'How? I've been asking around and nobody at work seems to know anything about it.'

'It was Tony who dobbed me in.'

My jaw dropped. 'You're kidding me. How did he know?'

'It was him who gave me the pot after his first visit. I'd never smoked the stuff before and I didn't want to risk taking it home. It would have been just my luck for that to be the one time they decided to do a bag search. I hid it in the shed and that time you caught me smoking it was after I'd done the dirty with Tony. You'd split up but I felt so guilty that I needed something stronger than a cigarette to de-stress me.'

'But how do you know he was the one who told Denise?'

'He told me when he called round for his stuff last night. We had a massive argument again, a load of stuff tumbled out, and that was one of the things. I think he was proud of being the one to break up our friendship. So sorry for blaming you for that too.'

'What a mess and what a git he is,' I said. 'Well,

it's over now. Tony's gone and I'm here and I've really missed you.'

'I've missed you too,' she said, squeezing my hand. She looked down and gasped. 'What the bloody hell's that? Explain yourself.'

'Oh. Rhys proposed to me on Christmas Eve'

'And you've been wearing the ring ever since? How have I not noticed?'

I smiled and nodded towards the Moses basket. 'Think you might have been slightly distracted.'

Maria smiled too. 'Do you think? So tell me everything. Was it really romantic?'

'It was lovely.' As I told her all about our engagement and then about Iris's wedding, it started to feel like it used to between us. Tony had done his best to destroy our friendship but he was the one who'd ended up losing us both. Couldn't have happened to a nicer bloke.

* * *

'How was Lighthouse Point?' I asked Nick after Rhys dropped me off at the cemetery later. Our grandparents and Dad had all loved the sea so Nick visited

Lighthouse Point every year on New Year's Day and threw in three single white roses at 11.02 a.m. – the day and time that Grandma, the final one of them to go, had died.

'It was fine. Absolutely freezing, though.' He shivered as though still feeling the chill. It was definitely a cold start to the year, but sometimes the seafront could be several degrees colder than slightly inland, especially if there was a strong wind.

We retrieved the bouquets of white roses from Nick's boot and made our way slowly up the cemetery path, Mum hobbling on her crutches.

Grandma and Granddad shared the same plot and their son-in-law – our dad – lay a couple of rows behind them. Dad's parents were still alive and in reasonably good health, living out their days in The Algarve. They claimed the warmer weather was better for their arthritis but Mum believed it was because they found it too emotional living in Whitsborough Bay, knowing that their son had been taken from them far too early. It had to be harder for Mum than them; she'd lost both parents and her husband yet she'd stayed in the same house and just got on with it. Who was I to judge anyone else's reaction to loss, though? Everyone handled grief in different ways.

As per tradition, Nick and I lay a bouquet each on our grandparents' grave and Mum lay the third one on Dad's. Standing together, we held hands as we took a moment to silently remember them or say a prayer before kissing our fingers and passing it on through each of the marble headstones.

I missed Grandma but only had vague recollections of Granddad who'd died when I was eight. As for Dad, who'd died two years earlier, there were images in my mind of being held up high by a tall, strong man, but I had no idea whether they were real or if I'd created them myself on the back of photos I'd seen of Dad and me together. I liked to think they were real.

'Everyone ready?' Mum asked, adjusting her hold on her crutches.

'I'm good,' Nick said.

'Actually, can we stay here a couple more minutes?' I asked. 'There's something I want to ask Nick and it feels appropriate to do it in Dad's presence.'

Mum and Nick looked at me expectantly.

'I know we haven't set a date yet, but Rhys and I

have started to think about what we want on our wedding day and I have a special request to make. Dad isn't here but there's someone who has always been like a dad to me as well as being my big brother. Nick, would you be willing to give me away?'

Mum gasped and I could tell from the expression on her face and the tears in her eyes that she loved the idea but didn't want to say anything until Nick had reacted.

Nick looked a little shell-shocked. Swallowing hard, he nodded. 'I'd love to. Thank you. I—' But he was obviously too choked up to say anything else because he grabbed me and gave me the biggest bear hug ever.

'That's such a lovely idea,' Mum said, mopping her eyes with a tissue. 'Your dad would be so proud of you both right now. And I know he'll be there in spirit on the big day itself, looking down on you, wishing he could be there for real.'

I lost it at that point and the three of us stood by the graves, hugging and crying.

51

Nick dropped me off at Izzy's shortly before three. Rhys must have been watching for me out the window because he opened the door before I'd had a chance to raise my hand to knock. One look at the anxiety creases across his forehead sent my stomach into spin cycle.

'What's happened? Is it Megan? Izzy?'

'No. They're fine. They're both asleep at the moment.' He shook his head. 'Mum phoned earlier. She's coming across with Dad and they want us to meet them at The Ramparts Hotel for afternoon tea.'

'When?'

'Today at four.'

My shoulders slumped. 'Seriously? Today? And at The Ramparts? Please tell me this is a wind-up.'

'I wish it was.'

The Ramparts Hotel was Whitsborough Bay's only five-star hotel; a grand building dating back to the Victorian era. I'd actually never been inside, but I knew it was posh. What was it with Ed and his need to splash the cash? What was wrong with a pint and a packet of crisps in The Old Theatre? And what was wrong with a bit of notice?

'I don't suppose that get-out-of-jail-free card is still available?' I asked.

Rhys put his arms round me, pulled me to his chest, and kissed the top of my head. 'I wish we both had one.' He pulled away and looked at me. 'Mum says he's promised to be on his best behaviour. They want to celebrate our engagement, apparently.'

I curled my lip up. 'I don't imagine your dad is particularly eager to welcome me into the family.'

'But Mum is, and hers is the only opinion I'm interested in.'

'I'm going to have to change, aren't I?'

'Why? You look gorgeous.' He stepped back to take in my outfit. 'Oh.'

'Exactly. I was wearing this at Sidney's and it's the sort of thing your dad would make a snide comment about. I've got nothing else posh, though.'

'What about the dress you wore for the wedding?'

'It hasn't been washed. Although... well, I didn't slop down it, which is a miracle for me. Maybe...' I'd hung the pale pink dress up on the outside of my wardrobe after the wedding as a reminder to check washing instructions in case it was dry clean only. It wasn't ideal but I could probably get away with spritzing it with perfume and wearing it again. It was that or leggings and a T-shirt. 'We'd better get back to the flat so I can change, then. Don't want to upset your dad by being late for the third time in a row.'

* * *

'Oh my God,' I whispered, clutching Rhys's hand tightly as we crossed the hotel lobby. 'It's posher than I imagined.' I was very aware of my heels clicking on the marble flooring as we navigated our way round a plinth in the middle of the lobby, on top of which rested an enormous vase filled with a stunning array of flowers and foliage. A sparkling chandelier dangled high above it, the many glass droplets catching the colours from the flowers and projecting them onto the walls and floor.

A suited man in his fifties approached us and directed us through the bar to where we'd find The Orangery where we could 'take afternoon tea'. I wanted to ask, 'Take it where?' but I wasn't sure he'd appreciate the joke.

The Orangery was beautiful. A large Victorian conservatory, it had a cream and grey patterned tile floor, round tables with large white wicker chairs, and planters with realistic-looking fake trees adding some colour. White fairy lights twinkled in the trees and around various pillars and there was a Christmas tree in one corner, decorated with a simple silver, blue and white colour scheme. A large black grand piano stood on a small stage to our right and a woman in a black cocktail dress was providing the music. I didn't know what it was called, but I recognised the song she was playing from the film *Casablanca*.

The restaurant was about two-thirds full but

there was no sign of Jenny or Ed. I glanced at my watch: 3.55 p.m. For once, we were early.

'Table booked in the name of Edward Michaels,' Rhys said to the maître d'.

'Very good, sir. If you would like to accompany me...'

Rhys and I followed him to the left where he indicated for us to sit at a table for six.

'Is this right?' Rhys asked. 'I thought it was a booking for four.'

'It says six, sir, but not to worry if that's our error.'

He pulled my chair out for me before passing us each a small leather-bound menu. 'The afternoon tea is a set menu, but we can make substitutions or accommodate any dietary requirements as explained here. There is champagne and tea coming as part of the meal, but would you like to order a drink while you're waiting for the rest of your party?'

'Could I have a glass of tap water, please?' I asked.

'Of course. And for sir?'

'I'm fine, thanks.'

The maître d' smiled. 'I'll bring a jug of water in case you change your mind.'

When he'd gone, I nudged Rhys. 'Do you think someone else is coming?'

He shrugged. 'Mum didn't say, but they could be bringing Debbie and her boyfriend, although it's been on-off for the past few months and I thought Mum said they'd split up for good a few weeks back. Who knows.'

A young woman appeared with a jug of water and poured me a glass. I sipped on it as I studied the menu. It all sounded delicious. I hadn't thought I'd be hungry after a big lunch with Mum and Nick, but my stomach had already started rumbling at the sight of the three-tiered cake stands bursting with finger sandwiches, scones, and cakes.

'They're late,' I said, putting my menu down later. I sat back in my chair, listening to the piano music. The pianist obviously favoured music from the movies because I recognised the current piece as the theme tune from *Titanic*.

Rhys looked at his watch. 'Ten minutes. That's not like my dad.'

Moments later, Jenny appeared, full of apologies. 'The car park was full, so your dad had to drop us off and go and find a space.'

'Us?' Rhys asked.

Jenny grimaced. 'Did I say "us"? Ooh, I'm so bad with secrets. Debbie's here, but you must promise to make out as though you're surprised. She's nipped to the ladies.' She popped her bag down on the table. 'Anyway, Happy New Year to you both and welcome to the family, darling girl. Let me see...'

I held out my left hand and she gently took it, moving it slightly so that the diamond could catch the light. 'Absolutely beautiful. I'm so thrilled for you both.' She gave me a hug, then moved round the table to hug Rhys. 'I need to hear all about the wedding plans, but we'd better wait until your father and Debbie are here, or I'll be in trouble for knowing more than they do.' She sat down beside Rhys.

'Who's the other chair for, Mum?' he asked.

There was no opportunity to answer because a tall, slim woman with curly dark hair rushed up to the table. 'Am I going to finally meet the woman who's stolen my baby brother's heart?'

I stood up and she grabbed me in a bear hug. 'I promise I am his sister and not some random serial-hugger.'

Debbie hugged Rhys, then I had to show her my

ring too. 'Exquisite,' she said. 'And you chose this?' She raised her eyebrows at Rhys.

'Oi. I have great taste, you know.'

Debbie laughed. 'Really? Has he ever told you about his double-denim phase, Callie? Or when he bleached the ends of his hair blond?'

'Debs!' Rhys cried.

'Is this true?' I asked.

Jenny nodded. 'There was a boy band phase too. He took guitar lessons and tried to spike his hair.'

Rhys hung his head in shame. 'I knew it would be dangerous to get you three in the same room.'

'Is there photographic evidence?' I asked.

Jenny and Debbie both nodded enthusiastically.

'Oh my goodness, I cannot wait to see that.'

I know it was evil of me, but I was pleased that Ed hadn't been able to find a parking space. It was adorable watching the warmth between Rhys, Debbie and their mum. Rhys didn't tend to talk about Debbie and I assumed their relationship was strained because she was 'the favourite' but I realised now that they had a great relationship and the reason he didn't talk about her was prob-ably down to him not seeing that much of her. Between his work, lifeguarding, Megan and me, he didn't have the time to visit. We'd have to rectify that.

'I apologise for my tardiness,' Ed said, silencing the giggles and stifling the mood. 'I should have planned better.'

'Dad.' Rhys nodded at him.

'Son.' Ed nodded back. So much warmth. Would it have killed Ed to smile or wish Rhys all the best for the New Year?

That spin cycle started in my stomach again as he looked towards me. 'Happy New Year, Callie.'

'Thank you. And to you.' I shuffled in my chair. Should I get up and shake his hand? Kiss him on the cheek? Give him a hug? Rhys hadn't stood up, though, and I was happy to take my cue from him. Thankfully Ed sat down and signalled to the maître d' who appeared with an ice bucket on a stand and poured us each a glass of champagne. I caught Rhys's eye and we both looked at the spare chair, but neither of us asked.

'A toast,' Ed said, raising his glass. We all followed suit and raised ours. 'We have three things to celebrate today. Firstly, to the New Year.'

We all copied the toast and took a sip. Ooh. Very nice.

'To Rhys and Callie's engagement,' Ed said, looking from Rhys to me and back to Rhys with perhaps a shadow of a smile on his face. It was better than a frown, though. 'Welcome to the family, Callie.'

Again, we echoed the toast and sipped.

'And, finally, a toast to another new member of the family.' Ed raised his glass and actually smiled this time. 'To my biological mother, Ruby.'

What? Rhys and I turned round as Ruby, a vision in a long red twenties-style gown, approached the table. 'Surprise!'

She wasn't wrong. How? When?

Jenny reached across the table and squeezed my hand. 'I told you your words would have an impact.' Her voice cracked as she added, '*You* made this happen.'

52

I felt as though I was having an out of body experience. Was that really me at a table in a posh hotel with Rhys's family... including Ruby? Any moment, I expected an alarm to go off and for me to wake up from a dream.

Over afternoon tea, the story gradually emerged. As Jenny had predicted, my words from our disastrous meal in Sidney's had hit home and Ed had spent the period between Christmas and New Year reflecting on what he wanted life after retirement to look like for him. The pair of them had been out for a meal with two couples they knew, both of whom were older and had been retired for several years.

They'd talked about finding new hobbies and spending time with grandchildren, children, and elderly parents. Ed had been very quiet on the way home as he'd considered his small but growing family and how he'd always pushed Rhys away, had done nothing to make me feel welcome, and how that could affect his relationship with any future grandchildren. And of course, he'd always refused to entertain the idea of meeting Ruby. He began questioning how he'd feel if anything happened to her and whether he'd be filled with regrets at not getting to know her.

'Can I ask a question?' I asked, waiting for Ed to nod before I continued. 'Why did you refuse to see her?'

Rhys squeezed my knee as though to say 'too blunt' but I wanted to know. Jenny had alluded to an incident at school and the need to control things, but it hadn't explained it.

'It's all right, darling,' Ruby said. 'I'm sure Edward has his reasons and we need to respect them.'

'I'd quite like to know too,' Debbie said, helping herself to another scone.

Jenny placed her hand over Ed's. 'You don't have to... Or I can say it if you want.'

Ed looked round the table then dabbed his mouth with his crisp white napkin and laid it across his plate. 'Fair enough. I'll give the explanation once, after which I don't want to discuss it ever again.' He straightened his shoulders and sat up taller as though trying to find the strength to share a painful memory. 'Every adopted child reacts to the news that they've been adopted in a different way. Some are hurt that they've been given up, others don't care, and others know it was for the best. I was one of the hurt ones, but not because Ruby had given me away. I'm not ignorant. I know it can't be an easy choice and that the mother usually thinks they're doing what's best for the child. In my case, being adopted might have been the best thing for me, but the couple who adopted me were not the best thing for me.'

Ruby's hand fluttered to her mouth. 'Oh, Edward. They were researched carefully. I was assured they were a good family.'

'I'm sure you did and I'm sure they were at the time. My adoptive parents were unable to have children of their own so, for them, I was a miracle. Initially. Unfortunately, I wasn't an easy baby and had several medical problems. None of them have had a long-term effect but my younger years were plagued with lack of sleep, difficulty in eating, and frequent trips to the hospital. I think the fantasy of parenthood versus the reality was a shock and it caused no end of arguments. I don't have a single childhood memory that doesn't involve them yelling at each other or at me.'

'Oh, Edward,' Ruby said. 'I'm so sorry.' I was at the opposite side of the table so I couldn't give her any comfort but I watched Debbie take Ruby's hand in hers.

'My adoptive mother's favourite phrase was, "I wish we hadn't adopted you," which was nice. My adoptive father's approach was to tell me that nothing I ever did was good enough. If I got less than an A, I hadn't tried hard enough. If I got an A, the assignment or exam had been "too easy". I couldn't win.'

I dared to glance at Rhys and could tell by his slightly raised eyebrows that this was how Ed had treated Rhys. I wondered if Ed even registered the irony of that.

'I learned to keep my head down, work hard, and try not to give them ammunition. When I was fourteen, I invited my two best friends round to work on a geography project. Mother didn't like me having friends round, but she was meant to be at a friend's house until early evening so I thought I was safe. Unfortunately, she had an argument with the friend and returned early to find three spotty teenagers creating a model of a volcano in the middle of her dining room table, with glue and paint everywhere.' Ed paused and took a glug from his champagne, then glanced at Ruby. 'This next part is going to hurt. I can stop now if you want.'

She shook her head. 'I had no idea. Please continue. I might as well know the full truth.'

Ed took another glug of champagne. 'Mother went ballistic, shouting and screaming at me. The usual, "I wish we hadn't adopted you," line came out followed by...' He paused again, looking at Ruby, but she nodded encouragingly. 'Followed by, "should have left you with your junkie whore of a mother". Sorry, Ruby. My mother destroyed our geography project, my friends ran off, and they told everyone at school that I was adopted because my real mother was... Well, you get the picture. School was hell after that. I never forgave my so-called friends and I never forgave Ruby.' He necked the rest of his drink and looked round the table. 'You asked.'

Wow! I tried to imagine what childhood must have been like for Ed. No wonder he'd turned out the way he had with adoptive parents like that and friends who'd betrayed him so badly.

'I'd never have let them have you if I'd known,' Ruby said, her hands twisting her pearls. 'I could not be sorrier.'

Ed nodded. 'You understand why it's been hard to make contact?'

'Goodness, yes. Oh, darling. I'd give anything to go back and change what happened to you.'

I held my breath while they stared at each other, Ruby's face etched with regret, Ed's with bitterness. Then he smiled. 'Yes, I do believe you would.' He raised his glass again. 'To fresh starts.'

'To fresh starts.'

Ed signalled to the waiter to bring more champagne and I looked across at Jenny, concerned about their drive home. She mouthed, 'We're staying here' to me. Phew!

'So what did you get for Christmas, Ruby?' Debbie asked.

'Oh, I was spoilt, darling,' Ruby said after a moment. 'Rhys and Callie bought me this most delightful teddy bear with a musical box in his tummy...'

The tension on the table lifted as Ruby described the teddy and everyone else chipped in with tales of their Christmas gifts before moving on to how they'd celebrated New Year's Eve. All the while, Ed steadily necked champagne.

Jenny saw me raising my eyebrows as he topped up his glass for the third time since finishing the sorry story of his childhood. 'Excuse me. I must go and powder my nose.' She looked pointedly at me.

'Me too,' I said, following her to the bathroom.

She checked nobody was in the cubicles before turning to me.

'You know Ruby well. How will she have taken Ed's story?'

'She's very resilient, but it will have upset her a lot. She'd rather know, though. She'll feel guilty about his bad childhood and blame herself for that, even though she couldn't have done more to make sure he was going to a loving home. But I think she'll look at the silver lining, which is that there's a very good reason why he never made contact. And, if I know Ruby, she'll spend the rest of her life making it up to Ed if he'll let her. Do you think he'll let her?'

Jenny shrugged. 'Today is huge for him. You've seen how much he's drinking so I know you realise that.'

'What happens next? Does it end today?'

She shook her head. 'Not if I have anything to do with it. No. Ed's a stubborn man—'

'Really? I'd never have guessed that about him.'

She laughed. 'He hides it well, doesn't he? He's a stubborn man, but that means that when he makes a decision to do something, he sees it right through. The reason this is so huge for him is that it was never about finding out answers or getting an apology. It was always about building a relationship and, after fifty-four years without one, he needed to be sure that's what he really wanted before meeting Ruby.'

The door opened and a couple of women came

in, gushing about the profiteroles. They smiled politely before disappearing into cubicles.

Jenny took my hands in hers. 'Our family has been broken but you've started to fix it. He's started with Ruby but I know that Rhys is next. Honestly, Callie, you're like a gift from heaven.' She drew me into a hug. 'Thank you for coming into our lives.'

53

It seemed that Ed was a happy drunk, which was unexpected as he'd seemed on edge and melancholy when we left the table. When Jenny and I returned from the ladies, he'd challenged Rhys to a scone-eating contest. Both had to smother a scone in jam and cream then eat it as fast as they could. If they licked their lips at any point, they incurred a five-second penalty. I'd done something similar with sugar doughnuts before but had never tried it with cream scones. Hilarious.

To further my surprise, Ruby decided to challenge the winner – Ed – and blow me if she didn't win! He demanded a rematch and ended up laughing so much that he snorted cream up his nose and had to retreat to the gents to sort himself out.

When he'd gone, I turned to Ruby. 'An unexpected start to the New Year, eh? How are you feeling?'

'I'm still a little stunned, darling. When Ian told me that my son was in reception, I thought someone was... what's that word you young people use these days? Planking?'

'Pranking?'

'That's it, darling. I thought somebody was pranking me, but there he was. Oh my goodness, Callie, he's the spitting image of Teddy. It was like stepping back in time.'

'And are you still annoyed with me for getting in touch with Teddy? Because it was an accident.'

She shook her head. 'Right now, my son is back in my life. He understands why I gave him up and he's not angry about it anymore. I'm not expecting it will be easy or perfect, but the main thing is that we're in contact. That's all I ever wanted and I'm led to understand that you made that happen too. You'll have to tell me more about this lecture you gave him.'

I smiled. 'Another day, perhaps. It was awful.'

Ed returned to the table, his face clear of jam and cream. 'I can't believe we just did that in a five-star establishment.'

'Darling,' Ruby said, 'I tend to find that the higher class the establishment, the more outrageous the japes. I was once staying at The Savoy and you wouldn't believe what Lord Harrington Pemberley and his brother did in the fountain...'

Sitting back in my chair, a feeling of contentment settled on me. Ruby was finally with her family, Ed was going to make amends with Rhys, Megan was in my life and Izzy had hopefully stopped playing silly buggers. Maria and I were friends again and Tony was out of the picture. And I had a wedding to plan. After a difficult four months or so, things were finally looking up. All I needed now was for Teddy to appear, fulfilling my Christmas wish, and for Nick to find love. I didn't understand why he was unlucky in love when idiots like Tony seemed to have the pick of whomever they wanted, but I was sure he'd find the right woman soon.

Sipping on my champagne, I tuned back into Ruby's story. I sometimes wondered if she made them up, but so what if she did? They were funny and she was a gifted storyteller. Mid-sentence, Ruby stopped and frowned.

'What's up?' Rhys asked.

'That music.'

We all fell silent and listened.

'It's your song,' I exclaimed. 'The one in the teddy.'

Ruby nodded, her head cocked to one side.

'Didn't you say it was in a film?' I asked. 'She's been playing music from films all afternoon.'

Ruby turned to me. 'Has she? Oh. That would explain it, then. For a moment, I thought... Never mind.'

'You thought it was Teddy?'

'Just an old woman being foolish.' She smiled a little too brightly as she looked round the table. 'Where was I? Oh yes, I was—'

A man's voice cut across her. 'You were in a theatre in Paris on my twenty-first birthday, looking as astonishingly beautiful as you do today.'

I swear that everyone at the table held their

breath at that very same moment, watching as Ruby turned and rose, her fingers pressed to her lips. Oh my goodness. The distinguished-looking gentleman with the posh voice standing by our table had to be...

'Teddy,' Ruby whispered.

54

It was like watching a scene out of a classic movie unfolding before our eyes. Ruby and Teddy stood face to face with their song playing in the background. They didn't speak. No words were needed because the expression on both of their faces said it all: love, regret, forgiveness. Teddy reached out and took both of Ruby's hands in his, drew them slowly to his lips for a gentle kiss, then they embraced. I felt like an intruder in an incredibly intimate moment, yet I wasn't able to look away because I was completely drawn into a love story that had spanned nearly seventy years.

Somebody on a table nearby dropped some cutlery onto the floor with a clatter and the spell between Ruby and Teddy was momentarily broken, both of them seeming to realise they weren't alone. They pulled apart but kept one hand firmly clasped as though they were both afraid to ever let go again.

Ruby turned to face the sea of expectant faces. 'This is Teddy.' She turned back to him. 'Teddy, this is… erm… this is my family.'

Teddy smiled at us all. 'Please forgive me for interrupting your meal. As soon as I heard Ruby was here, I had to come. Too many years have separated us already.' He turned to Ruby. 'Do they know who I am?'

'A couple of them do. Perhaps I'd better fully introduce you.' She indicated me first. 'This is Callie and, although I don't yet know how you found me here, I think she may be the reason you're in Whitsborough Bay today.'

I stood up, unsure whether to shake Teddy's hand, curtsy, or hug him. What was the protocol for a Lord? He saved me the decision, momentarily releasing Ruby's hand, pulling me into his embrace and whispering, 'thank you' over and over.

Ruby looked round the rest of the table when Teddy had taken her by the hand again. 'And this is my immediate family. My son, Edward, and my daughter-in-law, Jenny.' She took a deep breath and I guessed she was trying to decide whether the full truth should come now or later. 'My granddaughter, Debbie, and my grandson, Rhys, who is also Callie's fiancé. Rhys knows.' She paused and looked at me. I nodded encouragingly, hoping she'd find the strength to just blurt it out.

'I say *my* family,' Ruby said, 'but what I really mean is *our* family. Edward is your son, Teddy. *Our* son. Edward, this is your father, Teddy Latimer.'

Ed looked completely astonished. His eyes were wide and he kept opening and closing his mouth, but no words came out.

'*Our* son?' Teddy looked from Ruby to Ed then back to Ruby, mouth also agape. 'Was that why you disappeared?'

She nodded. 'Oh, Teddy. There is so much to tell you. So much. And Edward too...' She looked at Ed, shrugging. 'I wasn't expecting this today. I wasn't expecting any of this.'

Teddy kissed her hand again and smiled. 'And we

have all the time in the world because I am never, ever letting you go again.'

After that, there were tears, hugs, handshakes. Teddy's granddaughter, Amelia, had been loitering behind him, waiting for the right moment to step forward. I'd been so entranced by the reunion that I hadn't even noticed her. Teddy introduced her and she was clearly as astonished as Teddy to discover she had a whole new family. Two more chairs seemed to appear out of nowhere, followed by more champagne. This time, I didn't frown as Ed's glass was filled. If anyone needed a drink, he did. Not only had he decided to acquaint himself with his birth mother that day, but he'd unexpectedly met his birth father too. That was a lot to take in at once.

Seeing Ed and Teddy in such close proximity, it was obvious they were father and son. I wasn't normally good at spotting family resemblances but it was like someone had taken Ed and aged him thirty years, like they do on those missing person photos you sometimes see on the news.

'The gifts last night were from you?' I asked Teddy when the initial shockwaves had settled.

'Yes, they were from me.'

'The musical box was exquisite,' Ruby said. 'But how on earth did you get hold of something like that so quickly? Surely you only received Callie's letter last week?'

'I did, but the music box was something I commissioned over fifty years ago during our last months together. You'd gone before it was ready, but I always believed that, one day, fate would reunite us and it would be yours.'

Ruby touched her fingers to her lips and shook her head. 'I'm sorry, Teddy. I...'

'Not now, my darling. We'll talk about it later.'

There was silence for a moment so, of course, I had to fill it.

'I'm assuming it was you who delivered the gifts, Amelia?'

'Yes, it was. Please convey my apologies to the poor woman who kept having to answer the door.'

'She didn't mind,' I said. 'I think she was enjoying the intrigue. We thought... or rather I thought, that you might put in an appearance at midnight, Teddy.'

'That was the original plan,' Amelia said, 'But Grandpa wasn't well, were you?'

A murmur of concern rippled round the table

and Teddy laughed. 'Nothing serious so please don't panic. I'm asthmatic and I had a mild attack last night. Desperate as I was to see Ruby, I knew I'd be a wheezing mess if I went out into the cold night air so I stayed in and Amelia made the deliveries as planned. We decided we'd visit this afternoon instead but, alas, we couldn't get in.'

'There was an officious young man on security,' Amelia explained. 'Grandpa and I weren't sure whether Ruby had asked you to get in touch, Callie, or whether you were simply putting out feelers. If it was the latter, we didn't want to risk Grandpa being announced then turned away, but there was no getting past security without filling in the log and being announced as guests.' I could well imagine the challenge. We employed agency staff over the bank holidays and they did tend to be super strict, but rightly so.

'So Amelia politely enquired when he'd be finishing for the day,' Teddy said, 'and we returned half an hour after that only to discover that Ruby had already gone out with some visitors.'

'That would be us,' Debbie said. 'How did you

know we'd be here, though? I'm pretty sure we didn't tell security where we were going.'

'We met a lovely lady who was on her way out,' Teddy said. 'She asked if she could help and we explained that we were hoping to see Ruby. She told us you were here and, believe it or not, this is where Amelia and I have been staying so we must have passed you en route.'

'I only told Iris,' Ruby said. 'It must have been her and I daresay she recognised you from...' Colour pinched her cheeks. 'I'm embarrassed to say that we looked you up online, Teddy.'

Teddy laughed. 'There are some shocking pictures of me online. I hope you weren't too disappointed.'

'Nothing about you has ever disappointed me,' Ruby said.

Aww! They had to be the cutest couple ever.

'I think another toast is needed,' Ed said, raising his glass. He still had the look of a startled deer in the headlights, as though not quite able to believe the start to the New Year. 'To finding both my parents on the same day and to them finding each other. To Ruby and Teddy!'

'To Ruby and Teddy!'

EPILOGUE

Nearly three months later, exactly sixty-six years since the day they'd met on Teddy's twenty-first birthday, Ruby and Teddy finally said, 'I do'. The bride and groom might have been eighty-five and eighty-seven respectively by then but, as I'd always proclaimed, you're never too old to let love in and it's never too late to try again.

After so many lost years, Ruby and Teddy wanted to marry quickly. Ruby was a radiant bride in a deep-red early twentieth-century floor-length gown. It was the replica of one she'd seen Lady Mary wear in *Downton Abbey* and, I have to say, the seamstress had excelled herself. My twenties-style bridesmaid dress was pale cream but accompanied by a chiffon wrap using the same red floral lace as Ruby's dress so that I didn't look bridal. And, of course, I had my red heart-shaped necklace from Rhys, which matched perfectly. Teddy was dressed in a traditional tuxedo with a cummerbund and bow tie made from the same material as Ruby's dress.

As the happy couple took to the dance floor for the first time as husband and wife, I thought I was going to cry, but I just managed to hold on. Then the music started and Perry Como's velvety voice filled the room. That was it. The tears that I'd somehow managed to hold back all day burst through the dam and cascaded down my cheeks. With Ruby and Teddy finally together, the words seemed to take on a greater poignancy. They really had loved each other until the end of time, despite being apart for most of their lives.

'Should we shuffle with the oldies?' Rhys asked, offering me his arm when the music changed to something a little faster.

Smiling through my tears, I let him lead me onto the dance floor. Iris and William were there already, along with various members of Teddy's family. Ed and Jenny were waltzing round the room and Ed was actually laughing. Maybe the dance floor was his happy place. Well, somewhere had to be. We'd seen quite a bit of Rhys's parents over the past few months and, although it was going to take time to fully mend Ed's relationship with Rhys, I was impressed with the effort he was making. Rhys had shown them round the gardens at Bay View and I could tell from Ed's surprised expression that he wasn't just paying lip service when he said Rhys's work was extremely impressive. About time too.

'Happy?' Rhys whispered in my ear.

'I'm always happy when I'm with you.'

He pulled me closer and I rested my head on his shoulder, eyes closed.

'You got your wish, then,' he said.

'For Ruby and Teddy to reunite?'

'Yes, but also, at Iris and William's wedding, I said that next time we danced at a wedding, it could be ours. You wished for it to be Ruby and Teddy's instead.'

'I did, didn't I? And both wishes came true. I must be a fairy or a white witch.'

'Mum says you're a gift from heaven and I think

she's right. You've brought our broken family to-gether, and I don't just mean Ruby and Teddy, or Dad and me. I include Izzy and Megan in that too.'

'You're setting me off again,' I said, wiping my eyes.

'That wish you made for Ruby and Teddy to re-unite? You didn't let it float away like so many wishes. You made it come true. So I have a wish for you. I wish to make you as happy as you've made me and the rest of this family.'

I stepped back so that I could look into his eyes. 'You already do, Rhys. You don't have to wish it be-cause it's already happening.'

And it was. A year ago, I'd been seeing Tony, oblivious to the fact that he was married with four kids and had a roving eye. I'd thought I was happy and in love but, looking back, I'd been far from it. Since Rhys had come into my life, I'd known what true love was. Izzy and Tony had done their best to test us and tear us apart last year, but all they'd done was make us stronger. Ruby once told me that she'd always known that Rhys and I were made for each other and would last forever. She'd known what she was talking about because looking across at her and

Teddy gazing tenderly at each other as they made their way off the dance floor, I could see that they were made for each other and, despite the years apart, their love really had lasted forever. I remembered Ruby being adamant that there'd be no epilogue to their love story. I loved that I'd created one for them.

Izzy still had her awkward moments, but she never kicked up a fuss about me spending time with Megan, including overnight stays. She'd struggled being apart from her daughter at first but she'd started going out with her friend, Jess, and the adult company seemed to work wonders.

Maria continued to thrive, with Sofia being her world. I'd introduced Sofia to Megan and we'd taken the girls out a few times together which was lovely. Tony had pestered Maria to take him back for most of January, but we suspected he'd found someone else because, by February, the only contact she had with him was a weekly payment into her bank account. Exactly the way it should be.

Denise returned to Bay View in mid-January, a transformed woman. She would continue to face challenges with her mental health, but the harsh words and bullying behaviours at work were long gone and it was a pleasure to work with her this time round.

As for Rhys and me, we'd moved out of my flat and into a house. The flat had been far too small for Megan once she'd started walking. We'd also set a date for our wedding in early-October next year, booked the venue, and I couldn't wait to start looking at dresses and choosing the colour scheme.

Everything was looking rosy for the people I cared about. Except one...

'There's one more wish I'd like to make,' I whispered to Rhys.

'What's that?'

'I want our Nick to find what we have. I think I might have to throw some more coins into the wishing well.'

'Trust you to be making a wish for someone else instead of one for you.'

'I have everything I could ever want or need right now. I don't need to make any wishes for me.'

'I love you, Callie,' he said.

'I love you too.'

'Deeper than the ocean, higher than the sky, and longer than time,' he added.

Holding him even closer, I glanced across towards Ruby and Teddy again. Yes, their love really had been deeper than the ocean, higher than the sky, and longer than time. And I knew ours was going to be too.

ACKNOWLEDGMENTS

I hope you've enjoyed reading *Making Wishes at Bay View* and that you loved the pair of characters I've enjoyed creating the most. No, I don't mean Callie and Rhys (although I do love them, of course). I mean Ruby and Iris. I absolutely adore those two! I'd love to meet them in real-life.

Making Wishes at Bay View was never planned as part of the *Welcome to Whitsborough Bay series* but it was one of those happy moments where a seed of an idea grew into a tree. I'd secured a three-book publishing deal for the *series* and, a few months before the original first book was released, my publisher at the time suggested writing a short story relating to a character in the trilogy to give away for free as an indication of my writing. At the start of what is now the second book in the series, *New Beginnings at Seaside Blooms,* Callie's brother, Nick, collects the flowers for her wedding and I thought that a story about how Callie met her husband Rhys might be a lovely starting point. I'm not very good at keeping my ideas small, though, and a short story soon grew into a novella called *Raving About Rhys.*

My publisher ceased trading so I re-released *Raving About Rhys* as an independent author. Three years later, I was still thinking about Ruby and wondering what might have led to her having her baby adopted. Before long, I had another novel on my hands which I released as *Callie's Christmas Wish.*

I was thrilled to secure a publishing deal with Boldwood that would include new books but also some of my back catalogue. They were keen to take the original trilogy, but we agreed that it made sense to make this a four-book series, combining *Raving About Rhys* and *Callie's Christmas Wish* into one story. The fundamental story remains the same but Maria's behaviour is a little different in this revised version and there have been several nips and tucks along the way to create the story you've read. I have to say a huge thank you to my wonderful editor, Nia, for her valuable guidance, Dushi and Sue for spotting typos, repetition and inconsistencies, and the team at Boldwood Books for shaping the final version.

As always, my biggest thanks need to go to my husband, Mark, and our daughter, Ashleigh, for putting up with the limited time they get with me as I try (often unsuccessfully) to balance the day job with studies, writing and family life. They never complain when I drift off into a world with my imaginary friends, although hubby is guilty of laughing at me when I'm writing. I have a habit of acting out facial expressions and muttering dialogue which amuses him considerably. How rude!

Huge hugs of appreciation go to a team of beta readers – friends and family – who helped me smooth out the edges on the original versions. They bring different talents to this role, whether that be spotting typos, plot holes, slow moments, repetition, or challenging whether a situation is realistic. So a huge thanks to Joyce Williams (my lovely mum), Liz Berry, Susan Hockley, Jo Bartlett and Sharon Booth. Jo and Sharon are extremely talented authors whose work I highly recommend, so do check them out on Amazon.

An extra big thanks goes to Susan for being a beta reader on the original version of *Callie's Christmas Wish* because she had a particularly challenging year when I wrote it. Sadly, Susan lost her mum, Beatrice Lythgoe, in April 2018, aged 81. Susan's been a great friend since our school days so her mum features strongly in my childhood memories. When I started writing, Beatrice championed my work, reading and enjoying all my books. She was always keen to know when the next book would come out, which was so lovely of her. Beatrice had a career in nursing and midwifery before starting a family. As her family grew up, she became involved in local politics and, when we were at college, she was appointed as Mayor of Langbaurgh. How impressive is that? An inspiring woman, I see some of Beatrice's strength and spirit in Ruby. It therefore feels appropriate to dedicate this book to Beatrice. Rest in peace.

Thanks, as always, go to my virtual writing family – The Write Romantics – and huge thanks to my writing rock, Sharon Booth, for always being there through the highs and lows, providing advice, guidance, and friendship.

Finally, my thanks go to you, my readers. If you've enjoyed any of my books, it would be amazing if you could tell others by leaving a review on Amazon. Reviews make a massive difference to an author. You'll see some really long ones on Amazon, but you don't need to write an essay. A positive rating and a short sentence are equally welcome and hugely appreciated.

On a final note, I've mentioned a Perry Como song in the story. I wasn't personally familiar with the song or the piece of music but I found it after searching online for a tune popular in the 1950s that could feature in a musical box. I came across the Chopin piece and the Perry Como song as a result, and both fitted the story perfectly. I had hoped to include the lyrics at the start of the book for anyone who, like me, isn't familiar with the song. I applied for the rights to do this, waited months to hear back, was sent around the houses, and then drew a blank.

I've had to release this without the lyrics, which is a shame, but they are readily available online if anyone is curious. I did try, though!

Big hugs

Jessica xx

MORE FROM JESSICA REDLAND

We hope you enjoyed reading *Making Wishes At Bay View*.
If you did, please leave a review.

If you'd like to gift a copy, this book is also available as an
ebook, digital audio download and audiobook CD.

Sign up to Jessica Redland's mailing list for news,
competitions and updates on future books.

http://bit.ly/JessicaRedlandNewsletter

ABOUT THE AUTHOR

Jessica Redland is the author of eleven novels which are all set around the fictional location of Whitsborough Bay. Inspired by her hometown of Scarborough she writes uplifting women's fiction which has garnered many devoted fans.

Visit Jessica's website:
https://www. jessicaredland.com/

Follow Jessica on social media:

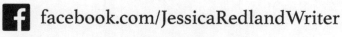 facebook.com/JessicaRedlandWriter

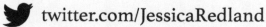 twitter.com/JessicaRedland

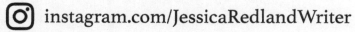 instagram.com/JessicaRedlandWriter

bookbub.com/authors/jessica-redland

ALSO BY JESSICA REDLAND

Standalone Novels

The Secret To Happiness

Christmas at Carly's Cupcakes

Starry Skies Over The Chocolate Pot Café

All You Need Is Love

Welcome To Whitsborough Bay Series

Making Wishes At Bay View

New Beginnings at Seaside Blooms

Finding Hope at Lighthouse Cove

Coming Home To Seashell Cottage

Hedgehog Hollow Series

Finding Love at Hedgehog Hollow

New Arrivals at Hedgehog Hollow

Family Secrets at Hedgehog Hollow

ABOUT BOLDWOOD BOOKS

Boldwood Books is a fiction publishing company seeking out the best stories from around the world.

Find out more at www.boldwoodbooks.com

Sign up to the Book and Tonic newsletter for news, offers and competitions from Boldwood Books!

http://www.bit.ly/bookandtonic

We'd love to hear from you, follow us on social media:

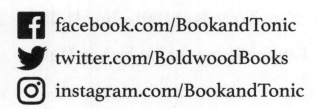

facebook.com/BookandTonic

twitter.com/BoldwoodBooks

instagram.com/BookandTonic

Lightning Source UK Ltd.
Milton Keynes UK
UKHW010651020921
389877UK00002B/254